Mary Lavin was born of Irish parents in East Walpole, Massachusetts, in 1912. She moved to Ireland at the age of ten, living first in Athenry, County Galway, and later in Dublin. In 1930 she entered University College Dublin and was working for her doctorate when she wrote her first short story, 'Miss Holland'. By 1942, eleven of her stories had appeared in such periodicals as the London *Good Housekeeping*, the *Atlantic Monthly* and *Harper's Bazaar*, and a collection of her short stories won the James Tait Black Memorial Prize. She continued writing up to the early eighties, producing some nineteen collections of short stories and contributing regularly to the *New Yorker*. She was awarded a Guggenheim fellowship in 1959 and 1961, she received the Katherine Mansfield Prize in 1961, and she was granted an honorary doctorate at UCD in 1968. In 1992, she was elected 'Saoi' by Aosdána, an affiliation of Irish artists, for outstanding achievement in literature. Mary Lavin lives in Dublin.

Thomas Kilroy is a playwright and novelist. He has received many literary awards, including the Guardian Fiction Prize and the Heinemann Award. He is a Fellow of the Royal Society of Literature.

In memory of Thomas and Nora Lavin

MARY LAVIN

in a Café

A new selection by
Elizabeth Walsh Peavoy

TOWN
HOUSE

Published in 1995 by
Town House and Country House
Trinity House
Charleston Road
Ranelagh, Dublin 6
Ireland

British Library Cataloguing in Publication Data. A catalogue record for
this book is available from the British Library.

ISBNs: 1-86059-000-4 (hardback)
         1-86059-001-2 (paperback)

Acknowledgements
Except for 'The Girders', which is published here for the first time, the
stories in this selection previously appeared in the following
collections, and we are grateful to the various publishers for
permission to reproduce them:

'In the Middle of the Fields' from *In the Middle of the Fields* (Constable,
London, 1967); 'A Family Likeness' from *A Family Likeness* (Constable,
London, 1985); 'Lemonade' and 'In a Café' from *The Great Wave*
(Macmillan & Co Ltd, London, 1961); 'Tom' from *The Shrine*
(Constable, London, 1977); 'A Cup of Tea', 'A Gentle Soul', 'Chamois
Gloves', The Widow's Son', 'The Will' and 'The Little Prince' from *The
Stories of Mary Lavin* (Constable, London, 1964); 'The Joy-Ride' from
The Becker Wives (Michael Joseph Ltd, London, 1946); 'The Convert'
and 'A Story with a Pattern' from *A Single Lady* (Michael Joseph Ltd,
London, 1951); 'Trastevere' from *A Memory* (Constable, London,
1972).

Cover illustration: *Girl in Blue* by Mainie Jellett, Private Collection,
Dublin, by kind permission of The Jellett Trust. We are indebted to
Bruce Arnold, author of *Mainie Jellett and the Modern Movement in
Ireland,* for help with the cover illustration.

Edited by Elizabeth Walsh Peavoy
Cover design by Wendy Williams
Typeset by Typeform Repro Ltd, Dublin
Printed in Ireland by Colour Books Ltd

Contents

* re-shaped by Mary Lavin since first publication

† first time in print

Foreword

When I was a young man interested in writing, Mary Lavin became an important presence in my life. It was in the fifties when Tom MacIntyre and I rang her up in Bective and contrived an invitation for ourselves to the Abbey Farm where she was living with the three girls, the first visit of many. I had seen Mary once before when she came to read to the English Society of University College Dublin at Newman House, a young widow in black, long black hair pulled back in a bun, eyes bright as buttons. What I remember most of that reading was an astonishing freshness in the description of flowers.

It was an education in books as well as a meeting with someone who became a dear friend. Which books? This is important, I think, in saying something about the kind of writer that she is and where she rests, securely, in our literary history.

I no longer have the copies of Turgenev's books nor of Flaubert's *Trois Contes* that she pressed upon me – lost, all lost in the migrations and the borrowings. But I can still recall how she talked about the death of poor Félicité in 'Un Coeur Simple' and the great parrot in the half-open heavens above her head. And I do have the copy of Tolstoy's *The Kreutzer Sonata,* still in its old yellow World's Classics wrappers, with its inscription from Mary, May 1960. This, she had told me, was a story that had profoundly influenced her when she had first started to write.

It was as if she had instinctively understood the inadequacies of the UCD degree in English of the day as a foundation for someone who wished to write. She was dead right, of course. What she was saying, too, in giving me those much-loved stories was: This is where I come from, these are my models. Mary Lavin is one of a generation of Irish writers who looked in the most natural fashion imaginable to the great European canon for examples to write by. There are younger writers, John McGahern and John Banville, for instance, who do so too. But

I say this now because it is a connection that is being lost. There is an impatience among many writers now with anything that doesn't have the immediacy of today's newspaper or television.

Her addiction to storytelling, though, also has to be seen as part of her make-up as a person, a huge curiosity about people, strangers, casual acquaintances and close friends alike. For her the stories they have to tell inscribe some profound truth about their lives. It is as natural for her as chatting in Grafton Street or in The Mews on Lad Lane, as natural as a glass of water. But she also carries these lessons from the masters, which gives her a great regard for the artifice of fiction, how the experience can be shaped by form and in this way how the rhythms of the ordinary can be not only preserved but enhanced.

She once said to me that she felt a story often grew out of an opening sentence. Simply sticking to her first volume, *Tales From Bective Bridge,* you can believe that she means this literally. 'Sarah had a bit of a bad name.' Or 'She was one of the most beautiful women they had ever seen and so they hated her'. Or 'The cat decided Miss Holland'. These are sentences that are already hatching. The hook is in place from the word go. But such sentences are not only beguiling in their promises, they also establish a particular tone, a way of telling that is at least as important as what is being told. That characteristic Lavin tone is at once sympathetic and demanding, highly moral in the way it negotiates human conduct but entirely flexible in its acceptance of the vagaries of experience.

I think she is also getting at something else here in her remark about first sentences. She is talking about the way language creates its own world, and its own readers too, in the process. This reverence for the act of writing is exemplified everywhere in her work. She has even written stories about the nature of fiction, stories 'with a pattern' like 'The Widow's Son'.

On another occasion I remember asking her, with that callow courage that you only have at a certain stage of your life, which story she would choose as the finest expression of her art. She said 'The Will'. Reading it again now I can see why. It is one of a body of stories – 'The Little Prince', 'Frail Vessel' and that remarkable novella 'The Becker Wives' are others – in which she explores, as no other Irish writer has done quite as well, a particular Irish setting, small town, genteel, familial, under threat from the forces of life's anarchy. It would be true to say that her high, early reputation was based upon this body of work.

The stories are always about a family, although the name, Conroy, Grimes, Becker, may change from fiction to fiction. The recurrent antagonism is that between a conniving, cold pursuit of material prosperity on the one hand and a flame-like spirit of passion on the other. The typical battlefield exists between sisters. In the language of the stories, one side is associated with darkness and heavy, clumsy movement, the other with mobility, adventuresomeness, even to the point of destruction. What these stories unveil is the mysterious, deadly antagonism in the world towards creatures of light and air, like Lally Conroy in 'The Will'.

There are, of course, many other kinds of Lavin stories. Indeed, when you get the chance to look at a selection like this one, that is precisely what emerges, variety.

For example, she has written with generosity about Irish Catholicism, but with her own implacable eye on its worst deformations. She can move from the very gentle irony of 'Chamois Gloves', one of the most delicate fictional treatments of girlhood in the nets of religious scruple, to the more hard-edged social dimension of religion on this island in 'The Convert', and on to the primal in 'The Great Wave', where religion collides with the forces of nature itself. There is a great range in these stories and they are clearly the work of a spiritual, if iconoclastic, writer.

My own favourite stories, and this obviously has to do with my own relationship with Mary, are those of widowhood, the first of which, I believe, was 'In a Café', from the early nineteen sixties. Quite simply, I know the territory of these stories as well as anything else in my life. I know the people who walk in them as I know kin, although everything here is fiction. In these stories she has looked into herself, but never in a limited, solipsistic way. Everything is shaped, subjected to a high degree of formal construction. To effect this kind of distancing upon one's own experience requires an immense inner strength on the part of the writer.

'In the Middle of the Fields', perhaps the greatest of these stories, begins with a passage of great resonance, a lyrical prelude that already contains the movements of emotion that are worked out in the story that follows. The passage is also a fine example, incidentally, of Mary Lavin's mature style.

In one sense it is a simple story, as great stories often are. A widow is alone, lonely in a house within the fields. A neighbour, a widower, comes to the house at night to talk about cutting the grass, but also to reveal his own broken feelings. What happens between them is one of those moments of total revelation, one of those awkward moments between men and women who have nothing in common except a need to be loved. The need is an unconscious one and as unconscious needs often do, it betrays itself in mistakes, misjudgements.

That is why the opening of the story is so apt, so beautifully appropriate in its suggestiveness, its elusiveness. The two characters are surrounded by ghosts in the night, ghosts out of the fields, strange influences beyond their control to which the growing grass of the fields is a constant witness, cyclical as the individual human life can never be. 'In the Middle of the Fields' is one of those works that achieve a harmony of all its parts that cannot be conveyed by mere analysis. It is both a highly personal work and at the same time one in which you can observe the artist moulding the material with consummate skill. I love this work because in it Mary Lavin the writer and Mary Lavin the person that I know, have become one.

Thomas Kilroy
April 1995

Preamble

I take this chance of selecting from my mother's collected stories from the inside track. I have never judged her writing from without, nor have I ever found her reputation to be intimidating. Thus, I bring the enthusiasm of a daughter to the lifetime gifts of a writer, wholly undepleted.

Mary had been re-shaping certain stories on and off since before I left Ireland in the late seventies, for inclusion in a collected volume. I returned home in September '92 to find the residue of this work, not yet in book form. I was invited to step into her shoes. This is the result. The re-shaped stories are 'A Cup of Tea', 'A Gentle Soul', 'Chamois Gloves', 'The Convert', 'The Widow's Son', 'The Will' and 'The Little Prince'. The original version of 'Lemonade', which begins with the child's departure from the United States, has also been included.

The story, as I know it, begins in 'In the Middle of the Fields'. A lonely young widow (Mary was forty-two when William Walsh died) attempts to come to terms with a set of circumstances that will make her existence viable. She plays out this new role, on a farm, deep in the countryside, with her three young daughters. We encounter some of the people who will help her to succeed.

Next we see the woman begin to embrace life again. She has made a fresh start. 'A Family Likeness', although written in the eighties, was actually conceived in the woods at Bective, County Meath, where Mary lived during her ten years of marriage.

Now the writer begins to tell of her childhood. In 'Lemonade', the child reminisces about her own submerged past, first in Boston where she was born in 1912 and where she lived for the first ten years of her life, and then in the west of Ireland. In 'Tom', the girl revisits her father's birthplace in County Roscommon, in the company of her father. This journey goes beyond memory and touches some of the relics of their joint past.

Here we reach a crossroads, which can be seen to be the start of Mary's 'either/or' stories. In 'The Girders', circa 1940, a young man unable to progress beyond a site where he is employed, is envisaged on the point of returning to Ireland. Yet it is a piteous homecoming and not a triumphant return that is predicted. Mary's father went hop-picking in Yorkshire before setting sail for Boston in the 1800s. Mary is fond of looking at life from an alternative point of view to the way that it has been lived. We see success paralleled by failure.

Now the child in the story progresses to her late teens. In 'A Cup of Tea', a female student of International Relations is tried by the conflict of her parents, or the girl in 'Chamois Gloves' grapples with her own internal conflict while professing her first vows in the noviciate. There is undeniable auto-biographical content in both of these stories. The emphasis in 'A Gentle Soul' is on premature love, making light of the sacrifices often demanded of youth. In 'The Convert' the final test becomes a spiritual bond, and the secrets of passion are eternally hidden from the young people involved. Thus the misunderstandings of inexperienced youth become the complicity of resigned middle age.

During the thirties Mary's father became overseer to a large estate in County Meath. The house was empty for most of the year, but was opened up for the hunting season. Mary visited her father there at weekends, travelling from Dublin where she was a college student, to be met at the station in Bective by the pony and trap, the very trap used by Crickem and Purdy in 'The Joy-Ride'.

While at University College Dublin, Mary signed a proviso that she would never wear the fur of trapped animals, and she refused to buy or eat veal in a restaurant because the calves were said to be kept in unlit quarters, which would blanch the colour of their meat. Her views were changing, and one observes changes in her characterisation and plot. We see visions of what people did, but also what might have happened were circumstances to have been otherwise. A story starts out, then becomes transmuted and passes through various procedures to become another type of story. We are conscious of how precious life can be.

'In a Café' – the café was called The Clog and it was situated in South King Street, Dublin. I don't think it lasted long, but it had the atmosphere of a still-life painting, and it gave Mary the niche she wanted into the artistic view of the capital. This was the Greenwich Village of Dublin, which Mary visited shortly after William had died. 'There could be nothing – oh nothing – glamorous about a widow.' 'In a Café' was the preliminary story to her later theme of widowhood. Mary Lavin, an only child, lived isolated from society, at one with the fields, cut off from all except for those members of the community who braved the stigma of her status, and came near. In many stories the priest was the person who made the jump necessary to make contact.

This was Dublin's *rive gauche,* where delicatessens existed side by side with a drayhorse van, delivering laundry or pigeon manure. The view is one of small backstreet cafés, the canal-side wharf, of houses and huckster shops where destruction abounds, so as to make it a hive of energy or pain. Mary's inventive description of Bohemian Dublin is new and exciting, coming from the pen of a convent-educated inhabitant of the Leeson Street complex.

Mary continued to revisit Bective for the holidays and at weekends during term time, but she lived most of her writing life in a mews at 11 Lad Lane, rear Fitzwilliam Place. Although she regarded the artist as classless, she was conscious of the strictures placed by society which marginalised those who had chosen a creative discipline such as her own. By earning her living from her writing, she gave the lie to those who ignored the values of an ideology deferring to material gain. Her first novel was serialised in the *Atlantic Monthly,* and she was what has been termed 'a *New Yorker* writer' for a decade. In 1990 her second marriage, to Michael Scott, ended in widowhood, and she was forced to seek a more retiring way of life.

In 'A Story with a Pattern', we are made aware of how forcible is the trajectory moving her characters along. Yet we are shown an alternative way of living. In 'The Widow's Son', Packy doesn't need his mother now and she must be made to step aside, or take responsibility for what has happened to her only son.

'The Will' is a story where the genealogy of family begins to reassert itself as being of prime importance to the individual. In 'The Little Prince', a new order begins to take over, as Bedelia tries to grapple with the truth, her loss of her brother Tom. Yet there is warmth in the telling despite the chill realities expressed.

The final story of the collection, 'Trastevere', brings us first to New York and then back to Rome, where the central character – the writer – and her elder daughter witness the tensions experienced by a young couple of their acquaintance. Thus the mother and daughter are a fuse leading to ultimate knowledge of a life that is fatally flawed.

During the later fifties my mother took her three daughters to Italy. Mary and I liked to perambulate along the river Arno in Florence, or through the pedestrianised Roman thorough-fares. I had been right over the Vatican Museum before I reached the age of fourteen. Yet there never seemed to be enough time to dally along those avenues, and somehow we both sought more from these sporadic trips to the continent of mainland Europe. In a way, getting this book together has been just that, a chance for me to perambulate with my mother, down along the walkways of her mind. Not to race, but to take the journey quietly at our own pace. And for this opportunity I am grateful to her, as I imagine you, the reader, are – grateful for being given a chance to dally with the writer, Mary Lavin.

Elizabeth Walsh Peavoy
April 1995

In the Middle of the Fields

Like a rock in the sea, she was islanded by fields, the heavy grass
washing about the house, and the cattle wading in it as in water.
Even their gentle stirrings were a loss when they moved away at
evening to the shelter of the woods. A rainy day might strike a
wet flash from a hay barn on the far side of the river – not even
a habitation! And yet she was less lonely for him here in Meath
than elsewhere. Anxieties by day, and cares, and at night vague,
nameless fears – these were the stones across the mouth of the
tomb. But who understood that? They thought she hugged
tight every memory she had of him. What did they know about
memory? What was it but another name for dry love and barren
longing? They even tried to unload upon her their own small
purposeless memories. 'I imagine I see him every time I look
out there,' they would say as they glanced nervously over the
darkening fields when they were leaving. 'I think I ought to see
him coming through the trees.' Oh, for God's sake! she'd
think. I'd forgotten him for a minute!

It wasn't him *she* saw when she looked out at the fields. It was
the ugly tufts of tow and scutch that whitened the tops of the
grass and gave it the look of a sea in storm, spattered with
broken foam. That grass would have to be topped. And how
much would it cost?

At least Ned, the old herd, knew the man to do it for her.
'Bartley Crossen is your man, Ma'am. Your husband knew him
well.'

She couldn't place him at first. Then she remembered.

'Oh, yes – that's his hay barn we see, isn't it? Why, of course!
I know him well – by sight, I mean.' And so she did – splashing

past on the road in a big muddy car, the wheels always caked with clay, and the wife in the front seat beside him.

'I'll get him to call around and have a word with you, Ma'am,' said the herd.

'Before dark!' she cautioned.

But there was no need to tell him. The old man knew how she always tried to be upstairs before it got dark, locking herself into her room, which opened off the room where the children slept, praying devoutly that she wouldn't have to come down again for anything – above all, not to answer the door. That was what in particular she dreaded: a knock after dark.

'Ah, sure, who'd come near you, Ma'am, knowing you're a woman alone with small children that might be wakened and set crying? And, for that matter, where could you be safer than in the middle of the fields, with the innocent beasts asleep around you?'

If he himself had to come to the house late at night for any reason – to get hot water to stoup the foot of a beast, or to call the vet – he took care to shout out long before he got to the gable. 'It's me, Ma'am!' he'd shout. 'Coming! Coming!' she'd cry, gratefully, as quick on his words as their echo. Unlocking her door, she'd run down and throw open the hall door. No matter what the hour! No matter how black the night! 'Go back to your bed now, you, Ma'am,' he'd say from the darkness, where she could see the swinging yard lamp coming nearer and nearer like the light of a little boat drawing near to a jetty. 'I'll put out the lights and let myself out.' Relaxed by the thought that there was someone in the house, she would indeed scuttle back into bed, and, what was more, she'd be nearly asleep before she'd hear the door slam. It used to sound like the slam of a door a million miles away.

There was no need to worry. He'd see that Crossen came early.

It was well before dark when Crossen did drive up to the door. The wife was with him, as usual, sitting up in the front seat the way people sat up in the well of little tub traps long ago, their knees pressed together, allowing no slump. The herd had come with them, but only he and Crossen got out.

'Won't your wife come inside and wait, Mr Crossen?' she asked.

'Oh, not at all, Ma'am. She likes sitting in the car. Now, where's this grass that's to be cut? Are there any stones lying about that would blunt the blade?' Going around the gable of the house, he looked out over the land.

'There's not a stone or a stump in it,' Ned said. 'You'd run your blade over the whole of it while you'd be whetting it twenty times in another place!'

'I can see that,' said Bartley Crossen, but absently, she thought.

He had walked across the lawn to the rickety wooden gate that led into the pasture, and leaned on it. He didn't seem to be looking at the fields at all, though, but at the small string of stunted thorns that grew along the riverbank, their branches leaning so heavily out over the water that their roots were almost dragged clear of the clay.

Suddenly he turned around and gave a sigh. 'Ah, sure, I didn't need to look! I know it well.' As she showed surprise, he gave a little laugh, like a young man. 'I courted a girl down there when I was a lad,' he said. 'That's a queer length of time ago now, I can tell you!' He turned to the old man. 'You might remember it.' Then he looked back at her. 'I don't suppose you were thought of at all in those days, Ma'am,' he said, and there was something kindly in his look and in his words. 'You'd like the mowing done soon, I suppose? How about first thing in the morning?'

Her face lit up. But there was the price to settle. 'It won't be as dear as cutting meadow, will it?'

'Ah, I won't be too hard on you, Ma'am,' he said. 'I can promise you that!'

'That's very kind of you,' she said, but a little doubtfully.

Behind Crossen's back, Ned nodded his head in approval. 'Let it go at that, Ma'am,' he whispered as they walked back towards the car. 'He's a man you can trust.'

And when Crossen and the wife had driven away, he reassured her again. 'A decent man,' he said. Then he gave a laugh – it, too, was a young kind of laugh for a man of his age;

it was like a nudge. 'Did you hear what he said, though – about the girl he courted down there? Do you know who that was? It was his first wife! You know he was twice married? Ah, well, it's so long ago I wouldn't wonder if you never heard it. Look at the way he spoke about her himself, as if she was some girl he'd all but forgotten! The thorn trees brought her to his mind! That's where they used to meet, being only youngsters, when they first took up with each other.'

'Poor Bridie Logan – she was as wild as a hare. And she was mad with love, young as she was! They were company-keeping while they were still going to school. Only nobody took it seriously – him least of all, maybe – till the winter he went away to the agricultural college in Clonakilty. She started writing to him then. I used to see her running up to the postbox at the crossroads every other evening. And sure, the whole village knew where the letter was going. His people were fit to be tied when he came home in the summer and said he wasn't going back, but was going to marry Bridie. All the same, his father set them up in a cottage on his own land. It's the cottage that's used now for stall-feds – it's back of the new house. Oh, but you can't judge it now for what it was then! Giddy and all as she was – as lightheaded as a thistle – you should have seen the way she kept that cottage. She'd have had it scrubbed away if she didn't start having a baby. He wouldn't let her take the scrubbing brush into her hands after that!'

'But she wasn't delicate, was she?'

'Bridie? She was as strong as a kid goat, that one! But I told you she was mad about him, didn't I? Well, after she was married to him she was no better – worse, you'd say. She couldn't do enough for him! It was like as if she was driven on by some kind of fever. You'd only to look in her eyes to see it. Do you know! From that day to this, I don't believe I ever saw a woman so full of going as that one! Did you ever happen to see little birds flying about in the air like they were flying for the divilment of it and nothing else? And did you ever see the way they give a sort of a little leap in the air, like they were forcing themselves to go a bit higher still – higher than they ought? Well, it struck me that was the way Bridie was acting, as she rushed about that cottage doing this and doing that to make him prouder and prouder of her. As if he could be any prouder than he was already and the child getting noticeable!'

'She didn't die in childbed?'

'No. Not in a manner of speaking, anyway. She had the child, nice and easy, and in their own cottage, too, only costing him a few shillings for one of those women that went in for that kind of job long ago. And all went well. It was no time till she was let up on her feet again. I was there the first morning she had the place to herself! She was up and dressed when I got there, just as he was going out to milk.

'"Oh, it's great to be able to go out again," she said, taking a great breath of the morning air as she stood at the door looking after him. "Wait! Why don't I come with you to milk!" she called out suddenly after him. Then she threw a glance back at the baby asleep in its crib by the window.

'"Oh, it's too far for you, Bridie!" he cried. The cows were down in the little field by the river – you know the field, alongside the road at the foot of the hill on this side of the village. And knowing she'd start coaxing him, he made out of the gate with the cans.

'"Good man!" I said to myself. But the next thing I knew, she'd darted across the yard.

'"I can go on the bike if it's too far to walk!" she said. And up she got on her old bike, and out she pedalled through the gate.

'"Bridie, are you out of your mind?" he shouted as she whizzed past him.

'"Arrah, what harm can it do me?" she shouted back.

'I went stiff with fright looking after her. And I thought it was the same with him, when he threw down the cans and started down the hill after her. But looking back on it, I think it was the same fever as always raging in her that started raging in him, too. Mad with love, that's what they were, both of them – she only wanting to draw him in, and he only too willing!

'"Wait for me!" he shouted, but before she'd even got to the bottom she started to brake the bike, putting down her foot like you'd see a youngster do, and raising up such a cloud of dust we could hardly see her.'

'She braked too hard!'

'Not her! In the twinkle of an eye she'd stopped the bike, jumped off, turned it round, and was pedalling madly up the hill again, her head down on the handle-bars like a racing cyclist. But that was the finish of her!'

'Oh, no! What happened?'

'She stopped pedalling all of a sudden, and the bike half stopped, and then it started to go back down the hill a bit, as if it skidded on the loose gravel at the side of the road. That's what I thought happened, and him, too, I suppose, because we both began to run down the hill. She didn't get time to fall before we got to her. But what use was that? It was some kind of internal bleeding that took her. We got her into the bed, and the neighbours came running, but she was gone before the night.'

'Oh, such a thing to happen! And the baby?'

'Well, it was a strong child! And it grew into a fine lump of a lad. That's the fellow that drives the tractor for him now – the oldest son, Bartley.'

'Well, I suppose his second marriage had more to it, when all was said and done.'

'That's it. And she's a good woman – the second one. The way she brought up that child of Bridie's! And filled the cradle, year after year, with sons of her own. Ah sure, things always work out for the best in the end, no matter what!' he said, and he started to walk away.

'Wait a minute, Ned,' she said urgently. 'Do you really think he forgot about her – for years, I mean?'

'I'd swear it,' said the old man. And then he looked hard at her. 'It will be the same with you, too,' he added kindly. 'Take my word for it. Everything passes in time and is forgotten.'

As she shook her head doubtfully, he shook his emphatically. 'When the tree falls, how can the shadow stand?' he said. And he walked away.

I wonder! she thought as she walked back to the house, and she envied the practical country way that made good the defaults of nature as readily as the broken sod knits back into the sward.

Again that night, when she went up to her room, she looked down towards the river and she thought of Crossen. Had he really forgotten? It was hard for her to believe, and with a sigh she picked up her hairbrush and pulled it through her hair. Like everything else about her lately, her hair was sluggish and hung heavily down, but after a few minutes under the quickening strokes of the brush, it lightened and lifted, and soon it flew about her face like the spray above a weir. It had always been the same, even when she was a child. She had only to suffer the first painful drag of the bristles when her mother would cry out, 'Look! Look! That's electricity!' and a blue spark would shine for an instant like a star in the grey depths of the mirror.

That was all they knew of electricity in those dim-lit days when valleys of shadow lay deep between one piece of furniture and another. Was it because rooms were so badly lit then that they saw it so often, that little blue star? Suddenly she was overcome by longing to see it again, and, standing up impetuously, she switched off the light.

It was just then that, down below, the iron fist of the knocker was lifted and, with a loud, confident hand, brought down on the door.

It wasn't a furtive knock. She admitted that even as she sat stark with fright in the darkness. And then a voice that was vaguely familiar called out – and confidently – from below.

'It's me, Ma'am! I hope I'm not disturbing you!'

'Oh, Mr Crossen!' she cried out with relief, and, unlocking her door, she ran across the landing and threw up the window on that side of the house. 'I'll be right down!' she called.

'Oh, don't come down, Ma'am!' he shouted. 'I only want one word with you.'

'But of course I'll come down!' She went back to get her dressing-gown and pin up her hair, but as she did she heard him stomping his feet on the gravel. It had been a mild day, but with night a chill had come in the air, and, for all that it was late spring, there was a cutting east wind coming across the river. 'I'll run down and let you in from the cold,' she called, and, twisting up her hair, she held it against her head with her hand without waiting to pin it, and she ran down the stairs in her bare feet to unbolt the door.

'You were going to bed, Ma'am!' he said accusingly the minute she opened the door. And where he had been so impatient a minute beforehand, she stood stock-still in the open doorway. 'I saw the lights were out downstairs when I was coming up the drive,' he said contritely. 'But I didn't think you'd gone up for the night!'

'Neither had I!' she said lyingly, to put him at his ease. 'I was just upstairs brushing my hair. You must excuse me,' she added, because a breeze from the door was blowing her dressing-gown from her knees, and to pull it across she had to take her hand from her hair, so that the hair fell down about her shoulders. 'Would you mind closing the door for me?' she said, with some embarrassment, and she began to back up the stairs. 'Please go inside to the sitting-room, won't you?' she said, nodding towards the door of the small room off the hall. 'Put on the light. I'll be down in a minute.'

But although he had obediently stepped inside the door and closed it, he stood stoutly in the middle of the hall. 'I shouldn't have come in at all,' he said. 'I know you were going to bed! Look at you!' he cried again in the same accusing voice, as if he dared her this time to deny it. He was looking at her hair. 'Excuse my saying so, Ma'am, but I never saw such a fine head of hair. God bless it!' he said quickly, as if afraid he had been rude. 'Doesn't a small thing make a big differ,' he said impulsively. 'You look like a young girl!'

In spite of herself, she smiled with pleasure. She wanted no more of it, all the same. 'Well, I don't feel like one!' she said sharply.

What was meant for a quite opposite effect, however, seemed to delight him and put him wonderfully at ease. 'Ah sure, you're a sensible woman! I can see that,' he said, and, coming to the foot of the stairs, he leaned comfortably across the newel post. 'Let you stay the way you are, Ma'am,' he said. 'I've only a word to say to you, and it's not worth your while going up them stairs. Let me have my say here and now and be off about my business! The wife will be waiting up for me, and I don't want that!'

She hesitated. Was the reference to his wife meant to put her at *her* ease? 'I think I ought to get my slippers,' she said cautiously. Her feet were cold.

'Oh, yes, put something on your feet!' he cried, only then seeing that she was in her bare feet. 'But as to the rest, I'm long gone beyond taking any account of what a woman has on her. I'm gone beyond taking notice of women at all.'

She had seen something to put on her feet. Under the table in the hall was a pair of old boots belonging to Richard, with fleece lining in them. She hadn't been able to make up her mind to give them away with the rest of his clothes, and although they were big and clumsy on her, she often stuck her feet into them when she came in from the fields with mud on her shoes. 'Well, come in where it's warm, so,' she said. She came back down the few steps and stuck her feet into the boots, and then she opened the door of the sitting-room.

She was glad she'd come down. He'd never have been able to put on the light. 'There's something wrong with the centre light,' she said as she groped along the wainscot to find the plug of the reading lamp. It was in an awkward place, behind the desk. She had to go down on her knees.

'What's wrong with it?' he asked, as, with a countryman's interest in practicalities, he clicked the switch up and down to no effect.

'Oh, nothing much, I'm sure,' she said absently. 'There!' She had found the plug, and the room was lit up with a bright white glow.

'Why don't you leave the plug in the socket, anyway?' he asked critically.

'I don't know,' she said. 'I think someone told me it's safer, with reading lamps, to pull them out at night. There might be a short circuit, or mice might nibble at the cord, or something – I forget what I was told. I got into the habit of doing it, and now I keep on.' She felt a bit silly.

But he was concerned about it. 'I don't think any harm could be done,' he said gravely. Then he turned away from the problem. 'About tomorrow, Ma'am!' he said, somewhat offhandedly, she thought. 'I was determined I'd see you tonight, because I'm not a man to break my word – above all, to a woman.'

What was he getting at?

'Let me put it this way,' he said quickly. 'You'll understand, Ma'am, that as far as I am concerned, topping land is the same as cutting hay. The same time. The same labour cost. And the same wear and tear on the blade. You understand that?'

On her guard, she nodded.

'Well now, Ma'am, I'd be the first to admit that it's not quite the same for you. For you, topping doesn't give the immediate return you'd get from hay –'

'There's no return from it!' she exclaimed crossly.

'Oh, come now, Ma'am come! Good grassland pays as well as anything – you know you won't get nice sweet pickings for your beasts from neglected land, but only dirty old tow grass knotting under their feet. It's just that it's not a quick return, and so – as you know – I made a special price for you.'

'I do know!' she said impatiently. 'But I thought that part of it was settled and done.'

'Oh, I'm not going back on it, if that's what you think,' he said affably. 'I'm glad to do what I can for you, Ma'am, the more so seeing you have no man to attend to these things for you, but only yourself alone.'

'Oh, I'm well able to look after myself!' she said, raising her voice.

Once again her words had an opposite effect to what she intended. He laughed good-humouredly. 'That's what all women like to think!' he said. 'Well, now,' he said in a different tone of voice, and it annoyed her to see he seemed to think something had been settled between them, 'it would suit me – and I'm sure it's all the same with you – if we could leave your little job till later in the week, say till nearer to the time of the haymaking generally. Because by then I'd have the cutting bar in good order, sharpened and ready for use. Whereas now, while there's still a bit of ploughing to be done here and there, I'll have to be chopping and changing, between the plough and the mower, putting one on one minute and the other the next!'

'As if anyone is still ploughing this time of the year!' Her eyes hardened. 'Who are you putting before me?' she demanded.

'Now, take it easy, Ma'am. No one. Leastways, not without getting leave first from you.'

'Without telling me you're not coming, you mean!'

'Oh, now, Ma'am, don't get cross. I'm only trying to make matters easy for everyone.'

But she was very angry now. 'It's always the same story. I thought you'd treat me differently! I'm to wait till after this one, and after that one, and in the end my fields will go wild!'

He looked a bit shamefaced. 'Ah now, Ma'am, that's not going to be the case at all. Although, mind you, some people don't hold with topping, you know!'

'I hold with it!'

'Oh, I suppose there's something in it,' he said reluctantly. 'But the way I look at it, cutting the weeds in July is a kind of topping.'

'Grass cut before it goes to seed gets so thick at the roots no weeds can come up!' she cried, so angry she didn't realise how authoritative she sounded.

'Faith, I never knew you were so well up, Ma'am!' he said, looking at her admiringly, but she saw he wasn't going to be put down by her. 'All the same now, Ma'am, you can't say a few days here or there could make any difference?'

'A few days could make all the difference! This farm has a gravelly bottom to it, for all it's so lush. A few days of drought could burn it to the butt. And how could I mow it then? What cover would there be for the "nice sweet pickings" you were talking about a minute ago?' Angrily, she mimicked his own accent without thinking.

He threw up his hands. 'Ah well, I suppose a man may as well admit when he's bested,' he said. 'Even by a woman. And you can't say I broke my promise.'

'I can't say but you tried hard enough,' she said grudgingly, although she was mollified that she was getting her way. 'Can I offer you anything?' she said then, anxious to convey an air of finality to their discussion.

'Oh, not at all, Ma'am! Nothing, thank you! I'll have to be getting home.' He stood up.

She stood up, too.

'I hope you won't think I was trying to take advantage of you,' he said as they went towards the door. 'It's just that we must all make the best we can for ourselves – Isn't that so? Not but you're well able to look after yourself, I must say. No one ever thought you'd stay on here after your husband died. I suppose it's for the children you did it?' He looked up the well of the stairs. 'Are they asleep?'

'Oh, long ago,' she said indifferently. She opened the hall door.

The night air swept in immediately, as it had earlier. But this time, from far away, it bore along on it the faint scent of new-mown hay. 'There's hay cut somewhere already!' she exclaimed in surprise. And she lifted her face to the sweetness of it.

For a minute, Crossen looked past her out into the darkness, then he looked back. 'Aren't you ever lonely here at night?' he asked suddenly.

'You mean frightened?' she corrected quickly and coldly.

'Yes! Yes, that's what I meant,' he said, taken aback. 'Ah, but why would you be frightened! What safer place could you be under the sky than right here with your own fields all about you!'

What he said was so true, and he himself as he stood there, with his hat in his hand, so normal and natural it was indeed absurd to think that he would no sooner have gone out the door than she would be scurrying up the stairs like a child! 'You may not believe it,' she said, 'but I am scared to death sometimes! I nearly died when I heard your knock on the door tonight. It's because I was scared that I was upstairs,' she said, in a further burst of confidence. 'I always go up the minute it gets dark. I don't feel so frightened up in my room.'

'Isn't that strange now?' he said, and she could see he found it an incomprehensibly womanly thing to do. He was sympathetic all the same. 'You shouldn't be alone! That's the truth of the matter,' he said. 'It's a shame!'

'Oh, it can't be helped,' she said. There was something she wanted to shrug off in his sympathy, while at the same time there was something in it she wanted to take. 'Would you like to do something for me?' she asked impulsively. 'Would you wait and put out the lights down here and let me get back upstairs before you go?'

After she had spoken, for a minute she felt foolish, but she saw at once that, if anything, he thought it only too little to do for her. He was genuinely troubled about her. And it wasn't only the present moment that concerned him; he seemed to be considering the whole problem of her isolation and loneliness. 'Is there nobody could stay here with you – at night even? It would have to be another woman, of course,' he added quickly, and her heart was warmed by the way – without a word from her – he rejected that solution out of hand. 'You don't want a woman about the place,' he said flatly.

'Oh, I'm all right, really. I'll get used to it,' she said.

'It's a shame, all the same,' he said. He said it helplessly, though, and he motioned her towards the stairs. 'You'll be all right for tonight, anyway,' he said. 'Go on up the stairs now, and I'll put out the lights.' He had already turned around to go back into the sitting-room.

Yet it wasn't quite as she intended for some reason, and it was somewhat reluctantly that she started up the stairs.

'Wait a minute! How do I put out this one?' he called out before she was halfway up.

'Oh, I'd better put out that one myself,' she said, thinking of the awkward position of the plug. She ran down again, and, going past him into the little room, she knelt and pulled at the cord. Instantly the room was deluged in darkness. And instantly she felt that she had done something stupid. It was not like turning out a light by a switch at the door and being able to step back at once into the lighted hall. She got to her feet as quickly as she could, but as she did, she saw that Crossen had come to the doorway. His bulk was blocked out against the light beyond. 'I'll leave the rest to you,' she said, in order to break the peculiar silence that had come down on the house.

But he didn't move. He stood there, the full of the doorway.

'The other switches are over there by the hall door,' she said, unwillingly to brush past him. Why didn't he move? 'Over there,' she repeated, stretching out her arm and pointing, but instead of moving he caught at her outstretched arm, and,

putting out his other hand, he pressed his palm against the
door-jamb, barring the way.

'Tell me,' he whispered, his words falling over each other,
'are you never lonely – at all?'

'What did you say?' she said in a clear voice, because the
thickness of his voice sickened her. She had hardly heard what
he said. Her one thought was to get past him.

He leaned forward. 'What about a little kiss?' he whispered,
and to get a better hold on her he let go the hand he had
pressed against the wall, but before he caught at her with both
hands she had wrenched her arm free of him, and,
ignominiously ducking under his armpit, she was out next
minute in the lighted hall.

Out there – because light was all the protection she needed
from him, the old fool – she began to laugh. She had only to
wait for him to come sheepishly out.

But there was something she hadn't counted on; she hadn't
counted on there being anything pathetic in his sheepishness.
There was something actually pitiful in the way he shambled
into the light, not raising his eyes. And she was so surprisingly
touched by him that before he had time to utter a word she put
out her hand. 'Don't feel too bad,' she said. 'I didn't mind.'

Even then, he didn't look at her. He just took her hand and
pressed it gratefully, his face still turned away. And to her
dismay she saw that his nose was running water. Like a small
boy, he wiped it with the back of his fist, streaking his face. 'I
don't know what came over me,' he said slowly. 'I'm getting on
to be an old man now. I though I was beyond all that.' He wiped
his facc again. 'Beyond letting myself go, anyway,' he amended
miserably.

'Oh, it was nothing,' she said.

He shook his head. 'It wasn't as if I had cause for what I did.'

'But you did nothing,' she protested.

'It wasn't nothing to me,' he said dejectedly.

For a minute, they stood there silent. The hall door was still
ajar, but she didn't dare to close it. What am I going to do with
him now, she thought. I'll have him here all night if I'm not
careful. What time was it anyway? All scale and proportion

seemed to have gone from the night. 'Well, I'll see you in the morning, Mr Crossen!' she said, as matter-of-factly as possible.

He nodded, but made no move. 'You know I meant no disrespect to you, Ma'am, don't you?' he said then, looking imploringly at her. 'I always had a great regard for you. And for your husband, too. I was thinking of him this very night when I was coming up to the house. And I thought of him again when you came to the door looking like a young girl. I thought what a pity it was him to be taken from you, and you both so young! Oh, what came over me at all? And what would Mona say if she knew?'

'But you wouldn't tell her, I hope!' she cried. What sort of a figure would she cut if he told about her coming down in her bare feet with her hair down her back! 'Take care would you tell her!' she warned.

'I don't suppose I ought,' he said, but he said it uncertainly and morosely, and he leaned back against the wall. 'She's been a good woman, Mona. I wouldn't want anyone to think different. Even the boys could tell you. She's been a good mother to them all these years. She never made a bit of difference between them. Some say she was better to Bartley than to any of them! She reared him from a week old. She was living next door to us, you see, at the time –' He hesitated. 'At the time I was left with him,' he finished in a flat voice. 'She came in that first night and took him home to her own bed – and, mind you, that wasn't a small thing for a woman who knew nothing about children, not being what you'd call a young girl at the time, in spite of the big family she gave me afterwards. She took him home that night, and she looked after him. It isn't every woman would care to be responsible for a newborn baby. That's a thing a man doesn't forget easy! There's many I know would say that if she hadn't taken him someone else would have, but no one only her would have done it the way she did.

'She used to have him all day in her own cottage, feeding him and the rest of it. But at night, when I'd be back from the fields, she'd bring him home and leave him down in his little crib by the fire alongside of me. She used to let on she had things to

do in her own place, and she'd slip away and leave us alone, but
that wasn't her real reason for leaving him. She knew the way
I'd be sitting looking into the fire, wondering how I'd face the
long years ahead, and she left the child there with me to break
my thoughts. And she was right. I never got to brood. The child
would give a cry, or a whinge, and I'd have to run out and fetch
her to him. Or else she'd hear him herself maybe, and run in
without me having to call her at all. I used often to think she
must have kept every window and door in her place open, for
fear she'd lose a sound from either of us. And so, bit by bit, I
was knit back into a living man. I often wondered what would
have become of me if it wasn't for her. There are men and when
the bright way closes to them there's no knowing but they'll
take a dark way. And I was that class of man.

'I told you she used to take the little fellow away in the day
and bring him back at night? Well, of course, she used to take
him away again coming on to the real dark of night. She'd take
him away to her own bed. But as the months went on and he
got bigger, I could see she hated taking him away from me at
all. He was beginning to smile and play with his fists and be real
company. "I wonder ought I leave him with you tonight," she'd
say then, night after night. And sometimes she'd run in and
dump him down in the middle of the big double bed in the
room off the kitchen, but the next minute she'd snatch him up
again. "I'd be afraid you'd overlie him! You might only smother
him, God between us and all harm!" "You'd better take him,"
I'd say, I used to hate to see him go myself by this time. All the
same, I was afraid he'd start crying in the night, and what would
I do then? If I had to go out for her in the middle of the night,
it could cause a lot of talk. There was talk enough as things
were, I can tell you, although there was no grounds for it. I had
no more notion of her than if she wasn't a woman at all – would
you believe that? But one night when she took him up and put
him down, and put him down and took him up, and went on
about leaving him or taking him, I had to laugh. "It's a pity you
can't stay along with him, and that would settle all," I said. I was
only joking her, but she got as red as fire, and next thing she
burst out crying! But not before she'd caught up the child and

wrapped her coat around him. Then, after giving me a terrible look, she ran out of the door with him.

'Well, that was the beginning of it. I'd no idea she had any feelings for me. I thought it was only for the child. But men are fools, as women well know, and she knew before me what was right and proper for us both. And for the child, too. Some women have great insight into these things! And God opened my own eyes then to the woman I had in her, and I saw it was better I took her than wasted away after the one that was gone. And wasn't I right?'

'Of course you were right,' she said quickly.

But he slumped back against the wall, and the abject look came back into his eyes.

I'll never get rid of him, she thought desperately. 'Ah, what ails you!' she cried impatiently. 'Forget it, can't you?'

'I can't,' he said simply. 'And it's not only me – it's the wife I'm thinking about. I've shamed her!'

'Ah, for heaven's sake. It's nothing got to do with her at all.'

Surprised, he looked up at her. 'You're not blaming yourself, surely?' he asked.

She'd have laughed at that if she hadn't seen she was making headway – another stroke and she'd be rid of him. 'Arrah, what are you blaming any of us for!' she cried. 'It's got nothing to do with any of us – with you, or me, or the woman at home waiting for you. It was the other one! That girl – your first wife – Bridie! It was her! Blame her! She's the one did it!' The words had broken from her. For a moment, she thought she was hysterical and that she could not stop. 'You thought you could forget her,' she said, 'but see what she did to you when she got the chance!' She stopped and looked at him.

He was standing at the open door. He didn't look back. 'God rest her soul,' he said, and he stepped into the night.

A Family Likeness

'Laura, it's nearly April. There might be primroses in the woods,' Ada threw out this idle comment while she and her daughter sat over mid-morning coffee, waiting until it was time to lift Daff. Daff was four, but she woke at cockcrow, and most mornings had to be put down again for a nap.

'What a good idea, Mother. Let's go over the minute she wakes.' Laura sprang up and went to the window to look across the fields towards the small beech wood on the rim of the property. Clearly she was picturing clumps of primroses dotting the brown loam under the trees, each one set like a posy made by hand in a collar of green leaves. 'I wonder if I ought to wake her? She's down long enough.' Laura was making for the hall. 'Daff?' she called softly up the stairs. Then she called a little louder. 'Daff?'

Ada was torn between a conviction that no child can ever get too much sleep and a hankering for her little granddaughter's chatter. Ada wished that Laura and Richard would give up that silly pet name. The name Daphne was so nice. 'It's a wonder you don't call her Dotty,' she said irritably when Laura came back to the table.

'Oh, drop it, Mother, please,' Laura said. They'd been over this ground once too often. But she didn't mean to offend. 'Whose baby is she anyway?' she added. This was a standing joke between them ever since Daff was born and had several times served to head off one of the sudden squalls that no amount of tact, no amount of love could stop from blowing up out of a clear sky.

Ada, who suspected she was being let down lightly, made a timid attempt to have the last word. 'It's not fair to such a pretty child,' she said.

'She is sweet, isn't she?' Laura said, to put an end to the argument, and when next moment there was a footfall on the upper landing both women rushed to the foot of the stairs, Ada to throw out her arms for Daff to jump into them, Laura to gather up an armful of wraps from the banister rail. For all the sunshine, there could be a nip in the air. 'Let's not waste a minute,' Laura urged, poking Daff's arms into the sleeves of a fleecy white coat Ada had bought her.

Ada closed her eyes. A child's arms were so fragile and when Laura turned and attempted to force her, too, into a coat, she pulled away. 'This coat is yours, Laura.'

'What matter?' Laura was so off-hand, Ada hesitated to protest further.

When Laura was growing up and quite plump, and she herself was still in full sail, Laura never disclaimed borrowing one of her dresses and blouses. Now it was Ada who was glad to avail herself of an occasional cast-off, a raincoat or dressing-gown, or even laddered stockings if the run was in the heel or thigh where it didn't really show. But this coat was so roomy, Ada sighed. Age had pared her to the bone like a field made spare by wintry winds. 'I could easily run up and get my own coat, Laura.'

'Why bother?'

Why indeed? With another sigh, Ada folded the coat around her, and the trio, all muffled up, set out for the woods. There was indeed a nasty nip in the air, but only in the shade of the house. When they got beyond the shadow of the gable it was really warm for the time of year. To get to the woods, they had to climb over a stile.

'Here, let grandmother help you, Daff,' Ada offered.

'Oh, leave her alone, Mother. She's well able to manage.'

Better than me, Ada thought ruefully when she had to be helped over the stile, not Daff. Daff was already manfully plunging through grass up to her middle. The growth was truly remarkable for April. It promised well for their finding at least a few primroses.

Laura was in great form. 'Let's make Daff a tossy-ball, Mother, like you used to make me when I was small. I never did figure out how you got the flowerheads all bunched up together without the stems showing.'

'Black thread. I used to bring a spool of it in my pocket. I wish we had thought of bringing one with us today.' Ada was not really attending to what Laura was saying. She was watching Daff progress. The long grass was heavy going for a four-year-old. Then her attention returned to her daughter. 'Tossy-balls are made with cowslips, not primroses, Laura.'

'Oh, well. Maybe we'll find cowslip too.'

'Not in the woods. They're only found in pasture, or meadow.' Ada looked around. 'There might even be some in this field.' She gave a violent start. 'Do I see cattle?' Instinctively, she grabbed Daff by the hand.

'Take it easy, Mother. The cattle are over at the far end. They only come back here to shelter for the night. Grass near trees is too sour for them. See. They're lying down. No wonder. It's a glorious day.'

Ada stifled her fears as best she could by watching Daff plodding valiantly onwards. To Ada herself, the wood was proving farther away than she'd bargained on. 'Ought we carry her, do you think, Laura?'

'You? Or me?' Laura's voice was scalding. 'You don't seem to realise it, Mother, but she's a big lump now. Sometimes you really astonish me. You know I'm not supposed to over-exert myself these days.' She gave Daff a poke in the back. 'Hurry up,' she said. But sensing Ada's disapproval, her next remark was transparently an attempt to please. 'This was a really good idea of yours, Mother.'

'I hope you won't be disappointed,' Ada said, non-committally. Her glance roved over to a grassy bank. In all truth, she was having misgivings herself about their outing. 'Now I come to think of it, a wood is not really the right place to find primroses either. Primroses grow best on a sunny bank.' She pointed, 'Like over there. Look. What did I tell you?' Indistinct, but unmistakable as the glow of stars in the Milky Way, masses and masses of primroses studded the green bank.

'Oh. Do you not want to go any farther, Mother? Is that it?' Laura asked. 'You could go back from here, if you wish, and I could take Daff to the edge of the woods and let her get a glimpse of …'

'Of what? The primroses are on the bank.'

'That's right.' Laura ceded graciously enough. 'Well, suppose you and Daff go over there and you sit down, while she picks a little bunch, and I go on to the woods. It's ages since I've been over there and it's important I keep fit.'

Fine as the prick of the smallest needle ever made, one with an eye so narrow it was quite impossible to thread, Ada's heart was pierced with sadness. Had her daughter seen that she was failing? She, who up to such a short time ago had been indefatigable, possessed indeed of far more energy than Laura herself had ever enjoyed.

'I don't want to sit down, Laura,' she said. With a pang she remembered the way her own mother had laid a querulous emphasis on some words. 'The grass may be damp,' she added meekly.

'Damp? That bank, with the sun pouring down on it since dawn?' Laura laughed, but glancing at her mother, she seemed to suffer a change of heart. 'I suppose it wouldn't be any harm for us all to take a short rest,' she said. 'Come on, Daff. This way.'

Why did she have to speak so peremptorily to the child, Ada wondered. 'The primroses are over there, dear,' she explained. When Daff didn't budge, she appealed to Laura. 'The child really is tired,' she said.

'All to the good. Maybe after this she might sleep through the night for a change.' Laura swung round savagely. 'Last night, she woke me at least three times.'

'I didn't hear a sound. Why didn't you call me?' Ada tried to keep her voice down.

'And if I did?'

Ada was not sure if her daughter meant she could be of no use or if she was insinuating that she might not have been prepared to get up and help. She looked dejectedly into the grass. 'Why didn't you call me?' 'Why?' she persisted.

Laura turned a cold eye on her. 'Haven't I heard you say often enough that there is no sweeter music than the crying of another woman's child.'

Oh, oh, oh! How Laura could twist words. Ada was outraged. 'Not your child, Laura. Not my own grandchild. Not Daff.' She could not remember having said such a thing unless perhaps to put some young mother at ease in a hotel if an infant had been wailing in the night. 'I do wish you had called me, Laura.'

'Don't go on and on about it. Please. It's not as if it was only last night. Every night is the same. I'm worn to a frazzle. I scarcely ever close an eye.'

They had started to walk on, when, nearing the headland, under their feet where the grass was scant, Ada saw a cow-pat. 'I thought you said the cattle didn't graze here,' she said, and hurrying, she made for the bank. From it she scanned the field. 'I don't see them anymore. Where have they gone?' she asked anxiously. There was more than one cow-pat. She saw several.

'Who cares?' Laura turned aside. 'Well, Daff? What do you think of the primroses?' The primroses were unbelievably plentiful. 'Can I pick them?' Daff asked in awe.

'Of course, darling.'

'This is how we do it, Daff.' Ada forgot the cattle. Burrowing, with fingers still nimble, down between the thick leaves of a large clump that bore twenty flowers or more, she grubbed close to the roots and pinched off a primrose with a long stem, cool and green, its base softly flushed with pink. 'We don't want to pull off their poor heads, do we?' she said gaily. 'And we'll only take one from each clump, so there'll be some left for other people to enjoy.' It was such a pleasure to guide the young mind. She was glad to see that Daff was watching intently. There ought to be no need of a scolding next time she beheaded a flower in the garden.

'For goodness' sake, Mother. They're only wild flowers. Let her enjoy them.'

'She could hardly be enjoying them more,' Ada said as Daff proudly held up a primrose with a stem as long as a beanstalk. 'It's precisely because these are wild that we can teach her to pick flowers properly.' She guided Daff's hand into the moist depths of another clump. Then, seeing that Daff had got the hang of things, she began to pick a bunch herself to bring back to her room, taking care to pick a few leaves to make a collarette for them. But when Laura, disregarding the fact that she was crushing several clumps, lowered herself down on the bank and lay back to bask in the sun, she was instinctively impelled to caution her. 'It's too early in the season for that, Laura.'

Laura sat up at once, but only the better to deliver an angry retort. 'I don't care if I get pneumonia. You haven't the faintest notion how exhausted I am, Mother. When I was Daff's age, you had servants to wait on you hand and foot.'

Taken off her feet by this outburst, Ada abruptly sat down. 'You are greatly mistaken, Laura. The only help I ever had was an incompetent local girl who came for a few hours to do a bit of cleaning. I never let her into the nursery.'

'More fool you.' Laura let her head flop back on the grass.

Ada stared. What had precipitated this attack? 'Your father, of course, was wonderful,' she said. 'If you woke at night it was him, not me, who walked the floor with you.'

Again, Laura sat bolt upright. 'Are you insinuating that Richard does not pull his weight? You forget he provides for us. The child is my concern.'

'No one is disputing that. Don't think, dear, I haven't noticed how tired you've been looking lately. It's not easy for me to see you so white and drawn.'

Laura, who lay with her beautiful face framed in flowers, made a move as if to sit up for the third time, but instead she turned her head and fixed on Ada a stare that went through her, not like a needle this time, but a pitchfork.

'Just exactly what are you trying to do to me, Mother? Bad enough to feel like hell without being told I look like hell.'

'Did I say that?' Ada stared miserably at the bunch of wild flowers in her hand. 'Here, Daff, you have mine,' she said. Daff shook her head, her interest in primroses was waning. The few she'd picked were scattered about on the grass. Ada left her own bunch down beside them, where it fell apart, the stems now looking more pink than green. Like worms, she thought, shuddering. She ought perhaps to dredge up from the time of

her own young motherhood some experience or other that
would show Laura she understood her fatigue. She hit on one
at once. 'My own mother used to drive me mad when you were
small, telling me I'd some day look back on those years as the
best years of my life.' But hearing herself repeat the timeworn
words, Ada felt that the adage was true. Then suddenly Laura
launched into a gratuitous and glowing reminiscence of her
grandmother, a reminiscence which, in the circumstances,
could be intended to hurt.

'Poor Grandmother. I used to feel so sad when you were
mean to her.'

'Mean? Me?' Ada winced.

Laura, who surely could see the wound she'd inflicted, was
in no way repentant. 'I loved her. She was such a dear little
thing, so gay and happy most of the time. She was always
overwhelmed with gratitude when I went up to her room and
listened to her stories. She had an unending store of them. We
had such fun. We used to laugh so much the two of us when we
were together.'

'At what?' Ada was disconcerted. And when Laura smiled
enigmatically she was goaded into self-justification. 'Towards
the end of her life your grandmother made things very difficult
for me. I can tell you that.'

'You didn't understand her. That was your problem,' Laura
said so smugly that Ada looked away in disdain. The sun still
spilled down but she felt chill as if it had gone behind a cloud.
'She used to brush my hair,' Laura added and closed her eyes.

To Ada there was something bogus about her daughter's
nostalgia. 'When it suited her,' she snapped. 'Any time I
needed her help she always seemed to have something more
important of her own to do.'

'Like what?' Laura opened one eye.

'This and that.' Ada was flustered at being pinned down.
'Well, for one thing, she was forever reading newspapers, even
papers a week old.'

'What else?'

'Let me see. She spent hours and hours cutting out snippets
of news that apparently had some special significance for her.

God knows why. The same with magazines. Oh yes, another thing, she had a collection of old postcards that she was always sorting.' Ada paused. Somehow these occupations of her mother's didn't seem sufficient to account for the awful clutter in that little room of hers. 'She used to hoard string and spend hours taking out the knots or tying together bits too small to be of any use. Your father often asked me to try and get her to keep her door shut. Of course, she never did. Your grandmother was a law unto herself.'

'I don't see that it mattered whether her door was open or shut, way up there at the top of the house. No one ever went up there, only him and me and whoever brought up her meals.'

'It was *me* who brought them up. Who else did you think? I always had to bring trays up to her because she never came down at proper meal-times. She was really wilful about small things. And if she did condescend to come down, it would be in her own good time, when the washing-up was done, the pots and pans put away, and the kitchen swept. You know how annoying that can be to a servant.'

'No.' As if the monosyllable was not sufficiently deadly, Laura went on. 'Old people can't be expected to be exactly normal.'

'She was the same as far back as I can remember,' Ada protested. 'I cannot recall her ever doing anything at the right time. When I was young, my meal was never on the table when I came home from school. She didn't even have the supper ready in the evening when my father came home tired and hungry from the office. She thought nothing of keeping us waiting while she attended to some fiddle-faddle.'

'Such as?'

'Oh.' Ada sighed wearily. Those memories of her mother were becoming too painful to contemplate. 'In those days, I think it was letter-writing,' she said apathetically. 'She'd sit for hours at the dining-room table dashing off page after page and then she'd go out to the pillar box before she'd pay any attention to us.'

'Letters to whom?'

'How do I know?' Ada was exasperated by this inquisition, but just then it was as if a shaft of light fell on the hand of that long-dead letter writer and she was confounded by what it revealed. 'Wait, Laura. I *do* know. She was writing to her own mother. To my grandmother. How could I have forgotten? She wrote to her every other day, long interminable letters.'

'I'm not surprised. She dearly loved her own mother. She was always talking about her,' Laura said dreamily. Then unexpectedly she opened both eyes and a look of amazement came on her face. 'Good Lord. Your mother's mother would be Daff's great-great-grandmother. You don't mean to say you remember her, Mother?'

'Why, yes of course I remember her. My mother kept a photograph of her beside her bed. I remember she had large dark eyes, soft and liquidy with a curiously vulnerable look, like a doe or a gazelle. I assure you too that my mother's constant talk about her made her a real presence in our house.' Again, Ada had a vision of the dead hand, barely able to constrain the love that sent its pen racing over the paper. 'I suppose I was jealous of my grandmother,' she said reflectively. 'I resented her place in my mother's affections, not only for myself but for my father too. I hated her. Although looking back now I realise she had a hard life. After all, she had twelve children. Can you imagine that? I suppose it was no wonder my own mother was so devoted to her, I may have been unfair as well as unforgiving.'

Laura surprisingly put out her hand and patted her knee. 'It's all so long ago, how can one say?' she said. 'And does it really make any difference now?'

Ada appreciated the gesture, even if the words were tactless. 'I'm sometimes sorry that I didn't listen more to her when she was talking about the past. I never seemed to have the time.'

'One can always make time,' Laura's mood had changed again. 'As I remember it, you expected her to be always at your beck and call just because she was living with you.'

Ada found this so unforgivable, she had to change the subject quickly. 'What is Daff doing?' she asked, although the child was only a few yards away and appeared perfectly happy. But as she spoke, Daff gave a rapturous squeal and she saw that, bored by the primroses, she had wandered back to the cow-pat and was

about to poke her fingers in it. 'Laura. Stop her,' Ada yelled.
She herself could never have got to her feet in time.

Laura stood up clumsily. 'Daff. Don't touch that, you little
fool,' she yelled, catching the child and shaking her. 'Do you
want to get filthy? Come away from there, at once.' Dragging
Daff after her she came back to the bank, out of breath.

'It was probably dried up,' Ada said, hoping to make light of
things.

'If she stuck her fingers in it, we'd soon know whether it was
dry or not.' Ada was chastened. Laura did look tired; she had
eased herself down on the bank once more and closed her eyes
again leaving Daff standing uncertainly in front of her.

Ada felt the child had done enough penance. 'You can play
anywhere you like, dear, as long as you don't get yourself dirty,'
she said. But Daff still stood unhappily waiting for her mother
to speak to her. After a minute, Ada had to resort to the
well-known bait for catching a parent's attention. 'Who is Daff
like, do you think, Laura?' she asked.

Laura did not rise to the bait. 'Who cares?' she said.

'That depends.'

'What do you mean by that?' Laura warily opened one eye.

'Well, you can be thankful that you resemble your
grandmother, my dear,' Ada said. To her dismay, she saw
Laura's expression change instantly from suspicion to
vexation. 'I know dear that when I said this before it upset you,
but …'

'Is it any wonder? When I was small you were always
threatening that I'd grow up to be like her.'

'Oh, I meant that I wouldn't have wished you to inherit her
character. But in her prime, my mother was a very beautiful
woman, and one couldn't wish better for you than that you'd
take after her in looks. Say what you like, you do. You are the
living image of her.

'You used to be upset, dear, because you knew her only when
she was an old woman. When she was young her face was like
the face on a Greek coin. And to the last her skin was smooth
and soft. It was that olive texture which never shows wrinkles,
unlike mine, or for that matter, yours. Don't misunderstand

me. I've always been proud of your porcelain skin, but that type
of skin is never as durable as an olive complexion.' Here, she
bent over and scrutinised her daughter's face. 'Laura. Are you
listening? I hope you put some protection on your face,
specially when you go out in the harsh wind. If you don't, you'll
wake up one day with broken veins. But to go back to the
resemblance between you and my mother. Do you know that
photograph of her wearing a white blouse in broderie anglaise,
with her lovely chestnut hair piled on the top of her head, the
one where she's holding me in her arms? She was very young
when that was taken.' Suddenly, Ada gasped. 'Why, Laura. She
must have been only your age then. Let me see.' She began to
make a quick count on her fingers. I simply can't believe it. You
are already older now than she was then. A year older at least.
No, two years. Laura, are you listening to me at all?' she asked.
She leant over her again. Laura was asleep.

Ada felt as desolate as if Laura had gone away and left her
alone. Then she remembered Daff. Daff was poking at
something with that twig. The cow-pat? No. But yes. The child
was stirring it up and now she had released upon the air an
utterly disgusting smell. Ecstatically then, the child began to
flick at it, sending the soft wet dung raining down on her dress,
her face and her shinning hair.

'Laura. Laura.' Ada shook her daughter. 'Quick. Wake up.
Daff's at the dung again.' Her own exhaustion was so great she
could not attempt to cope.

Lemonade

It couldn't last. Not all the lemonade anyway.

'Like another bottle?' Uncle Pauddy asked.

'Take one any time you feel like it,' said Uncle Matt. He took her inside the counter and showed her how to use the bottle-opener.

She had a few bottles just for the pleasure of prising off the caps, but she was really sick of lemonade. To hear the uncles, you'd think she never got any till she came to Ireland. On the boat she got plenty. Back in Boston, Pappa's friends often treated her.

'Whatever about you, Dinny,' they'd say, 'we can't let the child go home thirsty!' Though in fairness to the Irish uncles, she had to admit there was no ambiguity about the lemonade in Ireland. In Boston she never knew whether Mama or Pappa meant real lemonade, or the kind Pappa drank. It was confusing, like the night before they sailed for Ireland.

All Pappa's and Mama's friends had come to the house to say good-bye, that is to say, all Pappa's friends. Mama didn't want them.

'On our last night!' she sighed, when Pappa announced they were coming.

'I know, I know,' said Pappa, 'only it wasn't me who asked them. They invited themselves – out of the goodness of their hearts!' he added.

'– or maybe,' cried Mama – 'as a cure for the drought!'

'Oh come now, don't be bitter on our last night,' said Pappa.

And so they came, all the old cronies. There was barely room in the parlour for them all, especially with the trunks and boxes, strapped and corded with new white rope, in the middle of the floor, and on the top of one of the trunks, a big bunch of asters wrapped in wet newspaper.

'Don't sit on the asters, please!' Mama kept saying all evening.

'Wait a minute, wait a minute, boys,' cried Pappa, as the cronies came in the door, and he lifted up the red plush skirt that draped the table legs, and pulled out a crate. 'We can get rid of this box and make more room, if some of you give me a hand to empty out what's in it!'

Everybody laughed but Mama.

'Ah come now, ma'am,' said one of the cronies, and he pointed to the round tin seals, that were soldered to the twisted wire every place it was knotted. 'What harm can be in it, when it's covered with medals?'

Mama didn't heed him.

'Dinny, you gave me your solemn word –' she said.

'So I did! So I did!' cried Pappa, 'but it doesn't take effect till your ship sails, girlie! Come now, don't be a spoil-sport.'

The next minute the crate was split open, and Pappa ran into the kitchen and came back with a bunch of glasses, held by their stems like flowers.

'Now who's for lemonade?' he cried. Then he bit his lip. 'Gee, honey,' he said, and he ran over to Maudie. 'Amn't I the bad Pappa. I forgot to get real lemonade for you.'

It was because he was so sad, not because she was disappointed, that the tears came into Maudie's eyes.

'There,' cried Mama, seeing the tears, 'I knew something like this would happen!'

But Maudie dashed the tears away.

'I don't mind, Mama!' she cried. She shook Pappa's shoulder. 'Honest I don't!'

'Don't you?' Pappa looked up at her. 'Honest, girlie?' The happy look came back to his face. He had only one girlie now to placate. 'How about giving the child a little of what we have – well diluted, of course – to make up to her?' he whispered to Mama.

Mama was almost speechless.

'Dinny Delaney! – it's when you say things like that that I know I am doing right in –'

But Pappa clapped his hand over her mouth, and he spoke very low, so that no one could hear but Maudie.

'No more of that!' he said. 'Tut-tut. A bargain is a bargain. A little holiday – that was what we agreed to call it and you needed it badly, if anyone ever deserved it, it's you, girl. A little holiday. No reasons asked and none given. Isn't that what we decided? And don't forget it when you get the other side either.' He looked very cross for a minute, and stared down into the drink in his glass. Then he raised his eyes. 'Indeed, a little nip wouldn't hurt you either – for health reasons,' he added, quickly. 'I'm telling you, you needn't look so stuck-up about it and this time tomorrow you may be glad to remember my words, but the best preparation for a sea-voyage is a drop of this stuff here,' and he tapped the glass in his hand. 'I see you don't heed me, but I know what I'm talking about, and it was a bar-tender – wait! – what am I talking about, it wasn't a bar-tender at all but a steward on board ship, that told me himself about a young woman just your own age on one of his crossings, and she was so sick the ship's doctor thought it was all up with her, and so it might have been if it weren't for the steward's presence of mind in forcing a drop of drink down her throat. That's the truth I'm telling you, girl. And don't forget it either. And remember, if the child happens to get sick –'

Here, he went to sit down again beside Maudie, but Mama gave a scream.

'Mind the asters!' she cried. 'Oh, they're ruined,' she said, snatching them up and examining them.

They were getting a bit tattered. A lot of raggy petals had come undone and littered the floor like scraps of knitting wool.

'I did so want to have them with us on the voyage,' Mama wailed.

'How many times have you made the voyage, ma'am?' asked one of the cronies politely.

'How many times did I cross the Atlantic, Dinny?' Mama asked, but she didn't wait for his answer. 'Four times,' she said, 'counting this time, of course,' she added, scrupulously.

'You're not the whole way across yet girl!' said Pappa. 'There's such things as icebergs, you know,' he said, and he turned and looked soberly towards his guests. 'For all our advances in science and the like, we haven't got rid of the icebergs yet.'

'What are icebergs?' asked Maudie.

'Oh, they're nothing at all,' said Pappa, hastily, 'and anyway, who knows, but your Mama might get homesick yet and change her mind at the last minute, and then you wouldn't be going away at all!'

'Oh, but I *want* to go,' cried Maudie. 'I've told everybody I'm going, the teachers in school and all!'

'So *you* want to leave me too, do you?' he said, and he stared deep down into his glass that was empty now.

'Oh, don't start that kind of thing with her – with a *child*,' cried Mama. 'Naturally she's looking forward to the excitement. And anyway, she knows or she's been told rather that you're coming over to take us back in the spring.'

'Yes she's been told that, I know,' said Pappa gloomily. Why was his voice so peculiar though? And why did Mama raise her own voice and scatter her words to all sides.

'It will be Dinny's fourteenth crossing – when he comes over for us,' she said.

They were all amazed.

'Fourteen times across The Pond!' cried old Pa Spiddal, immeasurably impressed. His real name was not Spiddal at all. That was the name of the place he came from back in Ireland. He talked about it so much that he was never called anything else.

'That's true,' said Pappa, taking up again. 'And by rights, some of them crossings ought to count double because the crossings nowadays are not to be compared with the crossings when I first came out here. Oh, those early crossings! Did I ever tell you about the time –'

'I'm sure you did!' said Mama, hastily, but the others were greedy for it.

They were all Irish, but not born-Irish, and so taking part in this leave-taking of Dinny's wife and child had a two-fold nostalgia for them, a nostalgia for the old country, but also for the old people, now dead and gone, through whose eyes, only, they had ever seen that lost land.

'Well,' said Dinny, ignoring Mama, '– to give you an idea of the way we used to be tossed about in those days, I must tell you there used to be a rim around the tables to prevent the cups and saucers from sliding off on to the floor. No! wait a minute, I think that must have been on later crossings altogether – in the real early days, when I was a young lad making my first voyage, the cups and saucers were chained to the tables, they were enamel cups, or maybe tin but –'

'Dinny!' Mama's cheeks were blazing. 'Surely that was only in steerage!' she cried.

'Yes – sure it was steerage,' said Pappa, unembarrassed, and quite unaware of Mama's flushed face. 'I don't know what it was like in first class,' he said, 'although as I used to say in those days, there wouldn't be much differ if the ship went down.'

But although one or two of the old cronies laughed, Maudie could see that one or two of the women had caught each other's eyes. And just then, she felt a stealthy movement down near her feet, that dangled over the edge of the trunk, and looking down – stealthily too – she saw that old Ma Spiddal had reached out her foot, and, with the tip of her black buttoned boot, was gently, but persuasively, pushing apart the two big steamer trunks.

But Mama saw it too. She snatched up the asters.

'Is it the labels you want to see, Ma Spiddal?' she asked, crisply. 'Not but that steerage nowadays is nearly as good as first class in the old days,' she said, showing – no – forcing the labels under Ma Spiddal's nose, 'still, it's not worth our while looking into a few dollars here or there, like as if we were emigrants!'

'Ah, it's more than a few dollars difference, my dear,' said Ma Spiddal, with a mixture of grudgingness, envy, but above all, contrition.

'Well, it's Dinny's concern anyway, not mine,' said Mama more gently. She looked down with some surprise at the asters in her hand. 'I'd better put these in water!'

'Water!' Pappa shuddered violently, – 'a sacrilegious word on this night,' he said, and he dived into the crate again to bring up another bunch of bottles.

But Mama whispered something to him, and next minute Maudie felt herself being picked up bodily in Pappa's arms. And all the way up the stairs her head bobbed from side to side.

'Am I on the boat?' she cried. 'Is it sinking?'

'You see!' cried Mama to Pappa. 'I hope you're satisfied now with your old guffage! A nice time I'll have with her on the boat!'

'Well, I declare to God,' cried Pappa, 'anyone would think to hear you that it was my idea for you to go instead of –'

'Instead of what?' flashed Mama.

'Oh what's the use going into it now,' said Pappa, and he rummaged in his pocket. 'Here,' he said. 'I may as well give you the tickets now.'

Mama took them and looked at them.

'Single fare?'

'You'll feel freer that way,' said Pappa.

'We'll lose money by not getting a return.'

'Only if you come back,' said Pappa, queerly.

Sleepy as she was, those words went through Maudie's heart. And Pappa saw.

'Who knows, girlie? I may go over and settle down there myself,' he said, jocularly, but the jocularity didn't satisfy even him. 'Give me back those tickets for a minute.' He whipped out a pencil from his pocket and put a little cross on the back of one of the tickets. 'That stands for lemonade,' he said to Maudie. 'Show it to the steward on the boat and he'll understand. It's my mark. It means I'll pay for it when I go across next time – Mama will arrange things if there's any difficulty.'

Mama snatched back the tickets, in no way pleased, though.

'Can we never discuss anything seriously?' she said. 'Isn't it decided that you're coming over in March to bring us back?'

'That was the idea at the start,' said Pappa.

'Well?' said Mama.

'Well!' said Pappa. 'Oh, I'll go over all right,' he said, slowly, 'but who knows if we mightn't all settle down over there.'

Mama looked dubious.

'You mightn't find the company so much to your liking over there.'

'Oh, you're bitter, aren't you? Bitter to the last. Let me tell you something. Before I ever left an eye on you, I meant to end up in the old country. I don't remember the old tongue, though I heard it spoken on our own hearthstone by the old people. I didn't know what they were saying to be sure, but it was as natural to hear them at it as it was to hear the jackdaws above in the chimneys. I remember there was one saying that was always put at the end of the rosary by the fire at night, *Bás in Éirinn* – Death in Ireland to you – that was my mother's wish for us all, that we'd make enough to end up in the old country.'

'There's only one way of making that wish come true,' said Mama, bitterly, 'and I can't see you ever having means for anything at the rate you're going.'

'You're wrong there. Like you're often wrong! And property doesn't cost as much back home as it does here, you know. A fellow was telling me the other day there are farms going for nothing – they're giving them away, in Leitrim and Roscommon.'

'Is it down there!' cried Mama. 'Thank you for nothing.'

Pappa sprang up from the bed.

'There you go again. What use is it trying to plan anything with a woman like you. God Himself wouldn't please you! It's my belief that you'll be disappointed in Heaven when you get there!'

'I wouldn't be surprised if I was!' cried Mama, 'I'm so used to disappointments now. But I don't believe you know what you're talking about! Leitrim! Roscommon! I'd never have a soul to speak to from day-up to day-down!'

'Like here!' shouted Pappa. 'How is it I have friends everywhere I go?'

But at this the tears started into Mama's eyes.

'Don't ask *me* that question, Dinny,' she said. 'Isn't it in the answer to it that all the trouble lies, that is between us now, or at any time? Oh, I'm so tired, tired, tired.' She raised her head and seemed to listen distastefully to the voices and laughter that came up the stairs from the parlour. 'You'd better go down to them; they'll think something is wrong. Or are they going to stay all night?'

'Oh God, no!' said Pappa, and he brought up another bit of Gaelic for the occasion. 'I'll give them a hint, one more round and call it a *deoch an dorais* – a drop for the door!'

'Aren't we really coming back, Mama?' said Maudie, when he was gone down.

'Why do you ask that?' said Mama, sharply. 'Wouldn't you like to stay in Ireland with all your uncles and aunts, and go to a nice convent school where the nuns could put a polish on you?'

It was four o'clock in the morning, and, if there were any daylight to see it, the coast of Ireland could have been seen, like a thin string of seaweed drifting on the horizon. As it was, all that could be seen was the flash of the lighthouse.

'Wake up, Maudie, wake up, for your first glimpse of Ireland. Look!'

Through the porthole, misted over now with their breath, all Maudie could see at first was the same grey waste of waters that had washed outside it every day of the voyage, except that now it was lit with flashes from the lights in the engine room. When her eyes became accustomed to the dimness, she could see that far out it was lit too by white flashes of its own cold foam. Then, suddenly, in the distance, a black fist opened to let out a blue ball of light, and closed again, then opened to catch it once more – closed and opened, closed and opened, closed and opened –

'It wasn't really Ireland? It was only old rocks, wasn't that all?' she asked timidly later in the day, when they were in the tender at Cobh and still far away a green shore floated on the top of the water.

She was feeling very sleepy but she didn't fall asleep till they were in the train.

Then she sank back wearily against the red repp seats that smelled of dust and coal-fumes, and it really seemed as if she had only just closed her eyes when Mama was shaking her to wake and open them.

'Here, let me tidy you up,' she said. 'This is the next station but one to – there!'

Maudie knew she had nearly said 'home', but had changed it quickly to 'there'. Tired as she was, she sensed an apathy in Mama. Where now was the impetuosity that woke her up to see Fastnet Rock?

And then – suddenly – before the train had properly pulled up on the platform – wrenching open the carriage door, shouting, laughing, kissing Mama, and seizing up their baggage – were three of the handsomest young men Maudie had ever seen. It was the uncles, the fabulous uncles.

'But we're only at the Clare Junction!' cried Mama.

'We couldn't wait!' cried the uncles all together, like schoolboys. 'We took a sidecar and came up here to meet you. We'll ride on the train with you from here onward.' They crowded into their carriage. 'How are you, how are you? Welcome home at last. Time you came back!'

Maudie was overwhelmed. Such laughing! Such kissing! No wonder Mama missed them so much, and was always talking about them, and telling about their larkings and goings-on.

'Is there anybody there for here?' cried Uncle Pauddy, as the train came to a stop again. 'Mind the step, mind the step,' he cautioned, as they got out on the palely lit station. 'Take my arm,' he cried, as they stepped into the pitch black street behind the station.

'I know my way,' said Mama, irritably. 'What about the trunks?' But Uncle John-Joe was already loading the trunks on to a little trolley that was standing up against the wall.

'We use it for bringing the porter barrels out to the bottling shed,' he explained to Maudie. 'Did you ever hear of porter, I wonder?'

'Is it like lemonade?' she ventured. They all laughed.

'Poor Dinny!' said John-Joe.

'So you remember that after all the years!' said Mama.

'How is he, anyway?' said Matt, quickly.

'Oh, he's fine,' said Mama.

'I'm glad to hear it,' said Matt, soberly. 'He'll be over after you it's likely.'

'That's what he planned anyway,' said Mama, shortly.

'That'll be grand,' said Matt. 'We might persuade him to buy a little place over here and settle down in it for good.'

They were well out of the station now, in a narrow street with no footpath, walking abreast in the middle of the road that was soft and muddy.

'Don't tell me there was a Fair today,' said Mama, as she splashed into a puddle.

'Oh, indeed, yes,' said John-Joe, apologetically. 'Today was the second day of the big October Fair.'

'What a day I chose!' cried Mama.

'Come now,' said Matt. 'Don't start acting like a returned Yank.'

'That's what I am though, I suppose,' said Mama.

'Oh, not at all,' cried Matt. 'Sure you were only out there on a little holiday – you'll all be stopping home for good this time – wait and see.' He squeezed Maudie.

But Mama was going back reflectively on Matt's words.

'A holiday is it?' she said. 'Ten years! It was a long sort of holiday!' Then she laughed. 'According to Dinny, *this* is the holiday,' – 'Coming back is the holiday according to him!' They walked on a few steps more. 'I wonder which of you is right?' she said, but as they went around a corner, she suddenly clapped her hands. 'My old room!' she cried. 'All lighted up. Oh, how good of Cass! How is she? How is Cass? To think I never *asked* for her. Look, look Maudie,' she pointed to a pink light that glowed away at the end of the street. 'That was my room when I was a girl, that was my room in the gable-end,' she cried. 'Oh, I've been so homesick for that light, for that room.' She started to run. And when they got to the hall-door she made straight for the stairs, calling back over her shoulder, 'I forgot to tell you that the dwelling-rooms are over the shop.' But Maudie was staring about her enthralled.

All up the stairs, and all along the red-papered corridor at short intervals, fastened to the wall were red tin lamps. Behind each lamp was a fluted tin reflector that threw out a light so bright the red wallpaper seemed to bleed.

At last she got to the end of the corridor and she saw a small woman standing there.

'Cass!' cried Mama, and she ran forward.

'I didn't come down because –'

'Oh, why should you!' cried Mama, as they came together and kissed.

'Well?' said Cass, stepping back. 'How are things? How is Dinny?'

'Oh, he's grand – grand,' said Mama.

'I hope you weren't expecting to be in your own old room,' said Cass then. 'I moved into it, I didn't think you'd be back,' she added, defensively, 'unless on a holiday.'

'Oh, that's fine,' said Mama. 'Put us anywhere at all. I'm so tired I'd sleep on the floor!' But she stopped midway in the doorway of the room. 'What else is this but a holiday?' she asked.

Cass said nothing.

'Did you think I wasn't going back to him?' asked Mama.

At that Uncle Matt came up with a trunk on his back.

'We're going to make Dinny buy a place over here!' he said. 'And now, Cass, what about a cup of tea? And what will the child take? How about a bottle of lemonade? Eh?'

'Is it at this time of night?' cried Mama. 'Well, she'll have it in bed if so! I'll be undressing her while you're getting it,' and they went into their room.

'Will you be all right?' asked Cass, and she went out and closed the door.

When she was gone, Mama looked around the room.

'I must say I can't blame her for moving out of *this* room,' she said. 'I had no idea it was so ugly and dark. And over the shop! Listen!' From below there was a sound of feet echoing as if in an empty place. 'That's Pauddy getting your lemonade,' she said, and she frowned. 'Now, my *old* room was over the snuggery,' she said, as she pulled down the sheets. 'There was never a sound. I'm not complaining, of course. And, anyway, I know what's at the back of it all.' She lowered her voice. 'Jealousy! You see, I ought never to have had the best room, seeing I was the youngest daughter. But,' and here Mama whispered so low Maudie could hardly hear her, 'I was your grandma's favourite,' she said. 'She always spoiled me. Aunt Cass resented it. I didn't realise it till this minute. And, as I say,

I don't blame her for taking it when I went away. Only I do think she could have let me have it for this visit.'

So it *was* only a visit. How the limits of their stay swelled and shrank, although thinking of the glowing ruby walls and the beautiful fluted reflectors at the back of the lamps, she felt that she would never want to leave such a palace. Why, the windows had alternating panes in diamond shape of red and green glass. Stained-glass! A palace indeed! And on the landing just outside their door she had seen a big pedestal, on which stood a brass urn filled with ferns. And the pedestal was marble. Truly a palace!

The next day Maudie woke before it was light. She was up and dressed in a minute and out on the landing.

Oh, but where now was the bleeding red wallpaper? Alas, unlit, the lamps shed no sanguinary glow, and the fluted edges of the tin reflectors were blunt with rust. As for the marble pedestal! When she laid her hand on it, it had the soft warm touch of wood! The red veining was done with paint. The marbling only a fake. And moving across the veined surface, were – that settled it – little putty-coloured creatures like the ones that crawled on the pews in church – that Mama told her were wood-lice. She stood and surveyed. Ah well, it was very clever of them of them to make it *look* like marble. She was prepared for the stained-glass windows on the landing to be faked as well.

And true enough, they were only plain glass over which had been stuck transparent paper, patterned in diamond shapes of red and green. And where the paper didn't go all the way down to the sash, it was just plain glass, and you could see through it. Maudie bent down and put her eye close to it. It didn't even look out of doors, but down into the shop, and there was Uncle Pauddy looking straight up at her, and next minute he came to the foot of the stairs to meet her. That was when he took her behind the counter and showed her how to manipulate the bottle-opener.

'Have another lemonade. Go on!' he urged recklessly. At eight o'clock in the morning!

It was funny how sick she got of lemonade in no time at all. Now, it would have been different with biscuits, but no one had told her to help herself to a biscuit any time she felt like it, although there was a big case of them in the middle of the shop with a glass lid on it. It was Aunt Cass who was in charge of the grocery though, and right from the start Aunt Cass had been critical of the free hand the uncles had given her.

'Aren't you afraid you'll be sick?' she said.

'I'm never sick!'

'Oh, that isn't what a little bird told me –'

The meanness of that! Just for spite, Maudie opened the lid of the biscuit tin and took not one, not two, but three big biscuits.

'You won't appreciate them if you eat too many of them,' said Cass. Then, looking out of the window, she gave an exclamation. 'Ah,' she cried. 'there's a poor child who'd give her two eyes for a biscuit this minute!'

Maudie swung around to see. At the shop window, looking inwards – but only for an instant – was a girl about her own size. But oh, she was so thin, and her skin so dark, or so dirty, and she had such ragged hair hanging about her shoulders! And only a glimpse was to be got of her – for as Maudie looked out, the girl, with a glowering look on her face, slunk off around the gable.

'Why don't you give her a biscuit?' cried Maudie on an impulse of malice to Aunt Cass. Then she had a better inspiration. 'I will,' she cried, and plunging her hand once more into the tin she brought up a whole fistful of biscuits and ran towards the door.

'Come back here!' cried Cass. 'Come back here at once. This is going altogether too far!'

But Maudie was gone. She rushed out into the dark street. At first she thought the girl had vanished into thin air, but as her eyes got used to the dark, she saw that she was still there, in a corner between the gable and the big yard-gate, and her bony shoulders were hunched together the way angels are sometimes depicted in holy pictures, their wings wrapped around them till the white knobs of their wing-bones almost meet on their chests.

'Hullo!' Maudie spoke exactly as if she was talking to someone in no way peculiar or particular. 'Would you like a biscuit?' she asked.

'I've no money,' said the girl gruffly.

'Oh, but I'm giving it to you.'

'Why?' said the girl.

'Well –' Maudie drawled to gain time. 'I got them for nothing myself.' That ought to take the harm out of them.

The girl looked more scared than ever.

'You'll have to tell it in confession if you stole them,' she whispered. 'You'll have to tell the priest!'

And with a queer shudder, she was gone.

Maudie turned back into the shop. She saw uneasily that Cass was talking about her. And Mama was there too.

'Do you mean to say,' said Cass, very flushed in the face, 'do you mean to say you don't see any difference between taking them for herself and taking them to distribute in the street?'

'It shows the child has a charitable instinct, *I* think,' said one of the uncles.

'That's not the way I'd describe the instinct,' said Aunt Cass. 'But what is to be expected – the devil makes work for idle hands – what is to be expected when she's not where she ought to be – at school!'

'But Cass, my plans are so indefinite,' said Mama. 'And there's only the national school!'

'It was good enough for us, wasn't it?'

'Well, anyway, I'd have to ask Dinny about it,' said Mama feebly. 'I don't know what he'd say. But tell me,' she said more animatedly, 'where does that poor child go to school, the child we were talking about just now, Mad Mary's child? I know she's to be pitied, but I just can't believe she can be normal, living in that hovel, and with that creature for a mother –'

'Is that the girl I saw at the gable?' cried Maudie, 'the girl –'

'Don't interrupt!' said Mama, fretfully. 'It has nothing to do with you. As I was saying,' she went on, turning back to the others, 'it's not that I haven't the greatest pity for the child. It's just that I can't believe a child like that can be fit company for –'

Uncle John-Joe interrupted.

'And what do you think should be done with a child like that? Where should she be sent, if not to the local school?'

'Well!' Mama hesitated. 'I don't know, but I'm sure that in America –'

'America! America!' cried Aunt Cass, angrily. 'If it was so wonderful why did you take her away from it? As for making friends, I thought it was the company Dinny kept out there was one of your main objections to the place!'

Mama's eyes opened wide.

'Who told you that?' cried Mama.

'Who but you?' said Cass.

'Oh, Cass,' cried Mama then, 'you were always the same! A person might say one little word, only half meaning it, and you'd store it up for years in bitterness to throw it back in their face when they were least expecting it.'

'But you *did* say it!'

'Oh, what if I did!' cried Mama, and she turned to the uncles. 'She's put a different complexion on my words!' She looked around for Maudie and she threw her arms around her. 'Indeed,' she cried suddenly, 'it might be no harm to have the child away from the atmosphere in this house sometimes. Where's my hat? I'll go down to the convent right now!'

'Easy, easy!' said Uncle Pauddy.

But Maudie knew Mama. It wasn't only the lemonade that was coming to an end.

The school-house was at the far end of the town. As Maudie and Mama went up the street, beside them, running along in their bare feet with bulky satchels strapped to their backs, were a number of little boys.

'Are they going to my school?' Maudie asked.

'They have their shoes in their satchels, dear,' said Mama. 'They've come in from the country.' And suddenly she laughed. 'In my day they had to bring a sod of turf each for the teacher's fire. We brought a penny, the town's children I mean. I wonder if that old custom is dead? I must ask!'

Maudie was hanging back.

'Oh, Mama, look at those little cottages! Are they real?' There was a whole row of them, all dazzlingly whitewashed and all roofed with yellow thatch!

'Come on, dear,' said Mama. 'There's the convent. Look. Can you see it, out through that archway?' She pointed through an old stone archway that was right in front of them, and under which the road ran, as if it was nothing unusual at all for a road to run under the arch of an old abbey. As if it wasn't a road at all but a river! And as she and Mama went under it, Maudie shivered. It was cold and damp.

'Oh,' she exclaimed, for as she looked up at the glistening wet stones a big drop of icy cold water fell straight into her eye.

It was probably because of that she didn't see the cottage on the other side of the archway until they had nearly passed it, or it may have been that Mama pulled her closer to her side as they passed it, but anyway when she did look, she shivered again.

It was the same as the other cottages in a way, the same size, with a window to either side of the door – two eyes and a mouth – only this cottage had such sad eyes, and such a hungry mouth, and all around it was so dirty and dismal. There was grass growing out of the rotting thatch, as well as in the crevices of the tumbling walls, while around the door were pools of water. And in the pools there were green things growing – or was it moving? But Mama gave her a jerk.

'Don't stare like that,' she whispered. 'She'd think nothing of coming out and firing a stone at us, or emptying a basin of slop over us. She's done both before now to people, or that's what I've been told.'

So that was Mad Mary's! thought Maudie, but the next minute she felt so sad that the tears came into her eyes. Was this where that poor girl lived, the girl that had crouched at the gable? Was it here she lived in this awful, slimy cottage, in the shadow of the archway?

'What's behind the wall?' she asked, fearfully, because there were no more cottages now, only a wall of loose stones, entangled with ivy, and gappy in places, but never gappy or low enough to let be seen what lay beyond.

'Oh, it's only an old cemetery,' said Mama impatiently.
'There was a friary there long ago and that archway was part of
it. But this is the school!'

For they were going up a neat cement pathway now to a
school-house as neat as a shoe-box, with windows cut around
all its sides. And when they got to it, and Mama pushed open
the door, there were rows and rows and rows of scholars, and
all of them staring outward, with open mouths.

'Ah, here's our little Yank,' said a tall young nun, coming
forward and taking her hand. 'I don't suppose she knows any
of the other children yet?'

'I'm afraid not,' said Mama.

But just then Maudie saw a familiar face.

'I know her!' she cried, and she pointed to where, in the very
end form, and all by herself, the strange girl was sitting in a
ragged black dress. 'Can I sit with her?' she asked eagerly, but
she realised at once there was something wrong. The nun still
held her hand. Tightly.

'Oh, but wouldn't you like to sit up in the front, Maudie?'
she asked, and then, feeling Maudie pull back, she shot a look
at the girl in black. 'I don't think Sadie Dawe would want you
to sit beside her, anyway! I am sorry to have to say it, but Sadie
isn't very friendly. That's why she sits down there alone. Sadie
hasn't learned yet that we have to behave in a certain way if we
want people to like us, and be friends with us.'

It was such a lie! Maudie felt sure of that.

'I don't mind *how* people behave,' she cried, 'if *I* like *them*!
Perhaps she'll be friends with *me*.' And just like the drop of
water from the arch fell straight into her own eye, she smiled
straight into Sadie's eyes.

There was a moment of suspense. And then Sadie smiled
back, right into Maudie's eyes.

'Well, you may sit there for today,' said the nun, giving Mama
a conciliatory look, but Mama drew Maudie back for a last word.

'How can you be so like your father!' she whispered crossly.
'Why did you have to pick this child out of all the children in
the town?'

'I'm sorry, Mama,' said Maudie, but she knew it was not for the present she made apology. It was for the future. Then she slipped into the bench beside Sadie.

The impulse that made Sadie smile, however, had died away. As Maudie gave a sidelong look at her, she saw that she had averted her face, and on it was a sullen withdrawn look. Only once, when the nun was called to the door for a minute, Sadie turned her head.

'Which way did you come to school?' she asked.

Maudie looked her in the face.

'Past your house!' she said recklessly.

And after a minute that was like a shock of contact, Sadie not only smiled but gave a giggle. Emboldened by that laugh, Maudie whispered to her.

'What happens at play-time?' she whispered.

'They play!' said Sadie.

Maudie noted the pronoun.

'Don't you play?'

At last, Sadie turned fully around.

'They don't want me,' she said. 'It wasn't *true* what the nun said.'

'I knew!' said Maudie triumphantly. 'But I can be your friend, can't I?'

'Maybe nobody else will want you, now,' said Sadie darkly.

When the bell rang out for the break, though, a few minutes later, the other scholars all dashed out into the school-yard, and left them alone.

'I told you!' said Sadie.

They walked across the school yard.

'What do you do?' asked Maudie.

'I sit on the wall.'

'Not all the time?'

'All the time. But you don't have to stay with me if you don't want to stay.'

'I do want,' said Maudie staunchly.

'Why?'

Why? It was on the tip of Maudie's tongue to say it was because she was so sorry for her. She swallowed quickly.

'Because you're my friend!' she said.

And as Sadie climbed up on the wall, she climbed up as well. Sadie had her lunch in her pocket. It was in a greasy paper bag, and consisted of two slices of bread as thick as doorsteps, with a slab of butter in between as thick and hard as cheese. Maudie took out her orange.

'Is that all you've got?' asked Sadie, and Maudie was afraid she was going to offer to share the bread. But she didn't. 'The first day I came to school,' she said suddenly, 'the nun gave me an orange, and I bit it like an apple. I never had one before.'

Maudie was about to laugh until she saw Sadie's face.

'They all laughed at me,' Sadie said, 'even the nun.' She looked at Maudie.

'Do you know what I'd have done?' said Maudie – 'I'd have laughed too! I'd have *died* with laughing! And I'll tell you something! You'd have laughed too – if you saw someone else do it!'

But Sadie shook her head.

'I'd never laugh at anybody ever, ever,' she said, 'no matter what they did!'

Maudie dangled her legs for a while after that.

'That's queer, you know,' she said. 'I bet you'll be different when you grow up.'

'No, I'll never be different from what I am now,' said Sadie passionately. 'I'll never be different from what I was that first day I came to school.'

'I'm sure I won't change much either,' said Maudie, but without conviction, and then she saw that Sadie wasn't listening. She was staring out across the convent garden that lay on the other side of the school-yard to where, because of the falling ground, the friary ruin could clearly be seen, and under its shadow her own cottage. At the door of the cottage there was a figure standing. 'Is it your mother?' asked Maudie, fearfully.

'Yes,' said Sadie, shortly, and then as the figure went in from the door, her shoulders slumped with relief. 'I always sit where I can see her,' she said, 'because if I saw her coming up here I'd– I'd–'

There seemed no words, though, to express what she would
do in a circumstance so to be dreaded. 'You see, she did come
up once,' she said then, slowly. 'It was about me being told to
bring a sod of turf. She said I was to bring a penny, like the
town's children. It was all right, really, me bringing the sod of
turf, you know. I didn't mind, because the arch is the boundary
of the town and the country, and we're outside the arch, but
my mother thought they were making other distinctions.'

'And were they? Was that what she minded?'

'Oh, I don't know,' said Sadie. She sounded tired all of a
sudden. 'It wasn't that that mattered, it was the way my mother
came in the door.' Suddenly she put her hands over her face.

'Was she –' Maudie almost said 'mad.' 'Was she very angry?'

'No no, she was very quiet and spoke very soft and polite, but
what was awful was that everybody gave in to her, right away.
We had a monitress, but she called the nun, and they both gave
in and said it was all right for me to bring whatever she liked!'

'But wasn't that great?'

Sadie shook her head. 'It was awful,' she said. 'You see, they
were *afraid* of her.'

It was out.

As she listened, Maudie felt so terribly sad she could only sit
there dumbly, but after a minute she thought what a good thing
it was Sadie knew what people thought. There would be no
need to try and be tactful all the time.

'When did she get like that?' she asked casually, 'a bit queer,
I mean,' she added.

'I think she was always not quite right,' said Sadie slowly,
picking her words exactly, 'but she got worse after my brother
died.'

'Oh, I didn't hear about that,' cried Maudie.

'Nobody talks about it,' said Sadie. 'It was because of
something *she* did that he died.'

Maudie felt a terrible throb of fright in her throat, but the
next minute she was reassured.

'Poor Ma,' said Sadie, 'it was her ignorance. And someone
told her it would cure him, somebody bad it must have been,
or someone worse or more astray in the head than herself!'

'What was it?' breathed Maudie.

'Well, he had a rash. It was only a rash, but someone told her to wash him in' she paused, 'I couldn't tell you,' she said then, suddenly. 'Perhaps you can guess,' she added, her cheeks flaming. 'Anyway, there's the bell, we've got to go back to class.'

They didn't get another chance to talk till the bell rang at three o'clock. And then there was Mama, waiting for Maudie.

'See you tomorrow, Sadie,' Maudie called out. 'Keep my place for me!'

'I don't think there's any danger of your place being taken!' said Mama, coldly, 'and let me tell you, Maudie, that I'll take it as a favour if you don't talk too much about your new companion at the tea-table!'

But it was Mama herself, though, who talked about Sadie. Twice, twice at least, when Maudie came into the room she was talking about her to the uncles.

'And wasn't there another child?' she was asking the first time. She stopped at once when Maudie came into the room. 'Never mind, tell me another time,' she said.

But the next time she went out of the room they were at it again. They didn't hear her come back.

'Oh, how revolting,' cried Mama. 'It's like something you'd hear done in a primitive tribe!'

'Well, poor creature, she paid for her ignorance when the sores became infected and he died in terrible agony, the poor child.'

'Is it ever since that?'

'I suppose so,' said Uncle Pauddy, 'although she was never what you'd call in it. For a while after the marriage, and before the girl was born, she was normal enough and she used to keep the place fairly clean, she'd slap a bit of lime on the walls and one thing and another, but after a while she lost heart, and little by little she lost her grip.'

Just then Mama saw Maudie. 'I thought you were outside,' she said.

There was no more about the Dawes. Maudie didn't know what Mad Mary had done that was so disgusting and terrible, and she didn't really want to know.

'Were you very sad for your brother?' she asked next day when they were sitting on the school wall.

'Well, nothing was so bad when I had him, if that's what you mean,' said Sadie. 'We didn't ever talk about things – like you and I do, I mean – because he was too young. He was only seven. He didn't even have a proper coffin, and that wasn't because we were poor either. It was because he was small – it was only a little white-painted box.' Suddenly she turned to Maudie. 'When they put it down in the ground and threw the clay over it, I thought she'd go really mad, and I could see people looking at her, they all must have thought the same. I felt awful. Do you know what I wished, I wished it was me in the white coffin. It being white, and Tony being in it, didn't make it seem so bad to be dead. It didn't seem as bad as standing there, with all the people, and thinking she'd do something to make a final show of me for good and all.'

'But she didn't?'

'No, she didn't,' said Sadie, wonderingly, as if that was the first time she realised that this was so.

'I bet you were sorry for wishing you were dead too,' said Maudie. 'Wouldn't it be awful for her if she didn't have anybody at all?'

Sadie looked at her. 'I never thought of that,' she said slowly. 'I am always thinking about what it's like for me having her; I never thought of what it's like for her having me. I never even thought really hard anyway of what it was like for her not having Tony any more.' Suddenly she seemed struck by something. 'Would you like to see Tony's grave? She keeps it lovely. I will say that! And it's not easy to keep. It's not like the new cemetery where there's no weeds let put up their heads anywhere, the old friary is all weeds and briars. You no sooner cut them back from your own plot than they've rambled in again from the other plots.'

'He's not buried in the old friary, is he?' Maudie couldn't help exclaiming. 'Isn't that very creepy, having him buried just back of you?'

'I don't see what differ it makes him being there,' said Sadie. 'And it makes it better for my mother. She feels he's near her.

And people can't be prying on her and saying she spends too much time at the grave because they can't see her going in or out when she gets over the wall. There's a big gap at the back of the cottage, and Tony's grave is only a bit in from that. There was a big patch of nettles in the way, only she's flattened them down now by going in and out, and the sting is gone out of them. It's a lovely grave. She has lovely things on it, white marble roses, and a little silver dove with a leaf in its mouth. They've come off other graves, but she didn't steal them, you know, she just found them lying in the grass, because nobody keeps up the graves there any more, and the grass has spread out over everything like a big cover. It has even grown up over the headstones in some places. Of course they were small stones to begin with, I suppose, or broken. And some stones are sunk down into the graves where the ground has dropped. Did you know a grave can sink? If the coffin is cheap and caves in, the grave sinks down in the middle. Oh, you'd want to be careful there, I can tell you. You'd break your leg or twist your ankle in a minute, and it's not lucky to fall in a graveyard, did you know that? If you fall in a grave you'll be dead within the year!'

'I don't believe it!' said Maudie, but all the same she felt a thrill of excitement. 'How do you know? Who told you?' she asked.

'Oh, I don't know who told me,' said Sadie, 'but you learn a lot in a place like the friary, just walking around reading the tombstones. There's one man buried there with three wives buried along with him. What do you think of that? And the stone over him is split in two. I bet you don't know why?'

'It had to be moved so often, maybe, putting them all down?'

'No!' scoffed Sadie. 'The grave was robbed! Sometimes robbers used to dig up coffins of married women to get their gold wedding rings, and they thought they'd have a great haul with three wives in the one grave, but they got a land, because he used the one ring for them all. He didn't let it be put in the coffin with them, any of them, until he was dying himself and he had it put on his own little finger, but the thieves never thought of looking in his coffin.'

At this the bell rang. Sadie jumped down off the wall.

'Oh, I could tell you hundreds of stories,' she said.

'I didn't know a cemetery could be so interesting!' said Maudie.

'Oh, they're not all interesting!' said Sadie. 'The new cemetery is the dullest place you ever put a foot. I wouldn't be caught dead in it, though I spend a lot of time in the old friary. But of course I'm not like mother. I know that when you're dead, you're dead.'

'And doesn't she know that?' Maudie jumped down from the wall too.

'Wait till you see Tony's grave!' cried Sadie. 'I'll take you this afternoon.'

For the rest of the day, whenever she had thought of going to the old cemetery, Maudie's heart filled with pleasurable dread; but at four o'clock that afternoon when they climbed up on the wall, and then dropped down into the long yellow grass, she felt a different kind of dread: not so pleasurable.

It was true the grass was never cut. It was tough and matted. When they dropped down into it their feet were immediately netted and snared, at least that was how it felt to Maudie. Sadie took high springing steps and never stumbled. Was it true what she had said about falling in a cemetery?

'Oh, wait for me, Sadie,' she cried.

'Ssh, ssh,' said Sadie urgently. 'We don't want people to know we're here.'

Maudie looked back over her shoulder. There didn't seem much chance of anyone knowing. Always when she passed under the wall on the outside, she used to think this place was silent and still. Now it seemed as if it was the town outside that had gone silent, like a clock that had stopped, while all around them sounds that ought hardly to be heard surged into her ears. Their own feet on the matted grass sounded noisily. The wind, that only lightly stirred the ivy clambering over the headstones, yet caused the pointed leaves where they met the stone to send out a mysterious tapping. And somewhere in the grass to one side there was a strange sound, half sighing, half singing, as the wind went over a rusted tangle of wire.

'Oh, what is that?' she cried, drawing back. 'Is it a rat-trap?'

Sadie laughed.

'It's an immortelle,' she said, but it was impossible for her to make Maudie see what it had been before its glass dome was violated and its false flowers broken and lost in the weeds. 'Come on. I'm dying to show you our grave. I can see it from here,' raising her arm and pointing.

But Maudie had hardly ventured to take one step after her when unaccountably Sadie drew back.

'Perhaps you don't really want to see it. Perhaps you'll get stung with nettles. Perhaps we'll go another day!'

'There's something you don't want me to see!' cried Maudie, accusingly. And, knowing now where the grave was from the way Sadie had pointed, she ran ahead of her, full tilt towards it.

The grave was like a little glade in the forest of dock and old nettles. It was a small rectangular shape, as neat as any grave in the new cemetery, and it was decorated, oh so beautifully, with all kinds of things, jam-pots filled with wallflowers, little plaster figures, and, as Sadie said, broken pieces of marble statuary, a scroll, a little white cross, and yes, firmly bedded in the loosened clay, a white angel with outspread wings, with only one of them a little bit, only a very small bit, broken at the tip.

'Oh, but it's beautiful, Sadie,' she called back. 'It's just as you said. I don't see why you didn't want me to –'

Even as she said the words, though, she did see why Sadie had turned back. In the middle of the grave, among all the bits of mortuary marble and plaster, there was – or maybe she wasn't seeing right – Maudie went slowly forward – yes, it was a lemonade bottle, a full bottle, unopened.

Then Sadie came up to her.

'I didn't want you to see it,' she said slowly. Then she spoke terribly quickly. 'She doesn't do it very often; it's a long time now since she did it at all. I thought she'd given it up, or forgotten, or something. I wouldn't have brought you only I thought that she'd stopped it, but now – well, now you've seen!'

A vaguely oppressive feeling came over Maudie, although when she looked around the graveyard, except for Tony's plot, it was only like a big untidy garden. Yet she felt the oppression growing, and she felt she was going to cry.

Sadie stared at her incredulously.

'I thought you'd laugh,' she said. 'I thought you'd be finished with me when you knew she was as queer as all that. I thought you'd say it wasn't any wonder she was called, well, what she's called!'

Maudie wiped her eyes.

'Well, I suppose you could laugh at it too, if you looked at it another way,' she said, and she actually tried to laugh a bit. 'Does she think his ghost will come back and drink it?'

'I suppose so,' said Sadie, and they stood and stared at the lemonade. But, of course, it was a funny sight to see it sitting there on the grave. Maudie did feel that she might really laugh in a minute. She might have done so if only the sight of it had not reminded her of something else.

How odd it was that she had got so sick of the lemonade when the uncles were lavishing it on her at the start, and now, when they'd stopped forcing it on her, she'd got back all her wish for it! Wish for it? Why the sight of that bottle there on the grave was enough to make her throat as dry as blotting-paper. She closed her eyes and ran her tongue over her lips. She could just imagine the cap being prised up, slowly at first, and then jerking into the air, with millions of little beady bubbles welling upwards, and then pouring down the sides of the bottle. Not to lose one single bubble of it, she'd hold the bottle up over her head and let it roll down her throat. Oh, the longing that came over her! She opened her eyes. I'll have to go home, she thought. I'll have to humiliate myself. Even if it's only Aunt Cass that's in the shop, I'll have to humiliate myself and beg her for a bottle. I couldn't stand this.

But what about Sadie? Her glance fell again on the bottle stuck on the grave.

'I should think it would be to you she'd give it, and not waste it like this,' she said. She bent down and looked closer. The label was new and glossy. 'Is it the same bottle she puts every time?' she asked, but before Sadie could answer, in a clump of nettles to one side, under a bit of an old wall that once was part of the friary nave, she saw fragments of broken glass, one bit of bottle neck with the gilt cap still tightly clawed down upon its unopened top. 'Oh, what a waste! Sadie!' she cried suddenly, and she stooped down and picked up the bottle, 'wouldn't she be delighted, your Ma, if she came along and found it empty. If she thought he came back and drank it!'

'Do you mean we ought to spill it out?' Sadie asked aghast.

Maudie was taken aback.

'Well, we *could* do that,' she said, 'but that would be a worse waste, wouldn't it?' Remembering something Sadie had said herself the first day they met, she lowered her own voice. 'Waste is a sin,' she said. 'Of course, it's all right for your Ma,' she said, glancing at the broken bottles in the nettles, 'she's not *responsible*, I suppose. But I don't think *we* ought to spill it away. Anyway,' she said recklessly, and not looking at Sadie at all, 'I'm thirsty. Are you? It's very hot here!'

For a minute there was silence.

'I'm *very* thirsty!' said Maudie again.

Then Sadie seemed to get limp, and she said something so low Maudie barely caught it.

'I'm gasping!' said Sadie

'That settles it then! said Maudie, and she grabbed the lemonade bottle tighter, and looked around impatiently. 'How will we open it, that's the thing?'

A reckless exhilaration was sweeping her onward. She could see that Sadie was being swept along too. Her wild eyes were no longer at such odds with her face. And a rich red colour raced in her cheeks. And what was rarer, she cracked a joke.

'She ought to have left a bottle-opener!'

At the thought of Mad Mary, Maudie swallowed a gulp of air, but she was steadied by the thought that soon she'd be swallowing the fizzing golden lemonade. And after all, what they were doing was an act of charity.

'Would we break the neck of the bottle, do you think? We could hit it off a stone. Oh no, wait a minute.'

She darted over to the grave. There among the miscellany of plaster emblems and bits of marble, was a strip of metal with a Latin inscription. It might have been off a coffin, she thought, but the thought only made her giggle. She picked it up. 'This will do it!' she cried, and wedging it between the little tight teeth on the rim of the cap she pressed upwards with all her strength. 'Hurrah!' The cap flew up like a bird, and the foam came slowly after it, swelling upwards first and then falling down the sides of the bottle. 'Quick. Lick it,' she cried, 'don't waste a drop!' She held up the bottle in the air so that both of them, pressed together, could catch with their eager open mouths the ineffable stream.

It was while they still held the bottle over their heads that, under it, Maudie looked across the grave and saw Mad Mary.

At the sight of that figure, silent and still, in her black rags, and appearing like a spirit without any warning, all the fears of her that had till then been dampened down in her heart burst into flames of panic and terror. Not a limb could she move, not a part of her, not even her tongue, that had stopped in the middle of a lick. And after a second Sadie, too, saw her mother.

'Oh Jesus, Mary and Joseph! she'll kill us,' she cried out loud, as if the woman in front of them was deaf to them. 'She'll murder us!'

Were they far from the gap in the wall? Maudie wanted to turn and look, but to do so she would have to take her eyes off the woman. And her eyes were all she had to defend her. She stared into Mad Mary's eyes. And then, to Sadie's amazement, instead of running back, Maudie ran forward.

'We didn't mean any harm, you know,' she cried. 'It was only going to waste!'

'I know that, child; I know it *now*,' said Mad Mary, and she looked not at Maudie at all, but down at the little decked-out grave. 'He's gone beyond where I can do anything for him,' she said, 'and maybe it's as well.' She raised her eyes and looked at Sadie. 'It'd be fitter if I gave it to her. He was only a child, but sure that's all she is too.' She paused. 'And what more am I at times. Wasn't it only a child would have gone on like I did, putting food on a grave? If I'd gone on much longer like that I'd have been put away and the right thing for me.'

'Oh, that's no kind of talk!' cried Maudie.

Mad Mary looked at her.

'Whose child are you?' she asked, but she didn't listen to the answer. 'What did you do with the lemonade? Did you let it spill?' For the bottle had fallen from Sadie's limp fingers. 'Would you like some more?' she asked. 'Take her home to the cottage, Sadie,' she said, 'and I'll get some for the both of you.'

But enough was enough for one day.

'Let Sadie come back with me,' Maudie cried, 'and we'll get some from my uncles. And we won't have to pay for it,' she cried, appealing to Mrs Dawe. 'Think of all the money you've wasted,' she said persuasively, and she nodded towards the nettles, where a bit of bleached paper that had once been a glossy label now fluttered dry as a leaf between the stalks.

'Your uncles won't want the like of her with you maybe,' said Mad Mary dubiously.

'Why wouldn't they?' countered Maudie.

'That's right,' said Mad Mary. 'Why wouldn't they?' and she looked at Sadie as if she'd seen her for the first time. 'Do you never put a comb through your hair?' she said crossly.

'I think we'd better go, Mrs Dawe,' said Maudie politely.

'Good-bye, Ma,' said Sadie.

'I'll be with you as far as the gap in the stones,' said the woman. 'I'd be better employed doing a bit of readying at home than always readying this place.'

'Oh, but the grave is lovely!' said Maudie. 'The lemonade bottle spoiled it really. Didn't it?'

They all stood and looked back in agreement. Then they went out through the gap in the wall and Maudie and Sadie waved their hands at Sadie's mother and ran through the archway back into the town.

But oh, what was that at the gable-end of the shop?'

'A jaunting-car!' cried Maudie. 'A sidecar, I mean!' On the top of it was a big corded trunk, that the jarvey was just reaching up to take down. It was what was on top of the trunk that took Maudie's eye. A bowler hat!

'Pappa's!' she screamed. They were only two weeks gone from him. Triumph, she thought, triumph. Here he was following them. But she didn't know whose was the triumph, theirs or his. 'Oh, I must hurry!' she cried.

'I suppose I'd better go home,' said Sadie, sadly. And then she caught Maudie by the sleeve. 'I suppose you'll be going back to America now?' she said.

Maudie turned.

'Oh, I don't know,' she said. 'We might live here! And what does it matter –' she stopped. 'We'll always be friends. And anyway, once you get started, friends are easy to make, you'll see! But come on quick. We're sure of the lemonade now that Pappa's here – lots of it!'

Tom

My father's hair was black as the Devil's, and he flew into black, black rages. When he spoke of death, as he often did, he spoke of when he'd be put down in the black hole. You could say that everything about him was black except his red blood, his fierce blue eyes, and the gold spikes of love with which he pierced me to the heart when I was a child.

He had made a late, romantic, but not happy marriage. All the same, he and my mother stayed together their whole lives through. They drew great satisfaction to the end of their days on this earth from having kept faith with each other.

They had met on shipboard – on the S.S. *Franconia*. My father had gone to America when he was young, and was going back to Ireland to buy horses for the man he worked for in East Walpole, Massachusetts. My mother was returning home from a visit to a grand-aunt and grand-uncle in Waltham, where the grand-uncle was pastor of the Roman Catholic church.

My mother's family lived in County Galway. They were not very well off. They were small-town merchants who sold coal, seeds and guano as well as tea, sugar, and spirits. My mother was the eldest of twelve. It used to puzzle me that the eldest of twelve should go visiting in a land to which most Irish men and women in those days went as emigrants. Such a visit suggested refinement, and this was affirmed by her classic beauty, her waist – which was thin as the stem of a flower – her unfailing good taste, and her general manner. My father had set his eye on her the minute he went up the gangplank – she was already settled into her deck chair, reading a book.

They did not marry till three years later, when, after a correspondence conducted more ardently by him than by her, he sent her a diamond ring and money for her passage out again – this time to marry him. They were married from the parochial house in Waltham.

My mother hated living in America, and on three occasions when my father let her go to see her people he had to follow and fetch her home. When she spoke of her ocean crossing, whichever way she was going, my mother referred to them all as visits, until the last one, when, eastward bound and taking me with her, she knew she'd never have to go back. My father had drawn out some of his savings and given her money to buy a house in Ireland. She bought it in Dublin. Then he gave up his job, took the rest of his money out of the bank, and went to Ireland himself – for good.

My father never seemed to feel resentment against my mother for forcing him to return to the land of his birth. He may not have felt any; his savings, although modest, enabled him to cut a great dash in his native land. He had brought home with him a car that looked so large on the narrow Irish roads that when we went for a drive on Sunday it seemed at every minute as if the sides would be taken off it by the thorny briars in the hedges – hedges so high they made other cars look like cockroaches. Sitting up at the wheel of that car in a big coat with an astrakhan collar was a far cry from running barefoot across country in County Roscommon, where he had been born.

'Why didn't we go back to Roscommon to live?' I asked him one day.

His blue eyes blazed with contempt for my foolishness. 'I have to educate you, don't I?' he said. And I suppose he imagined, like all poor emigrants, that in the place of his birth, time would have stood still – the children going barefoot to school, doing their sums on a slate, and mitching every other day, until at last, like him, most of them would run off to England and thence to America with scarcely enough schooling to write their names.

Although my father had a deep and a strong mind, and was the subtlest human being I ever knew, he had had small schooling. He could read and write, but with difficulty. He came, indeed, from stock that had in the penal days produced a famous hedge-schoolmaster, and of this he was very proud. It may well have been his pride in this scholarly kinsman that led to his own premature departure from a one-room schoolhouse in Frenchpark. For one day the schoolmaster, in a poetic discourse on spring, invoked the cuckoo, and made reference to the cuckoo's nest. My father's hand flew up, and, without waiting for permission to speak, he gave voice to his shock and indignation. 'The cuckoo doesn't build a nest! She lays her eggs in another bird's nest!'

'Is that so?' The master must have been sorely nettled by this public correction. 'Well, boy, if you think you can teach this class better than me, come up to the blackboard and take my place.' Then, abandoning sarcasm, he roared and caught up his cane. 'I'll teach you not to interrupt me!' he cried.

'You're wrong there, too,' my father said. 'You'll teach me nothing more as long as you live.' And with that he picked up his slate and fired it at the master's head. Fortunately, for once his aim was bad, and he missed. Instead, he put a gash an inch deep in the blackboard, and in the hullabaloo he lit out of the door and down the road for Dublin. He was in such a rage he forgot to say good-bye to his mother, whom he never saw again in this life. He spoke of her to me three or four times, and I'm sure it was of her he was thinking on that occasion, leaning over a gate staring into the deeps of a field in a mood of utter blackness.

From Dublin my father went to Liverpool, from there to the potato fields in Scotland and the hop fields in Yorkshire and, finally, one Palm Sunday morning, he arrived in Boston, then a leading port. All he took with him to America were the memories of the boy he had been, running barefoot over the bogs and the unfenced fields of Roscommon with a homemade fishing rod in his hand, or maybe a catapult. That boy used to think nothing of running across country from Castlerea to Boyle, and even into Sligo. Towns that lay twenty miles apart were no distance to him – leaping stone walls like a young goat, bounding over streams like a hound, and taking the corner off a lake if there was wind to dry out his clothes. Whenever I think of what it is to be young, I find my mind invaded by images of a boy – a boy running over unpeopled land under a sky filled with birds. My father had made his memories mine.

My mother had her memories, too, but she had so many of them they seemed to take up all the room in her head. She never discarded duplicates. She had a hundred memories of summer evenings when she and her sister and cousins strolled around the rampart walls that enclosed the small town where she was born. There was the same tinkle of laughter in every one, and the same innocent pretence of surprise when the girls met their beaux taking the air in the same place at the same time. Winter evenings could have been reduced to the tale of one evening in one parlour, my mother at the piano, with her sisters in a half-circle around her singing high and the beaux in an outer ring singing strong and low. I was an only child, and when I was small I liked to think about those gay young people swaying back and forth, their mouths like swinging censers spilling song to right and to left. But I got tired of hearing about them, and in the arrogance of my own youth I thought those memories of my mother's had used up all passion in her. Long before I knew what passion was, I knew there was no passion between my parents. Not that my mother wasn't always telling me proudly about all the American women – that is to say, Irish-American – whose expectations had been dashed to the ground when my father arrived back from Waltham with her as his bride. And she displayed with amusement his bachelor trophies – a topaz tie-pin, a set of silver-backed brushes, and a half-dozen or so pairs of gold cuff-links. He had been the most eligible bachelor in East Walpole, she many times assured me. He was nearly fifty and had never been caught. It was my mother's code that nice girls never tried to catch a man but had themselves to be snared. She herself was thirty before she was snared.

Everyone thought she was much younger, she said, until the midwife took the opportunity of asking her age in a cloudy moment just as I was about to emerge into the world.

'Your father's admirers were all a lot older than that, though,' she told me. 'They must have been out in America for years to be able to buy those expensive presents, because you may be sure they left Ireland empty-handed.'

My mother's own trunk could not have been very heavily laden, but she based her estimate of what the others brought with them on the fact that they had travelled steerage. She travelled cabin. My maternal grandfather, as well as whole-saling grain and guano, was a shipping agent for the Cunard and White Star Steamship Lines, and my mother knew all about poor Irish emigrants, no matter what grandeur they later assumed.

My mother had a state-room to herself, and the courtesy of a reduced fare arranged by the Queenstown agents of the line. It was her firm conviction that no one – no woman, that is – could ever live down the stigma of steerage. Her state-room in cabin class was a symbol to her of how my father had lifted himself up by his marriage, he, of course, having gone steerage on his first crossing. By the time they met on the *Franconia* he had elevated himself to cabin, else they would not have met.

'He would never have been happy with any of those women,' my mother explained to me in East Walpole. I knew them all by sight. They were plump and jolly, and usually to be seen in the company of their husbands – at a ball-game, or watching a parade, or just sitting side by side with them in matching rocking-chairs on their front porches. My mother never rocked on her porch. She never went to a ball-game. She watched only one parade, and that was when the United States entered the First World War. Then she stood at the gate of our house on Washington Street – then a post road from Boston – to see the American boys marching to camp. She cried all the time, thinking of her brothers back home in Ireland. Mostly she stayed at home, doing embroidery or reading. She didn't believe in tagging after a man everywhere he went.

I had my doubts about the wisdom of this, and once made a sly reference to my father about his former admirers.

He looked at me with astonishment. 'They'd never have given me a daughter like you,' he said. 'You have not got your mother's looks, but you have her ways.' I understood that my mother's ways were an abiding source of his pride.

Sometimes I wondered if it was my father's lack of education that had kept my mother from marrying him in the three years that followed the voyage on the *Franconia*. He'd asked her as they parted on the quayside at Queenstown, she told me.

'But I took a dislike to him at first sight,' she said. 'I'd noticed him coming on board and I objected to the way he was staring at everyone, especially at me. I wasn't surprised when he came up to us and broke into our conversation.' She had become acquainted in the departure shed with two elderly English gentlemen, who had helped her find a porter to carry her steamer trunk and arranged with the steward to have her chair placed between theirs. They also urged her to choose first sitting, which was the sitting they favoured. Their company was most enjoyable, she maintained; it was they who made the voyage so pleasant. They were both married and spoke nicely of their wives, who hadn't accompanied them because this was a business trip. They showed her photographs of their wives, and said that their wives, too, had read and greatly enjoyed *The Weaver*, by John Parker, which was the book my mother was reading when my father caught sight of her from the gangplank.

It was in this book, that she'd left on her deck chair while she went down to the dining saloon on the second day out, that my father wrote his name. He scribbled it in the margin of the page at which she'd left it open. And after that, every time she vacated her chair he wrote his name on whatever page was open.

'It was a very cheeky thing to do,' my mother said. 'My sisters would have been horrified.'

Then one day, when she was playing quoits with the nice elderly gentlemen and the one who was partnering her put down the quoit for a minute to rest, my father picked it up and finished the game. Naturally, they won, my father and herself. And after that he partnered her into the finals, and victory. They were presented with a silver rose bowl, which he immediately gave her but which I never saw. It vanished into thin air during the three years that passed between playing quoits on shipboard and playing at marriage on dry land.

The two gentlemen between whose deck chairs my mother's had remained stubbornly placed used to tease her about Tom. 'He'll propose to you before we dock in Queenstown,' one of them prophesied, and the other agreed. They urged her to accept him. 'He's a good man, Nora,' they said.

'But I refused him!' my mother would insist, with a laugh that still rings in my ears. It was a pretty laugh; her face was only a small part of her charm. 'He had a cheek, scribbling in my book.' I think she had suspected from his handwriting his lack of schooling, and it would not be long until his letters proved her right.

I have often wondered what became of his love letters to my mother. What did she do with them? Surely bad spelling and grammar would not be cause for a woman to destroy her love letters? His letters to me, written the times she took me away from him to Ireland, told so much love it lies on the pages still, although the ink has faded and the paper frayed. I have them all treasured away. Among them there is one on pink paper that he wrote me after he'd come back to Ireland to join us. It was written on the eve of the Grand National, and he was going to Liverpool for the night. He had just had time to come to a hockey match in which I was playing left wing, but he hadn't been able to stay for the finish. I should explain that in his day he had been a great athlete, a champion hurley player, but at a time when everyone on the team was expected to score from any place on the field at any time and however he could. He wrote:

Dear Little Daughter,
This is a Pound For Pin Money and I hope ye will win. I was very Much Disopinted how you Plead you Seem to wait till the Ball Came to you that is Rong you should Keep Moving and Not to stay in the One Place. God Luck,
                                                                    Dadey.

'Dadey' is nothing unusual – just 'Daddy' spelled his way. I wish he hadn't written 'ye' for 'you' – it looks like stage Irish. But it also shows that my father never felt obliged to spell a word in the same way in the same sentence, much less the same page. It was as if he felt that he could give new meaning to a word with each new spelling – or, at least, a different inflection of meaning. It was as if for him a letter had a visual quality and could impart a message beyond its mere words. How often I saw him, after he had laboriously composed a letter, lean back from it the way a painter might stand back from his easel and, grabbing up his pen, jab at the page again, dotting an 'i' or crossing a 't' and adding 't's and 's's or doubling an 'l' or 'n' at a furious rate, until he felt he had given the composition a more powerful effect.

His letters to me must have roused at least as much love as was put into them. I keep them in the velvet-lidded box where my mother kept the trinkets he received from other women. In this box I also keep a few souvenirs that my mother herself seemed to treasure beyond their value: a silver Child of Mary medal, a gold-plated Communion cross, and a buttonhook of real but hollow silver. That buttonhook baffled me – it seemed to emphasise what I thought was the shallowness of her feelings. Why had she kept a thing like that throughout her life? It had been a casual gift, and an odd one, from a customer in her father's shop – a customer whom in her lifetime she always 'Mistered'. Mr Barrett – that was how she referred to him. It seemed a distant way to refer to any man.

'But he always called me "Miss Nora"!' she said when I questioned it.

Mr Barrett was a land agent on a large estate called Multyfarnham, a few miles outside the town ramparts. My mother met him one afternoon when she and her sister were picking the daffodils that grew in rings under the trees in such numbers they never regarded it as stealing to pick them.

'When he caught us, Mr Barrett said we were only thinning them out,' she explained. And she said it was to make sure she was happy in her conscience that he called that evening to buy a drink in her father's shop. 'Only a glass of port wine,' she hastened to add. 'He never drank anything else.' It was clearly a token drink to make his call acceptable to her family – as if anything could, it seemed from the tone of her voice. Why they disapproved I did not at first understand. 'I used to stay out in the shop talking to him for hours,' my mother went on. 'My sisters would be furious. We all played the piano, but I was the best. What made them mad with me was that I stayed out in the shop until closing time.'

'Couldn't you bring him into the parlour?' I asked.

'I thought I told you!' my mother cried. 'Mr Barrett was a Protestant!'

'Oh?' That was all I managed to say, but I looked with my first real interest at the crescent-shaped scar on her index finger. It was more than a crescent; it ran almost the whole way around her finger, like a ring. It was hard to believe it was not a real ring made of ivory or whalebone that had somehow sunk into her flesh and over which, like grass on a grave, the skin had grown. I don't think it would have been visible at all if her skin had not been the deep olive of a Galway woman's, which tradition credits to the wrecking of the Armada off the coast of Ireland. Even when my mother was an old woman, the texture of her skin was soft and smooth. And then, too, that scar shone bright as the sickle moon.

'I was polishing a glass for his port wine,' she said, 'and when the glass broke in my hand he pulled out his handkerchief and tore it into ribbons to bind up the cut. It was a silk handkerchief with his monogram on it.'

'Do you ever hear from him? Where is he now?'

'He's dead,' she said. 'He was found dead one morning in a little ditch that ran between the road and the woods. He used to take a shortcut over it when he was going home at night. He must have slipped on the plank across it. He fell face downward into the water.' She paused. 'There was only half a foot of water, but he drowned.'

'Was he drunk?' It seemed a natural question, and I didn't think I deserved the look she gave me.

'I told you, he only drank port wine,' she said, 'and never more than one glass.'

'How frightful!' I cried. 'Did you feel awful?'

'I didn't hear a word about it for two years. I didn't hear until the time I came back with you – an infant in my arms – to show you off to my family. It happened only a few days after I left for America to marry your father. I inquired about him the minute I came in the door – I was wondering if he ever called when I had gone.' She looked down at the scar on her finger. 'That's when they told me.' She paused again. 'But no matter what they said I knew he never drank to excess – only the one glass of port wine.'

I never asked my mother about Mr Barrett again, even when my father was dead and she might have been prepared to talk more about him.

My mother lived for twenty years after my father – her due, considering that was the difference in age between them. It was not a fair bargain, however, because he had had her beauty when he could proudly display it but she did not have his support when she needed it most. 'Poor Tom,' she'd say. 'If he only knew that I'd be left so long after him, to fend for myself,' or 'If only Tom could see me now, crippled like this, it would break his heart.' And while he had always spoken of death as being put into the black hole, she always spoke of it as 'joining Tom.' And the implication was that now wherever he was would be home to her. And a place of happiness, too.

She used to speak of him during those twenty years she survived him in much the same way that her sisters and brothers used to speak of him in his lifetime.

'Poor Tom,' she would say. 'He was so good to me.'

'Poor Tom,' *they'd* say. 'He is so good to Nora.'

One day when my mother had been dead for two years, I was paying a duty call on an unmarried aunt who kept house for one of her bachelor brothers. We were sitting in the little parlour that had been the scene in my mother's stories of so much brightness and laughter and song, but the day was dull, and our talk was sad, and we often fell silent. In one of those silences, my aunt picked up the newspaper and was glancing at it idly when she gave an exclamation.

'Listen to this!' she said. 'Yesterday some poor young man was found drowned in a small drain with only a foot of water in it. He was lying face downward. They thought he had drink taken, but from the evidence given at the inquest the coroner decided it was suicide.'

'Where did it happen?' my uncle asked listlessly, and when my aunt said it had happened in another part of the country his interest evaporated. But my aunt was devouring the print. She caught my uncle's arm and shook it violently.

'Suicide!' she repeated. 'Just like Nora's Mr Barrett.'

A hundred questions leaped to my mind, but I was silenced by the look on my uncle's face. 'What are you talking about?' he cried. '"Nora's Mr Barrett" – as you call him – was accidentally drowned. You know that as well as I do. What would Muggie think if she could hear you saying such a thing?' Muggie was the name by which my maternal grandmother had always been called by her grown-up family; it was meant to be an endearing diminutive, but to me it had always seemed more appropriate than they knew. In one way or another, she had smothered most of her children.

Had my mother known the truth about Mr Barrett? I wondered. Had my father? Had that knowledge had anything to do with his rare but terrible drinking bouts, and the less frequent but more terrible depressions that came down over him like a snuffer? I had seen that snuffer quench joy in him at times when he should have been happiest, looking over a gate at his pure-bred horses thudding across pastures flowing rich as rivers. Yet his face would darken, and I'd be sure he was thinking that, even before him, they would be put down in the black hole. Tie-pins and silver brushes, he knew too well, could outlast a million men and a million horses.

I was twenty. I had just finished my first university examination, and while I was waiting for the result my father decided to take me to Roscommon, to the place where he was born. He had taken me to Killarney, with its lakes, and Connemara, too. We had gone together to the Glens of Antrim and the Burren in full flower. But I knew these places were nothing compared to a bog land bathed in the light of his memory, a light he thought had no night and over which he thought no cloud could ever settle.

It was mid afternoon when we reached the town of Boyle and took the road to Frenchpark. What would he feel, I wondered, when he'd see the changes inevitable in the time since he'd last been there?

To my astonishment it did not bother him at all that where there had been golden thatch there were grey slates, where there had been ploughshares there were tractors. He hardly seemed to notice that the boys wore boots and not one girl had a waterfall of hair. His eager eyes fell short of these changes and fastened on unchanged mounds of earth, on unchangeable stone walls, and on streams that still ran over the same mossy stones. 'Look at that!' he would cry, stopping the car one place after another and pointing out with delight something familiar. 'Look at that five-bar gate! Many's the time I vaulted it. Look! Look! By god, that's the same old bank I put Dockery's ass over, digging my toes into its sides like it was into butter I was digging them!'

Then his eyes fell on something so exciting he could hardly speak. 'I didn't believe it'd be still standing. By all that's holy! It's the old schoolhouse!' he cried. 'God be with the master! I wonder if he's still alive.'

The little schoolhouse was no longer used as a school, of course. We had passed a large new school a mile or so back down the road. But Tom got out and stood staring at it. At last, he went over and tried the door. It was locked. He looked up, then, at the windows, which were very high up so the scholars of those days couldn't be distracted by looking out.

'I bet the mark of that slate is still on that blackboard,' he said, and suddenly he lifted me up as he used to when I was a child in Boston lifted up to see a parade. 'Can you see anything?' he cried.

'Only cardboard boxes piled up everywhere.' The classroom was evidently used as a storage place for the jotters and copybooks, erasers and pencils that had replaced the old slates and slate pencils of his day.

He set me down. 'But I'd guarantee the mark is still on that blackboard!' he said. He gave a laugh. 'If I thought the master was hereabout, I'd call and let him see you.' His eye travelled over the countryside again. 'There were eighty-four scholars in that little schoolhouse,' he said. 'And I could name every one of them.' As if I didn't know! I myself could sing out that litany of names: Micky Dockery, Tom Forde, James Neary, Ethel Scally, Mary Morrisroe, Paddy Shannon . . .

'Most of them went to America,' my father said, 'and I met many a one of them out there. I'd be in a bar and it crowded, and suddenly I'd see a face, and I'd know it at once for a Roscommon face. You wouldn't have to give me a minute till I'd put a name to the face as well. I'd leave my drink and I'd go over and I'd slap the fellow on the back and I'd call him by his name. But if he saw me coming he'd beat me to it. "By the hokey – it's not you, Tom?" And after that it would be round for round as long as either of us had a dollar in our pocket. And it wasn't only the fellows but the girls. I was with your mother and you one day in Boston sitting in Childs Restaurant, and I caught sight of one waitress that was shapelier than the rest, with red hair that could make you think the evening sun was on it. "Stop staring, Tom!" your mother said. She was easy embarrassed. But although the girl had her back turned to us I could have laid a five-dollar bill she was from the County Roscommon. "Wait till she turns around," I said, "and I'll give you her name into the bargain." But when she turned round she beat me at my own game. "Tom!" she screamed, and she left down the tray she was carrying and ran over to us and began shaking hands with your mother and taking you in her arms and throwing you up in the air. And everybody in the place gaping. With all the commotion it wasn't long till the manageress arrived on the scene, but seeing it was Molly Starky she turned away and let on to notice nothing. Molly wasn't the kind of girl any boss would attempt to put down. She'd have pulled off her apron and lit out of the place if anyone ventured to say a word to her. A real Roscommon woman! Do you know what happened when we'd finished eating and I asked for the cheque? She went over to the cash register and rang up a zero. "On the house," she said. That'll show you what she was like!' My father laughed.

He looked around him again over the flat land, where, among the new cement houses, there were still a few mud-wall cabins. But there was more grass growing out of their thatch than could be seen in the little fields around them. They, too, would soon turn back into the clay from which they were made. 'She lived over there,' he said, pointing to a cabin behind one of the new cottages. It seemed now to be a cow byre. He sighed. 'But that was a long time ago. I don't know if she's alive at all. There can't be many of the old folk left. There must be a lot of them laid to rest in –' He paused, and I waited for the familiar phrase about the black hole, but the memories of boyhood were too strong.

'In Cloonshanvil cemetery,' he said quietly, pointing to where in the distance I could see a small, walled cemetery, dotted with marking stones not much different from the rough field stones that surrounded the little plot.

'Is that where your parents are buried?' I asked, thinking of his mother, to whom he had never said good-bye. I thought he'd want to visit the grave.

But he shrugged. 'They're put down, somewhere there,' he said, with what I took at first to be a strange indifference. 'I sent money back to the priest one time and asked him to put a tombstone over them, but he returned it and said no one could find the exact spot.' A dark shadow fell over us both for a minute.

'It's a wonder he didn't keep the money to say Masses for their souls,' I said, and at that the shadow lifted and a smile broke like sunlight over my father's face.

'I never thought of that,' he said. 'Ah, but the priests that were going in those days weren't like the priests today. He was a gentleman even if he was a priest.'

We were walking back to the car when we saw an old man coming towards us on the road.

'Let's have a word with this old-timer,' he said, 'and see if there's anyone left around here that I knew in my young days.' The old man was so bent and was walking so slow that we got back into the car and moved forward to meet him. As we got nearer, my father took his hand off the wheel and nudged me. 'He's making his way to Cloonshanvil to save people the trouble of carting him there,' he said.

Yet when we drew level with him the old fellow looked spry enough for his age. His face was weathered by wind and rain, but he seemed as hardy as a wild duck. It wasn't poverty that had bent him double, either; he had a suit of good frieze cloth on his back and a pair of good strong shoes on his feet. As the car stopped, he came over to us with a courtesy not common today.

'Good day, sir.'

'Good day to you, sir,' my father replied, but I saw that he was staring at the old fellow with a puzzled look on his face.

'It's a fine day, sir, isn't it, thanks be to God,' said the old man. And, as my father had said nothing, he looked appraisingly at the car. 'That's a fine car you've got there, sir,' he said. 'I suppose it's visitors to this country you are? Is it wanting to know the way to Dublin you are, sir?'

At that my father gave a laugh. 'No,' he said. 'I know this part of the country well enough. I wish I had a dollar for every time I walked this road!' he cried with a jaunty note in his voice.

'Ah, I knew you were from America, sir,' the old man said. 'Sure Americans have plenty of money for travelling the world and going anywhere they like.' Then he frowned, as if he, too, were puzzled by something.

My father hesitated for a second, and to my astonishment he turned the key in the ignition and put the car into gear. But just before we drove away he leaned out. 'Did you ever hear of a young fellow called Danny Kelly?' he asked.

'Is it Danny Kelly? Usen't us two to sit on the one form beyond in the schoolhouse!'

'Is he still in these parts?' my father asked slowly.

The old man gave a dry chuckle. 'He is!' he said. 'He went to Scotland for a while, but his family brought him back here a while ago. And he'll never be leaving again.' With a jerk of his thumb, he pointed toward the Cloonshanvil cemetery. 'The Lord have mercy on him.'

'The Lord have mercy on him,' my father repeated, and both of them took off their hats. 'There was another young fellow by the name of Egan,' my father said then. 'Did you know him?'

'It would be a queer thing if I didn't! I'm called Pat Egan,' said the old man, but now his blue eyes filled with mild inquiry. 'If it's not an impertinence to ask, sir, where did you hear my name?'

Now, I thought. This is the moment. But my father was letting in the clutch.

'There was a fellow I knew in Boston that came from here,' he said. 'He told me if ever I passed this way to inquire about a few of the scholars that were in that schoolhouse there with him.' He nodded at the little school.

'And what was that man's name, sir, if you'll pardon my asking?'

My father seemed to expect the question, he was so ready for it. 'I declare to God I knew him as well as I know myself,' he said, 'but at this moment I can't recall his name.'

Pat Egan was satisfied. He laughed. 'Wait till you are my age, sir,' he said, 'and you'll be forgetting your own!'

We drove away.

'What do you make of that?' my father asked. 'Pat Egan and me are the same age to within a day. I didn't know him from Adam when we drew up beside him. But when we were a minute or two talking I knew him by a bit of a blood mark that you maybe didn't see at all, because it was under his left ear. But I remembered it, because the female teacher, when she'd be expecting a baby – which was every year – used to make him keep his cap on in class, pulled down well over his ears so that she wouldn't see it and it maybe bring bad luck on the child in her womb. I knew him by that blood mark. But he didn't know me from Adam!'

'Why didn't you tell him who you were?' I asked, looking back at the figure of the old man getting smaller and smaller behind us.

'I don't know,' my father said quietly, and then, to my surprise, he abruptly swung the car into a narrow lane on our left. 'There used to be a cottage up this lane,' he said, 'and many's the time I was in it. I near wore the seat off my pants sitting on an old settle that stood by the hearth. Rose Magarry was her name,' he said. 'She was my first sweetheart.' And now with every word he was giving light little laughs like a stream frolicking over stones. He was so lighthearted I thought I could tease him.

'Oh, you must have been a right boyo in those days,' I said.

He turned angrily. 'What makes you say that?'

'I was thinking about those tie-pins and cuff-links you got from admirers. That's all.'

'Is it them things?' he scoffed. 'A few dollars is all that kind of thing cost in those days. Gold was cheap in America then. The girls could earn as much as us men then. And some were earning more! They gave presents like that to every fellow they met.'

He had slowed down the car and was looking from side to side of the lane. 'We ought to have come on the cottage before now,' he complained.

We were passing a mound of dung that looked like rotted thatch, and among the nettles and elderberry bushes there were foxgloves and hollyhocks, twined together with honeysuckle, and a white rosebush gone wild. Hundreds of bees were buzzing over it, and white butterflies dancing. 'Do you think there might have been a cottage there at one time?' I said cautiously, because I was thinking that if it is true, as legend tells us, that nettles grow out of the bones of monks and men of combat, perhaps honeysuckle and roses grow from the bones of young maidens.

My father was looking where I'd pointed. 'You're right. That would be the spot. I knew I couldn't be so far out in my calculations. The old people would be dead, and she'd be married and gone. Come to think of it,' he said, 'I heard she was married and a widow into the bargain.' He looked ahead, to where there were four or five new cottages, the ground around them as bare as a hen run. 'We'll stop at one of those cottages and ask if anyone can tell us where Rose lives now,' he said. He winked at me. 'Just for fun.'

We stopped in front of the first of the cottages, at the back of which a young woman was hanging out wet clothes. She turned and stared at us, more aggressive than curious. But an old woman, who had been sitting inside the window, got up and came hobbling out.

As she came down the cement path, my father called to her, 'I'm sorry to bother you, ma'am, but I wonder could you tell me anything about a girl by the name of Rose Magarry used to live in that cottage back there.' He nodded back at the mound of rotted thatch and flowers.

The old woman had a touching simplicity. 'Magarry was my own name, sir,' she said. 'Would you be meaning me? I am called Rose. I married Ned Malone, but he's dead these twenty years.'

I looked anxiously at my father. He was gripping the steering wheel and staring straight in front of him. 'I was only wanting to ask because of a young lad that used to know her long ago,' he said stiffly. 'A fellow I met in America. He asked me to call.'

'And what would his name be, sir?' the old woman asked, and it broke my heart to hear the deferential note in her voice. But next minute she threw up her hands. 'Ah!' she said softly. 'Don't I know who that was! Tom! It's his son you are, sir, isn't it?' She darted close and peered into my father's face. 'Tom's son. Sure, you're the dead spit of him!' Then, stretching out her hands, she caught at his and went as if to drag him out of the car. 'How is he? Tell me, is he still alive? But wait, what am I thinking about, you'll come inside and be telling me over a cup of tea? And you too, miss?' she said, recalling my presence. But next minute she glanced back uneasily at the young woman who was all the time standing by the clothesline staring.

'You'll have to excuse us, ma'am!' said my father. 'We've a long journey ahead of us yet.'

There was a strange little silence.

'Ah well in that case, sir!' the old woman said then, and she seemed relieved. 'But wait a minute, sir,' she cried. 'I'll open the two sides of the gate, so you can turn your car in comfort.'

I waited till we'd turned and driven down the narrow lane and were back on the road. 'Why didn't you tell her?'

He said nothing for a long time. 'Why do you think?' he said, and the black mood that came down on him didn't lift till we'd crossed the Shannon.

The Girders

The broken checkwork of the steel girders against the sky, as he came near to the dockyard, filled him with his first fear of the new day ahead. When he reached the works and took off his coat to put on his blue canvas overalls, he felt the impatience of his nerves as they waited for the first noises of the day to begin; the voices of the other workers calling out their early morning jokes and the sounds of their feet on the boards of the wooden hut, as they took their tools from the lockers, and then the sounds of their feet on the gravel as they shuffled about waiting their turn to climb the metal ladder to the scaffolding overhead.

He didn't know what the building would be like when it was finished. There had been so many, many buildings on whose riveted iron frames he had hammered out a loud tirade of blows for a day's pay that now he scarcely bothered to find out what it was going to be; an insurance office, a bank, a row of flats, or a hospital.

All he did was hammer home great gleaming nails and bang together iron bars. Long before the buildings were completed, he was away in some other part of the city being signed on to another job of heavy work that needed only muscle and sweat.

He stretched out his glossy brown arm and bent it inwards to see again his bulging muscles, but there seemed to be no power in his hands, just as, walking along the street, there seemed to be no power in his legs. There was something the matter with him; he couldn't hide it much longer. He used to love his work, and now, as morning cleared its space on the window pane, he lay in terror of the day ahead, and the walk to the yards left him as tired as lifting the mortar-hods or raising the iron hammer.

It couldn't go on. The foreman knew that he was a steady man, and that he didn't try to shirk things, yet he noticed that every now and then as the foreman went the rounds, although he did not yell at him as often as he did at the other men, lately he used to stand near him for a longer time than usual, letting on to be examining a blue-print, or maybe talking to the man next him, but most likely all the time, or so it seemed to him, watching his work and counting the strokes of the hammer; listening to see if they rang true on the metal.

They rang true enough. The noise of every stroke went through his body, and the concerted noises of the thousand hammering men around him struck through his head and fell to the pit of his abdomen. The drill bored into his bones. And lately, when a siren wailed on the river, he felt himself running his tongue over his lips, and he noticed the other men looking at him.

Under their stare he tried to stop, but the strain of doing so made him worse, and the movement of his lips went on; an involuntary action of his muscles, not directed by a single thread of contact from the mind, a twitch. He felt they were watching him every time a loud and single stroke broke into the network of the regular noises and crashed its way through, drawing after it fragments of all the other noises as it fell away into the silence again.

The only time they did not stare at him was when the lunch whistle went, or the knocking-off bell at night. They were too busy then, pushing their way down the metal passage to get to the exit ladders. But, as for himself, he dreaded the knocking-off bell.

While he was working he felt that he could keep on automatically for ever, as a wheel will roll down a hill. Once he got his body to start working it went on working in much the same way that his lips twitched without conscious direction from his brain. But when the whistle blew at night he had to stop; let his forced energy run out, go out along the weary streets to his room, and there he was quickly smothered up in the close and stuffy feathers of sleep.

The feathers of sleep were no longer silken and soft, as they had been long ago, but greedy and clinging like the feathers of wet fowl. He had to start shaking them off in the middle of the night or he wouldn't be ready to get up when daylight came and the horns on the river shouted in the day.

It was the little voice of the lark that used to cheer the day inwards, over the fields, when he was a boy in his brass-knobbed bed at home.

Thoughts of home came into his mind almost every minute. At first they were sweet and welcome, but after a time they clung unpleasantly close to his mind and were as hard to brush away as the wet feathers of sleep. They upset him so much that when they came he did not know for the moment where he was, and he didn't know quite rightly what he was doing.

Once or twice when a plank showed a round knot in its wood, his eyes filled with tears because he was, in some queer inconsequential way, reminded of the small, grey faces of the clover leaves in the smooth fields at home. And once, some sound in the singing of the echo hammer-stroke rang so strangely in his ears that it seemed to him for the moment that it was summer-time long ago, in the old home-meadows, and that a great gold bee had buzzed up on a sudden, banging the brazen air like a gong. The impression was so strong that he started back with the sweet fright of it, and only for the arms of the foreman he might have fallen over the edge of the scaffolding plank.

The thought of this narrow escape kept his head clear for a long time after that. He did not want to die. If life, of late, was crazed and giddy, he knew that outside the city the world was still as sane and sweet as ever, and that as soon as he had put aside another thirty pounds he would be able to go back again to the fields. Once back, he would never want to leave there again. He would never be restless again. He would never be uneasy; never be hard to please. Another thirty pounds would be just enough, but lately it seemed as if they might be harder to make than the three hundred and twenty that lay in the vaults of the bank.

He used to think there was only a strip of railway line between him and the fields, but lately it seemed there was a barricade of steel and iron girders between him and the country, and that they grew higher every day. How could one man break his way through barricades it took two hundred men to lift up against the sky?

Desperately he raised the hammer once again, and as he did, he felt the weight of it tear at his armpits. Then, when it came to his shoulder-level, he felt the familiar sensation as it lost its weight and poised for a second motionless. And then there was another jerk as the weight asserted itself once more against his strength and once more dragged him down.

But all of a sudden, he felt that there was something wrong; the drag came from behind; the hammer was drawing him downwards, but it was not forward and down as expected, but down and backwards; backwards and downwards and into the unthinkable abyss of the street below.

His arms could not stop the course of the falling weight. His whole body could not stop it. He was drawn with a pitiless jerk down through the screaming air that flashed with a thousand colours and was cut with a thousand lines.

The days in hospital were much alike, until on one of them he wakened to a new atmosphere in the ward. At first he could not account for it. Everything was just the same, as far as he could make out with his eyes, and yet he was aware of some great and important difference. With a start he realised that it was in his own body. His body had sprung to attention at the chilly voice of dawn. Sleep had been outdistanced in an instant. But for his crippled legs he was the same as he was long ago before he came to the city, alert, clear and freshened by sleep, and ready for what the day demanded.

He looked around the ward. It was loud and cheery with white paint and laundered counterpanes. The nurses made sharp and clear-toned echoes through its rectangular length with the knocking of enamel on enamel. Through the wintry, eastern windows he saw the sudden day come up the sky, as a clamorous boy on roller skates comes up a quiet street.

And then he remembered that this was the day that he would be leaving the hospital and going home. The letter from his mother was on the iron tray with his medicines. The chart was gone from the white rail of his bedstead. When his clothes were brought in at eleven his overcoat would be with them; and his grey cap.

In the letter his mother said that she was getting a room ready for him at the gable-end of the house, so that he could see the whole farm without getting up out of his wheel-chair. In a few months, when the weather was warm, she said, he could be taken down to the copland to sit under the trees where he could see the people passing on the road and have a chat with anyone who had a bit of time to spare.

She had his bed thumped over, she said, by the boy in the yard, and she was collecting down to make him a few extra pillows. And if there was anything else he could think of that would make him more comfortable he was to write and tell her, because she wanted to have everything ready for him so he wouldn't miss the hospital.

'I don't think your mother need worry!' said one of the nurses, smiling at him, when he gave her the letter to read. 'There are very few people that miss the hospital!'

'But on the other hand, we'll miss you!' said the young probationer nurse, who was helping to make his bed.

And later when the two nurses had finished all the beds and were washing their hands in the washroom at the other end of the ward, they spoke about him again.

'I'll miss him!' said the young girl. 'And the other patients in the ward will miss him.'

'So will I,' said the older nurse, 'but I'm glad for his own sake he's going, because anyone could see when he came in here that he had his heart set on getting back to the country.'

'I believe he was raving about the hedges and the flowers when they brought him in. Is that true?'

'It is,' said the other nurse. 'I was there. I felt awful listening to him. It would break your heart! And we thought at the time that there was no hope for him.'

'Thank goodness he's getting his wish and going back to the country. He should never have left it. Anyone could see just by looking at him that he wasn't made for the city. Couldn't you just imagine him, with his face as brown as a berry and his sleeves rolled up, following a plough down a field?'

'He won't ever do that now, though,' said the young nurse, sadly.

'But he'll be where he wants to be. That's something! He won't be looking out night and day at the girders and the derricks the same as he was here! I think it was a shame, and I said so at the time, to put him in a ward where he would be staring out at the very place he was working on when he fell. Of course, there was no room in any other ward. It was too bad. I often saw him staring out at them, and he was hard put to it to keep the tears back.'

The young probationer went over to the roller towel on the wall, and jerking it towards her, she began to dry her hands.

'I thought he had tears in his eyes this morning, when he was staring out the window!' she said.

'Ah well!' The nurse straightened her cap. 'He won't be looking at them much longer. Horrible things! I hate looking at them myself. They're regular death-traps!' She shook the moisture from her nice white hands and took up another end of the towel.

'I think …' the young girl began.

'Hush,' said the older nurse, and she jerked her head slightly to indicate that the Sister in Charge had appeared at the other end of the ward.

The Sister in Charge always inspired awe by her appearance in the ward, because the young nurses associated her with the dignities and duties of her office, but as a matter of fact, this particular Sister was by nature kind and fussy, with chubby hands that were always folded in front of her and a smile for everyone.

'So we are going home today!' said Sister, when she came to the young man's bed, and then as she saw that he was staring out over the dockyard and that his eyes were filled with tears, she, too, wished for the thousandth time that he had not been put in a bed that looked out to that side of the building.

'Come, come!' she said, and she lifted the letter from the tray. 'Read your nice letter again and stop looking out at those ugly old cranes and pulleys. I only wish we had a nice view from our windows. But you don't need to worry about views! In two days' time you'll be looking out at the nice green fields and the cows and the grass, and little white chickens pecking on the ground. Won't that be nice?'

The chubby little Sister smiled and sighed, both at the same time.

'If I wasn't doing my little bit for God, I'd ask nothing better than that: to be in a country with a few little white hens, and the lovely brown eggs! Come now, like a good boy, read your letter again, and stop looking out at those cruel buildings. You'll soon be out of sight of them! You'll never see them again. It's a great pity you weren't put in another ward.'

It was a pity he wasn't put into another ward. That was what he was thinking himself. He looked down at the letter in his hand, and wished with all his heart that the kindly little Sister would flutter away to another bed.

When she did, he raised his head and looked out of the window again. He'd never see the girders again, nor the webbed shafts of the cranes. He'd see the trees and the fields, and he'd be looking at them for the rest of his life. He thought of them. The fields were a monotonous green. The trees were clumsy and stupidly twisted.

He looked out of the window again. Printed fast on the pale skyline was the mighty silhouette of the girders going upwards to the wintry sun. He knew that they were going up with a clarion of hammering and the triumphant fusilade of a drill. And they didn't look cruel at all. They looked kind of pretty. And the cranes looked as frail as the silk wings of a dragonfly that wouldn't harm a thing.

A Cup of Tea

'She'll take a cup of tea, no matter how late it is when she gets here. You can leave the kettle at the back of the stove where it will keep the heat without spilling over and putting out the fire.'

'All right, ma'am,' said the servant girl. She threw a baleful glance at her mistress, mother of Sophy, for whom all this trouble was being taken. She who had been expected since early morning and would, as likely as not, arrive late and keep them all from their beds. The young servant's back was nearly broken from all the work that had been done in the last few days. They had scrubbed every single floor in the house, cleaned all the windows, and had gone as far as waxing Sophy's room twice in the one day because Sophy's mother had marked it going in and out with clean curtains and extra pillows, bunches of flowers and hot jars.

'She needs a holiday after all the hard work she has done,' her mother said as she pushed the kettle further back on the stove, then changed her mind and put it back where it had been.

'I hope she'll pass the examination,' said the servant, in the hope of gaining a moment's rest by introducing a topic upon which her mistress was always talkative and garrulous.

'Oh, her examination!' It was almost as if Sophy's mother had forgotten that Sophy had done any examination at all, so absorbed was she in the thought that her only daughter was coming home again after a three months' absence. 'Yes, her examination!' she repeated carelessly as her eyes ran over the tray that was already set for Sophy's breakfast in bed next morning. 'Why, of course she'll pass. I expect she'll do very well, and get very good marks.'

'She's clever, isn't she?' said the young girl, in a tone of voice in which she was careful to mingle ingredients of envy, flattery, as a good farmer mixes his grasses when he lays down a meadow.

'Oh, she has a good brain, I suppose,' said Sophy's mother, in an offhand manner that far from deceiving the servant, emboldened her to sit back on her hunkers and rest her limbs.

'Why wouldn't she have brains?' said the young girl, 'I suppose she takes after her father?' And jerking her finger and thumb she pointed upwards in dumb show at the ceiling, for overhead was the study in which Sophy's father was buried in books and lost in the fumes of tobacco smoke. He was an amateur entomologist.

'What time do you intend to get that floor done? Do you expect it to take all night, with you sitting back taking your ease?'

The girl grabbed up the scouring brush again and began to rub it hastily on the big bar of soap that she had held indifferently in her hand while she had taken a short respite. Except for the noise of the brush going over the flagged floor there was no sound for a few minutes, but it was clear from the expression upon the face of Sophy's mother that she was still brooding on what the servant had said.

'There's a great deal of difference between a hobby and a degree from a University!' she said at last, 'Sophy has done one of the hardest courses in the University. There were only two girls in the Political Economy class and only one in the class for the Study of International Relations. Let her father spend all his time up there in his study with his books and his magnifying glass, but I don't think he'd make much sense out of Sophy's books. Did you ever see them? Heavy as a bible, with figures and diagrams clogging up every page. I never saw such books.' She relaxed somewhat and her face assumed the expression of satisfaction it had worn after Sophy's floor had been waxed for the second time. 'Of course, my husband is a great authority on insect life,' she admitted grudgingly.

Having little or no respect for her husband's reputation she was nevertheless aware that upon it her own importance depended. She was going to say more, but just then the young servant ran to the window, pulling off her apron.

'She's here, she's here,' she shouted excitedly, but before her mother could reach the door, Sophy was running down the hall towards them. She had let herself into the house with her key. Throwing her bag and scarf to either side, Sophy put out her arms to hug her mother. There was a clash of metal buttons and bracelets clanging against one another. The mother was reminded of the girl's father, how his watch-chain used to rattle against the buttons on his waistcoat when he attempted to embrace her. That was before he took to wearing smoking jackets around the house, with buttons of braided petersham, and gave up bothering to carry a watch of any kind. She banished the image from her mind. 'Stand back and let me look at you. You're very thin. I hope you're not trying to lose weight. How did the car drive up without my hearing it? Did you have a tiring journey? What time did you leave? I hope you had a stop along the road?'

The mother's eyes flew from Sophy's face to her waist, from her waist to her hair, and from her hair to her hands with the distracted, and haphazard, eyes of love. 'How did you get on in your examination?' Then before Sophy had time to answer any of the questions, she continued, 'Sophy you're too thin, and it doesn't suit you. It throws up your likeness to your father. I've often heard people commenting on it, but I never could see it myself. But I'd swear I was looking at him now. How odd I never saw the likeness before now. I thought it was only a slight resemblance in the way you held your head, but only at certain times, if you were upset or annoyed. I can't say it was ever anything definite. Nothing at all like the way you resembled my own sisters, in your walk and the way you hold yourself. But I suppose it's natural you should resemble him in something. It's a good thing you didn't inherit his disposition.' Instantly she regretted her last remark. Sophy's face, however, gave no sign of annoyance, as she moved away and bent to pick up her bag and gloves.

'How is he?' she asked. She sank down suddenly into an armchair in case her mother might think that she was impatient to go up to him.

Feeling she had let herself down by her torrent of words, the mother gave a little laugh. 'Why don't you run right up and see for yourself?'

'I've only just arrived,' said Sophy, 'there's no hurry.'

'He must have heard the car,' her mother said grudgingly. 'His study is on this side of the house. Please dear, don't sit down before you've seen him, if only for a few minutes. You need only say a word or two. If you sit down for too long you won't feel like going up to him.' The mother walked over and taking her daughter's arm, urged her to stand up and do what was required of her, as if Sophy might not otherwise comply with her wishes. 'And when you come down, we'll have a nice chat, and I'll hear all the news.'

Sophy got up slowly from the armchair. She put on a deliberate air of unwillingness, compelled by an impulse of compassion to play up to the pretence of reluctance with which her mother was deluding herself.

'Hurry dear,' said the mother, 'you'll be glad that you went up. He'd feel so hurt if he didn't know you'd got here safely.'

'Why doesn't he come down?' said Sophy, with a good appearance of resentment.

'He's coming to the final chapters of his latest book about his famous beetles. He only comes down for his meals because I insist, but I believe he spends the entire evening at his desk. I see the lights on under his door. That book will want to bring in queer profits to pay for all the lamp-oil he's burned in the last five years. Although who's going to buy that book is more than I can make out, unless there are more than I know of dried up unnatural people like himself.' Again the mother recollected the effect her words had on Sophy. 'Run up for a minute, to the door anyway. There's no need to stay.'

But as Sophy went out of the door dragging her feet, the mother knew in her heart that the girl would not come down again until she had to be called, perhaps more than once. As she listened, already she heard the girl's footsteps getting faster and faster. Soon she was taking the stairs two at a time. The mother thought of the lassitude and disinclination which Sophy had shown about going upstairs. Had she been pretending, and why? Her mother regretted her own polite pretence. She wanted to run out to the foot of the stairs and shout, 'Don't let me keep you. Go on, run up to your father. Tell him all your news. Don't even think of telling me anything.' But she didn't give in to her anger. Instead she kept her mouth shut tight and went out to tell the maid there was nothing more to be done and she could go off to bed.

The little maid was worn out. She sat on a chair in front of the range with her legs apart and her head bent as she tried to take a splinter out of her thumb by sucking it.

'Is your finger sore?' the mistress asked. 'Oh Peggy, you can go to bed now, and you can carry my daughter's bag up when you go.' She looked over at the pantry, then asked, 'Did you leave out a jug of milk and a bowl of sugar? If she didn't stop along the way, she'll be looking for a cup of tea when she comes down.'

The maid rose unsteadily to her feet and went into the pantry. She came out with a large jug of milk, but her face had a dubious expression, and when she came into the light of the kitchen she put the jug up to her nose, and smelling it she wrinkled up her face.

'Don't do that,' shouted her mistress, nearly causing the maid to drop the jug. 'Where did you pick up that disgusting habit?'

'I only wanted to see if the milk was sour. How could I find out without smelling it?' said the girl, not fully aware of where her error lay, but painfully aware of having been seen.

'The milk couldn't be sour. It's the afternoon's milk. Give me the jug.'

The girl looked with interest to see in what superior way its condition would be tested by her mistress.

Sophy's mother took the jug and for a minute she seemed to hesitate, then she began to move it deliberately round and round in concentric circles a long way from her nose, but presumably within the orbit of her olfactory organs, for as she did so she sniffed two or three times.

'There's no need to stick your nose right into the jug,' she said crossly, because the maid was correct in what she said, and the milk was just on the point of turning. 'You must have left it in the sun.'

The maid tossed her head and took out a hair-slide rather unnecessarily, since she fastened it in her hair again a minute later in the exact same place where it had been before. 'Don't put your hands to your hair in the kitchen,' said her lady absentmindedly, but she was looking around her. 'Where is the small saucepan? Oh, there it is. Rinse it out with clean water for me. And then you can go to bed. This milk is perfectly fresh, but it will do no harm to give it a boil. That will make sure of it for the morning. It will be cool before Sophy comes downstairs.'

The milk was well cooled when Sophy came down. Her mother had been up and down to her own room two or three times and had at last undressed and put on her slippers and dressing-gown. She walked heavily each time she passed her husband's study, but the talk and laughing inside may have prevented her footsteps from being heard. When she passed the boxroom under the stairs she heard the maid getting ready for bed.

'Oh Mother! I kept you up,' cried Sophy when she came down at last and saw the slippers and dressing-gown. 'Why did you wait up? Why didn't you call me?' Then she said at once, 'You really should have gone to bed.'

'I thought you might like some tea,' said her mother coldly. 'I kept the fire in. It was nearly out, but I was just in time to throw on a few logs.'

'Oh good!' said Sophy.

The mother's spirits rose. 'I have the tray set,' she said, 'I'll have a cup with you. I never take tea at this hour because it keeps me awake but I'll be awake tonight anyway, with excitement.' Her spirits rose higher. She forgot her hurt. 'I want to hear everything that happened since you went away. Begin at the beginning. I worried all night thinking of the long journey you had sitting in that cold railway carriage. They should have a proper heating apparatus. It's disgraceful. Did you meet anyone interesting going up in the train? Were you back on the right day? Were there any new people in your class?'

'I'm sure I told you all that in a letter,' said Sophy, taken aback at her mother's accurate memory of a day she had difficulty in recalling.

'I could hear it a dozen times,' said her mother. 'Tell me everything.'

'Oh, there's nothing to tell,' said Sophy taking up a biscuit and beginning to chew it.

'You found plenty to tell our father it seems, judging by the length of time you stayed up with him,' said her mother irritably.

Sophy looked up. 'Oh, we were only talking,' she said vaguely, for she could not remember much of the lazy banter that she and her father exchanged either. Tiredness was setting in. 'The exams were not too bad,' she said, 'the results will be in the paper.' She tried to remember something else to tell. 'The second paper on the first day was a bit hard, but I think I'll pull through all right.'

'I can hardly believe it's your final examination,' said her mother. 'How time flies! I lie worrying at night wondering if we did right in sending you to the University. It puts such a strain on a girl. I hope you'll stay home for a while after the results come out. Indeed, if you like I'll speak to your father about letting you stay home entirely. It's very nice to have a degree and feel independent, but there's no need to carry things too far and wear yourself out working when your father himself makes no attempts to add to his income, although he could earn more than any man in the town if he wasn't so odd.'

'You have the wrong idea, Mother. I had a definite idea in taking my degree.'

Her mother looked at her, at her glossy silk knees and her nice straight hair.

'You have plans made, have you?' she asked excitedly. 'Tell me them. I want to help.' She remembered the way she used to go into her own mother's room, years and years ago, to sit on her mother's bed, and brush her hair. Then she would tell her mother all about a dance she'd been to, the partners she had, who danced with whom, when she was away from home on a visit to relatives. She had even described the underwear her cousins wore, and the manner of arranging their hair, so that nothing would be unknown to her mother of the way her time had been spent during her short absence.

'One thing is certain,' the mother said, speaking these thoughts out loud, 'you have my mother's hands. I never saw anything so remarkable. She would have been pleased to know it, but I never thought of telling her.' She sighed and her faint sigh seemed to fill the air with ghostly memories and regrets. Sophy moved in her chair, and stared down at her hands self-consciously, but seeing a loosened piece of cuticle on the forefinger of her left hand she became absorbed at once in trying to tear it off with the finger and thumb of her right hand. She gave two or three sharp tugs but the loose piece of skin failed to break off. 'Don't,' her mother said, 'your finger will be sore all night. It will keep you awake.'

'I can't leave it alone,' said Sophy.

'You can. Stop looking at it. Forget about it. Tell me more about your examination. Go on, tell me about your friends and you'll forget all about it. The bit of skin will knit back into place.'

But Sophy could not forget about the dead bit of cuticle. It irritated her, and she kept at it. Her mother spoke again in a dreamy voice, as she sank back again into her reveries. 'Poor mother's hands were all blackened and hardened from work, but she wouldn't have grudged you your easy life. She would have been the first to congratulate you on your independence in going to the University. How it would have amused her to see your hands so much like her own. I wish I had thought of telling her. It's only when people are gone from us that we remember all the little things we could have done to please them.'

'Ah!' Sophy said triumphantly. She had torn off the bit of loose cuticle and she put her finger up to her mouth to ease the little sting. Then she looked around at the tray. 'How about the tea?'

'The kettle is at the back of the stove,' said her mother. 'It will be almost boiling. I'll poke up the fire and it will bring the water to the boil in a minute.'

'Is there any use bringing up tea to Father?' Sophy asked when her mother came back into the room with the kettle.

'You can if you like,' said the mother bending down to settle the kettle on the crackling logs in the grate. 'I know the reception I'd get if I interrupted him at his work! Anyone would imagine it was for my own good I'd gone up to him, to hear the way he'd turned on me for interrupting him on the few occasions I was unwise enough to enquire if he'd like anything before I went to bed.'

'Well, I'm dying for a cup of tea. I'm so thirsty!' Sophy said, breaking in upon her mother. 'All the way down in the train I was thinking of those dear old cups with the impossible birds on them.' She held up one of the frail cups and stared at its hand-painted pottery. But her mother understood the interruption and flushed.

'If that's the case it's a wonder you stayed upstairs so long,' she said bitterly, and once again, incongruously, she remembered the confidences that used to be exchanged between her own mother and herself long ago. It would have been such a relief, just once, to tell Sophy of some of the unpleasant things she had had to put up with while she was away. But Sophy was talking about the stupid old cup as if she wanted to stave off any chance of confidences. She was holding up the cup with both hands and staring at it with burning cheeks and bright eyes. How could she be so excited about an old cup that she had seen in the china closet ever since she was able to toddle!

'Is it meant to be a real bird?' Sophy asked. 'Is it a peacock? Is it a nightingale? Whoever saw such feathers! Whoever saw such colours!' Her voice was feverish and she asked question after question, laughing nervously at the same time.

'Give me the cup,' said her mother. 'The tea is ready.' She caught the small cup roughly. She disliked it with a sudden passion and could have thrown it on the floor only it was belonging to a set. She began to talk as normally and casually as she could. 'I'm looking forward to a cup of tea myself. Indeed, I'd take a cup every night if I had someone to take one with me. I used to love a cup at this hour. I don't know why I gave it up. You give up a great many things, one after another, when you are alone. Of course, I don't want company. I have my reading. I have my knitting.' All the same she didn't want to make things worse by her criticisms of Sophy's father.

Sophy looked at her mother's face which was bent over the fire and for a moment she envied the fine structure of bone that made the face so clear cut and attractive in spite of age, and she looked at the grey hair that was still so full of life that it sprang into curling tendrils whenever it escaped from the combs that held it up. Her own pale face and straight hair that she knew well gave her a resemblance to the face of her father, in spite of her mother's difficulty in seeing it, was now evident.

'The kettle is beginning to sing,' said her mother, just then. 'It's a good thing someone in the house has the heart to sing, as I often say to the maid, when your father has been particularly trying.'

Sophy looked around quickly for something with which she could again attract her mother's attention away from the abyss over which she hung dangerously. Her eyes fell on the photograph album that her mother had taken from her old home when she had left to get married. It was covered in faded blue velvet, with a large silver clasp. 'Did you paste in the picture of my class that I sent you at mid-term?' Sophy leaned forward and took the album on her knee. It fell open at the page upon which she had gazed so fervently as a child.

It was a photograph of her grandmother sitting in a wicker chair against a scenic screen of palm trees and the photographer's trellis balustrade. Around her, grouped in formal postures, were her daughters, Sophy's mother, and Sophy's aunts. They all wore long white dresses with long white sleeves and high necks and white hats that tilted under the weight of floppy silk roses. They all wore gold brooches, and gold bracelets, and they all had great masses of nut-brown hair. And they sat with their arms entwined around each other's waists, while those of them nearest to the chair upon which their mother sat, leaned back against her or looked up into her face. Sophy always had to pause a moment before she picked out her own mother from the group of charming girls. She remembered that her mother often told her that it took the photographer twenty minutes to try and pose them, spreading out his hands, exclaiming and above all entreating them to stop laughing just for one minute. And all at once she remembered other stories her mother used to tell her too, when she was a little girl and easily pleased, stories of beaux and bouquets, the pranks and the larks that were played upon each other, the singing and the piano playing that had gone on all day long. And she tried to feel sorry for her mother, sitting here now all alone in the evenings, filled with bitterness at some unfulfilled, foolish dreams.

Instead of a feeling of pity, however, Sophy felt impatience and irritability. Why did her mother marry the wrong man? Is it possible to be certain before it's too late that the man you are going to marry is the right man? Times have changed, she told herself. Women know more about men now than they did long ago. Marriages may break asunder now too, but they don't rot slowly. Her mother had taken up the sugar bowl. 'I hope you haven't given up sugar? It's so foolish of girls to try to be thinner than nature intended them to be.'

'Oh, I take sugar all right,' said Sophy. Then she could not resist a slight protest. 'I'm glad I take it because if I didn't I should hate to have you try and force me to do so, Mother.'

'Am I such a scold?' her mother smiled, and seemed to enjoy the remark as a joke. She passed the jug of milk. 'Put in the milk yourself. You say I always give you too much.'

But Sophy was staring into the jug.

'What is the matter with the milk?' She held the jug up to her nose.

'There's nothing the matter with it,' said her mother, looking at her anxiously.

'Ugh, there's a scum on it! Ugh, it's disgusting. What is it?'

Her mother relaxed with relief. Oh, she must have forgotten to take off the scum. 'I gave the milk a boil when you were upstairs. It wasn't sour, but it seemed on the point of turning. Boiling prevents that, but it doesn't make any difference to the milk. You wouldn't notice any difference in taste when it's in the tea. But I shouldn't have left the scum on it. That was stupid.' And she reached over and lifted off the scum with the back of a spoon. It crumpled up on the side like a ribbon of white silk. 'There's nothing disgusting about it at all. In fact, it's full of calcium and good for you,' she said when she saw her daughter's face.

'I hate boiled milk. It does give a taste to the tea,' said Sophy.

'Not at all,' said her mother, pouring out a cup. 'I often give it a boil at night.'

'Is there any milk in the kitchen that has not been boiled?' said Sophy, drawing her empty cup away as her mother went to pour tea into it. She stood up with the cup in her hand.

'I'm afraid not,' said her mother, 'but I assure you this is quite all right. You won't notice the difference when it's in the tea, I promise you. I wouldn't have done it otherwise.'

Sophy sat down and held out the cup. When it was filled she raised it to her lips and sipped at it.

'I get the taste of it distinctly,' she said, lowering the cup again.

'You couldn't, dear.' Her mother sipped hers. 'I don't taste it.'

'Well I do,' said Sophy, 'and what's more, I can't drink the tea.'

'But that's absurd,' cried her mother. 'It's just your imagination.'

'It's not imagination. I think you might have left a little milk without being boiled, when you know a cup of tea means so much to me after a long journey.'

'I tell you it makes absolutely no difference.'

'Oh Mother! Let's not argue about it. I can't drink the tea, that's all. Oh, why did you boil the milk?'

The mother sat looking at her own tea, for which she too had suddenly a great distaste. Why did she boil the milk? She tried to remember. It wasn't sour. And even if it was beginning to turn sour she should have kept back some of it until Sophy had had a cup of tea when she came downstairs. Why had she boiled it? Then she recalled how she had walked from room to room, moving the kettle, stirring the fire, and filling in the time with aimless actions while she was waiting for her daughter to come down.

'Perhaps if you hadn't stayed so long upstairs I might not have thought of boiling it.' She flung out the excuse without caring what effect it had. The whole week of anticipation and preparation was spoiled. The evening was spoiled anyway. Now everything was spoiled.

Sophy got up from her chair. There was no mistaking the black lines of fatigue, and the way her mouth drooped at the edge, as if in dismay. They must be acting the way her father and mother must behave.

'Don't harp on it Mother,' she said, 'now that it is too late.'

'That's right,' her mother said. 'Lose your temper now. Go upstairs and bang your door. After all the trouble I took preparing for you, this is all the thanks I get. It's good that I'm used to this kind of thing from your father!'

'Oh, leave Father out of it!' cried Sophy.

'Two of a feather!' cried her mother.

Sophy threw out her hands in her last appeal for peace. 'I wish you wouldn't react like this, Mother.'

'What other way can I take it?'

'You could admit that you made a mistake in boiling the milk without remembering whether or not I minded.'

'How stupid of you to mind. As a matter of fact I still don't see why you mind. I never could see why. At home we always gave the milk a boil after supper to keep it from being sour in the morning.'

'I never heard of it being done anywhere else,' said Sophy. 'You did a lot of things in your home that sound queer to me, if it comes to that.'

Her mother drew in a quick breath. 'I suppose you heard your father say that! He's always having a slap at my sisters.'

'He never even mentions them, if you want to know.'

'Oh, that doesn't deceive me. There are more ways of sneering than by word of mouth. And indeed, now that we're mentioning such things, let me tell you that your own attitude isn't what it might be at times. When the old cock crows, the young cock cackles.'

'Well, I can't help it, can I, if I'm like him?' said Sophy.

'There's no need to copy his ignorant traits,' said her mother.

Sophy stuck her fingers into her ears. 'I won't listen to talk like that. It's unjust. I never knew him to say or do anything that wasn't fair.'

'Maybe if you were at home a little more you might not have quite the same impression.'

Sophy ran to the door. 'I must say I'm glad I don't come home very often if this is the kind of reception I'd get. Good night!' She banged the door.

Sophy went out and up to the bedroom where the floor had been waxed twice over, and where the white muslin curtains floated back and forth gently as the breezes urged them.

While she undressed she thought of the girls in white dresses who vexed the photographer by laughing so much he could not pose them properly. And then she thought of the photograph of her father that hung in the hall, showing a stiff and straight young man, with serious and intelligent eyes. And suddenly she ran to her case and opened it, tossing up her blouses and handkerchiefs as she ran her hand to the bottom and took out a photograph in a small frame. It was a photograph of another young man, also straight and still, with serious eyes and a stern look, because these are the attributes which young men wish to appear to possess when they have their photographs taken. Sophy stared at the photograph, and then she ran to the mirror and stared at her own face. But she had not learned anything from looking at either face, for she sighed and got into bed.

Two or three times she leaned up on her elbow to hear if her mother had gone up to her own room, but she heard no sound, and several times she wanted to go down again and ask to be forgiven, but she knew that instead of coming to terms they would begin to argue again, so she lay still, and began instead to plan the things that she would do for her mother when she had money of her own to spend as she liked. But even this was difficult to do because her mother and herself so rarely liked the same things. The tears came into her eyes.

And then it suddenly seemed to Sophy that she had discovered a secret, a wonderful secret, that wise men had been unable to discover, and yet it was so simple and so clear that anyone could understand it. She would go through the world teaching her message. And when it was understood there would be an end to all the misery and unhappiness, all the misunderstanding and argument with which she had been familiar all her life. Everything would be changed. Everything would be different.

The footsteps that had stopped outside her door moved on, and then were silent. A door closed far away. The dream began to form again. People would all have to become alike. They would have to look alike and speak alike and feel and talk and think alike.

What a wonderful place the world would become. People would all look alike. They would all look like the girls in the photograph, with white dresses and linked arms. They would speak and think alike. They would all think like herself and her father. It was so simple. It was so clear! She was surprised that no one had thought of it before. She saw the girls untwine their arms, and lift up the hems of their long dresses and step aside to admit her as she passed into their company.

A Gentle Soul

I have just come back from the graveside where the people of these darker parts performed their last neighbourly duties towards Agatha Darker, my sister. Since our father died, six years after our mother, we lived alone in this house, we two, in silence and bitterness. And there were times when I used to wish this day upon us when she would be lowered into the clay that could be no blacker, nor colder, no more close, nor more silent, than her own black heart.

It would have served the same ends if I were to die myself I suppose, but perhaps the thought that I would have Jamey Morrow to face kept me from dying many a time in the long, long decades since I last laid eyes on him, or what was left of him under the old sacks they put over his face in the yard before they carried him home to his sister's cottage.

I was the only one in the yard when it happened, but I had my back turned, and I didn't know there was anything wrong until I heard the clatter of the mare's hooves and the crack like a shot of a gun when the side of the cart splintered against the piers of the gate. I didn't see Jamey at all when I first looked around. I only thought of the mare and how I could stop her, because after the cart struck the gate, the traces broke and she went off in a mad gallop down the lane. I often wondered afterwards that he didn't give a shout or a cry, but maybe it was lost in the clatter of the hooves and the rattle of the iron-rimmed wheels of the cart. Or else maybe it all happened so suddenly he didn't get his breath to shout, but was jolted out of the cart and down on the cobbles where – oh God, what an awful thing to happen to any man, the back wheel of the cart went over him. Over his head, I believe, but by God's mercy I didn't see that. When I saw him next he was lying on his back where he was thrown down. They said I ran over to him but I don't remember any more than just seeing him lying there in the muck and the dirt with his hands stretched out as if he was still straining after the reins. But I knew he was dead. They say I gave a scream and fell down on the cobblestones, and didn't come to again until they brought me to my senses after they carried me in to the house and put me down on the sofa in the parlour. But do you know the first thing I heard after the accident? It was Agatha's voice. She was saying something to my father. 'If only it hadn't happened in our yard.'

That was all it meant to her, that a man was killed, and that man Jamey Morrow who had worked for us for fifteen years, and whom we knew as long back as we could remember, when we were all of us small children. I can't remember a time when I didn't know Jamey Morrow and his sister Annie. I remember when their mother was alive, a poor sickly woman. Our own mother used to take us with her when she went down to the cottage with soup or medicine for the poor woman. 'She's not long for this world,' Mother used to say and she used to look at Jamey and Annie, and sigh, and tell us they would soon be orphaned. But that is only one of the ways that things seemed to work out the opposite of what might have been expected.

Who, for instance, could have thought when this country got its freedom, and the new government began to build ugly concrete bungalows for the labourers and farm workers, that a day would come when these would be fitter for human habitation than our stone farmhouses that were such a source of pride for us. Then we considered the countryside was destroyed by these hideous places. I remember well my father's rage when he heard the Morrows had put down their names to get one, and that it was going to be built on the frontage of James Lanigan's farm at a point just opposite to where our lane opened onto the road, just where Father said it would be an eyesore, every time we came down the lane. Although I was glad the Morrows were getting away from the damp hovel in the fields where they lived up to that time, even I wished they weren't going to be right at the end of our lane.

We loved our lane so much. We were proud of being nearly a mile back from the road, knowing that it was our own land with our own cattle to either side of us. We used to love going up and down it on the sidecar, especially in summer when the hedges grew as high as walls, and there were pink-and-white dog roses nodding in the breezes as we tilted to this side and that over the dried ruts in the ground.

I never thought a day would come when places lying back in the fields would be as good as worthless. But then who, among us, could have foreseen that even our thatched roofs in which we took such pride would become a curiosity for city people. I must admit that thatch can look very unsightly if it is neglected, and in time, it was not easy to get thatchers. Some of our neighbours had the thatch pulled down and had their places slated. The Lanigans, our nearest neighbours but one, had their roof covered with a galvanised tin sheeting, and I suppose it too looked better than ours which sometimes had rotted patches in it and new blades of grass sprouting out of the thatch. But our place didn't look a whole lot worse for that, because nothing could be done to straighten the old walls, that were crooked as well, which added to the old-fashioned look that somehow or other seemed all right with the thatch.

Ah well, I suppose it's comical now to think how we resented the new council houses, and thought they spoiled the countryside. To do ourselves justice, I must say that there was never any attempt to make the new places fit into their surroundings. Places like ours and the Lanigans', and others like them, were hedged around with privet and laurel to beautify them, and the windows and door were wreathed round in summer with woodbine and roses. All the same, I admit the Morrows' cottage was no better nor no worse than any other. In fairness to Agatha, I am prepared to give her credit for that one thing.

The Morrows didn't get a council house until Jamey was almost a grown man. There being only him and his sister, both of them unmarried, justified the Council passing over them for a long time. But they got one in the end.

Agatha and I were away at boarding school when the building of the bungalow began. It was well underway when we came home for our summer holidays.

'What in the name of the Almighty is that?' Agatha asked, when we came to our lane, and she saw the new walls going up just opposite to our gate. My father only shrugged his shoulders. 'The Morrows are getting a place at last, there's nothing we can do about it,' he said. He pressed his lips together, and gave the mare a lick of the whip so that she fairly leapt up the lane.

'I wouldn't mind so much if it was anyone but those Morrows,' said Agatha, when she and I were walking down the lane a few days later. She always hated them. I never knew why, and I don't know now, unless it could be that even before Jamey came to work for us at all, before he was a man you might say, when we were only youngsters going to school together, she might have seen that there was something in his eyes when he looked at me that wasn't in them when he looked at her. Even in those days, he seemed to be always crossing our path, as if indeed to provoke whoever held the reins of the pony. As I said, we went to the National School when we were small girls, until we were old enough to go away boarding, like all farmers' children did. But whereas the other scholars often had to walk three or four miles to the schoolhouse, and often barefoot, we who lived only a short distance from the village, always came and were brought back by our pony and trap. And when I said a few minutes ago that Jamey Morrow was always crossing our path, that was literally true because one of the things I clearly recollect about those days was the way he would start up suddenly almost out of nowhere, like a hare, right in front of the pony's head, and with a laugh, he'd dart across the road, to stare at us from the high bank on the other side.

'You fool,' Agatha shouted at him, and once I remember that she snatched the whip from the socket and rose up in the trap to lash out at him. But he only laughed, in what Agatha called an impudent way. That day, to goad her, he ran alongside the pony the whole way to the schoolhouse gate, and no matter how Agatha beat the poor animal under the shafts, we could not out-distance his grinning face. 'You fool,' Agatha shouted again, as we got to the wall of the schoolyard, when laughingly he vaulted over it. In her fury all Agatha could do was to give a final lash to the wretched beast whose poor legs were plaiting underneath from fatigue.

Here I think I should set down another thing I remember about those days. We used to unhitch the animal and tie her up in a covered shed at the side of the schoolhouse, with a nosebag of oats that we brought with us in the trap. Well, on this particular day when we were in school, I began to feel uneasy about the poor beast after such a walloping and at the first opportunity I went out to the schoolyard to take a look. But someone had put an old bit of sacking across the pony's back and cut a few fistfulls of grass too because there were green blades all around the ground under the pony's hooves and stuck between the animal's yellow teeth.

It wasn't Agatha who put on that sack. It wasn't she who had cut the grass. And it wasn't me. It could only have been one person, and when at that minute sensing there was someone else in the yard, I hardly needed to catch sight of him to know that it was Jamey Morrow.

I suppose you might say in a way, we were sweethearts as long ago as that, when our eyes met that day in the empty schoolyard, there was always the same look in Jamey's eyes that was in them ever after when we were alone.

I suppose too that is why I felt so odd the year we came home from boarding school for good, and our father told us that Jamey Morrow had come to him looking for work. I felt so strange, I had to sit down on the lid of my trunk. And that was nothing to the way I felt the next day when I went into the kitchen for something and there was Jamey standing at the back door with a bucket of calf meal in his hands waiting for me to scald it. Agatha was there too, but Jamey's eyes were on me. He never looked at her at all although she was in front of me, and I just stood in the middle of the floor, staring at him until I felt myself blushing and backed away into the shadow of a big grain bin we used to keep in the kitchen for the sake of dryness.

Oh, the look Jamey gave me that day. How often I was to tremble in case that Agatha too had seen it, or Father. How well I was to know that look in the years still ahead.

I think now that Father never saw, but I know that Agatha was aware of every glance that passed between us even when she was in another room with the thickness of two walls between her and us. But her pretended silence was part of the plan she pursued from the start, not to let on she noticed anything at all.

On the day of the inquest, she kept up the pretence of the accident not being any concern of mine, any more nearly than it would have concerned anyone to have a man killed in their own yard, in front of their own eyes, you might say, although I was clearly affected by it. At the last minute in the kitchen, when we were dressed and ready to go to the Courthouse and Father had the mare hitched to the sidecar, I pleaded with them both at once to let me take off my blue silk dress, but she only looked at me coldly, and asked what else I had that I could wear.

'Anything but this,' I cried in anguish, looking down at the blue dress. It was fitter to wear to a wedding than to an inquest.

'You know you have nothing else to wear for such an occasion, except your old foulard,' she said slowly and deliberately. My foulard was black, unrelieved except by a bit of jet beading on the bodice. It was part of the mourning clothes Father bought for us when our mother died. Agatha used to have one like it, but black suited her and she had worn it out in no time. Shortly before, I had seen her cutting it down into a petticoat. But black never suited me, and I didn't wear mine very often. It was as good as new.

'You look a sight in black, you know,' said Agatha when she saw me still irresolute. 'You look bad enough this morning as things are, God knows. Your face is all blotchy, did you know that?'

I neither knew nor cared, Agatha must have known that too, because in spite of her policy of pretending to know nothing, there were times when her malevolence could not be hidden, and it broke out. 'Do you want people to say that you went into mourning for your father's yard-man?' she said.

I know I ought to have given her the answer she deserved. I ought to have told her how little I cared what anyone thought about Jamey and me, at this moment, her least of all. But Father was waiting outside on the sidecar, and the door was open. There didn't seem to be any gain in upsetting him for nothing, because all the declarations I could ever make would not do Jamey any good, nor could my silence do him any harm, or so I thought at the time.

That was always my failing, not facing up to people, but it was only that day I was to learn that it was a failing. I used to think it was a good quality. I used to be proud of what I thought was my gentle nature. I used to think that people admired me for it, particularly when they knew Agatha was so hard.

Agatha was like Father. He and she were so alike in their ways they were more like a man and his wife than father and daughter. But I took after Mother.

Poor, poor Mother. She had always been timid, and when she became frail and delicate towards the end of her life, her timidity was almost cowardice. She let Father dominate her in everything, and she was always warning us to avoid saying anything to upset him in case, as she used to say, her voice sinking to a whisper, in case he would get a stroke, and 'drop'.

Oh, the dread of that simple word 'drop', when it came like that in a whisper, from my mother's lips. Such is the power of association that, in a storm, I never heard the wind drop without feeling greater terror in my heart than the fury of the storm.

Agatha evidently did not have the same fears as me of provoking Father's anger, or perhaps she was serene in the knowledge that there was nothing in her life that could stir him to any great degree of anger. This put her in a good position to incense him with stories about me.

Not that I had much to hide from him either before Jamey came to work for us, but as far back as I can remember I was mortally afraid of my father. But then I was afraid of Agatha too.

I was like Mother, you see. She was afraid of everything. I suppose I was taken after her, as they say. Indeed, she said as much to me one day shortly before she died. She had taken my hand in hers that was so thin and white. 'You're just like me, Rose,' she said. 'I'm glad I'm like you, Mother,' I breathed with love and tenderness, but she looked at me, with pity, and then she turned her head to one side, and I saw that her face was wet with tears.

'What is the matter, Mother?' I whispered, but all she could do was shake her head from side to side almost in admonition.

As if there was anything I could do then, or at any time, to make me other than I was. What happened at the inquest only proved that if I had a hundred lives to live I would have been the same cowardly creature all the time; and Jamey's dogged perseverance would have gained him nothing in the end, no matter how long he lived.

I would never have had the courage to face up to Father, to Agatha, to the whole countryside, and let it be thrown in my face that I'd go down to live in the cottage I sneered at so much when it was being built. I couldn't bring myself to think of such a thing, although many a time since then the thought of standing in one of those small rooms with Jamey was like thinking of a caress because, for all our love, we never stood as near together as those close and narrow walls would bring us.

We had never been alone for longer than a few uneasy minutes, in the yard we had only exchanged a few cautious words, while I scoured the milking pails for him, or worked the handle of the pump, while he rinsed them round with spring water. At such times Agatha was never far away, bound to return before too long. But those moments were terrible long moments for all that, when it would seem to me some pull seemed to be exerting itself between us, so that I often had to catch hold of something, the table or the back of a chair, in order to keep myself from moving nearer to him, or putting out my hand to touch him. Whether it was something inside myself that made me feel this pull towards him or whether he put pressure upon me deliberately by his eyes that were always full upon me whenever we met, I don't know. I only know that after such long moments passed, and Jamey had gone, or more likely when someone had come upon us, although my heart beat wildly at the thought of what the moment might presage, I was always glad that things were to remain vague for another while.

And so one summer after another came and went, and left us as it found us. And the cold hard winters came, and although they were longer in passing, they too passed and left things unchanged.

Oh, how bitter it was afterwards to think of how Jamey had endured those winters. Up at all hours of the night with ewes at lambing time, and yet first astir in the yard at frosty dawn. Many and many a time my heart was stabbed at the sight of him going about his labours, caked to the knees with mud, his clothes shapeless from all the wettings he got and the poor means he had of drying them.

It was some comfort to think of times, in the bitterest of weather, that I got a chance to call him to the kitchen window and hand him out a cup of hot tea when Agatha was occupied elsewhere. But for this it's likely he would not have stayed in such a backward place.

Of course in the summer, our place was not that bad. And the summer used to come so suddenly it would seem to reach full tide overnight, the hedges all frothing in blossom, and the cattle in the pastures wading through the great billows of grass, as if through water, while the meadows grew breast high. So high indeed that once, as we went down the lane in the sidecar and saw a man walking down a patch that ran through our meadow, it was only when the wind swayed the grasses that it could be seen he held by the hand a little girl in a pink sunbonnet.

Oh, the summers were beautiful, the summers were bountiful, they seemed to be made for lovers. I used to forget Agatha. I used to forget Father. But above all, I used to forget that there had been other summers when the hedges were just as thick with roses and the grass mounted in the fields like a flood, yet all those summers had passed and Jamey and I were, as we had always been, no nearer to each other.

So many summers!

Only a few days before Jamey was killed, I was standing at the door of the kitchen, and although the real summer had not yet come, here and there, like a spray of foam breaking before its time far out upon a distant wave, hawthorn had broken into blossom.

'The summer is nearly here,' said Jamey, rolling the water slowly round and round in the milk pail, and not looking at me at all.

'It makes me sad to think of the summer coming,' I said.

He stopped rolling the can.

'I was thinking of the summers long ago, when I was a child.'

He looked straight at me, then the old feeling of nervousness came over me, so much that I trembled, and instinctively I drew into the shelter of the doorway. Agatha had only gone down the passage to the dairy, where we could hear the sound of the clappers as she made up the butter. But Jamey was reckless that day. He let down the milk-can and came a step or two after me, as I drew back further into the kitchen. 'Why think of the summers that are gone?' he said. 'Why not think of the summers ahead?'

One would have thought those words were simple enough, and harmless too, but I read their deeper import so clearly that, terrified, I glanced over my shoulder in case he might have been overheard, and when I looked back again I saw on his face another look with which I was becoming familiar, it was not pity, it was not contempt. The nearest I could go to naming it was to say it was a look of accusation. 'More are gone than are to come,' he said. And again his voice had lost that eager questing note, it was flat and dull. He lifted the pail, and going to the pump, the clatter he made filled the yard.

Looking after him that day my heart was heavy. That is all there is between us, I thought, or ever like to be – looks of love, and looks of accusation.

Agatha was a long time in the dairy that evening. I need not have been so cautious. Yet when she came back into the kitchen half an hour later, you'd think our voices had left traces in the air from the way she stood on the threshold with the bowl of buttermilk in her arms, looking around her suspiciously. 'Who was that?' she asked, but she knew without being told that it was Jamey. 'It's well for you, that you have nothing more to do than give chat to the like of that fellow.'

That was Agatha's attitude from the start; to ignore the implications of the situation that was developing, and give her attention instead to surface irregularities, the way I idled, or the way Jamey's boots muddied the floor when he came into the kitchen.

It was hard at times to know whether or not she suspected anything. Sometimes it seemed impossible to think that she did not. Nothing except those dangerous inflammable looks had ever passed between Jamey Morrow and me. Those looks that showed how near the surface was the fire that would consume us all. On the other hand nothing had ever occurred behind Agatha's back that might not have passed between us in her presence. Agatha and Father would never have held up their heads if I had been carrying on with Jamey, and had run away with him.

Not that our plans had ever been put like that in words. Poor Jamey, he hadn't the right to speak plainly. I had never given him that right. But what was in his mind could not be stifled, and there was a purpose and a meaning behind every word he uttered. There was one day, when he came to the door of the kitchen, and called me by my first name, recklessly, not caring if he was overheard. By good chance we were alone. 'Did you hear the news?' he asked, his eyes bright and piercing as they searched my face.

I hadn't heard anything strange.

'About Molly Lanigan?'

I had heard nothing, but of course I knew at once what was coming.

'And Andy Fagan?'

Jamey nodded his head excitedly.

'Have they run away?' I spoke in a whisper, but when Jamey replied he was exuberant, and cried out loud. 'Yes, to Australia.'

There was a look of satisfaction on his face.

'But how did they manage?' I was very disturbed, very bewildered. Molly was the daughter of James Lanigan, our neighbour, and their way of life was the same as ours in so many ways. I couldn't see how they had been able to arrange things to make their getaway unnoticed by the rest of the household.

Perhaps old Lanigan was not as proud as our father, and did not set such a high standard for his womenfolk, allowing them to walk to Mass rather than take out the trap, even if the day was wet, and he took less heed of their appearance in the house too, with the result that Molly Lanigan sometimes went around the kitchen in the morning with old trodden-down slippers on her feet, or went about the yard in muddy weather with her feet stuck into a pair of her father's old boots, unpolished and unlaced. But whatever might have been old Lanigan's laxity in these respects, he and Father saw eye to eye when it came to estimating the difference between themselves and the labouring class. Old Lanigan especially had been greatly incensed at the scheme for giving them cottages. 'You'll see,' he said. 'All this will end badly. It will put them above themselves. A day will come when we won't be able to get one of them to lift a spade. More than that, you'll see the day when they'll be so full of themselves they'll be setting their caps at our daughters, and looking for wives among them.' Molly Lanigan was with her father that day, and how she and I giggled until we saw Agatha looking down her nose at us.

Molly was as pretty as a rose, with soft mossy hair, and softly tinted cheeks, the pink coming and going in them. People often said we were alike, Molly and I, but of course I wasn't anything like as pretty as Molly. All the same, people fancied they saw a likeness between us, and we were often taken for sisters. Well, we were more like sisters than Agatha and me, and I suppose that's what people meant. I felt more sisterly towards Molly, that much was certainly true, although Agatha never liked Molly. And one day she brought up her name with a glitter of malice. 'I hear people are beginning to talk about Molly Lanigan?' Agatha probed.

'I heard something about Molly too.' I had heard some talk, Jamey had hinted to me about her, but I didn't dream Molly would go as far as to give people grounds for talking openly about her.

'There's talk about the way she's carrying on with one of their own workmen,' said Agatha.

Father, who had evidently heard nothing, turned to Agatha with a look of concern. 'They'll have to try and put a stop to that kind of thing, before it's too late.'

So it was true? All at once I felt a strange feeling in my heart that I could not name. Then, with shame, I realised the feeling was jealousy.

'Molly and Andy Fagan,' I murmured, more to myself than to the others, more to hear if, coupled together, their names would seem less ill-assorted than were their persons.

My Jamey was so different from Andy, I told myself hastily, because I could not help feeling that for the one thing that united them, there must be a hundred things that would divide them. It would take Andy Fagan a long time to rise above his origins. Anyone would have to admit that Jamey in his old clothes, and up to his knees in mud, was still a cut above being a labourer. I thought that whatever was between Molly and Andy would be brought to an end, because not long after Agatha's malicious talk, Molly was packed off to Dublin. She went to stay with a sister of her father's who had the name of being a very strict woman.

It was easy to see what was at the back of this move. Molly was in Dublin for almost two years, without once being let home. You'd have thought that would have put an end to anything there had been between her and Andy. That was why I was so taken by surprise when Jamey told me about them going to Australia.

'But she was sent to Dublin to get her away from him,' I cried. I couldn't understand how they managed things at all.

Jamey gave a short laugh. 'That was old Lanigan's mistake, if he had left her at home he might have furthered his own plans better.'

I didn't understand him and I told him so.

'If old Lanigan had left her at home, it's likely she'd have found poor Fagan was driving too hard a bargain. The difference between what he had to offer and what she would have to give up for him was too great,' he said. Then he paused, and he gave me a look I'll remember till the day I die. 'Like others before her,' he said.

Do you see what I mean now about the way he was always hinting and insinuating, without ever daring to speak outright? 'I wonder will they ever come back,' I said, nervously, stupidly, if you like, because I only wanted to change the conversation. I didn't altogether succeed, for Jamey kept staring at me, head on, for a minute that I thought would never end, as if there were something I should do about it. And then he looked behind me at the yard, and the ramshackle pump, and he looked at me again straight in the face.

'Is it back to a place like this?' he said. Because at that time of the year, with the dreary stretches of mud that lay between one shed and another, one place was like another in our part of the country.

He gave a laugh. I didn't like that laugh. And I didn't like the look I saw on his face, it was not the familiar dogged look I used to know. I couldn't give it a name at all, but I felt a faint stirring of fear. I used to think I knew Jamey better than I knew anyone in the world. But all of a sudden I felt frightened. On Jamey's face I had expected to see nothing but the loving look with which I had grown familiar. Was there something I could do to change the way it was between us? The thought crossed my mind that for all his dogged devotion he might one day take a notion and walk out of the place without me. Then where would I be, left alone by his departure?

So when he was taken from me finally and quickly by death, I had one gleam of consolation in the thought that it was not by any act of his will or of mine that we were parted.

This was the thought that was uppermost in my mind the day we rattled along the road to the inquest. It made me feel less bitter towards Agatha at that time, and more pitying, because after all, I had my memories, and I thought no one could take them away from me. I was planning when day ended, and twilight began to descend on the countryside, I would wander across the fields to the old cemetery in which Jamey had been laid beside his parents, kneeling down among the cool grasses

I would whisper to him all the words of love that I had never spoken.

Ah Jamey, I would cry. Ah Jamey! And I would tell him all my love, tell him how I stifled it, and how I suffered from it, so great were my feelings of love. I thought Agatha or Father must surely notice my sensations. I had to clench my hands to prevent me from pressing them to my heart.

Father noticed something I think, because he looked at me sharply. 'Hold on to the sides there,' he said roughly. 'Do you want to be thrown out on the road?'

I hardly heeded him. In my mind I was still kneeling, penitent, in the moist grasses of the graveyard, at evening time. 'If only I had you back again,' I'd say. 'I'd go to the ends of the earth, wherever you wanted, and whatever you wanted of me I'd do now right this minute with you Jamey. Forgive me,' I'd cry aloud to all the countryside.

In spite of my dreaming I became aware at last that we had reached the outskirts of the town, and, for the first time I began to apprehend the embarrassment of the occasion. 'There are a lot of people in town today,' I said addressing Agatha, although between us of late there had been a great constraint.

I hardly thought she would speak, but she answered. 'What did you expect?' she said, stonily. 'They're here to gape at us!'

I suppose it was because I was so absorbed in my own feelings that I had not given much thought to the inquest. Now, however, at the last minute, I was filled with a nervous curiosity. 'Will we be asked questions?' I cried.

Agatha looked contemptuously at me. 'Why do you suppose they're bringing us here?' she said.

All at once my heart began to beat violently. 'They won't ask me anything, will they?'

Father looked around hastily. 'You'll be the principal witness, didn't you know that.' Then he looked at Agatha.

'Didn't you tell her she'd be the first witness?'

'She's not a fool, is she?' she muttered. 'Doesn't she know she was the only one in the yard when it happened.'

But Father wasn't satisfied. 'All the same, I thought you were going to talk to her,' he said.

We were in the town now and the mare had to pick her way carefully in the crowded streets. We had rounded the corner of Main Street, at the end of which was the Courthouse. I saw Annie Morrow, a pathetic figure in her cheap black clothes, making her way along. I'd have to make an opportunity to speak to her, but it was for Jamey's sake I'd do it, because to tell the truth, there was as much difference between him and her, well, as I suppose people would have said there was between him and me if they had been given an occasion for talking about us. But I was full of pity for her all the same, in spite of her mean appearance and her badly made clothes. 'There's Annie Morrow,' I said aloud. 'I suppose they'll have to ask her questions too.'

I thought my father at least would have felt something now that he had seen her. But he averted his proud, hard face, and looked straight ahead. 'You'll find she'll be well able to answer anything she's asked,' he said. 'Too well,' he added.

All of a sudden I knew there was something strange in Agatha's silence. She hadn't told me I was to be called as a witness. There was a strange bluntness about her. Something was breeding, something evil.

'Don't you know the Morrows and their like will throw all the blame of this upon us?' Father said.

'But it was an accident,' I cried. 'How could there be blame put on anyone?'

Father gave a jerk to the reins. 'It's easily seen you know little about the Morrows or their class,' he said. 'They're always looking for a chance to put down their betters. Don't you know they'll say the whole thing was due to some fault of ours; that the harness was broken or the mare was wicked, or some other such lie.'

I didn't think that anyone would go out of their way to tell a deliberate lie like that, much less in a Courthouse where they'd be on oath to tell the truth. But I didn't know either that a lie could take all kinds of forms, and that you could tell one just by saying nothing at all. 'I don't believe Annie Morrow would tell a lie,' I cried. 'Can't we prove the harness was all right. We can produce it. And doesn't everyone know our mare is quiet?'

We were drawing up at the door of the Courthouse by this time, and all Father would have to do when we got down from the sidecar would be to make a knot in the reins and throw it into the well of the car. The mare would stand in the shafts all day if necessary. She'd stand in the street outside the Courthouse today without being held or tied or anything. There wasn't an animal in the countryside that was as quiet.

'Everyone knows our mare,' I said, as I prepared to get down on to the footpath. It was not till then that Agatha spoke.

'The best animal in the world would turn sour if she was badly treated,' she said in her cold, cold voice.

I got such a strange feeling that I was not able to get down from the trap. I sank back on the worn leather cushions. 'You can't mean that Jamey ill-treated her?'

Agatha shrugged her shoulders.

'Who knows?' she said.

Then I found my voice. 'Agatha Darker, you know very well that Jamey Morrow never ill-treated an animal in his life.' But when I looked at her cold sneering face I turned around to Father. 'You know it, don't you, Father?'

Father was putting a knot in the reins. He threw the knotted leather into the well of the car before he answered.

'It isn't what we know, or do not know, but what we saw or did not see that will count in here,' he said, and before he put the whip into its socket, he motioned towards the Courthouse with it. 'You were the only one in the yard when the accident happened, if you say he didn't kick the animal they'll take your word for it. That's all there is to say about the matter. Come on! Get down!'

But I didn't get down. I felt so weak I thought my feet would go from under me if I tried to stand, much less to walk up through the crowd that was gathering at the Courthouse door, and all of them staring at us with a hostile stare. I recognised one or two of them as labouring men that were working on farms around about us. And I recognised two girls that were cousins of the Morrows. You'd have thought they would have been a bit sober-looking at such a time, but instead they had a saucy impudent look about them, as if the proceedings in the Courthouse gave them some sort of importance.

I could not help noticing when my sister Agatha got down from the sidecar on to the footpath, those girls lost a lot of their impudence. Agatha always had that effect upon people. She made them uncomfortable. They shrank back from her, as, with her head erect, she prepared to go into the Courthouse.

'Agatha!' I cried. She was my sister after all. Those people crowding around us were not our kind, and although I didn't want to side with Agatha and Father, I didn't want to side with them either. After all, I had to live with Agatha and Father, and now that Jamey was gone from me, I'd have to live with them for the rest of my life.

'Oh, Agatha!' I cried. 'Why do I have to answer questions? After all, I didn't see anything that happened. You and Father saw more than me. It was only when you ran out into the yard and I saw you put your hand up to your face that I looked around and saw him lying on the ground. And didn't I faint after that? What good will it do them to question me? I saw nothing!'

I did not know it then, but it was this moment for which Agatha was waiting.

Taking my arm she helped me down from the sidecar, and linking her arm in mine, she pressed me close to her, as we made our way up the steps of the Courthouse together, between the rows of gaping faces on either side. 'Of course you saw nothing. That's why it was so absurd of you to keep insisting that Jamey could not have provoked the mare. How did you know what happened? He could have kicked her a dozen times without you seeing him. We all know it is most unlikely that he did anything of the kind, but you couldn't swear he didn't, could you? Don't forget, you'll be on your oath?'

We were at the Courthouse at this time, but we had not gone in because we were waiting for Father to join us. 'You couldn't swear he didn't, could you?' Agatha again asked.

At that moment Father came up the steps.

'Could you?' my sister asked again. And this time I shook my head.

Oh, to think of the cleverness and malice that led me to that betrayal. Is it any wonder that I hated her from that moment to this moment, and that I will hate her until the last moment of my life on this earth. And to think that when that last moment comes it will be by her side I will be laid in the earth, and with her dust that mine will mingle, I, Rose Darker, that should by rights be laid alongside Jamey Morrow.

Chamois Gloves

It was an important day at the Convent of Our Lady of Perpetual Succour: three postulants were about to take their First Vows.

A beautifully fine day, thank God!

The sunlight glinted on the chapel windows, on the greenhouse roof, and on the windshields of the visitors' cars as they came up the driveway.

One or two cars were already drawn up in front of the chapel, which was a separate building to the left of the convent, and the tyres had made ridges in the loose, clean gravel. The gravel was really too thickly spread, because it rolled about under the feet of the relatives when they stepped out of the cars. No wonder there were no weeds! And in case even one small weed should dare to put up its head, Joe the gardener was standing by the yew hedge, with a hoe in his hand. But he was in his best suit, and he was wearing his hat.

On the other side of the hedge, magnificently unconcerned, two, no, three young nuns walking rapidly up and down were doing their spiritual reading. And finally, at an open window in one of the classrooms on the ground floor, the five small girls who were going to be bridesmaids at the ceremony were having their wreaths and veils put straight by a lay teacher.

The principal participants were out of sight, way up on the top storey of the noviciate, in their cells.

The cars were really beginning to arrive now. Two more were coming up the drive, and there was the sound of another changing gear down at the gates. The gates were situated at a bad point in the road, and they could not be safely negotiated in top gear.

In the basement of the convent an old lay sister peered upwards through a window below ground level.

Had they all arrived, she wondered. She was the Kitchen Sister, Ursula, and she was in charge of the luncheon which would be served after the ceremony. She looked back over her shoulder at a clock. In exactly fifty minutes, she calculated, they should be sitting down to table. But would they? Tch! tch! she said, as from yet another car, that scattered the gravel right and left, like peas from a pea shooter, there descended a whole family, father, mother, and three small children. 'I hope there won't be more than the number, like last year,' she muttered. People had no consideration, no manners, you might say. Some of them thought children didn't count. They ought to be taught a lesson. Children should not be put at the table at all. They should be put in a classroom and given a glass of milk and a plate of biscuits. But no, oh no, nothing will do the parents but squeeze the children around the big table in the parlour, upsetting everything, especially the numbers of knives and forks. Some father would try to accommodate one of these children by calling out, 'I have two forks,' as if the table had been laid wrongly. 'Ah, but they don't know any better,' said Sister Ursula.

She was the daughter of a small farmer, and it always seemed to her that the meals at the convent were very grand, and that the guests didn't properly apprehend the niceties. And if after the meal, a grapefruit came back untouched, or a piece of cutlery unused, she felt justified in saying, 'You can't blame them. Where did they see such things before?'

On the other hand, Reverend Mother, who came from a well-to-do merchant's family in the midlands, was always nervous in case everything was not correct, and on occasions such as this she hovered about the table adjusting the folds of the serviettes, and making minute alterations in the lie of the cutlery. It was a minor, but constant, source of embarrassment to her that they had no proper grapefruit spoons. She had not quite sufficient confidence to order them, but whenever a young nun's dower included a share of family plate, or when the convent received a bequest in the form of silverware, she eagerly rummaged through it. 'Are there no grapefruit spoons?' she would exclaim, and when there were not, it was manifestly difficult for her to conceal her disappointment, no matter how rare or how valuable were the other items.

Sister Ursula knew Reverend Mother's feelings about the spoons, and so, whenever she laid the table for visitors, she always gave the bowls of the teaspoons a squeeze to narrow them.

'Grapefruit spoons are long and pointed, you know,' she told the lay sisters. 'But who will notice the difference! Some people won't even have seen a grapefruit.'

Today, as she peered upwards through the ivy-framed window, she was inclined to think a lot of the cutlery would come back unused. Once professed, she was prepared to accept all the choir-nuns as ladies, but when it came to some of their relatives, she raised her eyebrows so that the band of starched linen across her forehead shifted its place and showed the ridge it had made in her skin. Ah! There was a familiar car. As usual, on the dot, Father Devancy. She bustled back to the range. Everything would be on time after all; Father Devaney would see to it. Thanks be to God.

The arrival of the priest's car was indeed a signal to all concerned. The young nuns pacing behind the yew hedge closed their breviaries and walked, not so much quickly, as purposefully, back to the convent. The five little communicants were bustled out of sight. Among the guests there was activity also. Some of the menfolk who had stayed sitting behind the wheels of their cars, got out and, pulling up their coats by the back of the collar, as if they were their own footmen, firmly followed their womenfolk. They, on the other hand, confident and chattering up to this point, now became ill at ease, and inclined not to know what was to be done. It was the men who were relied upon in the end.

'Well, what's keeping us?' they said, and they trooped up the steps before wiping their feet elaborately on the fibre doormat, and stepped onto the golden parquet as if it were brittle yellow glass.

In a few minutes, as if the chapel door had been a swallow hole and they had been sucked into it, everyone was seated on the inside. No longer blocked with people, the open door of the chapel gave a glimpse of hundreds of lighted candles, and it let out the first notes of the organ, peremptory, premonitory.

Meanwhile, in the noviciate which was separate from the main building, high up near the copper cupola, viridescent with verdigris, and on top of which, gay as a weather-vane, there shone a gilt cross, the three young girls who were about to be received, raised their arms and down over their bodies fell the beautiful white satin gowns they were to wear for their wedding with Christ. But although the cells were so high up in the roof, nevertheless the lower sashes were covered with a brass grille so that only the pigeons walking about on the cupola could see those beautiful bare arms.

On account of this brass grille, the postulants could not clearly see the cars arriving. They could only hear them as they came up the drive.

That's ours, thought Veronica, the youngest of the postulants. She recognised the sound of the engine, and a minute afterwards the noise of the car doors slamming. In a little while – the ceremony would be short really, and the luncheon would not take very long either – she would be with the family. A feeling of absolutely delirious happiness passed through her from top to toe. It was too bad Mabel couldn't be there, of course, but even that wouldn't spoil the marvellousness of it all. Oh, such joy!

But all at once she bit her lip. That was the trouble. She was too happy, far too happy, all the time, yesterday, today. Every single day since the day she first entered the noviciate, she hadn't had one moment of sadness or regret. Surely that wasn't right? Where was the sacrifice if there were no pain of loss, no anguish of indecision?

Take the other postulants! How many times during the past year had she been wakened in the small hours by a sound of sobbing in one of the other cells? It was subdued sobbing, but terrible to hear, all the same, in the darkness. She had never been able to tell whether it was Sister Assumpta or Sister Concepta, but from other indications she felt sure that in their souls, unlike her own, there was some struggle about which she knew nothing. Once, at recreation, Sister Concepta had asked her a strange question.

'Do you ever have dreams, strange ones?' But when Veronica had to admit she had not, Concepta had turned away with a worried expression.

That evening Veronica had confided in the Mistress of Novices, or Private Enterprise, as she was nicknamed on account of a famous reprimand she had made to a former novice whose zeal she considered excessive. 'We don't want any private enterprise in piety here.' Private Enterprise had listened for a minute and then commented. 'So you think God ought to have put more temptations in your way, do you?' she said. 'And might I ask what makes you think you'd be able to withstand them? Let me tell you, God knows what he's doing. And if, for some purpose of his own, he calls to his service the poor weak creatures as well as the strong ones, well then he arranges matters so that there isn't too great a strain put on us.' She spoke so sarcastically that tears had come into Veronica's eyes, but then, just before turning aside, the old nun smiled. 'At least, that's the only way I can account for my own perseverance,' she said.

Private Enterprise was always putting people in their place, yet in her disregard for their comfort, managing to make them feel fortunate in their lot.

And so, when out on the landing Veronica saw the pale faces of Concepta and Assumpta, even then, at the last minute, she felt an impulse to seek assurance one last time from the old nun. 'Look at their faces,' she wanted to say. 'Anyone can see the sacrifice they are making, while I am so happy.' Scandalised she realised that for her part, it was looking forward to the pleasure of seeing her family there that meant most. She was actually thinking beyond the ceremony, treating it as if it was of not much importance; the Great Day, for which she had been preparing every single day that had preceded it since she had entered the convent.

Perhaps after all she had no vocation? In panic she looked around. Where was Private Enterprise? Ah, there she was, plodding up the stairs. Veronica started forward, but before she could open her mouth, the old nun looked past her at Concepta and frowned. 'You're not going to be sick, are you?' she asked bluntly. 'You're very green in the face. Stop, Sisters!' she commanded them all, although just then they heard the faraway sound of the organ that had been a signal for them to start moving down the stairs. 'Better be on the safe side,' she muttered, and she disappeared into the small pantry on the landing. When she came out, she had a big enamel basin in her hand. 'I'll bring this down to the sacristy, just in case. I do wish you wouldn't dramatise so much, Sister!' she said irritably.

Humbly Veronica drew back. How glad she was she hadn't said anything.

And then, just before the postulants were given the signal to start moving, Private Enterprise held them up again. 'It will be all over in a few minutes,' she said reassuringly. 'Don't be nervous. Remember that in God's eyes every day of the past year was as important as today. You gave yourself to him every day. All that's happening today is that you're receiving the outward sign of your union with him. Don't be nervous. Think of how proud your people will be of you. Think of how soon you'll be seeing them.'

And so, when Veronica was walking up the aisle of the chapel, actually kneeling at the altar rails, she found herself thinking again of her family, and she didn't worry. It was a pity that Mabel wasn't able to come, but she would offer up her disappointment. She offered it up for Mabel, to bring her safely through her confinement.

And then, as if there was not to be even the smallest shadow on the day, as Private Enterprise had said, when they were in their black habits, ever such a short time afterwards, when the novices were led into the parlour, who should she see first of all, running over to her, but Mabel, yes, Mabel. She was running ahead of Mother, ahead of Father.

'Why, Mabel –' she cried. 'I thought –'

Mabel only laughed at how puzzled she was, and, all perfume as usual, she kissed her.

'What's this?' cried Father, when he and Mother came up to her. He pretended to draw back as he was about to kiss her. 'I didn't know nuns wore perfume.'

Several people in the parlour looked around in surprise.

'Oh, I suppose it rubbed off Mabel,' and then they all began to laugh. Indeed, by this time, at both ends of the parlour, where each of the other novices was surrounded by her own little group of friends, there were bursts of laughter like bursts of small artillery fire, until it seemed as if each burst ought by right to be accompanied by a little puff of smoke rising into the air.

As for the talk, it was easily seen the ceremony had been preceded by the Long Retreat.

'Did you really keep absolute silence for twenty-one days?' her mother asked, 'I mean absolute, absolute silence?'

'We can understand your mother's incredulity, Veronica,' said Father. 'Can't we, Mabel?' He was always teasing Mother.

'Oh, indeed!' cried Mother. 'I often wonder why some people were given tongues at all!'

To Veronica, it was just like being at home. She had forgotten, really, how they teased each other, Father and Mother, and how they all talked so much, all together too. Ever so slightly – she couldn't help it – Veronica felt superior to them, even to Father. In the Community Room at Recreation, the conversation was always happy, but somehow there was a difference. It wasn't so – so scatterbrain! But realising this might be spiritual pride, she checked herself quickly. Anyway, she wanted to hear about Mabel. She still didn't understand how she was able to be with them.

'Don't look so puzzled, darling,' cried Mabel herself just then. 'You're an auntie for the past fortnight. We couldn't let you know because of this silly old long retreat. I simply couldn't bear to miss being here, and so I got round the old doctor and made him give me a cocktail.' Seeing that Veronica didn't understand, Mabel reddened slightly. 'Nursing home slang, pet,' she said. 'Don't let it worry you: an injection to induce me, that's all.' But she was still a bit red in the face, and an awkward silence seemed to have come over their part of the parlour.

Not that Veronica had really taken in what Mabel said. She only comprehended that the baby was born, but a nervous feeling came into her stomach, and she didn't want to hear any more details. Just to know that everything was all right was enough. And that would have been an end to it if Euphemia had not joined them just then.

Euphemia was Veronica's aunt, and she was now twenty-seven years in the Order, but she considered herself a real woman of the world for all that. Even the name which she had taken in religion was used by all the family instead of her name in the world, which most of them had forgotten, certainly Mabel and Veronica could not recall it. Euphemia seemed to go in for compromise. On this occasion she took Mabel up quite sharply. 'I must say I'm surprised at you, Mabel. I didn't think you'd settle for being smart. In God's good time, that was the old-fashioned way. And the best way in the long run. Things are best left in the hands of Nature. Of course, it's an altogether different story if there are sound medical grounds for interference in the natural order, which I take it was not how it happened in your case?'

Long ago, when Veronica and Mabel were at school, they used to boast about their Aunt Euphemia, because she was so broadminded. You'd never think she was a nun at all. You could say anything to her. 'She's the kind of nun I'd like to be, if I had to be a nun at all,' Mabel used to say.

Well, Veronica didn't want to be that kind. She hoped she wasn't priggish, but if God ordained that certain things were to be outside her experience, she didn't want to know anything about them. And anyway, there were times, in the chapel, that she had seen Euphemia's face across from her in the transept among the choir-nuns, when she was still a postulant. It had seemed to her that there was something unreconciled in Euphemia's expression. Was it possible, she had often wondered, that for some people there was a struggle to be fought out, time after time, every day anew, even *after* taking the vow of chastity? She looked at Euphemia again, and now she was wondering if this was happening right at this minute.

But just at that moment, Sister Concepta came and whispered to her. One of Concepta's visitors had been at school with Mabel and she'd like to meet her again.

'Bring her over, of course!' cried Mabel, overhearing the whisper, and staring with curiosity across the parlour.

The friend turned out to be much older than Mabel. She was in the Senior School when Mabel was still in the Lower School. And she was married long before Mabel, as could be seen by the size of the big child, four or five years old at least, who was with her, staring up at them all from under an unkempt fringe.

The child stared most of all at Veronica.

'Is *her* hair cut too, Ma?' she demanded.

'Oh, Judy, keep quiet. You are tiresome,' cried the mother. 'How dare you say such things.'

'But you said in the car –'

'Never mind what I said! and stop staring. Where are your manners?'

The child's eyes were riveted on the starched linen band across Veronica's forehead. Everyone felt embarrassed for a minute. Then Father Devaney, who had been talking to Reverend Mother, detached himself and took the child by the arm.

'Well, little girl, what is your name?' he asked, and before the child had time to say any more he had led her towards a glass door that looked out upon the garden. There, on a strip of vacant grass, some pigeons were walking decorously up and down. 'Why don't you try and catch one,' Father Devaney said, and he opened the door. When Judy ran out, the pigeons rose into the air with a flurry.

'Oh, look, so many of them,' cried Veronica's mother. 'It's like St Mark's!'

'Only these are not so tame,' said Euphemia, implying familiarity with the place. Those were the words she used. What she really meant was, when had our mother been to Venice?

'Oh, do look at them,' cried Mother again, moving over to the glass door.

Reverend Mother too moved over to the door. 'Sometimes when they are walking up and down, we say they are reading their Office, they look so solemn,' she said. She conceived it as part of her duties always to make a mild joke on occasions like this. Certainly everyone laughed. Following her lead too, everyone, except Veronica and Father, moved over to the glass door.

Father laid a hand on Veronica's arm. 'Let's stay on this side of the ship to make weight,' he said. Veronica laughed. As a family, analogy was irresistible to them. She knew exactly what he meant. The pigeons had acted upon the company as a floating canister or a bottle will act upon the passengers of a ship, drawing them all to one side to lean over the deck-rail, and the insignificance of the object that focused so much attention, making explicit a boredom that they would hardly otherwise have realised.

Everyone was getting bored, there was no doubt about it. Much as she loved her own people, Veronica kept thinking of what would happen when the visitors left, and the novices took their place for the first time in the community.

There was a restlessness in the parlour. Her mother put her head out of the French window. 'Couldn't we go outside?' she asked, intending to give the impression that she was complimenting the garden. But in reality she was giving the effect of criticising the parlour.

Reverend Mother's narrow cheeks reddened profusely. Was the room stuffy? Was she at fault in not having had the glass doors open? She nodded her head vigorously at a young nun, who rushed to unhook one side of the door. 'Perhaps you'd like to see the garden.' Reverend Mother didn't address the whole company but speaking generally, stepped out into the air. As they were leaving the parlour, Father looked over his shoulder at Veronica. 'You must have a good greenhouse,' he said, because, now that it was empty of people, the parlour seemed to be full of ferns, dotted about everywhere in ornamental pots.

Veronica looked back. Even when she was a child, visiting Euphemia, the parlour had always fascinated her, with its strong odour of beeswax, and the stiff unrelaxing arrangement of its furniture. Once it was the only part of the convent she knew, and it hinted at deeper discipline and coldness to be found beyond it. 'It's a lovely room, isn't it?' she said impulsively. But her mother had come back and was within earshot once more. 'Personally I can't abide pot plants,' she said. And then impulsively she looked straight at Veronica. 'Aren't you ever lonely for home, darling?' she asked bluntly.

It was so easy to see the course her thoughts had taken. She was thinking of the drawing-room at home, always filled with masses of cut flowers, simply masses of them.

Veronica didn't want to hurt her mother, but she wasn't one bit lonely. It even seemed to her now that cut flowers were out of place anywhere except on the altar. But naturally she wasn't going to say that.

Anyway, at last, perhaps only for a moment, she was about to be alone with Mabel. Something or other engaged the attention of the rest.

'Well, old thing?' said Mabel. 'You look marvellous in your habit. Of course, you looked divine in' – but Mabel just couldn't bring herself to use the words 'wedding-gown' – 'in the satin gown,' she said quickly. 'But then who wouldn't cut a dash in that?' She looked critically at her sister. 'It takes a good figure to look well in that rig-out, although I can't deny, figure or no figure, you look a bit like a penguin, my dear.'

It was an old joke. When they were at school they always called the nuns penguins.

Veronica laughed. 'Do you know, Mabel –' she began, but their mother was calling Mabel. 'Isn't it about time someone made a move to leave?' Mother said.

'Oh, bother!' said Mabel to Veronica. 'I wanted to have a word with you. Oh, nothing in particular, just a little chat like long ago, but I dare say I'll get a chance again. Or perhaps I could pop in and see you tomorrow before my train leaves, if that's all right?'

Veronica didn't know. 'I'd have to ask permission to have a visitor,' she said.

'Good lord!' cried Mabel. 'It's plain to be seen I'd never have made a nun.'

Euphemia and Father Devaney joined them just then. 'God help us, Mabel, if we had to depend on the like of you to fill our convents,' said Father Devaney. He was an old friend of Mabel. 'In the name of God, what have you got on your fingernails?'

'Oh, go on now, Father, don't take the good out of that nice sermon you gave us. It was all about us poor mothers. It's the mothers of this world who deserve their crowns in heaven, I can tell you. Do you know what time the baby woke this morning?'

'It's a bit soon for you to complain, Mabel,' said her mother. She had a vague feeling that the topic of baby feeds was not quite seemly on this particular occasion. It might be different if the baby were on a bottle. Anything to prevent Mabel from saying something indiscreet. 'I don't know what you have to complain about, compared to our generation. When I think of what we suffered.' She turned to Father Devaney. 'Do you know, Father, these young people are so smart they've put an end to the pain of childbirth. A young doctor has written a book about it. All the young women are reading it. Mabel never left it out of her hands the whole nine months, and the doctor claims or at least Mabel says he claims, that having a baby is a pleasure now. Did you ever!'

But suddenly she stopped short. She had jumped into the conversation so hastily that she was now going too far herself. And to make matters worse, she had fallen foul of Mabel.

'The theory of painless childbirth is nothing to joke about,' Mabel said stiffly. 'After you feel the first contraction –' But Father, *dear* Father, came up just then and put his hand firmly on Mabel's shoulder. 'Another time, Mabel dear, another time,' he said. 'You've had your thunder. This is Veronica's day.'

Veronica's day! They all looked at her proudly.

'Are you happy about me now, Mother?' Veronica asked impulsively, because she knew her mother had had misgivings about her entering the convent.

'Of course, my dear,' said her mother. 'I only wanted you to be sure you knew what you were doing.' Unaccountably, there was another moment of awkwardness. 'I do feel we ought to start going –' she said again abruptly.

Very shortly, it was all over, the Great Day.

Once more wheels were crunching the gravel and there were car doors slamming.

Until the last car disappeared, the three newly professed choir-nuns stood at the hall door, and then turned uncertainly, back into the convent. What did they do now? A mild consternation stirred in them. They saw Private Enterprise, without a glance at them, going down the corridor leading from the chapel to the noviciate, and passing through that little door, more familiar now than all the doors of home, through which they would pass no more. Like the doors of home, it too was closed to them now.

Veronica glanced at the big clock in the hall. It was only five o'clock.

Suddenly she realised that she was so tired she could hardly stand.

Then Reverend Mother approached them.

'Sister Eucharia will tell you your new duties,' she said. Then she looked in particular at Veronica. 'Why, you look exhausted, Sister,' she said. 'I think you had better go to bed tonight, as soon as you've had your tea. In fact you'd better have your tea right now and then go straight to your cell.'

A great feeling of relief came over Veronica. It had been a terrible strain, really, the whole day.

As the other two, Concepta and Assumpta, moved away after Sister Eucharia, Veronica stood for a minute in the empty hall. Then she went down the corridor towards the Refectory. Fatigue had brought a certain dejection, and her shoulders drooped slightly. It was God's prerogative to say that he made things easier for some nuns than others, but exhaustion was not much to offer up to him. And she was really more tired by the business of being with her family, than by the upheaval caused by what she had given up.

Just then, however, a voice called after her.

'Just a minute, Sister.' It was Reverend Mother again. 'I think your sister must have left these behind. Will you be seeing her soon again, or will we post them back home?' In her hand she had a pair of chamois gloves. 'Perhaps you could keep them till you see her?' said Reverend Mother.

Veronica took the gloves and bowed to Reverend Mother.

Sister Ursula who was in charge of the Refectory was not to be seen, but the tables were laid, and Veronica sat down and ate some bread and butter, and took a glass of milk from the big jug on the side-table. That was enough for her. She wasn't hungry anyway, only tired, deadly tired.

As she passed back along the corridor to her new cell, no longer the one where she had changed out of her white satin dress into her habit, she could hear the choir starting the Tantum Ergo. Benediction was nearly over. But as she reached the landing, she noticed a small hand-basin on one side of the wall, with two taps which meant there was hot water as well as cold. In her hand she still held Mabel's gloves.

Tired and all as she was, it suddenly occurred to her that it would be nice to wash the gloves and give them back clean. Chamois gloves were so easily soiled. And she and Mabel always made a point of never wearing the same pair twice without them being washed.

Impulsively taking off her stiff linen cuffs, and leaving them on the shelf over the hand-basin, Veronica ran the hot tap. Steam rose up in a cloud. She made a lather, pulled the gloves on her hands, and plunged them into the water.

Oh, that slimy feel of wet chamois! How well she remembered it. She might almost have been standing in the little wash-up pantry at the top of the house which she and Mabel had used all their lives. It used to be a housemaid's pantry in the time of the previous occupiers, but she and Mabel then had it for their own use. Very rarely did their mother go up to it, and when she did, she closed her eyes in horror at its condition. 'This place is a disgrace,' she used to say, 'I do wish at least you wouldn't keep it so littered.'

It was really a dump, with steamy walls and shelves littered with unsightly broken combs and used jars of cold cream, discarded boxes of powder and make-up, and dozens of perfume sprays, and goodness knows what else. Because it was never cleaned or tidied except when something clogged up the handbasin, and more than once the down-pipe got clogged with hair combings, and they had managed to free it with a knitting needle. It was pretty disgusting that little pantry, compared with the rest of the house that was really so beautifully kept. Mother never tolerated anything that wasn't beautiful.

Yet she and Mabel had spent most of their time up there, gossiping and exchanging confidences, when they were supposed to be brushing their teeth, buffing their nails, and attending to their skin and hair.

It was there, one afternoon, that she plucked up courage to tell Mabel her own plans.

But all at once Veronica couldn't bear to recall any more. Two big tears welled into her eyes and coursed down her face. To think she'd never see that little pantry again. Mabel's pots and tubes on the window-ledges and on the edges of the cracked hand-basin were all she could think about now. Filled with memories of faulty sanitary ware, steamy walls and a litter of broken tubs, Veronica stood powerless.

What of her guardian angel, and all the other girls' angels? What bouquet or spiritual offering had they to bring? After a few seconds Veronica had to laugh to herself. She dried her eyes and rinsed out the gloves. She may have waited until the last moment, but it did appear as though she had got herself on the right track at last. The other girls may have had a more reasonable offering to make, she only gave up a jar or two of paint, and a steamy old pantry, when she added her sacrifice to the rest. She really was saying no to life. All her fatigue was dispelled in an instant, and cupping two tears in her palms, her angel sped for Heaven.

Veronica grabbed the gloves and took them to her cell to hang up and dry. In a few minutes she was fast asleep.

The Joy-Ride

The two butlers stood outside the door and watched the overseer's car go down the driveway. Crickem, a lank, pimply fellow, the younger of the two, turned around and looked up at the solid mass of the manor house behind him, all of hewn granite, three storeys high, and showing a frontage of fourteen windows and a colonnaded porch.

'I suppose he thinks the old house would run away,' he said, and he spat contemptuously into the dewy grass beyond the granite steps.

The overseer had just gone away for three days. The likelihood was that he had gone to the Galway Races, but the butlers had been given to understand that he was going to Dublin on business.

It was seven o'clock in the morning. The dew was still on the ground. And the two lackeys stared disconsolately at the wheel-tracks of the departed car that were printed fast on the dewy moisture of the gravel. The younger man was even more disconsolate than his companion. He had counted on their being given at least one day out during the overseer's absence. Purdy, the older fellow, did not really care one way or the other, but for Crickem's sake he was ready to abuse the overseer.

'If you were working for him as long as me you wouldn't have expected anything better,' he said, and he too spat into the dewy grass.

The estate on which the manor house stood occupied some four hundred acres of the best land in Meath and was owned by a young man not yet of age, who was heir to at least two other estates as well, in both of which he appeared to have more interest than in this one. The countryside, however, was consoled for his never visiting this estate, and for the likelihood of his never bothering much about it, by the fact that the overseer was himself a man of such gentlemanly habits, who ran the house on a scale that approximated to their idea of ownership, and treated them with what they regarded as a proper rudeness and contempt.

It was generally believed in the district that Malcolm would eventually purchase the property for himself, and in this assurance the countryside relied upon no knowledge of the overseer's financial position but rather upon the fact that he had an aquiline nose, called them all by their surnames, and wore a yellow tie printed over with a pattern of foxes' heads.

The house was certainly kept in good order. The owner might walk into it at any hour and find it not only habitable but exceedingly comfortable and pleasant. Malcolm believed that the best preservative for anything was constant use, and so the rooms were unshuttered every day, the fires lighted, the furniture dusted, and the windows kept clean. The curtains were always hanging. There was no dismal shrouding of pictures and chandeliers. There was no rolling up of carpets; the house was kept in running order.

And for this order, Crickem and Purdy were solely responsible. They comprised the entire indoor staff. Crickem, the young man, was responsible for the care of the front part of the house, for the airing of the rooms and the preservation of the furniture. Purdy helped, but although he too was a butler by training, he was, on account of his age, and the lesser likelihood of his being able to pick and choose his jobs, forced to undertake a few other chores, such as the preparation of the food, the making up of the overseer's bed, the polishing of his boots, and, of late, although it was understood to be a temporary arrangement, the laundering of the overseer's shirts, and the pressing of his trousers. Recently, these multifarious duties had induced Purdy to abandon the wearing of his black suit, and although the two men worked together amicably enough, it occasionally galled the older man to see Crickem going about resplendent in his black suit with the silk lapels, his white shirt and his black tie. To counteract any extra authority which Crickem's black suit might give him in the eyes of the outdoor workers, Purdy took care to keep his own black suit always in sight, hanging on a coat-hanger from a nail on the kitchen dresser.

Purdy was a small man of about forty, with a bald head and a round belly. His glossy face wore at all times a timid look, which was absurd on one of his age and bulk, but a natural timidity had in his case been increased by the feeling of vulnerability that comes to people who have come to feel that their security is dependent on a single thread. In spite of this timidity and sense of dependence, however, two days after getting his salary Purdy seldom had a penny in his pocket, for as regularly as pay-day came around, Purdy put on his black suit and his bowler hat and went down to the village to empty the contents of his pay-envelope on the counter of the local public house.

Lest, however, such improvident behaviour with money should seem to be inconsistent with the expression of timidity and dependence that sat upon Purdy's features, it is necessary to revert to an incident in Purdy's past to which Purdy himself never willingly referred at all, and which, in all but one particular he had effaced from memory. It was this: Purdy was a married man. Or perhaps it would be more correct to say that twenty years ago he had been married for a period of six weeks, to one Amelia Purdy, a housekeeper, whose idea of marriage having proved somewhat different from that of the young Purdy, a separation had been mutually sought and mutually granted. To this Amelia Purdy however, Purdy paid every week one third of his salary in alimony, the alimony being by the provision of the Court, sent direct to Mrs Amelia Purdy by Purdy's employer. The sum, therefore, which Purdy got in his envelope each week represented the legal residue over which he had full liberty. Now, in spite of a poor opinion of women in general, and of Amelia in particular, Purdy was able all the same to discriminate between virtues and faults, and the fact that Amelia proved difficult to live with did not blind Purdy to the fact that she was an exceptionally thrifty woman, with the double capacity of making money and keeping it. And Purdy knew that not one penny of that alimony would be squandered by Amelia, that not one penny of it would, as it were, be let go down a crack in the floor. It would, on the contrary, be saved up carefully, and as likely as not more would have been added to it, until it must by now represent a tidy sum in the vaults of Amelia's bank. Yes, that alimony must, by now, have accumulated into a tidy heap. And in Purdy's mind, that alimony was still his money. He had never lost this feeling of ownership over it, as for that matter, he had never lost his feelings of ownership over the tall and forbidding Amelia. And it was always at the back of Purdy's mind that if all went to all, if the worst came to the worst, if, that is to say, he was really up against it, he could patch things up with Amelia. Two could live easily on the interest from that accumulated alimony. Without adding another penny to it, two could live on it in comfort. So, every Friday night Purdy went down to the village and confidently emptied his pockets.

Yet, in spite of having Amelia and her alimony to fall back upon, Purdy had no wish to jeopardise his job at The Manse. And so Crickem, who in a short and rapid career had occupied some thirty to forty jobs, was able to enliven himself any time he wished by taking a rise out of the older man. When restrictions and duties weighed heavy on him he used to glance slyly at Purdy.

'After all,' he would say, 'there's no obligation on us to stay here. Nobody can force us to stay. We can walk out any minute we like!'

And after this, or some such remark, he had nothing to do but sit down and watch the absolute terror that would come into Purdy's eyes.

On this particular day, the day of the overseer's departure, Purdy was more placid than ever under the restrictions that irked his callow companion. A day out coming in the middle of the week would not be much use to him with his salary all spent. But he hadn't forgotten what it was to be young, and so when the overseer's car had gone out of sight, he put his hand on the young man's shoulder and patted him understandingly.

'I know how you feel,' he said, 'but there's no reason why we should both stay in all the time. If you like you can take a day out and I'll be able to manage.'

'Oh, what fun can a fellow have alone?' said Crickem irritably shaking off the patting hand. 'I don't see why we can't both get out. As I said before, the house isn't going to run away, is it?'

'No,' said Purdy seriously, 'but I wouldn't like to go out and leave no one here.'

'If it's bolted and barred what can happen to it?' demanded Crickem.

'But it won't be bolted and barred,' said Purdy. 'I got particular orders that the shutters were to be taken down as usual.'

Crickem snorted. 'That was to tie us down,' he said, savagely spitting out once more.

Purdy moved over to the door.

'There's no use standing out here in the cold,' he said. 'Are you coming inside?' And when Crickem had stepped in after him Purdy automatically bolted and barred the hall door, and put up his hands to close over the heavy shutters inside the door. But suddenly he stopped. 'What's the use of locking up?' he said. 'We'll be opening the house again in an hour or so?' He let his hands drop. 'As long as we're here,' he said then eagerly, 'why don't we take down all the shutters?' For Purdy was not at ease about Crickem, and he felt that the sooner the house was laid bare and open, the windows thrown up and the doors unbarred, the sooner Crickem would see the necessity for someone to remain in charge of it.

But Crickem pushed him aside impatiently and clattered the shutters into place over the door.

'Wait till we decide what we're going to do,' he said ominously, and in case the old fellow would burst with apprehension, he turned around more tractably. 'We'll have our breakfast first in any case,' he said. 'It's too early to open the house anyway. The dew is still in the air. It would do more harm than good to open up the place at this hour! Come on!'

Tightly shuttered now, the hall was as dark as a vault, except for the pale streaks of yellow sunlight that came through the joinings of the boards. These gave no light, beyond their own long narrow reflections on the floor, and were little better than strokes of paint to guide the two butlers back to the kitchen regions.

In the back regions the windows were without shutters, protected only by black bars and railings. Here the cold north light was permitted to make its bleak entry through high sashed narrow windows overhung with ivy. The two men turned into the kitchen.

In the kitchen the two butlers took their breakfast without any further reference to the day in front of them, but Purdy was uneasy, and from time to time he glanced nervously at Crickem, and wondered what was in his mind. The young man, he thought, had a peculiar look in his eye, and his eye was, moreover, directed on him, Purdy.

Crickem, as a matter of fact, who had never spent more than a year in any job, had for some time past been feeling that his term in this one was running short. He was familiar with this unsettled feeling although he could never decide whether it was a premonition of dismissal, or a contributory factor to it. At any rate it made him reckless. And although a few hours of stolen liberty would not make much of a meal for a reckless young man, a piquant sauce would be added to it if he could induce the cautious Purdy to eat the same fare. The young man had already got a good deal of satisfaction out of shaking Purdy up with the suggestion that they both take a day out and he knew that now the old fellow was suffering the discomfort of suspense. But the suspense must not be drawn out too long. The next thing to do was to give him a false impression of security. Crickem stood up suddenly and with an elaborate air of resignation he walked over to the door.

As he expected, Purdy nearly strained a blood vessel in his anxiety to get to this feet and comply with this suggestion, which he no doubt took to mean that there would be no more talk about illicit outings. Crickem had to hurry out the door ahead of him to hide the smirk on his face.

The usual procedure in this matter of opening up the shutters was for Purdy to take the left of the house and Crickem

the right. They began with the windows to each side of the hall
door, and then Purdy went into the drawing-room and Crickem
into the library. From then on they saw no more of each other
until they emerged into the hall again after a complete round
of the house, although as Purdy carefully folded back each
shutter under his care, he could hear, in the distance, the
clatter made by Crickem who was less particular about the noise
he made. On this morning, however, while Purdy made his way
around the rooms on the left, there was nothing distant or faint
about the clatter that came from the other side of the house.
Clatter after clatter sounded through the house, and in the
brief moments between the clatters, there were ear-shattering
sounds as of someone recklessly plunging about in a dark room.
Purdy tried to feel amused. After all there was no one to hear,
no one to be disturbed, no one to worry in case any damage
might be done. If this was the only advantage Crickem took of
the overseer's absence things would not be too bad.
Nevertheless, Purdy felt himself quake every time there was a
flat clatter on the other side of the house, and after a few
minutes he found himself counting the clatters. The fellow
ought to be at the last one soon. Only about one more to be
done, Purdy estimated, and he carefully let down the hasp on
the last window on his side of the house, and silently folded
back the shutters. But the deafening clatter that came at the
same time from the other side of the house was not the last. It
was immediately succeeded by another. And that was
succeeded by another. And then, as Purdy made his way back
to the hall the clatters continued one after another, and if
possible, one louder than another.

That was strange! Purdy hurried along towards the hall. Had
he miscalculated the number of windows on the other side? He
had always taken for granted that there were about the same
number on each side. How then was he finished today so much
sooner than Crickem? Even as he hurried along there was
another and then still another violent clatter in the distance.
But this time, strange to say, it seemed to Purdy that the
clattering came from one of the rooms that he himself had
shortly vacated.

Purdy opened the door of the passage leading in to the hall. Here in the bright light from all the opened rooms that radiated from it, he and Crickem would join company to engage upon the next task of the day. But as Purdy rushed into the hall this morning, to the accompaniment of another deafening clatter somewhere behind him, to his astonishment the hall was just as it had been at seven o'clock that morning; as dark as a vault, the only possible difference being that in the yellow streaks of sunlight from the cracks and joinings of the shutters, particles of dust danced deliriously like midges and there was a smell of dust in the air.

Purdy stood like one bewitched. Hadn't he himself opened one of the shutters in this hall? And the other rooms, opening off the hall, why was there no light coming from them? He groped his way over to the drawing-room and fumbled in the dark for the handle of the door. It was a minute or two before he grasped that the door was wide open, and beyond it the drawing-room yawned as black as a pit.

Like a sleepwalker Purdy put one foot inside the threshold of the drawing-room. There was no mistake. It was a black pit, slashed only with the familiar yellow streaks where the re-shuttered windows let in cracks of light. Purdy stood with his mouth opened and gaped into the blackness. Far away, this time unmistakably to the left of him, there was a last and violent clatter, and after a few moments there was a sound of footsteps and whistling coming along the passage. The next minute Crickem opened the door leading into the hall.

'Are you there, Purdy?' he called out, and in the thin light from the regions behind him, Purdy saw with a sinking heart the unmistakable grin of mischief on the young fellow's face. 'Come on!' cried Crickem. 'Now we can do what we like. Malcolm may be smart, but he's not smarter than me. He gave orders to open up the house, did he? Well his orders were obeyed. We opened up the house. But there was nothing said about closing it again. That's where we have him! Come on now, let's get out of this dungeon. What are you doing standing there in the dark?'

Crickem held open the passage-door, and beckoned to Purdy towards it. He wanted to hurry the old fellow back to the lighted regions where he could see the expression on his face. He wanted to get a laugh at the old chap's fright.

But, when Purdy emerged into the lighted hall Crickem got a surprise. Purdy's face had changed. There was no doubt about that. But to Crickem's astonishment instead of a look of fright, Purdy's face wore an entirely unexpected expression. It was not fright. It was not nervousness. It was not even disapproval.

Crickem stared.

Purdy, yes, Purdy, had undergone some extraordinary change. He was transformed. And on his face there was what could only be called a grin.

Yes, Purdy was grinning.

And the outer was only a reflection of the inner change. Something had happened to Purdy in the few minutes when he realised the way Crickem had compromised between obedience and revolt. Something had stirred inside in him. And what had stirred was a memory of youth. This was the kind of compromise that had characterised every boyish prank that Purdy had ever dared upon. A feeling of boyish irresponsibility had come over Purdy, and all of a sudden looking at Crickem, Purdy forgot that he was fat as a barrel, bald, and middle-aged, and timid, and that he was moreover married to a six-foot shrew to whom he paid one-third of his salary in alimony. It seemed to him, that he and the raw youth in front of him, who was thin as a pea-rod and pimpled with the bad-living of youth, were partners cut to the one pattern. He chuckled and rubbed his hands together. Then as Crickem stared at him in astonishment, Purdy's eye fell on Crickem's trouser leg, and it appeared to him all of a sudden that if there was any difference at all between them it was in the manner of their attire.

'Just a minute,' he said, as Crickem opened the kitchen, and dashing in ahead of the young man Purdy grabbed his black suit off the nail of the dresser, and disappeared up the servants' staircase. A minute later he too was resplendent in black and white, a proper butler; a proper dandy.

In his black suit, it would not be correct to say that Purdy still
felt like a boy; rather he felt like a young man; exactly indeed,
as he used to feel twenty years ago when he was apprenticed to
the head waiter in the Centreside Hotel in North Great Georges
Street, Dublin, where pranks and larks and sprees were the
order of the day. Purdy looked himself up and down, and yet
he hesitated to go downstairs. In the old days he had a name
for thinking up pranks, and now he felt it was up to him to keep
pace with Crickem. It was up to him to take some daring step
on his own two feet. Crickem had gone a good bit. He, Purdy,
must go one better. He sat down on the side of his bed and
thought furiously for a moment or two and then a look of great
daring came over his face, and standing up he made his way up
to the overseer's dressing-room. A few minutes later he was
going down the passage to join Crickem, trying not to run in
his excitement, and what he had of straight black hair was
plastered as close to his head as paint, with liberal handfuls of
the overseer's hair lotion that came in specially prepared
proportions all the way from Dublin, and of which the overseer
was himself so careful he used only as much as moistened the
palms of his hand, while on the elderly butler's feet, instead of
his usual square-toed boots of black leather, there were a
high-polished pair of Malcolm's bright yellow shoes, with
pointed toes.

The monkey was up in Purdy. He was ready to spend the day
in pranks, one more daring than another, but all of them
somehow of the same nature as using the boss's hair oil and
wearing his yellow boots. For these were the pranks that had
been popular in the Centreside Hotel, twenty years back. These
were the larks they had when Purdy was a boy.

Crickem however was not a boy. And when Purdy came into
the kitchen the young butler looked at his foolishly-plastered
pate, and at the pointed boots that made him walk like a
spinster on the tops of his toes, and he felt he was in danger of
being put into a ludicrous position. He didn't want any tom-boy
pranks.

'Well, what are we going to do?' he said brusquely. 'The
house is bolted and barred. The doors are all locked, the

windows are shut. There's no need for us to sit around the place all day.'

A twinge of returning apprehension shot through the joy that filled Purdy's soul. He looked at Crickem.

'What could we do?' he said half-heartedly, but no sooner had he said it than he took confidence. There was nothing to do. Crickem might be filled with daring, but what was there to do at ten-thirty in the morning, in the heart of the country, four miles from the nearest town, and two miles from the railway station from which the only outgoing train had already departed some two hours! Purdy took heart again. He felt he might even show off a bit.

'It's a pity there isn't another motor car!' he said. 'We could go for a jaunt somewhere.'

In spite of himself, Crickem was impressed.

'Can you drive?' he asked.

Purdy couldn't drive, but he didn't let himself down.

'What's the use of being able to drive,' he said, 'when there's no car!'

Crickem stared at him. Had he underestimated Purdy? But Purdy was a new man. This wasn't the old Purdy.

'The petrol might be missed,' said Crickem, determined to put him to the test.

'Pouf!' said Purdy. 'There are plenty of petrol stations between here and where I'd go!'

Curiosity overcame Crickem.

'Where would you go?' he asked, and he was humble as a pupil at the foot of the Master.

Purdy waved away the question deprecatingly.

'What's the use of talking about it!' he said. 'There's no car, and that's the end of it!'

Inside the tight yellow boots that pinched his toes, Purdy seemed to be rising up taller and more lofty. Peaks of daring loomed up ahead of him, and rising on the pointed toes of the overseer's boots, Purdy got ready to scale those peaks. But rising, he fell.

'God be with the times,' he said, 'when you didn't have to bother with cars and petrol, and when, if you wanted to go for a joy-ride you had nothing more to do than to walk down to the yard and hitch up a pony and trap!'

'A pony and trap!' Crickem sat up. 'Purdy!' he cried, running over to Purdy and slapping him on the back. 'Purdy! You're a genius!'

This was when Purdy first felt his feet slip. He saw disaster ahead. What did Crickem mean? Why was he so excited? Purdy trembled in his boots. His jaw shook. His eye wobbled. And he stared open-mouthed at Crickem. Crickem saw his advantage.

'Oh well,' he said patronisingly, 'If you didn't think of the idea, you put it into my head.'

'What idea?' asked Purdy in a small weak voice.

'The pony and trap!' cried Crickem, and then the whole significance of the affair became clear to him. He saw through Purdy's pretence of daring. 'Do you mean to say you didn't know there was an old pony cart down in the yard?' he cried, and he rubbed his hands together with delight in Purdy's discomfort. 'I don't know what I was doing down there, but I remember one day when I was poking about in the stables I saw an old trap pushed into a corner of one of them.'

Purdy's vague prognostication of coming disaster resolved itself into a certainty. Instantly he recalled what he had not thought of for years, that away at the back of one of the stables, stowed in away behind a few rusty and out-dated farm implements, which like itself had long ago been supplanted in use by mechanical implements, there was, indeed, as Crickem said, an old pony cart. Instantly it rose in a vision before Purdy's eyes; a dilapidated but undeniably entire pony trap of the kind used for the nursery governesses in the days of horse transport; the body painted to resemble basketry, the shafts, wheels and the sockets of the gig-lamps painted black with yellow stripes, and the whole vehicle, shafts and chassis, dulled with dust, and draped with cobwebs as a cheese is shrouded in muslin. Desperately Purdy clutched at the one possibility that remained.

'It's all covered with dust and cobwebs,' he said. 'It's probably falling to pieces.'

'Not at all,' said Crickem. 'Those old traps were made to last for ever. Come on! Let's go down and have a look at it!'

Purdy could do no less than follow and although he did so reluctantly he gave the impression of being in a greater hurry than Crickem because, with his short, fat little legs, he took two or three steps to every one of the long lanky butler.

'See! It's covered with cobwebs,' the little fellow panted again, when he followed Crickem into the inner depths of the stable a few minutes later.

But the cobwebs, alas, only proved that the old trap had been left undisturbed and intact and that it had escaped the usual fate of such outmoded vehicles. None of its various portions had been detached for other uses. And when Crickem pushed an old swing-plough out of his way and caught the shafts of the pony-cart and pulled it out of the dark stable on to the sunlit cobblestones, there it was, as good as the day some distracted governess had driven it into the yard for the last time. There were the yellow-buttoned leather cushions, piled one on top of the other. There was the fringed rug, folded neatly on the seat, although no doubt riddled inside with moths. And there, above all, like a mast on a schooner, the small yellow whip stuck up from the whip sockct, with two white sails of cobweb hoisted to either side of it.

Without waiting to brush aside the shrouding webs and spider strings along which the startled spiders were scurrying on short black legs, Crickem caught up the shafts and setting himself between them, began to run up and down the cobbles, dragging the trap behind him.

It was the sight of Crickem between the shafts that gave Purdy another moment of hope.

'A pony!' he exclaimed. 'We've no pony!' and he could not keep the elation out of his voice.

But Crickem turned around in the shafts and with a jerk of his head he indicated the loose boxes at the other end of the yard.

'What's wrong with those nags?' he asked, and he let the shafts drop on the ground with a clatter. Purdy was speechless.

There were only two horses kept, but they were the apples of the overseer's eye.

'The hunters!' he gasped.

'Sure!' said Crickem. 'If they're as good as Malcolm says they are they'll go like lambs under the trap.' He looked critically in the direction of the loose boxes, over the half-doors of which the two horses looked out at them with mild equine curiosity. 'We'll take the bay,' he said.

Now, if there was anything to choose between the two horses, the excess of excellence in his owner's eyes, rested with the bay.

'The bay!' said Purdy weakly, like a man in a dream, and he followed Crickem over to the largest of the stalls, where a handsome bay horse, with a white star on his face, drew back its head with a nervous tremor.

To lead out this magnificent animal and throw the harness over her, was only a matter of moments, and as Crickem expected, right from the moment she was led up to the trap, she showed herself willing and ready to draw it. Freely of her own accord she backed into the shafts and stood waiting to be hitched.

But at this point there was a small delay as Crickem wrestled with the intricacies of the harness.

He had started confidently enough and thrown the neck collar over the animal's head, the breeching across its back. He had fastened the traces to the wagon. But when he had done all this between the shafts and the bay mare there still hung down a bewildering number of leather straps that had not been pulled through the brass buckles, also of considerable numbers, on the upper parts of the harness.

Crickem scratched his head and stood back from the job.

'Just a minute! Just a minute!' he said, as if poor Purdy was complaining of the delay. He surveyed the hanging leathers. 'The main thing,' he said, catching up the belly-band and mistakenly plaiting it with the trace, 'The main thing is to get the horse secured to the wagon. It doesn't matter much how you do it.'

Purdy, in the pointed boots, wobbled on the cobblestones in his indecision as to whether or not he should let this erroneous idea be put into practice. On the one hand they wouldn't get far but on the other hand, he shuddered to think of what might happen to the wagon on that short journey – to say nothing of what might happen to the handsome bay mare whose legs, to Purdy's troubled eye, looked as fragile as glass.

Meanwhile, as Purdy hesitated, Crickem had again tackled the job. Twice he succeeded in buckling all the buckles, but twice it was necessary to unbuckle them again. And in the course of the latter effort he had once inadvertently loosened the traces and let the shafts fall to the ground with a splintering crash, and three times he had run in and out under the bay mare's belly. But still the mare and trap were as independent of each other as they were when the mare was in her stall and the trap was in the stable.

And under the stress of coping with these unlooked-for obstacles, Crickem, who for purposes of his own usually treated Purdy as an equal, was reaching that point at which his patience was worn so thin that truth was likely at any minute to make a sudden fissure. Several times he knocked into him as he ran from one side of the trap to the other. And although Purdy stood at a good distance from the scene of this activity, Crickem began to mutter at him under his breath.

'Can he find nowhere else to stand?' he muttered at one moment.

'How is it some people haven't the wit to get out of a person's way?'

In the course of this muttering, however, during which he had once again let the shafts fall, and twice again run in and out under the horse's belly, Crickem chanced to glance at his companion. Before Purdy had time to efface it, on his glossy countenance was a supercilious smile.

'Well?' demanded Crickem. 'What are you smiling at? Eh?' He had reached the point at which he would readily have kicked the mare, but for an instinctive feeling that a horse was not perhaps the best animal in the world with whom to engage upon a kicking match. By the gleam in his eye when it fell on Purdy it looked as if he might satisfy his impulse by kicking his fellow man. But suddenly the gleam faded.

'Look here!' he said, partly sneering, and partly in earnest, 'you're not by any chance an expert at this job?'

Purdy said nothing for a moment. Then he stooped down and caught up the belly-band. In an instant it was slipped into position, and Purdy darting around the mare had secured it in its buckles on the far side. Then the trace was slipped into its hook. Every strap was tightened and buckled, and in a few minutes nothing remained to do but jump into the trap and they would be on their way, fully equipped and as smart as paint.

Positions were once more reversed. Purdy was top-dog again. He sprang into the trap, and caught up the whip. And then on another impulse he sprang out again and threw the reins to Crickem.

'Wait a minute!' he said. 'We must bring something to eat with us.'

For he was once again back in the old days when the staff of the Centreside took their annual outing, and in those days there was always a fat hamper of food strapped under the axle of the wagonette.

'Can't we stop on the way and get something to eat in a public house?' asked Crickem, who was impatient to go spanking down the road.

Purdy looked at him with pity for his inexperience.

'You can't leave a horse on the side of the road, you know!' he said, and his little legs twinkled as he sped across the yard towards the house.

He was hardly inside the larder however when he heard a step in the yard, and there was Crickem.

'I tied the reins to the yard door,' said Crickem quickly, anticipating the look of disapproval on Purdy's face.

Only slightly relieved, Purdy again turned his attention to the food he had collected, and laid on the table. It was a mixed lot; a loaf of bread and a slab of yellow cake, a tin of sardines, a hunk of dry cheese, and in a small stone crock to keep it from melting there was a pound of strong butter. But chief among all these was a large ham-bone on which there was a certain amount of ragged pink meat.

Crickem looked critically at this collection.

Then he went into the larder, and after poking on an upper shelf he came out a few minutes later with another loaf and a bottle of green pickles. Purdy eyed the pickles. He regretted not having seen them. They seemed to give Crickem back some of his advantage over him. He looked around to see if he could go one better than the green pickles. After a minute he clicked his fingers.

'Where are the keys of the wine cellar?' he asked.

Crickem nearly let the bottle of pickles fall on the floor. So great a temerity overpowered him completely.

'Don't you know every bottle in the cellar is counted and listed,' he said. 'There's no chance of taking a bottle without it being missed.' But as he saw that Purdy was continuing to look around for the key of the cellar he looked at him with admiration. 'Are you going to take a bottle?' he asked.

'We'll see!' said Purdy. 'We'll see!' in the tone of one speaking to a child. 'Let me find the key first.'

The truth was that Purdy had suddenly remembered that several years before, Malcolm had ordered a case of liqueurs among which there had been one or two bottles of curacao for which he could not acquire a taste and which he intended to return. They had never been returned however, and if his, Purdy's, memory was correct, they were stowed away in a dark corner of the wine cellar. It was almost a certainty that these bottles of curacao would not be missed or that if they were missed it would be possible to persuade the overseer that they had been sent back to the wine merchant. On the other hand, the whole affair of the liqueurs had taken place before the arrival of Crickem, and he would not be aware that there was anything to mitigate the enormity of Purdy's daring.

When however the key of the wine cellar was located and the wine cellar was opened, a little difficulty arose as Crickem ran in ahead of Purdy, smacking his lips and uttering exclamations.

'What will we take?' he cried, and he rubbed his hands and smacked his lips. 'How about a bottle of sherry!' He snatched up a bottle of sherry and ran out of the dark cellar to told it up to the light, but almost at once he ran back again, exclaiming and rummaging in the shelves. 'How about port? How about claret?' In all his transports he was careful, however, to cede the choice to Purdy, for with the choice went the guilt. 'What are you going to take?' he cried.

'Just a minute; just a minute!' said Purdy, and he began to take out bottle after bottle and search around in the dark recesses at the back of the vaults.

'Clever lad!' said Crickem. 'You're taking from the back where it won't be missed.'

But Purdy spurned such a suggestion.

'I'm looking for something in particular,' he cried. 'Confound the dark. Here! Light a match for me.'

But ten, twenty, matches were lit and burnt out to the tip, and still Purdy's bottles had not come into view.

'Oh let's take anything,' said Crickem, getting tired of lighting match after match. 'There's only one match left anyway,' he said as he hastily dropped the second last match and sucked his singed fingers.

Purdy faltered. Could it be that he had been mistaken? Could the curacao have been returned after all? And if this were so, what then? He had got himself into this fix. He would have to take something. He couldn't let himself down. Crickem was about to strike the last match.

'Wait! Give me that match,' cried Purdy, and taking it into his own hand he struck it carefully and guarding the flame with his hands he crawled into the last, the sole remaining vault of the wine cellar. In the shelter of the vault the flame burned brightly, and quickly ran along the thin stick of the match. Already Purdy felt the heat; he would soon have to blow it out or drop it. In despair he ran his eye around the vault.

'Ah!' Just as the flame had reached his finger-tips, just as he felt the first nip of pain, there, in the far corner of the vault, shrouded, as the trap had been thick white with cobwebs, were the three fat bottles of curacao. Eager as a mother's gaze upon her first-born, Purdy's eye fell on them. Then the match went out and they were plunged in darkness, but Purdy grabbed the bottle-necks with unerring accuracy. A minute later he crawled out backwards into the light, and triumphantly held up the bottles.

Crickem was not so elated. He looked at the labels.

'What does this stuff taste like?' he asked, and he regretfully eyed the tried and trusted sherries and ports that lined the upper vaults. But again he decided to share the taste and dispense with the guilt of the choice.

It was a true summer day. The sun shone out brilliantly, and the fields were bright and busy with the activities of harvest; some yellow with uncut corn, others pale with bleaching stubble. Some dulled with hay still in the sward, others brilliantly green with aftergrass, and spotted all over with cocks of hay. While overhead the sky was a clear deep blue.

The two butlers set out at the pace set by the bay mare, a steady brisk pace. They took the Slane road, that ran through the richest deepest part of Meath, and soon they were going up hill and down, the countryside hidden from them at one moment as they dipped into a small valley between high ditches and revealed at the next moment when there was a rise in the road, or when they rolled up over one of the many railway bridges that rose up like hoops in the flat parts of the land to give a magnificent view across the entire county, with its plains diversified by pasture and grain, and shadowed by the woodlands of its great demesnes. But Purdy and Crickem, when they stood up in the trap, as they did at every other turn of the road, did so not to view this magnificent panorama but to wave their hats and shake their hands at the harvesters inside the hedges, and to blow kisses at the girls.

The sight which so delighted the two gallants, was, however, hardly to be compared with the sight that they themselves presented to the people at whom they waved. For the bright scene of summer comes and goes, but the country people who casually raised their heads at the sound of the high-stepping mare, were left staring open-mouthed with astonishment when they saw the two butlers bowling along the road in their outmoded vehicle. Those that were near enough to the road dropped their forks and rakes and lustily waved their straw hats. A few old men ran out towards the road, and taking the pipes from their puckered mouths called out hoarsely:

'Have the old times come back again!'

But it was the women who were most excited. It was the women who felt intuitively that there was something illicit about the two men in black frock-coats jogging along in a horse and trap. And something in themselves responded. Their eyes grew bolder and they threw out their bosoms brazenly.

'There's a sight for sore eyes!' cried Purdy as they passed one field where the workers were all women and young girls. They were tossing hay that had evidently heated in the cocks and had to be remade.

'What we want now,' cried Crickem, 'is two girls of our own.'

But to make a choice; that was going to be the difficulty.

'Look at those for girls!' cried Purdy, pointing to the other side of the road, where there was a knot of young girls sitting on a gate. They had come out to the fields with lunch pails for their menfolk, and now they sat on the gate in their bright cotton frocks and blouses and their flashing white aprons.

'There's a sight for you,' he cried again delightedly, as the women, emboldened by their numbers, looked at them with flashing eyes, and pushed each other forward with false screams and a lot of laughing. And those that pushed others forward, with a rowdy hand or a coarse gesture, offered themselves more urgently with their bright bold eyes.

And the two men on the pony cart drank in the intoxicating sensations given them by the women, as their nostrils and their open mouths drank in the sweet rushing air. But still they did not stop the mare, who cantered gaily onward. Clusters of women were dangerous. Might not the ones that were boldest in offering themselves be the most resentful if their offers were accepted. Might not the triumphant chariot career be turned into a rout, and might they not end, if they stopped, by having to scramble back into the wagon with ignominy, and depart in a hail of derisive taunts, perhaps even of stones. No. They could not risk stopping until they were sure of themselves.

And yet, girls were necessary to make the escapade complete.

'We must get a couple of girls. We won't be right without them,' said Crickem over and over again.

They were frank enough with each other about it.

'No use!' they would say as they passed group after group of women, merely waving at them and raising their hats. 'No use! They're bold enough at a distance.'

'Wait till we're passing through some town,' said Crickem. 'We'd stand a better chance with the town girls.'

'Oh, yes, town girls are the thing,' Purdy agreed.

'Whenever you see a crowd of girls together,' said Crickem, 'you can make up your mind you have a poor chance of picking up with one of them. They wouldn't give in to each other that they like that kind of thing. Wait till we come across a couple of girls by themselves. You'll see we'll come across plenty like that. When you see two girls sitting on the side of the bank you stand a chance with them. And the cooler they are the better your chance, many a time. These ones that roll their eyes and toss their heads know they're safe with the crowd. But two girls sitting on a bank! That's a different thing. What are they doing on the bank? What's in their mind if it's not the same thing that's in your own mind? See!'

And Purdy saw.

All the same when, not long after this profound remark, the two gallants passed a high bank on which were sitting two girls with saucy hats, and bright flashing stockings, still they did not stop.

And why? Well, it was probably Purdy's fault. When they first sighted the two girls, Crickem sat up with an eager smirk.

'What did I tell you?' he demanded.

But although he too sat up, Purdy felt a pang of uneasiness. Certain failures of the past came to his mind for the first time in years. Certain miscalculations he had made with Amelia were recalled to him in a rush. And his heart misgave him. Supposing the girls were to turn him down! Suppose they were to snigger when he took off his bowler hat! Supposing, in short, that both of them should want to have Crickem, and want to sit on either side of him, and let him put his arm around them, one in each arm, while he, Purdy, sat alone in the back of the trap, rolling over the countryside, a butt for the jeering of everyone they passed on the road.

They were almost abreast of the girls.

'Good-looking, aren't they?' whispered Crickem.

Purdy pressed his lips together and then opened them with an inspired remark.

'Do you call that good-looking?' he asked. 'I must say I'd like something better on my knee than one of those skinny creatures.'

Crickem turned around. He was astonished; so astonished in fact that he forgot to corroborate his own impression and they passed by the two girls on the bank, who unable to believe their eyes, were sitting up looking after the trap with their mouths wide open. Crickem stared at Purdy. This was the bald little fellow, who was paying alimony to some shrew of a wife, and whom in the matters of women he had always treated with contempt, and yet two of the best turned-out dolls you could ask to see were not pretty enough to satisfy him. Well! Crickem shook his head. He began to lose faith in his own judgement. Perhaps the two on the bank had been a bit flashy. Perhaps there would be better to be had further up along the road. The young man sighed. But then he took heart again. The day was young.

Just then two more girls appeared, walking in the middle of the road ahead of them. At the sound of the horse's trot on the road the girls turned and looked back over their shoulder. Ah! Here was something. One of the girls had red hair and carmine cheeks. Her teeth were flashing, and in her eyes there was just the right amount of impudence and independence. Crickem sat up again and over his face came the familiar smirk. He didn't look at the other girl at all.

But Purdy did. He saw at once that she was the foil that has ever and always appeared beside the heroines of history, literature and romance. He saw she was fat, plain, pale, and pasty-faced. And he surmised much worse. In all likelihood she would have a tendency to buck-teeth, a squint, or bandy legs. And there was no doubt in his mind that she would fall to him. Instantly he pictured Crickem with the red-head sitting beside him, blowing hot and cold upon him, with her chilly manner and her warm inviting eyes, while he, in all likelihood, would hardly have room on the other seat, with the fat creature's arm laced around him like a vice. Oh, he knew those plain women. He knew those ones that didn't like men. The world wasn't all Amelias! He felt the sweat break out on him. Perhaps after all there were worse faults than Amelia's faults.

The mare raced forward. The girls had moved to the side of the road, the red-head indeed merely moving in a few paces, but already, as Purdy suspected, the foil was going into her tricks. It was she who would be expected to attract their attention; to effect an introduction. With an artificial squeal the fat girl suddenly scrambled up on the ditch and called out to her companion to do the same, thus making an opportunity for the men to get their names.

'Crissie! Crissie! A runaway horse! Get up or you'll be killed!' She screamed again. And then linking the two parties together, she pointed a fat finger at Crissie and called out to the occupants of the on-rolling trap. 'Tell her to get out of the way,' she cried. 'She'll be killed. Oh! Oh!' And she began to scream again without ceasing.

Purdy looked at Crickem.

Crickem's eyes were fastened on Crissie, who, calm and immovable, indifferent to danger, refused to step aside an inch, and glancing collectedly at the trap, called out reprovingly to her friend.

'Don't be silly, Polly. The horse is as quiet as a lamb. And anyway I expect these gentlemen have the animal well under control.' As she spoke, Crissie raised her eyes and they were filled with messages of apology for Polly. But all the messages in those charming eyes were directed at Crickem, and at Crickem alone.

Didn't he know it would be like this! Purdy felt the sweat break out on him again. And the fat creature's name; Polly! That was the last straw.

Once more he would have to take action, and take action quickly.

'Which of them is the worst?' he whispered under his breath to Crickem. 'Which will you have; the fat one or the one with the bandy legs?'

'Bandy legs!' Crickem's smile faded. He almost rose up in the trap. But it was too late. They were on top of the girls and all that could be seen of the saucy red-head was her face. Her legs, bandy or otherwise, were now hidden from them by the mare's girth as they passed them by, without slackening pace. But it must have been the red-head that Purdy had called bandy-legged, for, high on the ditch, plain to be seen, was Polly. And Polly's legs were not bandy. In fact Polly's legs were so fat they would easily have borne the weight of five or six Pollys.

The moment was lost. They had trotted past. And again Crickem did not look back. He turned in amazement to Purdy.

'You don't miss anything, do you?' he said, in awe. 'I didn't see anything wrong with the red-head. When did you get so particular. I thought I was particular, but you beat all I ever came across!' Then he looked back regretfully. 'We'll never get a girl at this rate,' he said, but Polly and Crissie had been left behind in a sweep of the road, and there was no further chance of seeing how far Crissie's legs belied the saucy confidence on her face.

Meanwhile the day rolled on, and the wagon rolled on, and the countryside rolled past them in the opposite direction, and since it was a summer day of unusual warmth and brightness, it need hardly be stated that the galliards met and passed many a pretty girl on the way. But something had happened to Crickem; some chord in his confidence had snapped, and it was he now who was anxious to show Purdy that he too was a bit particular. They no sooner came in sight of a pair of legs on the road in front of them than Crickem began to criticise the girls.

And then there was the hamper tied to the axle. There was no sense sharing it, it was small enough for two people. It was better to eat it, while they had the chance.

'There will be plenty of time afterwards,' said Purdy, 'for picking buttercups,' and he gave Crickem a dig in the ribs in case the young man might miss the meaning expressed in this fragrant phrase of bygone days.

It was about four o'clock in the afternoon when they pulled in under a shady chestnut tree at the side of the road, tied the mare to the tree, and got out the ham-bone and the bottles of curacao.

'I didn't know I was so hungry,' said Crickem, filling his mouth with cheese.

'Did you see the corkscrew anywhere?' said Purdy, and, rummaging in the hamper with their mouths full, neither of them as much as turned to look at a buxom buttercup that went down the road beside them, leading her cows home from pasture. And when she passed a second time, having no doubt milked the cows in the interval, they were still less aware of her than before, for there had been more meat than you'd imagine on the ham-bone, and the green pickles were heavy. Our friends had overeaten, and asked no more than to lie on their backs, with their hats over their faces, and snore. Buttercups might spring up all around them, and yet cause them no disturbance. The only disturbance they experienced came from within. The curacao made them feel slightly sick.

But as they lay replete under the throbbing sun, through their drowsy minds there wandered visions of all the women and girls they had passed on the roads, and in the fields; all the Crissies and the Pollys; all the buxom women that had stood at the cottage doors, and all the blushing slips of girls that had hid their faces and giggled at them. And they were almost as surfeited with visions of hips and thighs, dimpled elbows, and bosoms and bellies, as they were with green pickles.

Purdy, in particular, was worn out.

At last, however, the chill of the early harvest eventide began to steal its way through the grasses under them, and the shade of the tree to which the mare was tied, began to spread its shade upon them. The mare was the first to feel the evening deepening around her, and her sensitive skin quivered as the shades fell blue about her. She began to kick the iron bars of the gate to which she was tied, with an impatient hoof, and to rattle her trappings.

The two butlers sat up.

'How about heading for home?' said Purdy. The day had been long enough for him.

But Crickem, at the first chill touch of the evening air, was restored to his full vigour.

The false feeling of satisfaction fell away from him in an instant, when he stood upon his feet, and the pricks of the chill evening were less insistent than the pricks of his thwarted desires.

Where had the day gone? How had it wasted away like this? He looked at Purdy. It was the old fellow's fault, he thought. If the old fellow hadn't been so particular they might have had a girl apiece now. It would be cold going back in the trap. It wouldn't have been a bad thing to have a hot arm around your middle to keep you warm. Crickem grew warmer at the very thought. They might even have got a couple of girls who would have gone back with them to The Manse. All those empty rooms! All those big beds! What an opportunity lost! A feeling of positive hatred for Purdy shot through him, and he glared at him, but Purdy wasn't looking. Purdy was patting the mare, and rubbing his hand over her haunches that were dappled with dried sweat marks and rough with dandruff and loosened hairs. The day had told on the mare.

'We'll have to give this animal a good rub down when we get back,' he said.

Crickem said nothing. He stood sneering at the crumbled tails of Purdy's coat, and the glossy seat of his pants all stained with grass. He wanted to do something to annoy him. He wanted to make him sting. He wanted to take the complacent look off his glossy fat face. And he knew how to do it.

He walked over to the chestnut tree and untied the mare. He helped Purdy to hitch her without saying a word, but when they sat up on the trap he had the familiar smirk on his face that Purdy knew and dreaded.

'Wouldn't it be a good joke,' he said then, breaking the silence, as if casually, 'wouldn't it be a good joke if the old Manse was burnt to the ground when we got back!'

Crickem had calculated fairly correctly. Purdy was stung, but not as badly as the young man would have wished. His fat cheeks shook all right, but he controlled his start with a little laugh.

'Oh, I don't suppose that's likely to happen,' he said, and endeavoured to forget such an evil suggestion as quickly as he could. Crickem, however, had left something out of his calculations, and that was the effect upon himself of his own remark. No sooner had he uttered it, however, than a superstitious feeling began to form inside him. He wished he had kept his mouth shut, and when Purdy gave a watery smile in his direction and pretended to take the joke in good part, the smile was not more watery than the smile on Crickem's own face. It was Crickem who had to break the silence that he had drawn down on them.

'I wonder could we be blamed if the old place did take fire?' he asked, 'I mean, could we be held responsible?'

He looked at Purdy, whom he had begun to hate less acutely in the last few minutes, and when Purdy looked around to answer him he was struck for the first time at how young his companion looked; a mere youth, thought Purdy in surprise; gawky, inexperienced. He was a bit worried, but not as worried as he had been before they set out. His was the worry of the cautious person that sets in before the deed is done, not the worry of the reckless that waits till the deed is beyond repair.

'There's no use worrying about it now,' he said, in an effort to reassure his companion, who fidgeted nervously on his seat.

And with this, Purdy flicked the whip in the air, and pointed out over the valley below them, for they had entered upon the Slane road again, and indicating the magnificent panorama of Meath, he admonished his companion to enjoy it.

'Look at that view!' he cried. 'Where would you see the like of it!'

And indeed it was beautiful. Although they had passed along this road earlier in the day, its beauty was not so evident, their excitement had clouded their minds and the human activity in the fields had distracted their eyes from the landscape. But now, there were no women in bright red blouses in the foreground. There were no girls in white aprons sitting on the gates. The eye flew over the empty fields to the far rim of the sky where the irregular patches of trees were deepened with blue mist. Trees and bushes, and even the far fields seemed a deep blue under this evening mist. And the blueness everywhere made the vista more immense. Even in the hayfields near at hand the yellow cocks were insignificant beside their own great blue shadows stretching out on the stubble beside them.

'A magnificent view!' cried Purdy again. 'There's no doubt about it, but a horse and trap is the only way to see the countryside. Such a view. You can see the countryside for miles around.' He stood up in the trap and looked all around him, as they rolled up one of the hooped bridges of the railway.

Crickem, who up to this had not paid much heed to Purdy's comments on the view, became somewhat more interested. He too stood up in the trap, but he faced forward, and stared ahead over the wide sweep that now lay immediately in front as well as below them for the road swept around a bend at this point.

'We ought to be able to see The Manse from here,' he said, and he tried to distinguish between the various masses of trees upon the sky line.

'Are you still afraid it's on fire!' said Purdy, and he laughed good-humouredly. The day had been so full and satisfying for him. He had forgotten his fidgets and fears.

Crickem bit his lip with vexation.

'It's all very fine for you to laugh,' he said, 'but if I were you I wouldn't be so gay. I don't like to think of the way you were playing with those matches in the wine cellar. Are you sure you stamped on them all? You should always stamp on a burnt match. You never know when it might smoulder and catch light again.' But Purdy laughed more heartily.

'The walls of the cellar are lined with brick,' he said.

Crickem said nothing for a minute.

'Think of all the straw from the wine bottles that was on the floor!'

'Oh come! Come!' said Purdy, patronisingly, 'Buck up! I can tell you if the old Manse was on fire we'd have no difficulty in seeing the smoke.' He pointed out again over the vast view with the handle of the yellow whip, and at the same time he opened his mouth and drew in such a deep breath that the buttons on his coat were strained to the limits of their thread and the top button popped open. 'Have you no poetry in you? Have you nothing to say at the sight of that sky! Look at those trees over there in the distance! Look at that mist hanging in the air!'

Crickem made an effort to shake himself up.

'Mist is for heat,' he said, at random. 'It will be another hot day tomorrow.' He stared into the distance morosely. 'It's just like smoke,' he said. 'Isn't it? Blue smoke!'

'Now you're talking,' said Purdy. 'That's just what it's like; blue smoke.' And the better to appreciate this poetic comparison he slackened his hands on the reins and let the mare break her gait. They proceeded at a walking pace, and Purdy gazed ecstatically over the scenery.

'Look at that clump of trees directly in front of us, now,' he said. 'Do you see the clump I mean,' he pointed with the end of the whip and then with a fat finger, and then he began to give more explicit directions. 'Move over nearer to me,' he said to Crickem. 'Run your eye along my finger.' Then he stopped up. 'Wait a minute,' he said, and he pulled the reins short and stopped the mare. 'Do you see that tree in the middle of that field?' he asked.

'Yes,' said Crickem listlessly.

'Well, run your eye along in a straight line from that. Do you see a spire a bit to the left? You do? Very well, now keep your eye on that spire, and raise it a few inches to the far side. Did you do that? You did? Well! What do you see?'

'I see the spire,' said Crickem, still more listlessly.

'Good,' said Purdy. 'Well, if you see the spire you must see the clump of trees I mean because they're just beyond the spire.'

'I see them,' said Crickem.

'Well!' said Purdy.

'Well what?' said Crickem.

'Don't you recognise them? They're the trees of The Manse or I'm greatly mistaken.'

'Oh!' said Crickem, and sat up with greater interest.

'Do you think it is?' he asked, for now he had located the clump of trees and was giving all his attention to it although it looked very similar to all the other patches of woodland in the plain below them.

'I'm sure of it,' said Purdy. His chest swelled. 'It must be one of the finest places in the county,' he said. A feeling of pride possessed him. 'Our place must be one of the best wooded places in the county. Look at those trees! Look at the way the mist is thick in them! I bet it's as dark as night in the middle of some of those copses now.'

The mist was certainly deeper. It not only lay in the crevices of the trees and bushes but seemed to rise up over them like a vapour to meet the evening clouds of a still deeper blue that were beginning to gather in the sky.

'I never saw anything so like smoke as that mist,' said Crickem, become touched in spite of himself by the serene expanse below.

'That was a good description of yours,' said Purdy. 'A poet couldn't have put it better. Look! Wouldn't you swear it was smoke! And look at those clouds! You'd swear they were clouds of blue smoke hanging in the air.' Then a playful impulse came over him; once more he poked Crickem in the ribs. 'What's this you said,' he asked. 'Wouldn't it be a good joke if it was smoke!' And he threw back his head and laughed. Purdy laughed, and laughed, and as he laughed the reins slipped loose and the mare moved over to the side of the road and began to crop abruptly at the long damp blades of grass that grew up through heaps of stones left on the side of the road by the road-menders.

'Oh, shut up!' said Crickem, and he caught at the reins. 'Are you going to drive, or are you not? Give me the reins if you're not able to drive the animal.' He gave the reins a vicious tug that caused the animal to throw back her head and show her long yellow teeth stained with the green sap of the grass. 'As I said before,' said Crickem, when Purdy wiping the tears of laughter from his eyes took control of the reins again, 'As I said before it wouldn't be such a joke on me as it would on you. It wasn't my idea to go fooling about with matches in a dark cellar.'

Purdy's fat sides shook with laughter. Crickem had a longing to give him a push and topple him out of the trap on to one of the heaps of stones. He bit his lips and glared at the skyline.

'You'd laugh on the other side of your face,' he said, 'if a few sparks came up out of that clump of trees!'

And then, just as he spoke, the young man's mouth fell open, and clutching Purdy by the arm he nearly dragged him off his seat. The reins fell to the floor of the vehicle.

'Purdy!' he cried. 'For God's sake. Look! Did you see sparks that time?' For hardly had he let the words pass from his lips than up from the distant blue trees there flew a covey of red sparks.

For a moment Purdy thought he was being fooled, but unmistakably again a flight of bright sparks flew into the sky.

'Fire!' cried Crickem. 'It's a fire. What did I tell you! It's The Manse! The place is on fire. I knew it! I knew it! I had a feeling about it.' He became suffused with fear. His face was a sickly white. 'You and your mist!' he screamed. 'I said all along it was smoke. "It's like smoke," I said. You can't deny that!'

But Purdy was staring at the distant smoke, that unmistakably now twisted up over the lovely wooded copse, and mingled with the evening clouds.

'It may be just a fire in the woods,' he said dully, but his voice did not carry conviction.

He appeared to be stupefied. Then suddenly he sprang to his feet, and standing up in the cart he caught the ends of the reins and slapped the back of the mare. 'How long will it take us to get back?' he cried, as he fell back into his seat when the mare broke into an unsteady gallop. But Crickem too had scrambled to his feet, and tottering from side to side unsteadily in the galloping trap he held on to the dash-board with one hand and with the other he tried to catch and drag the reins out of Purdy's hands.

'Wait a minute,' he yelled. 'Wait a minute. Think what you're doing. It's the other way we ought to be going! If the place is on fire we had better get out of the county as quick as we can.'

'What do you mean?' cried Purdy. 'Sit down you young fool or you'll fall out of the trap,' and he held tight to the reins.

Crickem tugged harder at the reins. 'Do you realise,' he yelled, 'that we may be held responsible for going out and leaving the place with no one in it.' He gave another violent tug at the reins to try to get them from Purdy and the baffled animal suddenly rose on her hindlegs, not like an animal given to such habits but as one sorely perplexed.

'Let go of the reins you fool,' cried Purdy. 'Do you want to upset us into the ditch!'

'I don't care if I do,' said Crickem. 'I'm telling you the best thing we can do is leave the outfit here and make across the fields to the nearest station. We might get a train to Drogheda that would get us to Dublin tonight. In Dublin we'd get the mail boat and get out of the country altogether.'

'Are you mad?' Purdy wrenched the reins back into his own control, and leaned over the trap to pat the haunch of the trembling animal in the shafts. 'If we didn't turn up it might be said that we set the place on fire!'

'And what else did we do?' cried Crickem. 'Curse those matches. Curse you and your bottles of fancy syrup – the damn stuff made me sick into the bargain.'

'We didn't do it on purpose,' said Purdy, 'and if we get back we might be able to help to put out the fire.'

He looked wildly over at the distant trees, where the heavy clouds of night and the clouds of smoke were now mingled together, the underside of them illuminated occasionally with dreadful pink reflections. Night was coming, and with it the nature of the fire was becoming more plain.

'We might be able to do something,' he cried. 'It might be only the stables. It might be only a fire in the woods.' He lashed the mare forward again, and then as Crickem still stood tottering on his feet, he gave him a push. 'Sit down if you don't want to fall out of the cart,' he said. Then on a second thought he glanced at the young fellow again, with contempt. 'If you don't want to go back, I'll let you out,' he said. 'But I'm going back!'

Crickem skulked in the seat without answering. Then in a mealy voice he muttered something under his breath.

'What did you say?' called Purdy.

'I said it wasn't my idea to go fooling about in the cellar, with matches,' said Crickem vindictively, 'And it was you struck the last match!'

For several minutes then they careered along the road in silence, Purdy standing and lashing the mare onward, Crickem sitting crouched up in the trap, his face bleakly fixed in the direction of the glow that grew brighter minute by minute in the darkening plain.

But as Crickem sat hunched up and staring at this glow, the dark masses of tree and shadow to the left of the bright glow was suddenly pricked here and there with white points of light. For a moment the young man stared at these lights without interest and without comprehension. But all at once he threw up his head.

'Purdy!' he shouted. 'Look at the lights!'

'What about them?' said Purdy irritably. 'They're the lights of the town.'

'I know that,' cried Crickem excitedly. 'I know it. But don't you see, they're beyond the fire. Beyond it! Do you hear me!' He screamed the words at Purdy. 'It isn't the old Manse at all. It's some other place. Do you hear me? Some other place!' And half shouting and half crying he staggered to his feet again, and leaned out over the horse's back.

Purdy could not believe the evidence of Crickem's eyes, and, continuing to lash the mare forward, he strained his own eyes over the distance. But as he stared his hands grew looser on the reins and the jaded animal instantly slackened her pace, and after a minute dropped into a walk.

'You're right, Crickem!' said Purdy at last, and flopped back into the seat, wiping the sweat from his face with the flat of his palm. The mare came to a dead stop.

The two butlers sat in the motionless trap. The night air cut into them. The sweat broke freely from them. The mare, too jaded to graze, gave occasional short erratic crops at the dank unseen grass under her feet by the wayside.

'Well!' said Crickem after a few minutes. 'What do you think of that!' He laughed awkwardly. He was feeling ashamed. For a minute he wondered if he could pretend he had been joking all the time, that he had known all along it was not The Manse that was on fire. But he was too fatigued and broken down by the strain to sustain the effort of pretence. He merely sat in the seat, slumped where he had been crouched.

But after sitting a few minutes like this, Crickem looked at Purdy who was sweating profusely and seemed as if he might sit where he was all night.

'Well!' said Crickem. 'That gave us a jolt all right.' He laughed again weakly. Then he nudged Purdy. 'Well! Why are we sitting here? Let's get on our way again.'

But Purdy, who had risen to the occasion when danger had threatened, was deflated now; he sat stolid on the seat.

'What would we have done if it was The Manse?' he asked, and he turned heavily to Crickem. 'How would we have faced Malcolm?'

But Crickem was in no mood for these speculations. It was getting downright cold. His fingers were beginning to get numb.

'Look here,' he said, 'if you don't want to get home, I do. Give me the reins. Move up there,' and stepping across the short stiff legs of Purdy he took his place on the driving side. The whip he could not take; it was clamped fast in Purdy's fist as if in the fist of a dead man. Bending the reins, Crickem lashed at the jaded mare who began to move forward again, her legs plaiting under her with fatigue.

Crickem himself was in excellent spirits.

'I always said I was a lucky fellow,' he said. 'I have the luck of the devil. I don't know why I was worried about the fire at any time. Nothing like that ever happens to me. I never yet got into a scrape I couldn't get out of again. I'd get out of hell if I ever got in. But I won't!' He poked the inert Purdy. 'Sit up, Purdy,' he said. 'We're coming to a village.'

There was an unusual stir in the small village.

'We must ask where the fire is,' said Crickem. 'Do you know I believe it's Liscard!' he said.

Liscard was a neighbouring demesne and the two men from The Manse had some acquaintance with staff there.

'I wonder would we go up and look at it,' said Crickem, as Purdy did not answer, for on their right now, quite near, they could hear the commotion of people shouting and the air was filled with the nauseating odour of charred wood.

'Do you want the horse to drop dead under us?' said Purdy then. He didn't want to see the fire. It made him shudder to think of it. It reminded him too much of what might have been.

'I think it would be a bit of sport to go up,' said Crickem. 'I wonder if his lordship was there when the fire broke out. If he wasn't you can imagine the sweat old Evans was in.'

Evans was the foreman at Liscard.

'Poor Evans!' said Purdy. He knew him a long time.

'Poor Evans my eye!' said Crickem. 'I'd just like to see him now.' He turned around. 'I bet he's hopping like a frog. Come on. Be a sport,' he said. 'Let's go up the road a bit. Think of the game we'd have looking at old Evans. And think of the fat old cook. She'd be a nice bundle to catch in a sheet! And think of the maids! Think of them screeching! Think of them jumping out of the windows into a sheet with their skirts blown out like balloons.' He slapped his thigh and roared laughing. 'Think of their petticoats!' he said, almost choking with laughter. 'Think of their drawers!'

But Purdy was thinking of Bina. Bina was the cook.

'Poor Bina!' he said.

There had been times when he had thought that if it had not been for Amelia! Ah well! There was no use in such vain thoughts.

'Will you come?' said Crickem for the last time. 'I'll tell you what we'll do. We'll tie the old nag to a tree and cut across the fields. Not that there's any need to tie the old bag of bones to anything; it's taking her all her time to put one foot before another.'

Purdy came to life.

'If we tie that animal to anything,' he said, 'we'll tie her to the door of a public house. I'm badly in need of a drink.'

Crickem hesitated another minute.

'All right,' he said. Perhaps when the old fellow was warmed up with a few whiskeys he'd feel differently about going to the fire. 'Get on, you trollop!' he said, lashing the mare again.

The village was only a hundred yards away, but it took them five minutes to beat the mare over the ground.

'We'll have to give her a bucket of beer too!' said Crickem in high fettle. 'We'll never get her home if we don't. We have another six miles to go if we have a yard to go.'

Purdy was scanning the dark village street for the lighted door of the public house.

'It's seven miles from here to the front gate of The Manse,' he said absentmindedly.

Crickem snapped his fingers.

'I'll tell you what we'll do,' he said. 'We'll get a bit of oats from the publican here in this place, and stable the old jade for a while. She'll never make the seven miles without a rest. And we can go across the fields to the fire. She'll be as fresh as a filly when we get back. How is that for a good plan?'

They had reached the small public house and Crickem drew rein, an entirely unnecessary gesture for the animal had come to a natural stop at the barrier of light that flooded out through the doorway of the public house.

The young man sprang to the ground.

'Are you sure it's all right to leave the mare,' said Purdy, looking at the dejected animal whose head drooped down between its forelegs.

Crickem made no answer. He had disappeared into the lighted bar, where bottles and glasses gleamed silver and gold in the light of a hanging oil-lamp. The place had an air of activity most unusual in a small village. The counter was ringed with wet marks as if numberless glasses had been filled and emptied across it in recent minutes and several empty glasses still remained on it.

There had evidently been a big trade done in the last few hours. Those who were quenching the fire had found frequent necessity also to quench their thirst. Behind the counter there was not only the publican but a young girl in a red jumper, an elderly woman, and a small boy, all members of the publican's family who had been drafted at short notice to cope with the unusual situation.

When Purdy and Crickem made their appearance the publican, who had evidently been taking a rest, hurriedly stirred himself again to remove the soiled glasses, in armfuls from the counter. The stout woman snatched up a cloth to wipe them. The young girl in the red jumper sprang to activity, and pushing back her black hair with a sweep of her hand came forward and asked them what they wanted to drink.

'You seem to have had a busy evening,' said Crickem to the young girl, pointing to the soiled floor, but leaning over the counter to stare at her.

'It's the fire at Liscard,' said the girl. 'The whole village is up there. And it's giving them such a thirst. Every other few minutes there's a crowd rushing back here to wet their throttles.'

The stout woman moved over nearer and seeing that Purdy and Crickem were alone, and were not the vanguard of another rush of trade, she ceased from wiping the glasses and joined in the talk.

'I suppose you're going up to see the sight too, people are coming from far and near to see it,' she said. 'I wish we could go up there. I believe it's a sight you'd never forget. One whole side of the house is gutted,' she sighed. 'It's a sight worth seeing. But we can't leave here. We got a glimpse of the flames out of one of the windows upstairs, but every time we got to the window a rush started here below and we had to come down again.' She pointed to the young boy. 'Even the young lad had to stay and help. It's a great pity. It would have been such an education for him. But it's a bad wind that doesn't blow someone good,' she said, as she took the coin that Crickem tossed down on the counter.

Meanwhile the publican had said nothing, but was staring at Purdy with a peculiar expression. Purdy who had been in the place once or twice hoped that the publican did not recognise him. He had not spoken a word, but had taken up his glass and begun to stare into it. He wished that Crickem would not keep up the chatter.

The woman drew out a till under the counter and threw Crickem's coin on to the heap of silver and copper coins that jostled each other like a shoal of live fish.

The publican was still staring at Purdy. Suddenly he edged the woman away from the counter, and took her place, leaning out across the board on his bare arms from which the blue shirt-sleeves were rolled back.

'That was a terrible thing that fire,' he said, and he addressed himself to Purdy.

'Was there much damage done?' said Purdy, forced into talk.

'Damage enough,' said the publican moodily. Then he looked up. 'The other place was worse,' he said. 'The other place was burnt to the ground, I hear.'

'The other place! What other place?' said Purdy.

'The publican looked curiously at him.

'Didn't you hear?' he said.

'What?' said Purdy.

Crickem was leaning across the counter, with one eye on the publican and the other upon the stout woman as she stood with her back to him washing the glasses. He had succeeded in making a not altogether unwilling captive of the young girl's hand.

'It's the most curious thing that ever happened in my time,' said the publican to Purdy. 'Two big mansions to go on fire in the one day, and within a few miles of each other.'

At the other end of the counter Purdy saw Crickem drop the girl's hand. His own body was growing cold.

'Two big fires?' he asked in a faint dim voice.

'Within a few miles of each other,' said the publican. 'Did you ever hear anything like it. Some say the sparks from the other place must have blown across the river and set fire to this place.' He jerked his thumb over his shoulder to indicate the scene of the local fire.

The stout woman joined the conversation again.

'We were all out on the hill at the back of the shop looking at the flames of the other fire, so we can't complain too much about not seeing this one. We saw something anyway, didn't we, Packy?' She tousled the head of the small boy.

'It was a better blaze than this one,' said the child in a shrill bragging voice. He was humiliated at not being out with the other young boys leaping and yelling in the flickers of the fire.

'It was worse than this one, all right,' said the publican. 'They saved the best part of the house up at Liscard. Only the servants' quarters were burned and there was talk of tearing them down anyway. But the other place was burned to the ground I believe.

They got the fire under control in time at Liscard, but it seems the other place was empty. There was no one in it at all.'

Purdy saw Crickem moving over nearer to him. He looked up. Crickem's face was as drawn and white and the pimples stood out on it like lumps in porridge.

The two butlers looked at each other.

'Did you hear that?' said Purdy.

'I did,' said Crickem, and as if the publican spoke another tongue and Purdy was an interpreter, he spoke again to Purdy.

'Ask him where the other fire was, can't you?' he prompted.

But Purdy had begun to tremble. His lip shook, and he felt his eye beginning to twitch. His head reeled, and when he looked up at the publican it was Amelia's face that floated for a moment before his eyes. He opened his mouth to speak, but instead he suddenly turned back to Crickem.

'Let's get into the air,' he gasped, and he stumbled out into the darkness, followed at once by the dazed Crickem.

The publican looked after them. The publican's wife and the young girl exchanged glances with each other.

'What ails those fellows?' said the girl, peeved at the gallant Crickem's abrupt departure.

The publican stretched out an arm to embrace the two empty glasses the men had left down so hastily.

'I thought I knew the small fat fellow,' he said. 'I thought he was a butler at The Manse.'

The woman scoffed.

'Didn't you see they were strangers,' she said. 'They knew nothing at all about the fire up there.'

'That's right,' said the young girl. 'They were strangers. They didn't even ask where the other fire was, although you'd imagine even strangers would have asked that!'

She looked at her wrist and put it up to her lips. It was red from the way the young man had gripped her, before he took such a sudden notion to dash away.

The Convert

At half-past three in the afternoon, while Elgar was up in the storeroom over the shop, he heard Miss Mongon calling upstairs to Maimie, and he knew that everything was over. Now, he would have to call to offer his condolences.

All week, when it was whispered about the town that Naida was sinking rapidly, it was of her parents he thought, and not of Naida at all. Would they expect him to call and enquire of her? Or would it only distress them to see him? If only he had not let so long pass without going to see them. That was what made things difficult now. It was nothing else. If only he had called to see them four years ago, as he intended, when he and Maimie came back from their honeymoon! Only for Maimie he would have gone.

'They'd give a nice reception to you,' she said.

'Not when I tell them I came to apologise.'

'For what?' said Maimie, slyly.

'For the way I left the house that morning,' he said.

Maimie smirked. 'Is that all?'

Poor Maimie; given her marriage hadn't been all she had hoped, it made her feel better to think that she had taken him from someone else. They weren't long back from Dublin when she began to repeat some nonsense she picked up from the customers in the shop. 'I hear Naida Paston is complaining of bad headaches. That's something new, isn't it? We never heard anything about her having headaches before now, did we?'

He guessed at once what was in the back of her mind. 'You ought to know,' he said shortly. 'You were her best friend, weren't you?'

Another day, when they were sitting down to their dinner, in the stuffy room behind the shop, she looked across the table at him. 'I hear Naida is no better,' she said, and then she took up her knife and fork. 'It must be true, what my mother used to say, that a girl that's jilted is never the same afterwards.'

He could have struck her. But by that time she was expecting Birdie, so he could only look at her with contempt.

'Don't look at me like that!' she cried. 'Don't forget the night she came bursting into this very room and made such a scene.'

Oh, that night! Only for thinking about it he might have made another effort to visit the Pastons, perhaps after Birdie was born, while Maimie was in bed, and could not stop him. It was for the child's sake he wanted to make up with them that time. It would be nice for her to be friends with people like the Pastons, and not be completely smothered by her mother and her mother's people. Yet at the last minute, when he had brushed his suit and was ready to go out the door, he faltered. Perhaps Maimie was right and they would not forgive him, although no matter what Maimie or anyone else might say, the only thing the Pastons could hold against him was the way he stole out of their house that morning he ran off with Maimie. Even now, four years later, it gave him a sick feeling to think of the way he threw his suitcase out of the window and let himself out after it. He had acted like a son of the house who if he were caught would have been locked up in a closet until the train had left the station. Instead of that he was practically a stranger. Well, if not exactly a stranger, at least there were limits to his familiarity. After all, he was paying his way, and although they were very kind to him, he used to spend the greater part of his time in his room studying.

Just because they were of his own persuasion was no reason for him to feel any constraint upon his liberty. Quite truly, even before he met Maimie at all, his religion had influenced him very little. If it was a factor, it was only inasmuch as there were few other Protestants in the locality, and the Pastons had very few callers. Except for Maimie, Naida did not seem to have any friends at all. And Maimie had probably pushed her way uninvited into the Pastons' house, out of curiosity, when they

first arrived in the town. As indeed she had done on one
occasion a few days after he came to stay, when he was walking
up and down the lawn before supper with Naida.

'Who is this?' he asked in surprise as he saw her coming
towards them across the grass.

'Oh, it's Maimie Sully,' said Naida. 'She's my best friend,' she
added hastily, but he saw that she looked back uneasily at the
house, and he guessed that whatever Naida might feel, the
visitor was not well regarded by her parents.

Not that Maimie herself seemed to mind what they, or
anybody else, thought of her. It was true that just once, as she
came up to them, she gave a little nervous glance, just as Naida
had done, at the windows of the house. But almost at once she
gave a defiant little laugh and came forward. Before she spoke,
that little laugh spoke for her. It seemed to say, I know you don't
want me here, but that's always the way with people until I'm a
little while with them, and then they won't let me go away!

Her actual words were more formal. 'I hope I'm not
intruding, Naida,' she said. 'I didn't know your guest had
arrived.' While she spoke, her eyes went past Naida and took
him in from head to foot, and he knew that she was telling a
lie. But he was flattered. 'Naida was telling me about you,' she
said. 'You're at Trinity College, aren't you?' The words were
simple enough, but there was something unaccountable in the
way Maimie said them, and her lively eyes were upon him all
the time. 'What are you studying?' she asked, without waiting
for his reply.

It was the typical question, but instead of seeing the abyss that
yawned between them at that moment, he saw only her eyes
gaze upon him, and he laughed good-humouredly.

Maimie didn't stay long that day. Glancing at the little gold
watch on her wrist, she sprang to her feet. 'Oh dear. I must fly!
Owdie Hicks will be waiting for me.'

'Who is Owdie Hicks?' he asked impulsively.

'He's one of my admirers,' said Maimie.

When she was gone his thoughts still dwelt on her. 'Where
does she live?' he asked Naida, as they walked back towards the
house.

'Her mother keeps a shop in the town. You can see the back of the house from here.' Naida pointed at the back windows of a house which was in full view of the Pastons' property.

He didn't see Maimie for several days after that, but once or twice when he took out his books to study under the trees, and Naida came and sat down quietly beside him, he looked instinctively at the back windows of Sully's house. Did Maimie ever look out and see them? It was a wonder she had not made another visit.

Then one afternoon when he went into the town on a message he ran into her in the street.

'Oh, hello. How are you getting along?' she asked, but she didn't give him time to answer. 'I was telling Owdie Hicks about you. I was telling him how glad I was that you were so nice.' She paused for a minute, and then went on with a laugh, 'For Naida's sake, I mean! She's one of my best friends, you know, and I always said she wasn't such a dry stick as people thought. I always said that you couldn't expect her to have followers, like the rest of us, when there were no young men in the town for her,' she explained with emphasis, and then she laughed again. 'There are plenty of my kind, but as I said to Owdie, I knew someone of her own would turn up some day, someone like you.'

Was she trying to provoke him? He ought to have been annoyed, but instead he felt irritated with Naida. Had she been talking about him? And what had she been saying? It did not occur to him that Maimie's words could have been calculated to have the effect they had upon him.

'I think you must have been misinformed about my relations with the Pastons,' he said stiffly, but when he saw that she was still laughing at him, he got irritable. 'Anyway, I don't know what you're talking about,' he said. 'Naida is only a child, she's used to solitude.'

'She's the same age as me,' Maimie said then, slowly and deliberately. 'Do you think I'm a child?'

There was no mistaking the meaning behind her words. There was no ignoring the invitation in her eyes. All of Maimie was in the look she gave him at that moment, all her boldness, all her vulgarity, and all her vanity, but also there was all her provocative charm, and her appetite for admiration. That look she gave him was his undoing. From that point onwards, there was no going back. It was only a matter of weeks until the tremendous evening when it was all settled between them. He had made up his mind to throw up all that was in his way – his studies, his religion, everything, and run away with Maimie.

How had Naida heard about their plans? – he had often wondered. And how would he be in Sullys the very night she made that ignominious visit to the house? How had it happened that she had not been stopped in the hall, or in the passage, but had surprised them alone in the stuffy parlour at the back of the shop, he with his arm so foolishly wound round Maimie's waist? He had often suspected Maimie of enjoying that outrageous scene. When he tried to pull his arm from around her waist, she had caught his hand and held it there. The things she said! He couldn't remember them now, but he knew they poured out from her like a flood of dirty water. So different from Naida, with her single passionate cry.

'Is it true?' Naida's cry rang in his ears to this day. To this day it wrung his heart. 'You can't do it,' she cried, when he made no reply.

Maimie had bridled. 'What do you mean?' she cried, and thrust herself between them. 'Naida Paston, I don't know who let you into my house to behave like this, but I know one thing. You're not going to prevent me from having him just because you couldn't get him for yourself.'

Oh, how had he listened to that? She might just as well have raised her hand and struck her friend in the face.

Naida drew back as if indeed she had been struck. Over her face there had come an expression that he would never forget as long as he lived. It was as if in that moment for the first time, she had seen how she must appear to Maimie, perhaps even to him.

'Oh!' she cried, and her hands flew to her face. 'Oh!' she cried again, and turned to him. 'That's not what I meant at all!' she said, and desperate with entreaty, her eyes had sought his. 'You know that, don't you?' she begged. 'It's only that –' She paused, and put her hand up to her forehead, as if she had become confused, or as if she had felt some tension there, or some pain. Yes, she had put up her hand to her head that day. He recalled it distinctly. She must have had those pains in her head even that night, four years ago. Why, if so, it couldn't possibly be said they had anything to do with him, that her weakness had been brought on grieving over him. Yes, she had put her hand to her forehead that day, he was sure.

'It's only that –' she said. But seeing that she could say no more, for one moment his eyes met hers. In the same way two birds draw near, for an instant in mid-air, almost crashing together, and seeming to cross beaks, as if it were to kiss, and then with a lightning twist, circling divinely, they have gone on their ways again. Are they mating? Have they some message to exchange, or is it, just, that finding themselves together alone in the blue air, with the animal and vegetable world stretched far below them, they become intoxicated with a feeling of recognition, of being in that great blue element, two creatures exactly alike? Will they meet again? Are they parting for ever? It matters not. Feather by feather, till they fall to the clay, they will be alike, those two.

'Naida!' he cried.

But she burst into tears and ran towards the door. Another moment and they heard her footsteps running along the street outside.

'Well!' Maimie had caught his arm and put it round her waist again.

'I ought to be glad I got you when some people are ready to go to such lengths for you.'

That warm, soft body; it had seduced him again in a moment!

Well, that was four years ago, and even now, Maimie could, if she liked at any time, make a fool of him again. Yes, the mother of a big child like Birdie, and expecting another child, Maimie still had the same hold over him. He went to the window and looked out. In the yard under the window their little girl was hopping about on the cobblestones. She was well named, a chubby creature, all body, hopping about on little thin legs that she nevertheless put down firmly under her with every hop she took, so that inside her little patent-leather shoes one could imagine her small toes tightening down in their grip upon the ground.

She was the image of Maimie. She was like her in appearance, and like her in character, and by imitation she was like her in a hundred small mannerisms. Not for the first time, but perhaps more poignantly than ever before, he felt a stab at his heart, and the painful love he had for the child tightened its stranglehold on him.

Apart altogether from the natural bond of paternity, he was drawn towards this child in another way, as if her differences from him, her likeness to her mother, gave him an obsessive attachment to her, the bond of the wrongdoer to his victim.

What was she doing now? He tapped on the glass, but the child, absorbed in play, did not hear. After watching her for a few minutes, he tapped again. This time Birdie's attention seemed to have been caught, because she turned around, and looked back at the house. But she did not raise her head to the upper windows, and in a lower window someone else must have been watching her too, because she ran back to the house and for a minute he could not see her until she ran out again to the middle of the yard with a slice of bread in her hand.

Who gave it to her?

He listened to the sounds from below. There was only the sound of the servant-girl whistling at her work, and a clatter of dishes in the sink.

Maimie was probably still lying down after the heavy meal she ate at midday. Except for a feeling of drowsiness after eating, her second pregnancy was having no ill effect upon her.

A curiosity about the unborn child entered his mind for the first time. Would it be like Birdie? Much as he loved her he hoped it would not be like her. He did not want this child, also, to be all Maimie. He did not want it to be like her, or like any of her family in any way. And yet he did not want it to be like him either.

What did he want? He stared out of the window, and as he did a forgotten image awakened in response to his question. On the mantelpiece in the Pastons' drawing-room there had been a photograph in a little silver frame. The stand at the back was broken, and more often than not it lay upon its face, but he had taken it up one day and looked at the picture. It was a picture of a little girl with limp yellow hair hanging docilely down by the sides of her thin face, from which the large eyes looked out with a steady and serious regard. At the time it had seemed to him that the child was plain, but now he knew that the look upon its face was the look that he yearned for, but never would see, upon the face of a child of his own. For the child in the picture was Naida.

Naida! All at once he was assailed by thoughts of her, and his mind was invaded by such poignant memories that he put his hands to his head as if in physical pain.

He could not stay alone. He opened the door and plunged into the passage. The small steep stairway before him might have been a black hole down which he flung himself headlong.

'For Heaven's sake! What kind of a way is that to come down the stairs?' Maimie was feeling too comfortable and heavy to be more than mildly annoyed. She had come downstairs when Miss Mongon, her assistant, called up to her about Naida, and she was now behind the counter in the shop. Miss Mongon was at the other end putting on her hat to go out to her tea. There was only one customer, Owdie Hicks, if he could be called a customer. He was leaning across the counter, gossiping with the two women. Maimie looked at her husband, and then she stared behind him into the hall. 'You brought the plaster down from the ceiling,' she said, seeing small flakes of lime particles floating indolently downward through the air, like snow at dusk, in the dark hallway behind him. Elgar looked back over his shoulder. He felt foolish, foolish, the more so because he had an idea that a conversation had been interrupted. What was keeping Miss Mongon there? It was because of her he felt ill at ease. As for the presence of Owdie Hicks in the shop, that did not bother him. It looked intimate but it was only the familiarity of old friends. But his awkwardness would be interpreted differently to an outsider. It would be seen to be jealousy. He looked jealous! It galled him that anyone should think him jealous of a poor wretched creature like Owdie Hicks. He forced himself to affect a false jocularity. 'What are you two plotting?' he asked, but he knew by a contemptuous flash in her eyes that Maimie was aware of his insincerity.

More obtuse, Owdie pointed to the counter. 'What do you think of those?' he asked. The counter was littered with snapshots with sticky glossy surfaces. 'I took them yesterday.'

'And he developed them last night,' said Maimie.

Owdie picked up one and passed it to him. 'What do you think of this one?' he said. 'That's the best, in my opinion. That ought to make a good enlargement.'

It was a snapshot of Birdie, and it was a good likeness.

Elgar nodded. Owdie took the picture back.

'It's her mother over again,' he said, and he stared at the picture. Then he looked up and laughed. 'I'll wait for her, if you'll only let me have her, don't forget you owe me one. It was you who stole her mother from me.'

Elgar looked away from the stupid white face. He did not look at Maimie either. The joke was stale. But not to Maimie. It could bring a blush to her warm face any day.

Their relationship was contemptible. If there were some iniquity in it, he could have endured it better. And yet, in his heart, he knew that even by his contempt he wronged them, and that it was not pusillanimity that kept them apart, but that for all their ogling and double meanings they were curiously innocent.

Where had they come by this integrity? Was it bred in them, or was it inculcated in them by their religion? He looked at them and wondered.

For Owdie Hicks would never marry. Already he had the neglected look of a man with no ambition for the regard of any woman. And Maimie, whatever caprice or vanity had made her want himself for a husband, she would be faithful to him without question; perhaps never fully conscious of any disappointment in her desires, daily attributing it to the annoyances of the day, to the weather, or to the strain of looking after the child.

Whereas he –? Abruptly, on the brink of this abysmal question, he shrank back.

Miss Mongon was ready for the street at last, but for her gloves, into which she was trying to squeeze her chilblained hands, as she came into the middle of the shop.

'Since you waited so long, you may as well wait a bit longer,' she said to Owdie, 'and there'll be two to choose from,' she said looking at Maimie and laughing.

He did not understand what she meant, but the familiarity of her manner, the intimacy in her voice revolted him. And then Maimie said good-humouredly, 'Oh, the next will be a boy!'

Was it possible they were talking about her condition in those terms of loose familiarity?

'Boys take after their mothers,' Miss Mongon said, laughingly showing the insides of her teeth decorated with tartar. 'Girls take after the father.'

Owdie looked down at the snapshots that he still held in his fat hand. 'That wasn't the case here,' he said, and then he looked up at Maimie. 'If I had known your children would take after you, I'd have been a bit more forceful four years ago.'

Elgar looked at him in unexpected pity. Behind the foolish words, he felt there was both disappointment and regret. But as he saw Maimie's gratified smile his contempt for the two of them returned. Maimie knew what Owdie meant, but she wanted to hear the compliment repeated. 'What do you mean, Owdie Hicks?' she asked, simpering.

Owdie had been leaning over the counter, facing inwards towards where, behind Maimie's back between the glittering bottles of whiskey, a big mirror in gilt frame gave back the shop, and all that was in it.

'Look!' He pointed his stout forefinger to where, between the glittering bottles, his own pallid face was reflected. 'How would you like one of your children to have a face like that?' he asked, and he gave a laugh, but the bitter little laugh was lost in the loud laugh that came from Miss Mongon. It surprised them all, and in particular Elgar. He looked straight at the elderly spinster, and for the first time he began to read the malevolent suspicions in her face. All at once, the shop assistant's inciting presence was unbearable to him. With a crash he brought his fist down on the counter.

'I may not have said as much in words,' he said, 'but you, all three of you, know that I detest this kind of thing; this vulgar talk about a matter that –'

He could not find words delicate enough for his meaning. He knew that his voice was shaking with the unusual vehemence of his feeling, and he was trembling too. He was upset further by the look of complete bewilderment on Owdie's face. Owdie thought he had gone out of his mind. Elgar turned to Maimie. 'I won't have this,' he shouted, 'I won't have it, do you hear me?' But the look that was upon Maimie's face made his head swim. She was looking back at him defiantly. She seemed to be indicating that whatever was wrong in their marriage, could not be put right by the ineffectiveness of a shout. He was disregarded completely. Then all his will was determined to say something to hurt her. But Elgar could not think of anything. All he could think of were his own outraged feelings. 'I won't put up with such talk. Not in our house.' He stopped, but a violent surge of emotion forced him on to say more, something he didn't mean to say. 'Not today,' he cried. 'Today of all days!'

Today of all days? Unawares, even from the wells of deepest feeling, those words had gushed forth.

Maimie flushed. For an instant her eyes held his, and then she glanced nervously at the others, at Owdie and Miss Mongon. They, however, were still subdued by Elgar's first shout. After it they did not appear capable of hearing anything more. Indeed, Miss Mongon stood as if pasted to the floorboards.

Husband and wife looked at each other, a long, inscrutable look.

Elgar was aghast at his own outburst; above all, at his final words. What did he mean? He hardly knew, but to his relief he heard Owdie talking again to Miss Mongon, easily and naturally.

'Well, so long! I suppose you'll hardly be back before I leave.'

But Miss Mongon was powerless to go. A thought had been stirred in her mind, and she was irresistibly urged to give utterance to it.

'She's being waked this evening, isn't she?' she said.

It didn't appear necessary to her to mention any name, but once again Maimie flushed, and Elgar, watching, saw his wife's eyes tearing Miss Mongon's words apart to see if she spoke in ignorance or in malice.

'Is it Naida Paston you mean?'

Never in his life had he heard that edge in Maimie's voice. But it was Owdie who answered Miss Mongon.

'In the house, I suppose,' he said, and Maimie's sharp cry was not noticed.

Was Owdie clever enough to have spoken on purpose to cover Maimie? Elgar was grateful to him in any case. The danger was passed.

'God forgive me,' Miss Mongon said, 'but I always think it's a lonesome thing to leave a coffin all night in an empty church. It gives me the creeps to think of it being left there.'

'It's the custom of the Catholic Church,' said Maimie sharply.

'I am aware of that.' Miss Mongon was weak and docile again. 'But feelings are feelings,' she said, with another little spurt of defiance. 'I'd rather be waked in my own house like Protestants.'

'Maggie Mongon –' Maimie had started.

'Perhaps it's not a dogma of faith,' said Owdie, interposing again, 'I mean to say we may not be obliged under pain of sin in this matter.'

But Maimie wasn't interested in dogmas and doctrines.

'If you ask me, it's a matter of common sense,' she said. 'I can tell you, if you had a corpse in the house for a few hours, you'd soon see the sense of taking it to the church!' She shuddered. 'Why do you think people fill the house with flowers?' She shuddered again. 'Ugh!' she said. 'Ugh!'

In their experience, neither Owdie nor Miss Mongon had ever found death anything other than chill and alienating, but with Maimie's words, malodorous fears overlaid their hearts. And they too shuddered.

'Yes,' said Maimie, crudely, cruelly, 'if it weren't for the way they're covered up with a shroud, you'd see them beginning to change colour after a few hours!' Absentmindedly, she examined the skin on her own living hand. Miss Mongon's flesh felt clammy. Then a thought struck her.

'They don't wear shrouds, do they!' she asked. 'Protestants, I mean?'

Maimie was taken by surprise, and still unnamed, Naida flashed into their minds again.

'What do they wear, I wonder?' asked Owdie.

'I think I heard someone say they're laid out in a white dress, the women, I mean,' said Maimie, who was reluctantly drawn into the conversation. Involuntarily, she turned to her husband. 'Elgar, you ought to know,' she said, 'what will she wear?'

But when he looked at her oddly, she stamped her foot at him.

'Naida, I mean,' she said impatiently. 'You ought to know.'

In a Café

The café was in a back street. Mary's ankles ached and she was glad Maudie had not got there before her. She sat down at a table near the door.

It was a place she had only recently found, and she dropped in often, whenever she came up to Dublin. She hated to go anywhere else now. For one thing, she knew that she would be unlikely ever to have set foot in it if Richard were still alive. And this knowledge helped to give her back a semblance of the identity she lost willingly in marriage, but lost doubly, and unwillingly, in widowhood.

Not that Richard would have disliked the café. It was the kind of place they went to when they were students. Too much water had gone under the bridge since those days, though. Say what you liked, there was something faintly snobby about a farm in Meath, and together she and Richard would have been out of place here. But it was a different matter to come here alone. There could be nothing – oh, nothing – snobby about a widow. Just by being one, she fitted into this kind of café. It was an unusual little place. She looked around.

The walls were distempered red above and the lower part was boarded, with the boards painted white. It was probably the boarded walls that gave it the peculiarly functional look you get in the snuggery of a public house or in the confessional of a small and poor parish church. For furniture there were only deal tables and chairs, with black-and-white checked tablecloths that were either unironed or badly ironed. But there was a decided feeling that money was not so much in short supply as dedicated to other purposes – as witness the paintings on the walls, and a notice over the fire-grate to say that there were others on view in a studio overhead, in rather the same way as pictures in an exhibition. They were for the most part experimental in their technique.

The café was run by two students from the Art College. They often went out and left the place quite empty, as now, while they had a cup of coffee in another café across the street. Regular clients sometimes helped themselves to coffee from the pot on the gas-ring, behind a curtain at the back, or, if they only came in for company and found none, merely warmed themselves at the big fire always blazing in the little black grate that was the original grate when the café was a warehouse office. Today, the fire was banked up with coke. The coffee was spitting on the gas-ring.

Would Maudie like the place? That it might not be exactly the right place to have arranged to meet her, above all under the present circumstances, occurred vaguely to Mary, but there was nothing that could be done about it now. When Maudie got there, if she didn't like it, they could go somewhere else. On the other hand, perhaps she might like it? Or perhaps she would be too upset to take notice of her surroundings? The paintings might interest her. They were certainly stimulating. There were two new ones today, which Mary herself had not seen before: two flower paintings, just inside the door. From where she sat she could read the signature, Johann van Stiegler. Or at least they suggested flowers. They were nameable as roses surely in spite of being a bit angular. She knew what Richard would have said about them. But she and Richard were no longer one. So what would *she* say about them? She would say – what would she say?

But what was keeping Maudie? It was all very well to be glad of a few minutes' time in which to gather herself together. It was a different thing altogether to be kept waiting for a quarter of an hour.

Mary leaned back against the boarding. She was less tired than when she came in, but she was still in no way prepared for the encounter in front of her.

What had she to say to a young widow recently bereaved? Why on earth had she arranged to meet her? The incongruity of their both being widowed came forcibly upon her. Would Maudie, too, be in black with touches of white? Two widows! It was like two magpies: one for sorrow, two for joy. The absurdity of it was all at once so great she had an impulse to get up and make off out of the place. She felt herself vibrating all over with resentment at being coupled with anyone, and urgently she began to sever them, seeking out their disparities.

Maudie was only a year married. And her parents had been only too ready to take care of her child, greedily possessing themselves of it. Maudie was as free as a girl. Then, if it mattered, she had a nice little income in her own right too, apart from all Michael had left her. So?

But what was keeping her? Was she not coming at all?

Ah! The little iron bell that was over the door, it too, dating from the warehouse days, tinkled to tell there was another customer coming into the café.

It wasn't Maudie though. It was a young man, youngish anyway, and Mary would say that he was an artist. Yet his hands at which, when he sat down, he began to stare, were not like the hands of an artist. They were peculiarly plump soft-skinned hands, and there was something touching in the relaxed way in which, lightly clasped one in the other, they rested on the table. Had they a womanish look perhaps? No; that was not the word, but she couldn't for the life of her find the right word to describe them. And her mind was teased by trying to find it. Fascinated, her eyes were drawn to those hands, time and again, no matter how resolutely she tore them away. It was almost as if it was by touch, not sight, that she knew their warm fleshiness.

Even when she closed her eyes, as she did, she could still see them. And so, innocent of where she was being led, she made no real effort to free her thoughts from them, and not until it was too late did she see before her the familiar shape of her recurring nightmare. All at once it was Richard's hands she saw, so different from those others, wiry, supple, thin. There they were for an instant in her mind, limned by love and anguish, before they vanished.

It happened so often. In her mind she would see a part of him, his hand, his arm, his foot perhaps, in the finely worked leather shoes he always wore, and from it, frantically, she would try to build up the whole man. Sometimes she succeeded better than others, built him up from foot to shoulder, seeing his hands, his grey suit, his tie, knotted always in a slightly special way, his neck, even his chin that was rather sharp, a little less attractive than his other features.

But always at that point she would be defeated. Never once voluntarily since the day he died had she been able to see his face again.

And if she could not remember him, at will, what meaning had time at all? What use was it to have lived the past, if behind us it fell away so sheer?

In the hour of his death, for her it was part of the pain that she knew this would happen. She was standing beside him when, outside the hospital window, a bird called out with a sweet, clear whistle, and hearing it she knew that he was dead, because not for years had she really heard bird-song or bird-call, so loud was the noise of their love in her ears. When she looked down it was a strange face, the look of death itself, that lay on the pillow. And after that brief moment of silence that let in the bird-song for an instant, a new noise started in her head, the noise of a nameless panic that did not always roar, but never altogether died down.

And now, here in the little café, she caught at the table-edge – for the conflagration had started again and her mind was a roaring furnace.

It was just then the man at the end of the table stood up and reached for the menu-card on which, as a matter of fact, she was leaning, breasts and elbows, with her face in her hands. Hastily, apologetically, she pushed it towards him, and at once the roar died down in her mind. She looked at him. Could he have known? Her heart was filled with gratitude, and she saw that his eyes were soft and gentle. But she had to admit that he didn't look as if he were much aware of her. No matter! She still was grateful to him.

'Don't you want this too?' she cried, thankful, warm, as she saw that the small slip of paper with the speciality for the day that had been clipped to the menu card with a paper-bin, had come off and remained under her elbow, caught on the rough sleeve of her jacket. She stood up and leant over the table with it.

'Ah! thank you!' he said, and bowed. She smiled. There was such gallantry in a bow. He was a foreigner, of course. And then, before she sat down again she saw that he had been sketching, making little pencil sketches all over a newspaper on the table, in the margins and in the spaces between the newsprint. Such intricate minutely involuted little figures. She was fascinated, but of course she could not stare.

Yet when she sat down, she watched him covertly, and every now and then she saw that he made a particular flourish: it was his signature, she felt sure, and she tried to make it out from where she sat. A disproportionate, a ridiculous excitement rushed through her, when she realised it was Johann van Stiegler, the name on the new flower paintings that had preoccupied her when she first came into the place.

But it's impossible, she thought. The sketches were so meticulous, the paintings so – impressionistic.

But the little bell had tinkled again.

'Ah! Maudie!'

For all her waiting, taken by surprise in the end, she got to her feet in her embarrassment, like a man.

'Maudie, my dear!' She had to stare fixedly at her in an effort to convey the sympathy, which, tongue-tied, she could express no other way.

They shook hands, wordlessly.

'I'm deliberately refraining from expressing sympathy – you know that?' said Mary then, as they sat down at the checkered table.

'Oh, I do!' cried Maudie. And she seemed genuinely appreciative. 'It's so awful trying to think of what to reply back! – Isn't it? It has to come right out of yourself, and sometimes what you'd like to say is something you can't even say out loud when you think of it!'

It was so true. Mary looked at her in surprise. Her mind ran back over the things people had said to her, and the replies.

Them: It's a good thing it wasn't one of the children.

Her: I'd give them all for him.

Them: Time is a great healer.

Her: Thief would be more like, taking away even my memory of him.

Them: God's ways are wonderful. Some day you'll see His plan in all this.

Her: Do you mean, some day I'll be glad he's dead?'

So Maudie apprehended these subtleties too? Mary looked hard at her. 'I know, I know,' she said. 'In the end you have to say what is expected of you and you feel so cheapened by it.'

'Worse still, you cheapen the dead,' said Maudie.

Mary looked really hard at her now. Was it possible for a young girl, a simple person at that, to have wrung from one single experience so much bitter knowledge? In spite of herself, she felt she was being drawn into complicity with her. She drew back resolutely.

'Of course, you were more or less expecting it, weren't you?' she said, spitefully.

Unrepulsed, Maudie looked back at her. 'Does that matter?' she asked, and then, unexpectedly, she herself put a rift between them. 'You have the children, of course!' she said, and then, hastily, before Mary could say anything, she rushed on. 'Oh, I know I have my baby, but there seems so little link between him and his father. I just can't believe that I'm wheeling him round the park in his pram; it's like as if he was illegitimate. No! I mean really. I'm not just trying to be shocking. It must be so different when there has been time for a relationship to be started between one's children and their father, like there was in your case.'

'Oh, I don't know that that matters,' said Mary. 'And you'll be glad to have him some day.' This time she spoke with deliberate malice, for she knew so well how those same words had lacerated her. She knew what they were meant to say: the children would be better than nothing.

But the poison of her words did not penetrate Maudie. And with another stab she knew why this was so. Maudie was young, and beautiful. Looking at her, it seemed quite inaccurate to say that she had lost her husband: it was Michael who had lost her, fallen out, as it were, while she perforce went onward. She didn't even look like a widow. There was nothing about her to suggest that she was in any way bereft or maimed.

'You'll marry again, Maudie,' she said, impulsively. 'Don't mind my saying it,' she added quickly, hastily. 'It's not a criticism. It's because I know how you're suffering that I say it. Don't take offence.'

Maudie didn't really look offended though, she only looked on the defensive. Then she relaxed.

'Not coming from you,' she said. 'You know what it's like.' Mary saw she was trying to cover up the fact that she simply could not violently refute the suggestion. 'Not that I think I will,' she added, but weakly. 'After all, you didn't!'

It was Mary who was put upon the defensive now.

'After all, it's barely two years – less even,' she said stiffly.

'Oh, it's not altogether a matter of time,' said Maudie, seeing she had erred, but not clear how or where. 'It's the kind of person you are, I think. I admire you so much. It's what I'd want to be like myself if I had the strength. With remarriage it is largely the effect on oneself that matters I think, don't you? I don't think it really matters to – the dead! Do you? I'm sure Michael would want me to marry again if he were able to express a wish. After all, people say it's a compliment to a man if his widow marries again, did you ever hear that?'

'I did,' said Mary, curtly. 'But I wouldn't pay much heed to it. A fat lot of good the dead care about compliments.'

So Maudie *was* already thinking about remarriage? Mary's irritation was succeeded by a vague feeling of envy, and then the irritation returned tenfold.

How easily it was accepted that *she* would not marry again. This girl regards me as too old, of course. And she's right, or she ought to be right. She remembered the way, two years ago, people had said she 'had' her children. They meant that it was unlikely, unlooked for, that she'd remarry.

Other things that had been said crowded back into her mind as well. So many people had spoken of the special quality of her marriage, her's and Richard's, their remarkable suitability one for the other, and the uniqueness of the bond between them. She was avid to hear this said at the time.

But suddenly, in this little café, the light that had played over those words, flickered and went out. Did they perhaps mean that if Richard had not appeared when he did, no one else would have been interested in her?

Whereas Maudie looked so attractive now, when she must still be suffering from shock, what would she be like a year from now, when she would be 'out of mourning,' as it would be put? Why, right now, she was so fresh. Looking at her one felt there was no other word for it but virginal! Of course she was only a year married. You could hardly call it being married at all.

But Maudie knew a thing or two about men for all that. There was no denying it. And in her eyes at that moment was a strange expression. Seeing it, Mary remembered at once that they were not alone in the café. She wondered urgently how much the man at the other end of the table had heard and could hear of what they were saying. But it was too late to stop Maudie.

'Oh Mary,' cried Maudie, leaning forward, 'it's not what they give us. I've got over wanting things like a child. It's what we have to give them. It's something –' and she pressed her hand suddenly to her breasts, – 'something in here.'

'Maudie!'

Sharply, urgently, Mary tried to make her lower her voice, and with a quick movement of her head she did manage at last to convey some caution to her.

'In case you might say something,' she said, in a low voice.

'Oh, there was no fear,' said Maudie. 'I was aware all the time.' She didn't speak quite so low as Mary, but did lower her voice. 'I was aware of him *all the time*,' she said. 'It was *him* that put it into my mind, about what we have to give.' She pressed her hands to her breasts again. 'He looks so lonely, don't you think? He is a foreigner, isn't he? I always think it's sad for them; they don't have many friends, and even when they do, there is always a barrier, don't you agree?'

But Mary was too embarrassed to let her go on. Almost frantically she made a diversion.

'What are you going to have, Maudie?' she said loudly. 'Coffee? Tea? And is there no one to take an order?'

Immediately she felt a fool. To whom had she spoken? She looked across at Johann van Stiegler. As if he were waiting to meet her glance, his mild and patient eyes looking into hers.

'There is no one there,' he said, nodding at the curtained gas-ring, 'but one can serve oneself. Perhaps you would wish that I –'

'Oh not at all,' cried Mary. 'Please don't trouble! We're in absolutely no hurry. Please don't trouble yourself,' she said, 'not on our account.'

But she saw at once that he was very much a foreigner, and that he was at a disadvantage, not knowing if he had not perhaps made a gaffe. 'I have perhaps intruded?' he said, miserably.

'Oh, not at all,' cried Mary, and he was so serious she had to laugh.

The laugh was another mistake though. His face took on a look of despair that could come upon a foreigner, it seemed, at the slightest provocation, as if suddenly everything was obscure to him – everything.

'Please,' she murmured, and then vaguely, '– your work,' meaning that she did not wish to interrupt his sketching.

'Ah, you know my work?' he said, brightening immediately, pleased and with a small and quite endearing vanity. 'We have met before? Yes?'

'Oh no, we haven't met,' she said, quickly, and she sat down, but of course after that it was impossible to go on acting as if he were a complete stranger. She turned to see what Maudie would make of the situation. It was then she felt the full force of her irritation with Maudie. She could have given her a slap in the face. Yes: a slap right in the face! For there she sat, remote, her face indeed partly averted from them.

Maudie was waiting to be introduced. To be *introduced*, as if she, Mary, did not need any conventional preliminaries. As if it was all right that she, Mary, should begin an unprefaced conversation with a strange man in a café because – and of course that was what was so infuriating, that she knew Maudie's unconscious thought – it was all right for a woman of *her* age to strike up a conversation like that, but that it wouldn't have done for a young woman. Yet, on her still partly averted face, Mary could see the quickened look of interest. She had a good mind not to make any gesture to draw her into the conversation at all, but she had the young man to consider. She had to bring them together whether she liked it or not.

'Maudie, this is –' she turned back and smiled at van Stiegler, 'this is –' But she was confused and she had to abandon the introduction altogether. Instead she broke into a direct question.

'Those are your flower pictures, aren't they?' she asked.

It was enough for Maudie – more than enough you might say.

She turned to the young man, obviously greatly impressed; her lips apart, her eyes shining. My God, how attractive she was!

'Oh no, not really?' she cried. 'How marvellous!'

But Johann van Stiegler was looking at Mary.

'You are sure we have not met before?'

'Oh no, but you were scribbling your signature all over that newspaper,' she looked around to show it to him, but it had fallen on to the floor.

'Ah yes,' he said, and – although she couldn't be certain, of course – she thought he was disappointed.

'Ah yes, you saw my signature,' he said, flatly. He looked dejected. Mary felt helpless. She turned to Maudie. It was up to her to say something now.

Just then the little warehouse bell tinkled again, and this time it was one of the proprietors who came in, casually, like a client.

'Ah good!' said van Stiegler. 'Coffee,' he called out. Then he turned to Mary. 'Coffee for you too?'

'Oh yes, coffee for us,' said Mary, but she couldn't help wondering who was going to pay for it, and simultaneously she couldn't help noticing the shabbiness of his jacket. Well – they'd see! Meanwhile, she determined to ignore the plate of cakes that was put down with the coffee. And she hoped Maudie would too. She pushed the plate aside as a kind of hint to her, but Maudie leaned across and took a large bun filled with cream.

'Do you mind my asking you something about your work?' said Mary.

But Maudie interrupted.

'You are living in Ireland? I mean, you are not just here on a visit?'

There was intimacy and intimacy, and Mary felt nervous in case the young man might resent this question.

'I teach art in a college here,' he said, and he did seem a little surprised, but Mary could see too, that he was not at all displeased. He seemed to settle more comfortably into the conversation.

'It is very good for a while to go to another country,' he said, 'and this country is cheap. I have a flat in the next street to here, and it is very private. If I hang myself from the ceiling, it is all right – nobody knows, nobody cares. That is a good way to live when you paint.'

Mary was prepared to ponder. 'Do you think so?'

Maudie was not prepared to ponder. 'How odd,' she said, shortly, and then she looked at her watch. 'I'll have to go,' she said, inexplicably.

They had finished the coffee. Immediately Mary's thoughts returned to the problem of who was to pay for it. It was a small affair for which to call up all one's spiritual resources, but she felt enormously courageous and determined when she heard herself ask in a loud voice for her bill.

'My bill, please,' she called out, over the sound of spitting coffee on the gas stove.

Johann van Stiegler made no move to ask for his bill, and yet he was buttoning his jacket and folding his newspaper as if to leave too. Would his coffee go on her bill? Mary wondered.

It was all settled, however, in a second. The bill was for two eight-penny coffees, and one bun, and there was no charge for van Stiegler's coffee. He had some understanding with the owners, she supposed. Or perhaps he was not really going to leave then at all?

As they stood up, however, gloved and ready to depart, the young man bowed.

'Perhaps we go the same way?' and they could see he was anxious to be polite.

'Oh, not at all,' they said together, as if he had offered to escort them, and Maudie even laughed openly.

Then there was, of course, another ridiculous situation. Van Stiegler sat down again. Had they been too brusque? Had they hurt his feelings?

Oh, if only he wasn't a foreigner, thought Mary, and she hesitated. Maudie already had her hand on the door.

'I hope I will see some more of your work sometime,' said Mary. It was not a question, merely a compliment.

But van Stiegler sprung to his feet again.

'Tonight after my classes I am bringing another picture to hang here,' he said. 'You would like to see it? I would be here –' he pulled out a large, old-fashioned watch, '– at ten minutes past nine.'

'Oh, not tonight, I couldn't come back tonight,' said Mary. 'I live in the country, you see,' she said, explaining and excusing herself. 'Another time perhaps? It will be here for how long?'

She wasn't really listening to what he said. She was thinking that he had not asked if Maudie could come. Perhaps it was that, of the two of them, she looked the most likely to buy a picture, whereas Maudie, although in actual fact more likely to do so, looked less so. Or was it that he coupled them so that he thought if one came, both came? Or was it really Maudie he'd like to see again and that he regarded her as a chaperone? What was it?

There was no knowing, however, and so she said goodbye again, and the next minute the little bell tinkled over the door and they were in the street. In the street they looked at each other.

'Well! if ever there was –' began Maudie, but she didn't get time to finish her sentence. Behind them the little bell tinkled yet again, and their painter was out in the street with them.

'I forgot to give you the address of my flat – it is also my studio,' he said. 'I would be glad to show you my paintings at

any time.' He pulled out a notebook and tore out a sheet. 'I will
write it down,' he said, concisely. And he did. But when he went
to hand it to them, it was Maudie who took it. 'I am nearly always
there, except when I am at my classes,' he said. And bowing, he
turned and went back into the café.

They dared not laugh until they had walked some distance
away.

'Well, I never!' said Maudie, and she handed the paper to
Mary.

'Chatham Row,' Mary read, 'number 8.'

'Will you go to see them?' asked Maudie.

Mary felt outraged.

'What do you take me for?' she asked. 'I may be a bit
unconventional, but can you see me presenting myself at his
place? Would *you* go?'

'Oh, it's different for me,' said Maudie, enigmatically. 'And
anyway, it was you he asked. But I see your point – it's a pity.
Poor fellow, he must be very lonely. I wish there was something
we could do for him – someone to whom we could introduce
him.'

Mary looked at her. It had never occurred to her that he
might be lonely. How was it that the obvious always escaped
her?

They were in Grafton Street by this time.

'Well, I have some shopping to do. I suppose it's the same
with you,' said Maudie. 'I am glad I had that talk with you. We
must have another chat soon.'

'Oh yes,' said Mary, over-readily, replying to their adieux, not
as Maudie thought, to the suggestion of their meeting again!
She was anxious all at once to be rid of Maudie.

And yet, as she watched her walk away from her, making her
passage quickly and expertly through the crowds in the street,
Mary felt a sudden terrible aimlessness descend upon herself
like a physical paralysis. She walked along, pausing to look in
at the shop windows.

It was the evening hour when everyone in the streets was
hurrying home, purposeful and intent. Even those who paused
to look into the shop windows did so with direction and aim,

darting their bright glances keenly, like birds. Their minds were all intent upon substantives; tangibles, while her mind was straying back to the student café, and the strange flower pictures on the walls, to the young man who was so vulnerable in his vanity: the legitimate vanity of his art.

It was so like Maudie to laugh at him. What did she know of an artist's mind? If Maudie had not been with her, it would have been so different. She might, for one thing, have got him to talk about his work, to explain the discrepancy between the loose style of the pictures on the wall and the exact, small sketches he'd been drawing on the margins of the paper.

She might even have taken up his invitation to go and see his paintings. Why had that seemed so unconventional – so laughable? Because of Maudie, that was why.

How ridiculous their scruples would have seemed to the young man. She could only hope he had not guessed them. She looked up at a clock. Supposing, right now, she were to slip back to the café and suggest that after all she found she would have time for a quick visit to his studio? Or would he have left the café? Better perhaps to call around to the studio? He would be back there now.

For a moment she stood debating the arguments for and against going back. Would it seem odd to him? Would he be surprised? But as if it were Maudie who put the questions, she frowned them down and all at once purposeful as anyone in the street, began to go back, headlong, you might say, towards Chatham Street.

At the point where two small streets crossed each other she had to pause, while a team of Guinness's dray-horses turned with difficulty in the narrow cube of the intersection. And, while she waited impatiently, she caught sight of herself in the gilded mirror of a public house. For a second, the familiar sight gave her a misgiving of her mission, but as the dray-horses moved out of the way, she told herself that her dowdy, lumpish, and unromantic figure vouched for her spiritual integrity. She pulled herself away from the face in the glass and hurried across the street.

Between two lock-up shops, down a short alley, roofed by the second storey of the premises overhead, till it was like a tunnel, she saw a doorway. Away at the end of the tunnel a door could clearly be seen even from the street, because it was painted bright yellow. Odd that she had never seen it in the times she had passed that way. She crossed the street.

Once across the street, she ran down the tunnel, her footsteps echoing loud in her ears. And there on the door, tied to the latchet of the letter-box, was a piece of white cardboard with his name on it. Grabbing the knocker, she gave three clear hammer-strokes on the door.

The little alley was a sort of cul-de-sac, except for the street behind her and the door in front of her. There was no aperture of any kind. As for the premises into which the door led, there was no way of telling its size or its extent, or anything at all about it, until the door was opened.

Irresponsibly, she giggled. It was like the mystifying doors in the trunks of trees that beguiled her as a child in fairy-tales and fantasies. Did this door, too, like those fairy doors, lead into rooms of impossible amplitude, or would it be a cramped and poky place?

As she pondered upon what was within, seemingly so mysteriously sealed, she saw that, just as in a fairy tale, after all there was an aperture. The letter-box had lost its shutter, or lid, and it gaped open, a vacant hole in the wood, reminding her of a sleeping doll whose eyeballs had been poked back in its head, and creating an expression of vacancy and emptiness.

Impulsively, going down on one knee, she peered in through the slit.

At first she could only see segments of the objects within, but by moving her head, she was able to identify things: an unfinished canvas up against a splattered white wainscot, a bicycle-pump flat on the floor, the leg of a table, black iron bed-legs and, to her amusement, dangling down by the leg of the table, dripping their moisture in a pool on the floor, a pair of elongated, grey, wool socks. It was, of course, only possible to see the lower portion of the room, but it seemed enough to infer conclusively that this was indeed a little room in a tree, no bigger than the bulk of the outer trunk, leading nowhere, and – itself its own end.

There was just one break in the wainscot, where a door ran down to the floor, but this was so narrow and made of roughly-jointed boards, that she took it to be the door of a press. And then, as she started moving, she saw something else, an intricate segment of fine wire spokes. It was a second before she realised it was the wheel of a bicycle.

So, a bicycle, too, lived here, in this little room in a tree-trunk.

Oh, poor young man, poor painter, poor foreigner, inept at finding good lodgings in a strange city. Her heart went out to him.

It was just then that the boarded door – it couldn't have been a press after all – opened into the room, and she found herself staring at two feet. They were large feet, shoved into unlaced shoes, and they were bare to the white ankles. For, of course, she thought wildly, focusing her thoughts, the socks are washed. But her power to think clearly only lasted an instant. She sprang to her feet.

'Who iss that?' asked a voice. 'Did someone knock?'

It was the voice of the man in the café. But where was she to find a voice with which to reply? And who was she to say what she was? Who, to this stranger, was she?

And if he opened the door, what then? All the thoughts and the words that had, like a wind, blown her down this tunnel, subsided suddenly, and she stood, appalled, at where they had brought her.

'Who iss that?' came the voice within, troubled.

Staring at those white feet, thrust into the unlaced shoes, she felt that she would die on the spot if they moved an inch. She turned.

Ahead of her, bright, shining and clear, as if it were at the end of a powerful telescope, was the street. Not caring if her feet were heard, volleying and echoing as if she ran through a mighty drain-pipe, she kept running till she reached the street, kept running even then, jostling surprised shoppers, hitting her ankles off the wheel-knobs of push-cars and prams. Only when she came to the junction of the streets again, did she stop, as in the pub mirror she caught sight again of her familiar face. That face steadied her. How absurd to think that anyone would sinisterly follow this middle-aged woman?

But suppose he had been in the outer room when she knocked. What if he had opened the door? What would have happened then? What would she have said? A flush spread over her face. The only true words that she could have uttered were those that sunk into her mind in the café, put there by Maudie.

'I'm lonely.' That was all she could have said. 'I'm lonely. Are you?'

A deep shame came over her with this admission and, guiltily, she began to walk quickly onward again, towards Grafton Street. If anyone had seen her, there in that dark alleyway! If anyone could have looked into her mind, her heart!

And yet, was it so unnatural? Was it so hard to understand? So unforgivable?

As she passed the open door of the Carmelite Church she paused. Could she rid herself of her feeling of shame in the dark of the confessional? To the sin-accustomed ears of the wise old fathers her story would be light-weight, a tedious tale of scrupulosity. Was there no one, no one who'd understand?

She had reached Grafton Street once more, and stepped into its crowded thoroughfare. It was only a few minutes since she left it, but in the street the evasion of light had begun. Only the bustle of people, and the activity of traffic, made it seem that it was yet day. Away at the top of the Green into which she turned, although the tops of the trees were still clear, branch for branch, in the last of the light, mist muted the outline of the bushes. If one were to put a hand between the railings now, it would be with a slight shock that the fingers would feel the little branches, like fine bones, under the feathers of mist. And in their secret nests small birds were making faint avowals in the last of the day. It was the time at which she used to meet Richard.

Oh Richard! she cried, out loud, as she walked along by the railings to where the car was parked. Oh Richard, it's you I want.

And as she cried out, her mind presented him to her, as she so often saw him, coming towards her tall, handsome, and with his curious air of apartness from those around him. He had his hat in his hand, down by his side, as on a summer day he might trail a hand in water from the side of a boat. She wanted to preserve that picture of him forever in an image, and only as she struggled to hold on to it did she realise there was no urgency in the search. She had a sense of having all the time in the world to look and look and look at him. That was the very way he used to come to meet her – indolently trailing the old felt hat, glad to be done with the day; and when they got nearer to each other she used to take such joy in his unsmiling face, with its happiness integral to it in all its features. It was the first time in the two years since he'd been gone from her that she had been able to envisage him.

Not till she had taken out the key of the car, and gone straight around to the driver's side, not stupidly, as so often, to the passenger seat, not till then did she realise what she had achieved. Yet she had no more than got back her rights. No more. It was not a subject for amazement. By what means exactly had she got them back though in that little café? That was the wonder.

A Story with a Pattern

The table was getting blistered with wet blue rings as glasses
were laid down carelessly. The ashtrays were overflowing with
fine white ash that blew softly over the slippery mahogany every
time a breath of air came in through the wide-open windows,
which, as a matter of fact, was not very often, for the afternoon
was still, and the room was hot and crowded.

The first noise of the party had died down, and here and
there groups of people with common interests had sorted
themselves out from the crowd, and stood together, talking in
low tones.

Coming towards me across the room, was my hostess, and the
middle-aged man that she guided by the elbow was staring at
me boldly.

'Here is someone who is anxious to meet you!' said my
hostess, and then being called from the other end of the room,
she pressed my arm, and made an excuse, and hurried away
without any attempt to make me acquainted with the man who
evidently had some slight acquaintance with me already.

I could only look at him, and wait for him to speak.

'How do you do!' he said, and he put out his hand, and shook
mine heartily. 'I'm glad to meet you! I've read a number of your
stories, and I want to tell you what I think of them. You've got
talent! Did you know that? You ought to take up writing. Take
it up seriously, I mean! Give your time to it!' He paused.
'There's a lot of money to be made out of writing. Did you know
that?' Then he lowered his voice. 'It's not everyone that can
write, you know. It's not everyone has the time! It's not
everyone has the education!'

And there and then, my new acquaintance gave me his opinions on books and writers in general. He had a high opinion of both, but although he had read a great many of the former he had never until this moment met one of the latter.

And while he talked I tried to sum him up. He was evidently one of those men in whom an eagerness for knowledge had developed only when it was too late for schooling to supply it; when he had entered upon some occupation or trade which had cut him off irrevocably from all chance of remedying his deficiencies. At times, however, he had a surprisingly adequate vocabulary, employed correctly and aptly, but this was probably acquired second-hand by listening to others.

Before the man had uttered three words I had seen that he was poorly educated, but before he had uttered a dozen I saw that it was a great loss to himself – and indeed to others – that this had been so, because his mind was eager and quick, and curious in the best sense of the word. The affair was irremediable now, however. He had all the faults one would expect. He was dogmatic where he should have been humble, forthright where he should have been delicate, and above all he confidently gave as original, opinions that were unfortunately original only to himself, having been evolved by him in slow processes of thought, but which were commonplaces to people who knew how to avail themselves of the world's depository of knowledge. Men such as he waste great quantities of mental energy working out simple problems that have long ago been solved by others, and they waste precious time as well, so that middle-age often finds them, after years of inquiry and application, in a state of mental immaturity at which a clever schoolboy might be able to laugh with justice. But there is this to be said for them also: old age, when it comes, finds them still eager, still vehement, still consuming their own energy, and death they regard as but another problem to be tackled, and to that problem they can also bring an open mind, unhampered by the stale opinions, the false findings, and the unsuccessful probings of others.

His opinion might be worth hearing after all.

'Which of the stories did you like best?' I asked.

He looked at me. 'I beg your pardon,' he said, 'did I say I liked them? I thought they were written with a good style, and I thought you brought the people in them to life, but I don't think that I remember saying that I liked them.'

Now this, you will admit, was disconcerting.

'Yes,' said my friend. 'Your stories have a great many good qualities, but I wouldn't exactly say that I liked any of them.' As he repeated this he looked at me with his head a little to one side as if he would be better able to judge my reaction to his words by holding himself that way. And then, evidently discerning that I had been somewhat taken back, he put out his hands, one to either side of me, and pressed me together as you'd press a concertina. 'Don't be offended,' he said. 'Remember that I know nothing at all about the subject. You might be right; for all I know. All I can do is give you my opinion; that is to say, tell you what I think. And what I think, if I might venture to put it bluntly, is that your stories in their present form, good as they are, will never appeal to a man. They may appeal to women. But they'll never appeal to men. A man would only read a page or two of your work, and then he'd throw it aside. Because,' he paused, 'because a man wants something with a bit of substance to it, if you know what I mean? A man wants something a bit more thick, if you understand.'

And carefully pinching off a piece of the smoke-laden air around us, he held it between his forefinger and thumb to show me just how thick men liked their reading matter.

'Now your stories,' he said, 'are very thin. They have hardly any plot at all.'

'But don't you think . . . ?' I said, beginning to explain a point, but he brushed my unfinished sentence away, together with a bothersome blue-bottle that had come our way at that moment.

'And the endings,' he said. 'Your endings are very bad. They're not endings at all. Your stories just break off in the middle! Why is that, might I ask?'

I'm afraid that I smiled superciliously.

'Life itself has very little plot,' I said. 'Life itself has a habit of breaking off in the middle.' I knew I was not being very explicit, but after all, his criticism had been casual enough! Perhaps I had become annoyed.

He, however, remained very affable, and he took up my argument blandly.

'But don't you see?' he exclaimed. 'It is just because life seems vague and disorderly, because it seems purposeless and chaotic, that people turn for distraction to books! We turn to books because in them we hope to find that the author, with a keener eye than ours, has been able to make a selection from the multiplicity of incidents that crowd upon us, and present them in a manner that will show that there is after all some relation between cause and effect.' He drew a deep breath. 'Only for books I would, long ago, have fallen into despair myself! But instead of that I read for a solid hour every night, before I put out the light. And so,' here he slackened the grip which he had retained upon my arms, and spread his hands out wide to either side of me, like great flat, protective wings, 'and so although I may not know much about writing, I can give you a plain man's opinion about your work. And mind you I may be able to give you some useful information!' He stopped for a moment. 'By the way,' he said quickly, 'would you mind telling me – I'm not asking out of curiosity mind you, and there's no impertinence meant – but I'd like to know if you make much money out of your stories?'

'Well,' I began slowly, in order to gain time, and find a suitable answer for the question. 'Well, you see . . .' I began.

But he cut me short again. 'I see nothing,' he said, abruptly. 'Don't tell me that you're not interested in whether your work sells or not, because that's only nonsense, if you'll excuse my saying so! Only a fool would say a thing like that. If you said that to a jackass he'd kick you, if you'll pardon the expression. Why do you write stories if you don't care whether they're read or not? And how can people read them if they don't buy them? Be reasonable about the matter! Admit that you'd like your stories to sell. And, as I said before, if you take my advice, they might!'

'What is your advice?' I said at last, testily enough it must be admitted.

'My advice is to give your stories more shape, to give them more plot; to give them more pattern, as it were!'

'That would be distorting the truth!' I said, and I was about to explain further.

'Why do you say that?' he cried, interrupting me. 'There may be times when life seems formless, and when our actions seem to be totally unrelated to each other, but for that again there are thousands of times when incidents in life not only show a pattern, but a pattern as clear and well-marked as the pattern on this carpet!'

He glanced down and my eyes followed his, to stare at the brilliant and constantly recurring medallions of the soft pile under our feet.

'I don't believe you could tell me one incident out of all the thousands!' I said.

'Will you put me to the test?' said he.

'If there is time,' I said, looking around, but no one appeared to have any sign of going.

'There's plenty of time. Let me see now . . .' And he paused.

'You can't think of one!' I cried.

'Can't I?' said he. 'If I'm having any trouble at all it's trying to choose one out of all the incidents that are crowding my mind into a state of confusion.' Still he paused for another space, and I was going to laugh at him when he looked up and cleared his throat.

'I'll tell you what I'll do,' said he. 'I'll tell you one of my father's stories, to save me having to make a choice among my own.'

'Your father read it in some old book, I suppose?'

'Oh, no, he didn't. I'm not going to cheat. This is a real, true story, and I often heard my father tell it. It's about a man that lived in the same town as him, long ago. They went to the same school, and they played together too, on wet days and the like, not indeed that Murty Lockhart was able to play very much. But that's all part of the story. Will I go on with it?'

I said that I wanted very much to hear the story, but I think my main reason for encouraging him to go on was that I wanted to hear how he would tell it. For, since the time he first came

over to me with such a sophisticated manner, a change had
taken place in both his manner and his voice, and even in his
very vocabulary. With his first words about Murty Lockhart the
emphasis he had been laying on every second word
disappeared altogether and he became instead, unsure, halting
and inclined to look at me questioningly in between every
sentence. And when he was speaking a short time, I noticed
with interest that it was not his voice at all I was listening to, but
the voice of his father who had told the story to him. His
memory had stored not only the incidents of that story but the
very words in which it had been told, and the very voice of the
man who first strung them together. It was the voice of an aged
and credulous man telling an incredible story with a kind of
fright at its seeming purport. And as he told the story the very
name of Murty Lockhart seemed to fill him with awe for he
always uttered it in a lower voice than the rest of the sentence.

'When Murty Lockhart used to come to the parlour window
of his house and look up and down the street from it, the people
of the town who happened to be passing by at the time would
say to each other, "Will you look at that devil up there thinking
out some new badness," or "Hell isn't bad enough for that
fellow – Look at him piercing out at us with his eyes!"

'What they really meant, of course, was that three shillings
was more than enough rent for his ugly, jerry-built houses,
much less the ten or eleven shillings they'd be paying him.
Murty owned pretty near all the town. I suppose, too, that he
often heard what was said about himself and his houses,
because you know, don't you, the way voices in the street float
in through the windows in a country town, not like in a city
where they are beaten down by the noises of the trams and
buses. Oh, yes, he heard all that was said about him, never fear,
but he took no offence, or, if he did, he never let on to it. He
probably knew as well as everybody else that what is said out
loud is better than what is said in a whisper, and that all that is
said is seldom meant in any case. Let that be as it may, anyhow,
but I may as well tell you that he himself was the very one that
seldom or never said what he meant. It was either the bitter
word covering up the soft thought or the soft word covering up

the bitter thought. No one ever knew how to take him, or where they were with him, after he grew up. But my father used to say that as a child you couldn't find a sweeter disposition than Murty's in the length and breadth of the country, not if you were looking for a month of Sundays. But when he grew up he got sort of soured and even those that played with him oftenest in his own back garden were turned against him by his manner; all but my father, that is to say. But there again, my father never pitied him like the rest did, not even when he was a little nipper sitting by the window watching the other children racing up and down outside. My father didn't pity him. It would be more correct to say he was kind of scared of him. Well, maybe not scared, but a bit in awe of him, if you like. And what's more, he never lost that feeling he had about him through all the years afterwards, even when Murty got so well off that the pity of the town was turned into envy. Yes, indeed, the pity of the town turned into envy all right as time went on, because, as the people got older, they put less store on flashing limbs and red faces and began to think that when Murty owned half the town he wasn't in need of much pity, no matter what way his legs were!

'By the way, I forgot – did I? – to tell you that poor Murty had club feet?

'Yes, I forgot to tell you that. Wasn't that stupid of me, now? That's the most important part of the whole story, or pretty near!

'Yes, indeed, poor Murty had club feet from birth. That was why, you see, he couldn't knock around like the other young hooligans in the town. That was the reason why they had to come into his back garden if they wanted to play with him. Even then they had to take good care it was something quiet and easy they played, like catchers or conkers. They couldn't even give high catchers. If they did, or if there was the least sign of roughness, Murty's mother would pull aside the lace curtains and tap on the glass. It wasn't much fun playing with him, as you can imagine, specially for kids that were just after hearing news of the Boer War that was on at the time, and were leaping inside their boots to be off playing Zulus or having skirmishes in the lanes. But kids are good at heart, as you've noticed no doubt, for all their contrariness at times, and they often and often gave up their games to come and play with little Murty. And dare any new kid say anything about his feet; or about anybody's feet for that matter – you know how touchy kids are – or there would be another kid ready to shut him up, double quick, or clip him under the jaw if need be! They were always ready to champion the poor kid. That was another reason afterwards why they found it difficult to understand how Murty could be so hard on them when they were all grown up – he and them, just because he had the upper hand on account of a bit of money. You see, his father left him a bit when he died; a bit more than Murty or anyone else expected. I suppose he felt the poor fellow needed more than most, on account of his feet. Anyway, Murty got the money and he didn't waste time in putting it to use. And he put it to such good use it wasn't long till he put himself above everyone in the whole town. I often thought when my father would be telling me about him that maybe he never liked having the kids championing him the way they used. Maybe he resented it. Maybe he didn't, though. I don't know. Nobody knows.'

At his point the story-teller stopped suddenly and looked at me.

'I suppose,' he said, 'that's where you'd end the story if you were telling it; with Murty not knowing why he was bitter against the town and the town not knowing either? But that's not where my story ends. That's not even the middle of it. Wait till you hear!'

He leaned back against the wall and continued.

'I always think it was curious, don't you, the way my father never felt any pity for him? He used to say that Murty's sort of yellow-coloured eyes used to fascinate him. He used to say, too, that he didn't think his feet were so terrible either, if it came to that. What was there to be gained after all, he used to say, by running the streets like lunatics the way the other kids and himself used to do? My father would have preferred reading to running any day. He always had his nose stuck in a book, or a Fourpenny Illustrated. It used to get on his own father's nerves to see him at it. His father and mother were always shooshing him out like a hen out of the house. So you can see, can't you, that my father would look on Murty as a privileged person in many many ways since he could sit all day reading a book and nobody would say, aye, yes or no to him.

'Murty used to sit at the window, sometimes reading, sometimes scribbling, and sometimes only sitting, and my father used to be a bit envious of him when he'd sweat past with a piece of rope between his teeth pretending he was a prairie horse, in some game or other he couldn't get out of, that the other kids were after planning. Later on when they were all a bit older it was more or less the same thing in a different way. Murty would be sitting at the window and my father would be rushing off to the ball-alley, that the parish priest had built for the young men, outside the town, and he used to look up and wave at Murty as much as to say "Well for you." If he had a second at all he used to turn to the door to say hello to him and look over Murty's shoulder at the book in his hand while he was promising to come in for a while on the way back if he got a chance. And then, as he ran down the street, and out onto the road, his mind would be filled with the pictures he had glimpsed in Murty's book; pictures of stars and planets, and comets, and flaming meteors.

'My father always had a great curiosity about the sky and the stars and such-like things. In his day there wasn't as much known as there is now about astronomy, and what was known was not to be found out, either, I may tell you, by buying a Sixpenny Paper cover. No, indeed, if you wanted to find out anything about anything at all in those days you had to read through a queer lot of print, in a queer lot of books; books that cost a nice penny, too, and were hard enough to come by even at that. Nowadays you can find out almost anything from a few pages in the middle of the Sunday paper. But not so then. I often wish he had lived long enough to see how easy it is to know everything there is to be known, because he was a man with a great respect for knowledge. Do you know, I think that he prized it higher than any other one thing. So you can see –

can't you? – how he sort of envied Murty, club feet and all, and
had a sort of awe of him as they both got older.

'Do you know? I've just thought of something I never hit on
before in all the times I turned over this thing in my mind. I
bet you anything you like, my father thought that Murty would
discover something or other about the Other World! Could
that ever have been the idea at the back of his mind, do you
suppose? Because, now that I come to think of it, I often heard
him saying that if a man thought for long enough, without his
ever opening a book at all, he ought to be able to tell at the end
of a long time whether there was a God or not! Maybe he
thought Murty might get some strange knowledge by all his
brooding and thinking. And maybe he thought that, if he did,
he would let him share the secret. Do you suppose he could
have had that in his head? Whether he had or not anyway he
wasn't as horrified as the rest of the town when he heard what
happened to Murty, because he always felt that Murty was
creeping up closer and closer on the mysteries of the world,
every hour he sat by the window, with his curious yellow eyes
fixed on the rim of the sky, or what there was to be seen of it
between the church opposite and the corner of the
schoolhouse roof. But, of course, he didn't expect for an
instant the thing would have the terrible turn it had, nor that
anyone else would be dragged into it but Murty himself. He
certainly would not have thought the one to be dragged into it
would be Ursula Merrick, such a quiet, serious girl with smooth
yellow hair and deep blue eyes. If it had even been a dark-haired
girl; but there was nothing dark about Ursula at all. She looked
brighter than most people, and happier, too, although, true
enough, her happiness seemed deeper and slower-moving than
other people's. Poor girl! May the Lord have mercy on her soul!
She died a year after she married Murty.'

He stopped. 'Am I telling this very badly?' he said, looking at
me uncertainly. 'Wasn't I a bloody fool to try telling a story to
a professional story-teller?'

'Remember my bad endings,' I said.

'Oh, not bad,' he said, 'just weak. Anyhow, it isn't the way it's
told that matters in this story, it's the story itself. All you have

to know is what happened, and it doesn't matter much how you hear it. I only want to show you that things are not always as vague and pointless in life as you would have us believe in your stories. Will I go on?'

'Do, of course.'

'I was telling you about the way Ursula Merrick got drawn into the thing, wasn't I? Well, I should have told you first that Murty grew up to be so clever that when his father died and left him a few hundred pounds he wasn't a half-year older before he had doubled the sum by buying an old ramshackle hovel across the street, and building it up into a fine new shop and letting it out to a butcher, or maybe it was a baker, I forget which, that came to the town from Kinnegad. It was put up cheap, but it had a fine showy front to it, and the stand couldn't be bettered, on the main Dublin road, and the fellow that rented it was ready and willing to give Murty whatever money he asked for it! He asked enough to justify him in buying another tumbledown place further down the same street and tearing it down too and putting up another fine-fronted shop. He let the second one to a chemist.

'He did all this speculating, I may tell you, without as much as going outside the door of his own house. He figured it all out on paper and set a few men on the job. By the time the second shop was built people were beginning to look with less pity at him when he sat at the window-pane inside. And by the time he owned a block of houses, three more shops and, as well as that, a farm outside the town, as he did in a short number of years, there was hardly one remembered he had club feet at all. Murty himself, indeed, seemed to have pretty near forgotten it too, judging by the way he began to go out and about, to this place and that, leaning on his stick as lightly as if he carried it for swank. He was looked up to by everyone everywhere he went, although this was as much from fear as from respect, because by this time he had a finger in everyone's business and, if he didn't own the house a man lived in, he owned the ground under it, or had some hold on the place. You can see, therefore, that although they were a bit surprised they weren't altogether astonished when they saw he was paying attentions to Ursula

Merrick. In fact, you know how it is in those country towns – they had got so used to him by this time and, considering his money, and the way he was looked up to and that, most people thought that the girl was doing well for herself. And the night they heard she was going to marry him they never gave a thought to his feet at all and went around telling each other what a stroke of luck it was for the girl. Maybe an odd young person here and there gave a kind of shudder, but that was all, and, getting used to the idea, they thought she had feathered her nest well, and that she would have the laugh at the other girls, who had married young shop-boys and mechanics without a penny to their name, when she'd be driving round in her motor car and giving meat-teas to everyone that came to visit.

'But when Ursula and Murty were married a few months and there were no signs of the motor car, and no signs of the meat-teas, and no signs in any other direction either of the fact that she was any better off than before, the talk began. First one old woman and then another began to say he was mean to her like he was to everyone else, and that she was looking back on her bargain, and that she had no right to marry a man like him, anyway. Any bit of scandal that came into their heads was out on their tongues a minute after. The rumours flew round to such an extent there was a regular swarm of them flying after her every time she put her foot outside the door. And would you believe it, the town turned against her in no time and people began to say she got her deserts for marrying a poor cripple just to get the use of his bit of money! They never thought for a moment she married him for any other reason, and I don't suppose it would have mattered what they thought, the poisonous old rips, if Murty himself didn't begin to wonder at his luck in getting her, when he came home every night and looked across the table at her: at her lovely face and her lovely yellow hair lit up with the candlelight. She must have been very good-looking, by all accounts, and the finest and fittest and best set-up man in the county might have wondered at his luck in winning her, much less a poor creature like himself with blunted feet and his shoes having to be made specially for him over in London!

'Murty began to think there must have been a string to his bargain somewhere and he no sooner thought this than he was dead set on finding it, and cutting it if he could. It was funny the way he first got suspicious; funny, I mean, the way a little thing can drag down such a lot on top of us if we don't leave it alone. Murty began to get suspicious when Ursula wouldn't order a fur coat for herself and wouldn't hear tell of getting a motor car. He noticed, too, that she put very little store on the trinkets and fancies he brought home to her if he had occasion to go to another town for a few hours. Even the servants in the house used to remark on the way she left them lying about, as if she put no more value on them than if they were junk. When he gave them to her she used to smile, they said, and thank him very much, but as likely as not she'd walk out of the room a minute or two after, and leave them lying about where anyone that had a mind to it could pocket them and walk off! She gave the impression, if you know what I mean, of not caring whether they were stolen or not; good things too, you know, brooches and little fur capes and bits of china. Murty used only laugh at first and tell the servants to put them away in a safe place till she missed them some day. But seldom or ever Ursula thought of them again. And after a while Murty got uneasy.

'You see, Murty, like everybody else, thought that Ursula had married him for his money, and that the more of it he let her see, the happier she'd be, and the less she'd be likely to feel bad when he couldn't go careering round with her to dances and evening parties, the way he imagined other young married couples did. The first day ever he saw her he set his heart on having her, and by that time, being accustomed to buying anything he fancied, he thought that he could buy her too. He was pretty badly in love with her, and although as he was getting to know her, I imagine, he must have had an odd doubt whether he'd get her as easy as he thought, nevertheless when she did agree to marry him it never crossed his mind it was for any other reason but because of his money.

'Now the strange part of the thing is that Murty would have seen nothing at all objectionable in her marrying him for his money. He was as proud as the devil with everyone, but he was as humble as could be with Ursula. He thought he could never buy her enough to keep her from regretting her decision. But when he saw she would rather go off walking in the rain than ride in a car, and that she'd rather wear a bit of velvet ribbon round her neck than a string of beads, he began to worry. So you see it was when he began to doubt that it was with his money he had got her, that the real trouble started, the very opposite of what the old back-biters in the town were thinking, as is often the way. Murty began to ponder over the whole thing and he tried hard to find another reason why she should have married him, and apart from money or love there aren't many reasons, you'll agree. She hadn't married him for his money, she made that plain enough, and he never, at any time, let himself think that the girl could have had any love for him. It was too bad he hadn't the least trace of conceit in him. If he had, things might have taken a different turn. If he had he might have found out in time what he learned too late, that Ursula Merrick, strangely enough, was in love with him before she married him, and not only that but that she became what you might call pitiably in love with him after her marriage. I say pitiably because she was one of those people whose feelings are deep and troublesome to them and they dare not show them to others. And I'd say pitiably in any case in the light of what happened in the end.

'Only for what happened, I suppose, I wouldn't be telling you the story at all, because I never yet heard a happy love story that was worth the breath used in telling it. It's only when all else around is dark and bitter that a glorious blaze of love like hers is shown up against the darkness. Yet I often thought when my father would be telling me about them, that it was a terrible pity Murty hadn't held a candle up to the big mirror over the fireplace, and taken a good look at his face one night without minding the rest of him. If he did he might have seen that years of studying and thinking had given his face a strong and stern kind of a look that made him as near to being handsome as he could well go without being so by nature. If he did he might have been able to put himself in Ursula's place for a minute and see some reason why she chose to spend her life face to face with him, if I might put it that way. Indeed, without going

to that length at all he might have found time to remember
that a girl like Ursula would have noble reasons, whatever they
might be, for everything she did. But he didn't think. He just
accepted other people's opinions about his marriage, which
just goes to show that even a man that has spent his whole life
in the pursuit of wisdom can fall as far from it as any fool, if he
fails for a minute to think for himself and lets lesser people do
his thinking for him. And if he had to have the opinion of
others, and the best of us can't resist it at times, it was more
than a pity he didn't look for it from my father, because I believe
my father would have seen quicker than any man alive, and told
him quicker, too, that Ursula Merrick was in love with her
husband just as I told you she was, and that she wouldn't have
married him if she wasn't.

'I told you before, didn't I, that my father was always kind of
fascinated by Murty? Well, I suppose you might say my father
was half in love with him himself, let alone Ursula, because love
is a strange thing, although you can't talk as broadly about it
now as you could once, because people think they are so well
up now that they feel they must snigger and sneer and put two
meanings on every word you say. But I think I'd be right in
putting it like that, talking to you, and say without fear of being
taken up wrong, that my father was a sort of in love with Murty
all his life. He would have been the very person then, I think,
to have made Murty see how fond his wife was of him, and how
happy she was ever and always to be in his company without any
greater entertainment in the way of drives or visitors.

'She used to sit, my father often remarked, as quiet as a mouse
whenever there was company, outside the arc of the firelight
with her head bent over a piece of sewing and only her white
hands showing clearly in the smaller arc of the lamp on the
table beside her. Murty often had my father and a few others
in to talk and argue, and sometimes one of them would read
out a passage aloud from some special book or other he had
got hold of in the city. Ursula would be silent all evening, and
my father thought for a long time that she was weaving her own
thoughts with a needle as silent as the steel one in her hand,
unheedful of what they were saying, but one night he noticed

that she left the door ajar when she went into the dining-room to set decanters on a tray and spread some biscuits out in a fan on a plate, as a small refreshment for the men. And once or twice he saw her come to the jamb of the door and stand there for a minute, and he knew then that she was listening all the time and probably grudging the space of floor she had to cross on her way for the refreshments, because it took her away from the conversation and left her likely to lose the continuity of what was being said.

'Now it's a hard thing for us in this age to realise how strange it must have been for women in my father's time, if they happened to be exceptionally intelligent and did not succeed in smothering their intellectual curiosity in the worries of domestic affairs. An odd one of them here and there, I know, cut through their obstacles and wrote books and poems, and travelled impudently around like men, but they were the rare ones, and if the truth were told they may have been more men than women in any case. But the quiet ones, the ones that were like Ursula, the ones with minds more receptive than creative, they were really and truly to be pitied. They probably went through life with a hunger for knowledge that even the richest harvest of personal experience was not enough to satisfy. When you think out in a wide stretch like that to either side of the story of Ursula and Murty you see at once, what nobody saw at the time, that it was a wonderful thing for her to meet a man like Murty, and to marry him, and live always within the radius of his wisdom and knowledge and within the magic circle of his talk, day and night. For Ursula was one of those women with rich accumulating sort of minds that stored up strange things they heard from time to time and wove them into her own life slowly, and after a long time had passed. Do you know that kind of woman? Perhaps if herself and Murty had been given another few years and she had gained confidence and courage to talk freely to him, he might have realised the bonds that bound her to him. But although she was one of those intelligent women who are almost a trouble to themselves they're so intelligent, she had no education beyond a general one such as is got in a country convent school, and even that benefited her little, because she probably found her own thoughts more interesting than anything that was chalked up on the blackboard. She looked into her own mind for the answers to all her questioning, and relied on her sensitive nerves more than she relied on the words of the rosy-faced nuns. But, since the greatest thinkers of all times have oftentimes had access to no deeper source of knowledge than hers, it is very possible that she could have talked better to Murty about life and death and the mysteries of man than any of the friends he invited in for that purpose; the parish priest, the doctor and, an odd time, my father, although my father, like Ursula, was only an amateur of philosophy, and one that listened more than he spoke.

'My father listened more than he spoke for the same reason that Ursula listened and never spoke; neither of them could have put their thoughts into ordered sentences and both could have been put on the dunce's stool by a single technical term. But they sometimes talked to each other, you see, and my father got to know how deep she was, deeper even than Murty he sometimes felt, as he listened to her untidy talk and saw the depth of her eyes. He used to watch her, too, in the church. He used to watch her stealthily from a dark end of the pew and he knew by her face she was not praying but forcing her mind to travel deeper and deeper into places of mystery and ignorance. Her eyes would be open wide like eyes that were dead.

'Now! you know now the kind of girl she was, you can see, can't you, how wonderful it was for her to sit and listen to Murty and his friends talking about things she'd never hear other women talk about – and all the time she sat silent under the lamp, sewing a piece of cloth, and not saying a word. You can imagine how she must have felt at night lying beside him in the dark and knowing that his mind was not banging aimless as a bat against the windows and walls of their house and the things of everyday, but that it was flying out with her own over dark unislanded seas of thought. Anyone with an eye in his head, my father used to say, afterwards, would have known by looking at her that she wouldn't be happy with the most robust and handsomest man in the country unless his mind was as edgy as Murty's, and that, by the same way of looking at things, she would always and ever have been as happy with Murty as she was for a short while, even if he was paralysed as well as crippled! But it wasn't till after it was too late that this was realised, and then the only kindness that could be done to him was not to mention her name, for fear Murty would hear it and fly into a fury of grief at the sound of it.

'It was a wonder he didn't do himself harm in one of those fits of grief. People were always nervous when they saw him going around alone, and the servants were almost too scared to sleep in the house with him. But my father said that when he didn't kill himself the night the child was born, it wasn't likely he'd do it after. My father knew he'd never kill himself. My father, you must remember, looked on all that happened as the strange working of mysterious powers, and he felt that Murty Lockhart only began to live on that terrible night, even though his new life was dearly bought. My father felt that on that night Murty passed into the knowledge of the mysterious workings of God, that he was all his youth seeking, and that Ursula too, poor girl, was timidly trying to probe. Of course my father was a staunch believer, and that accounts for the turn he gave to the whole thing when he was telling it. You might put a different interpretation on it, and call it a strange coincidence, but in either case you'll have to admit there was a pattern in the events, and that the beginning worked around to the end in as perfect a circle as ever anyone saw.

'No matter what way you look on the thing, however,' said my companion taking out a blue silk handkerchief and wiping his face with it, 'it's a good story. But I wish you could have heard my father tell it. I've told it badly enough up to now, but I'm afraid I'll make a proper mess of the end of it, although that's the most extraordinary part of it entirely. Well, anyway, to go on with it –

'Once Murty got suspicious he lost all balance and let his mind narrow in on itself until he had only one thought, and that was the thought that Ursula had married him for some reason he didn't yet know; and of course in a certain manner of speaking that was true too, but it was not from any deception or crookedness that that reason was kept from him, but from a mixture of dignity and modesty. It was from such reasons of modesty too that she was so slow about telling him that they were going to have a child. She didn't tell him until she was carrying it for several months. Perhaps she wanted to shorten the time of waiting for him by keeping it a secret as long as ever she could. Who knows! Anyway, the tragedy was to be, it seems, and she didn't tell him in time. While she was laying up her secret joy for him he was hoarding and storing distrust of her in his heart. Then one day some old rip in the town made herself busy enough and good enough to offer Murty a bit of friendly advice on how he should treat his wife while she was in that condition. Those were the very words the old devil used, and Murty didn't know what she was talking about, not being a man given over much to talking with women. You can imagine him asking her "what condition?" and then pulling himself up short and remembering that there was only one significance put on most long words by women of that old one's type. You can imagine him realising what was meant by her talk and realising too the laughing-stock he'd be all over the town when she went off and told the news that he didn't know his own wife was going to have a child. At this part of the story you'd pity him all right, but by the time he got home he was in a terrible rage. It was more than queer she didn't tell him, he thought. So it was – we all are agreed on that – but she wasn't an ordinary girl and you can't have it both ways. He went straight into the house and took one look at her and went out again. She must have thought it odd, but she was too preoccupied with her plans and thoughts to think long of anything those days. The servants thought nothing at all of it at the time, but afterwards it was the first thing that leaped to their minds. The day it happened they were too busy to think, because they were getting the attic ready. The attic was never used, but it had fine wide rooms with far views out from it, and neither noise nor dust seemed able to climb as high as it. She was going to open it up as a room for the child. They were getting it ready on the quiet, because they were in the know and it was to be nearly as big a surprise to Murty as the news of who was to use it! The day she decided to tell him was the day they were putting the finishing touches to the rooms. She just decided that a suitable time had arrived and she left down a duster she had in her hand and went downstairs and told him at about ten o'clock in the morning before he went out on his day's work inspecting his properties. She was so excited she probably didn't notice how quietly he took the news and how quickly he went out afterwards. In fact, she didn't have time to tell him about the attic, he went out so abruptly, but she thought nothing of it, he was always a bit abrupt, and so she decided she'd tell him later in the day and she went upstairs again and she went on with the directing of where to put this, and where to put that, and she was happy as a thrush. Indeed, the servants were remarking on how happy she looked a minute before Murty's step was heard outside the front door and the way her face lit up when she said: "Here's my husband, back again. Now we'll tell him about the way we're fixing up the attic." The two servant women were are happy as herself, because it was expected that Murty would take his hand out of his pocket for more than to bless himself when the day came. Certainly there wasn't one of them had the least suspicion of the dreadful tortured thought that had found its way into his mind. It was so vicious, so tortured, so misbegotten a thought, and most of all so unwarranted, that it would make you think after all that there might be something in the old people's saying that there's a twisted mind in a twisted body. The thought Murty had in his mind was so wrongful that I don't believe even you, listening to me here, could have any idea of what it was, and you'll be just as surprised as the servants and Ursula herself, poor girl, when he came out with it, standing at the foot of the banisters, looking up at the three women where they stood half-way up the stairs, their arms filled with blankets and pillows. Ursula was clutching the banisters they say, and staring at him as if a devil had looked out at her through his eyes. It was all so sudden. They were going up to the top of the house to put the last touches to the rooms and the older of the two maids, who was in the family long before Ursula came into it, was eyeing her like a mother as if she doubted the wisdom of her climbing up three flights of stairs. Just as they were on the third step they heard Murty coming up to the hall-door outside and turning the key in the lock. Ursula stopped and waited till he came in and then she called down to him gaily and asked him to come upstairs she had something to show him. He made some excuse and gave her a dark look. She started to tease him very prettily and to coax him to change her mind, but he went on down the hall and didn't even turn round to answer her. The colour that hadn't been in her cheeks for several months came back with a violent flutter.

' "You don't have to come," she called down to him, "If you're not interested in the rooms that are being got ready for our own child!"

'She probably expected him to be softened out of whatever caprice of anger he was in. Who knows what she expected, but everyone knows a pure girl like her didn't expect what she got, anyway. He turned around with a snarl that held all the months' bitterness.

' "How do I know it's my child?" he shouted.

'They were all deafened and blinded and stupefied at his words. He stared at them and they staring back at him like ghostly people from the valleys of death. Then he shouted out all his suspicions in a storm of words, as if by their stinging spate he could bring back the fluttering blood to their faces again. And it wasn't until Ursula fell down on the step of the stairs where she stood that he stopped the mad words that were pouring out of his mouth.

'They got her to bed and the doctor came and no one as much as thought of Murty during the next forty-eight hours when her untimely labour was on her. He went over to my father, who lived across the road, and told him the whole story; told him how he loved Ursula so much it got to be a torture to him to think how unworthy he was of her. It wasn't until after he was married to her he said that the real torture of loving her came on him. Before they were married he only wanted her for her body but afterwards he wanted her thoughts and – his voice sank – her love. He told my father he knew she was in love with someone, because she used to keep saying over little words of gentleness in her sleep such as no one heard from her during the day. Then, when he heard she was going to have a child and when she didn't run to tell him, he began to think that he had found the reason why a healthy girl like her had married a cripple-foot like him. Even to my father Murty was ashamed to put his meaning any plainer, but my father knew what he meant. He watched her, Murty said, and he knew by the passionate look on her face that she was carrying the child of the lover she talked with in her sleep.

'And then, as Murty spoke it all came clearly to my father, as things sometimes do, that Ursula was in love with Murty and Murty didn't know it even yet. All that night they sat downstairs in my father's house watching up at the lights that were burning high in Murty's house. There were dim red rays in some rooms from the colza oil lamps that were lit before statues. There were bright pink lights from paraffin lamps whose wicks were turned up to their highest. And sometimes a light was seen to travel from window to window as a lamp was hurriedly caught up and carried from one place to another. Sometimes a lamp was snatched up hastily and carried downstairs so quickly that the shadows it struck from banister to banister fell on the window-panes like bitter blows of a stick. And the hurrying lights told a tale of worry and dread to the watchers across the street.

'All that night my father tried to make Murty see that his wife had married him because she loved him, and that she probably loved him even more after she was married, but his words had to pierce through too much doubt and misery, and so when morning paled the window-panes across the street and left only a hard gilt core of lamplight where there had been a glaze of gold, Murty was still saying over and over again that he wanted to believe all my father said, but that he would have to have proof. It was the same old obstinacy he used to show in the arguments they had had many a night in the past.

' "This is another thing, Murty," said my father, "where there can be no proof. You must have faith."

' "Faith is a poor substitute for proof," said Murty with a glitter of despair in his eyes.

'My father went out and left him sitting by the grey powdered grate while he went out to find out how Ursula was, and he thought as he went, of how queer Murty was, even as a child, sitting between his mother's lace curtains, his eyes boring the distance, eyes that had seemed to him even then, as if they would pierce the mysteries of darkness. But, when he came back across the street a few minutes later he did not want to see those eyes, as he told Murty that Ursula was dead!'

The story-teller stopped and as I was overcome with such a feeling of horror at the turn the story had taken, I did not realise that it was not finished until his voice went on once more, lower and more uncertain.

'You see,' he said, 'my father was scared to look him in the face in case Murty'd see he was keeping something back from him; the news that was spreading poisonously over the whole town, that Ursula Lockhart had died giving birth to a stillborn child – whose feel were clubbed.'

We were both silent then, he from the strain of the story, I from the chill that had swept across me from the ending words of it. Then he spoke.

'Write out that story some time,' he said self-consciously. 'That's the kind of story to write!'

'But I can't write that! How can I?' I said. 'That's your story.'

'A story on the tongue is nobody's story,' he said.

'Write it down yourself then!' I said.

'I'm not a writer,' he said, and I must admit he said it indignantly.

'If I was, I'd miss hearing half of what goes on in the world, like you do,' said he. 'If you're wise you'll do as I say and write that out and get it printed. If you do, people will begin to think something of your work instead of throwing it into the waste-basket.'

'But afterwards? I'll have to go back again to my old methods.'

'Why?'

'Because I won't always be able to find stories like this to tell. This was only one incident. Life in general isn't rounded off like that at the edges; out into neat shapes. Life is chaotic; its events are unrelated; its . . .'

'There you go again!'

'But surely even now, you will admit . . .' I said, beginning to enter the discussion again, but this time my friend the story-teller glanced at me in a most peculiar way; you might almost say with dislike.

'Please don't start that nonsense again,' he said, and he casually walked away.

The Widow's Son

This is the story of a widow's son, but it is a story that has two endings.

Once there was a widow, living in a small neglected village at the foot of a steep hill. She had only one son, but he was the meaning of her life. She lived for his sake. She wore herself out working for him. Every day she made sacrifices in order to keep him at school in the town, four miles away, because there was a better teacher there than the village dullard by whom she herself had been taught.

She made great plans for Packy, but she did not tell him about her plans. Instead she threatened him, day and night, that if he didn't turn out well, she would put him to work on the roads, or in the quarry on the other side of the hill.

But as the years went by, everyone in the village, and even Packy himself, could tell by the way she watched him out of sight in the morning, and watched to see him come into sight in the evening, that he was the beat of her heart, and that her gruff words were only a cover for her pride and her joy in him.

It was for Packy's sake that she walked for hours along the road, letting her cow graze the long acre of the wayside grass, in order to spare the few poor blades that pushed up through the stones in her own field. It was for his sake she walked back and forth to the town to sell a few cabbages as soon as ever they were fit. It was for his sake that she got up in the cold dawning hours to gather mushrooms that would replace other foods that had to be bought with money. She bent her back daily to make every penny she could, and as often happens, she made more by industry, out of her few bald acres, than many of the farmers around her made out of their great bearded meadows. By selling eggs alone, she paid for Packy's clothes and for the greater number of his books.

When Packy was fourteen, he was in the last class in the school, and the master had great hopes of his winning a scholarship to a city college. He was getting to be a tall lad, and his features were beginning to take a strong cast. The people of the village were beginning to give him the same respect they gave to the farmers' sons who came home from their fine colleges in the summer, with blue suits and bright ties. And whenever they spoke to the widow they praised him up to the heavens.

One day in June, when the air was so heavy the scent that rose up from the grass was imprisoned under the low clouds and hung in the air, the widow was waiting at the gate for Packy. There had been no rain for some days and the hens and chickens were pecking irritably at the dry ground and wandering up and down the road in bewilderment.

A neighbour passed.

'Waiting for Packy?' said he, pleasantly, and he stood for a minute to take off his hat and wipe the sweat of the day from his face. He was an old man.

'It's a hot day!' he said. 'It will be a hard push for Packy on that battered old bike of his. I wouldn't like to have to face into four miles on it on a day like this!'

'Packy would travel three times that distance,' said the widow, 'if there was a book at the other end,' with the pride of those who cannot read more than a line without wearying.

The minutes went by slowly. The widow kept looking up at the sun.

'I suppose the heat is better than the rain!' she said, at last.

Absentmindedly, as he pulled a long blade of grass from between the stones of the wall and began to chew the end of it, the neighbour said, 'You could get sunstroke on a day like this!' He looked up at the sun. 'The sun is a terror,' he said.

The widow strained out farther over the gate. She looked up the hill in the direction of the town.

'He will have a good cool breeze on his face coming down the hill, at any rate,' she said.

The man looked up the hill. 'That's true. The hottest day of summer you would get a cool breeze coming down that hill on a bicycle. You would feel the air streaming past your cheeks like silk. And in the winter it's like two knives flashing to either side of you, and it could peel off your skin like you'd peel the bark off a sally-rod.' He chewed the grass meditatively. 'That must be one of the steepest hills in Ireland. That hill is a hill worthy of the name of a hill.' He took the grass out of his mouth. 'It's my belief,' he said, earnestly looking at the widow, 'it's my belief that that hill is to be found marked with a name in the Ordnance Survey map!'

'If that's the case,' said the widow, 'Packy will be able to tell you all about it. When it isn't a book he has in his hand it's a map.'

'Is that so?' said the man. 'That's interesting. A map is a great thing. A map is not an ordinary thing. It isn't everyone can make out a map.'

The widow wasn't listening.

'Here he is. I see Packy!' she said, and she opened the wooden gate and stepped out into the roadway.

At the top of the hill there was a glitter of spokes as the bicycle came into sight. Then there was a flash of blue jersey as Packy came flying downward, gripping the handlebars of the bike, his bright hair blown back from his forehead. The hill was so steep, and he came down so fast, that it seemed to the man and woman at the bottom of the hill that he was not moving at all, but that it was the trees and bushes, the bright ditches and wayside grasses, that were streaming away to either side of him.

The hens and chickens clucked and squawked and ran along the road looking for safe places in the ditch. Packy waved to his mother. He came nearer and nearer. They could see the freckles on his face.

'Shoo!' he cried, at the squawking hens that had not yet left the roadway, but ran with their long necks straining forward.

'Shoo!' Packy's mother lifted her apron and flapped it in the air to frighten the hens out of Packy's way.

It was only afterwards, when the harm was done, that the widow began to think that it might, perhaps, have been the flapping of her own apron that frightened the old clucking hen, and sent her flapping out over the wall into the middle of the road.

The old hen appeared so suddenly above the grassy ditch and looked with a distraught eye at the hens and chickens as they ran to right and left. Her own feathers began to stand out from her. She craned her neck forward and gave a distracted squawk, and fluttered down into the middle of the hot dusty road.

Packy jammed on the brakes. The widow screamed. There was a flurry of white feathers and a spurt of blood. The bicycle swerved and fell. Packy was thrown over the handlebars.

It was such a simple accident that, although the widow screamed, and although the old man looked around to see if there was help near, neither of them thought Packy was badly hurt, but when they ran over and lifted his head, and saw that he could not speak, they wiped the blood from his face and looked at each other desperately, to measure the distance they would have to carry him.

It was only a few yards to the door of the cottage, but Packy was dead before they got him across the threshold.

'It's only a knock on the head,' screamed the widow, and she urged the crowd that had gathered outside the door to do something for him. 'Get the doctor!' she said, pushing a young labourer towards the door. 'Hurry! Hurry! The doctor will bring him around.'

But the neighbours that kept coming in the door from all sides were crossing themselves, one after another, and falling on their knees, as soon as they laid eyes on the boy, stretched out flat on the bed, with the dust and dirt and the sweat marks of life on his dead face.

When at last the widow was convinced that her son was dead, the women had to hold her down. She waved her arms and wrestled to get free. She wanted to wring the neck of every hen in the yard.

'I'll kill every one of them. What good are they to me, now? All the hens in the world aren't worth one drop of human blood. That old clucking hen wasn't worth more than six shillings. What is six shillings? Is it worth poor Packy's life?'

But after a time she stopped raving, and looked from one face to another.

'Why didn't he ride over the old hen?' she asked. 'Why did he try to save an old hen that wasn't worth more than six shillings? Didn't he know he was worth more to his mother than an old hen that would be going into the pot one of these days? Why did he do it? Why did he put on the brakes going down one of the worst hills in the country? Why? Why?'

The neighbours patted her arm.

'There now!' they said. 'There now!' That was all they could think of saying, so they said it over and over again. 'There now! There now!'

And years afterwards, whenever the widow spoke of her son to the neighbours who dropped in to keep her company for an hour or two, she always had the same question to ask, the same tireless question. 'Why did he put the price of an old clucking hen above the price of his own life?'

And the people always gave the same answer.

'There now! There now!' they said. And after that they sat as silently as the widow herself, looking into the fire.

But surely some of those neighbours must have been stirred to wonder what would have happened had Packy ridden boldly over the clucking hen? And surely some of them must have pictured the scene of the accident again, altering a detail here and there as they did so, and giving the story a different end. For these people knew the widow and they knew Packy, and when you know people well it is as easy to guess what they would say and do in certain circumstances as to remember what they actually did say and do in other circumstances.

So perhaps if I tell you what I think might have happened had Packy killed that cackling old hen, you will not accuse me of abusing my privileges as a writer. Knowing the whole art of storytelling without taking notes, I lean no heavier now on your credulity than I did by telling you what happened in the first instance.

In fact, it is sometimes easier to invent than to remember accurately, and were this not so, the art of the storyteller and the art of the gossip would wither in an instant.

The story begins in the same way. There is the widow, grazing
her cow by the wayside, and walking the long road to the town,
weighed down with a sack of cabbages to help pay for Packy's
schooling. There she is, fussing over Packy in the mornings in
case he would be late for class. There she is in the afternoon
watching the battered clock on the dresser for the hour when
he will appear on the top of the hill at his return. And there,
too, on a hot day in June, is the old labouring man coming up
the road, and pausing to talk to her as she stood at the door.
There he is dragging a blade of grass from between the stones
of the wall, and putting it between his teeth, he chews on it
before he starts to talk.

'Waiting for Packy?' the old man says, and then he takes off
his hat and wipes the sweat from his forehead. 'It's a hot day.'

'It's very hot,' said the widow, looking anxiously up the hill.
'It's a hot day to push a bicycle for miles along a bad road with
the dust rising to choke you, and the sun striking sparks off the
handlebars!'

'The heat is better than the rain, all the same.'

'I suppose it is,' said the widow. 'All the same, there were days
Packy came home with the rain dried into his clothes like
starch, they stood up stiff.'

'Is that so?' said the old man.

'Yes, when he took off his clothes they stood stiff like boards
against the wall, for all the world as if he were still standing in
them.'

'You may be sure he got a good spoiling in those days. There
is no son like a widow's son. A ewe lamb!'

'Is it Packy?' The widow turned away in disgust. 'Packy never
got a day's petting since the day he was born. I made up my
mind from the first, that I'd never make a softie out of him.'

The widow looked up the hill again, and set herself to raking
the gravel outside the gate as if she was out on the road for no
other purpose. Then she gave another look up the hill.

'Here he is now!' she said, and she rose such a cloud of dust
with the rake they could hardly see the glitter of the bicycle
spokes, or the flash of his blue jersey as Packy came down the
hill at breakneck speed.

Nearer and nearer he came, faster and faster, waving his hand to the widow, shouting at the hens to leave the way.

The hens ran for the ditches, stretching their necks in gawky terror. And as the last hen squawked into the ditch the way was clear for a moment before the whirling silver spokes. Then, unexpectedly, up from nowhere it seemed, came an old hen who, clucking despairingly, stood for a moment on the top of the wall and then rose into the air with the clumsy flight of a ground fowl.

Packy stopped whistling. The widow screamed. A shower of grit skidded as the wheel braked. Packy swerved the bicycle to bring it to a halt on the hill.

For a minute it could not be seen what exactly had happened, but Packy put his foot down and dragged it along the ground in the dust. Then he threw the bicycle down with a clatter on the hard road and ran back. The widow could not bear to look. She threw her apron over her head.

'He's killed the clucking hen,' she said. 'He's killed it. He's killed it.' She let her apron fall back into place, and ran up the hill. The old man spat out the blade of grass that he had been chewing and ran after the woman.

'Did you kill the hen?' screamed the widow, and as she got near enough to see the blood and feathers she raised her arm over her head, and her fist was clenched till the knuckles shone white. Packy cowered down over the carcass of the speckled fowl and hunched up his shoulders as if to shield himself from a blow. His legs were spattered with blood, and brown speckled feathers were stuck to his hands, and to his clothes, and strewn all over the road. Some of the light white inner feathers were still swirling with the dust in the air.

'I couldn't help it, Mother. I couldn't help it. I didn't see her till it was too late!'

The widow caught up the hen and examined it all over, holding it by the breast bone and letting the long neck dangle. Then, catching it by the leg, she swung it and brought down its bleeding body on the boy's back, in blow after blow, spattering blood all over his face and over his clothes and all over the white dust of the road.

'How dare you lie to me!' she screamed, gaspingly, between the blows. 'You saw that hen. I know you saw it. You stopped whistling. You called out. We were watching you. We saw.' She turned to the old man. 'Isn't that right?' she demanded. 'He saw the hen, didn't he? He saw it?'

'It looked that way,' said the old man, uncertainly, his eye on the dangling fowl in the widow's hand.

'There you are!' The widow threw the hen down on the road. 'You saw the hen in front of you, as plain as you see it now,' she accused, 'but you wouldn't stop to save it because you were in too big a hurry home to fill your belly! Isn't that so?'

'No, Mother. No! I saw her all right, but it was too late to do anything.'

'He admits now that he saw it!' The widow turned and nodded triumphantly at the onlookers who had gathered at the sound of the shouting.

'I never denied seeing it!' said the boy, appealing to the onlookers as to his judges.

'He doesn't deny it!' screamed the widow. 'He stands there as brazen as you like, and admits for all the world to hear that he saw the hen as plain as the nose on his face, and he rode over it without a thought!'

'But what else could I do?' said the boy, throwing out his hand, appealing to the crowd now, and now appealing to the widow. 'If I'd put on the brakes going down the hill at such a speed I would have been put over the handlebars!'

'And what harm would that have done you?' said the widow. 'I often saw you taking a toss when you were wrestling with Jimmy Mack and I heard no complaints afterwards although your elbows and knees would be running blood and your face ridged like a cattlegrid.' She turned to the crowd. 'That's as true as God. I often saw him come in with his nose spouting blood like a pump, and one eye closed as tight as the eye of a corpse. My hand was often stiff for a week from sopping out wet cloths to put poultices on him and try to bring his face back to rights again.' She swung back to Packy. 'You're not afraid of a fall when you go climbing trees, are you? You're not afraid to go up on the roof after a cat, are you? Oh, there's more in this than you want me to know. I can see that. You killed that hen on purpose, that's what I believe! You're tired of going to school. You want to get out of going away to college. That's it! You think if you kill the few poor hens we have there will be no money in the box when the time comes to pay for books and classes. That's it!' Packy began to redden.

'It's late in the day for me to be thinking of things like that,' he said. 'It's long ago I should have started those tricks if that was the way I felt. But it's not true. I want to go to college. The reason I was coming down the hill so fast was to tell you that I got the scholarship. The teacher told me as I was leaving the schoolhouse. That's why I was pedalling so hard. That's why I was whistling. That's why I was waving my hand. Didn't you see me waving my hand once I came in sight at the top of the hill?'

The widow's hands fell to her sides. The wind of words died down within her and left her flat and limp. She didn't know what to say. She could feel the neighbours staring at her. She wished that they were gone away about their business. She wanted to throw out her arms to the boy, to drag him against her heart and hug him like a small child. But she thought of how the crowd would look at each other and nod and snigger. A ewe lamb! She didn't want to satisfy them. If she gave in to her feelings now they would know how much she had been counting on his getting the scholarship. She wouldn't please them! She wouldn't satisfy them!

She looked at Packy, and when she saw him standing there before her, spattered with the furious feathers and crude blood of the dead hen, she felt a fierce disappointment for the boy's own disappointment, and a fierce resentment against him for killing the hen on this day of all days, and spoiling the great news of his success.

Her mind was in confusion. She stared at the blood on his face, and all at once it seemed as if the spilt blood was a bad omen of the future that was his. Disappointment, fear, resentment, and above all defiance, raised themselves within her like screeching animals. She looked from Packy to the onlookers.

'Scholarship! Scholarship!' she sneered, putting as much derision as she could into her voice and expression.

'I suppose you think you are a great fellow now? I suppose you think you are independent now? I suppose you think you can go off with yourself now, and look down on your poor slave of a mother who scraped and sweated for you with her cabbages and her hens? I suppose you think to yourself that it doesn't matter now whether the hens are alive or dead? Is that the way? Well, let me tell you this! You're not as independent as you think. The scholarship may pay for your books and your teacher's fees but who will pay for your clothes? Ah-ha, you forgot that, didn't you?' She put her hands on her hips. Packy hung his head. He no longer appealed to the gawking neighbours. They might have been able to save him from blows but he knew enough about life to know that no one could save him from shame.

The widow's heart burned at the sight of his shamed face, as her heart burned with grief. But her temper, too, burned fiercer and fiercer, and she came to a point at which nothing could quell the blaze till it had burned itself out. 'Who'll buy your suits?' she yelled. 'Who'll buy your boots?' She paused to think of more humiliating accusations. 'Who'll buy your breeches?' She paused again and her teeth bit against each other. What would wound deepest? What shame could she drag upon him? 'Who'll buy your nightshirts or will you sleep in your skin?'

The neighbours laughed at that, and the tension was broken. The widow herself laughed. She held her sides and laughed, and as she laughed everything seemed to take on a newer and simpler significance. Things were not as bad as they seemed a moment before. She wanted Packy to laugh too. She looked at him, but as she looked at Packy her heart turned cold with a strange new fear.

'Get into the house!' she said, giving him a push ahead of her. She wanted him safe under her own roof. She wanted to get him away from the gaping neighbours. She hated them, man, woman and child. She felt that if they had not been there things would have been different. And she wanted to get away from the sight of the blood on the road. She wanted to mash a few potatoes and make a bit of potato cake for Packy. That would comfort him. He loved that.

Packy hardly touched the food. And even after he had washed and scrubbed himself there were stains of blood turning up in the most unexpected places; behind his ears, under his fingernails, inside the cuff of his sleeve.

'Put on your good clothes,' said the widow, making a great effort to be gentle, but her manners had become as twisted and as hard as the branches of the trees across the road from her, and the kindly offers she made sounded harsh. The boy sat on the chair in a slumped position that kept her nerves on edge, and set up a further conflict of irritation and love in her heart. She hated to see him slumping there in the chair, not asking to go outside the door, but still she was uneasy whenever he as much as looked in the direction of the door. She felt safe while he was under the roof, under the lintel, under her eyes.

Next day she went in to wake him for school, but his room was empty, his bed had not been slept in, and when she ran out into the yard and called him everywhere, there was no answer. She ran up and down. She called at the houses of the neighbours but he was not in any house. And she thought she could hear sniggering behind her in each house that she left, as she ran to another one. He wasn't in the village. He wasn't in the town. The master of the school said that she should let the police have a description of him. He said he never met a boy as sensitive as Packy. A boy like that took strange notions into his head from time to time.

There was no news of Packy that night. A few days later there was a letter saying that he was well. He asked his mother to notify the master that he would not be coming back, so that some other boy could claim the scholarship. He said that he would send the price of the hen as soon as he made some money.

Another letter in a few weeks said that he had got a job on a trawler and that he would not be able to write very often but that he would put aside some of his pay every week and send it to his mother whenever he got into port. He said that he wanted to pay her back for all she had done for him. He gave no address. He kept his promise about the money but he never gave any address when he wrote.

And so the people may have let their thoughts run on, as they sat by the fire with the widow, many a night, listening to her complaining voice saying the same thing over and over. 'Why did he put the price of an old hen above the price of his own life?' And it is possible that their version of the story has a certain element of truth about it too. Perhaps a great many of our actions have this double quality about them, this possibility of alternative, and that it is only by careful watching, and absolute sincerity, that we follow the path that is destined for us, and, no matter how tragic that may be, it is better than the tragedy we bring upon ourselves.

The Will

'I couldn't say what I thought while he was here,' said Kate, the eldest of the family, closing the door after the solicitor, who had just read their mother's will to the Conroy family. She ran over to her younger sister and threw out her hands. 'I cannot tell you how shocked I am, Lally. We had no idea that she felt as bitter against you as all that. Had we?' She turned and appealed to the other members of the family who stood around the large red mahogany table, in their stiff black mourning clothes.

'I always knew she felt bitter,' said Matthew, the eldest of the sons. 'We couldn't mention your name without raising a row.'

'She knocked over the lamp, once,' said Nonny, the youngest of the unmarried members. 'In her last years she always kept a stick beside her on the counterpane of the bed, and she tapped with it on the floor when she wanted anything. But one day someone said something about you, I forget what it was, she caught up the stick and began to bang the bed rail with all her force. The next thing we knew the lamp reeled off the table. The house would have been burned down about our ears if the lamp hadn't quenched with the draught of falling through the air.'

'Still, even after that, we never thought that she'd leave your name out of the parchment altogether. Did we?' Kate corroborated her every remark by an appeal to the rest of the family group. 'We thought she'd leave you something anyway, no matter how small.'

'But I don't mind,' said Lally. 'Honestly I don't. I wish you didn't feel so bad about it, all of you.' She looked around from one to the other beseechingly.

'Why wouldn't we feel bad?' said Matthew. 'You're our own sister after all. She was your mother as well as ours, no matter what happened.'

'The only thing I regret,' said Lally, 'was that I didn't get here before she died.' The tears started into her eyes.

'I don't think it would have made any difference whether you got here in time or not. The will was made years ago.'

'Oh I didn't mean anything like that,' said Lally in dismay, and a red blush struggled through the thickened cells of her skin. 'I only meant to say that I'd like to have seen her, no matter what, before she went.' The tears streamed down her face then. They ran freely because she made no attempt to dry them, her mind being far away, thinking of the days long ago before she left home at all. But the tears upset the others, who felt no inclination to cry. Having watched the old lady fade away in a long lingering illness, they had used up their emotional energy in anticipating grief. Their minds were filled now with practical arrangements.

'Don't upset yourself, Lally,' said Kate. 'Perhaps it all turned out for the best. If she had seen you she might only have flown into one of her rages and died sitting up in the bed from a rush of blood to the forehead, instead of the nice natural death that she did get, lying stretched out with her hands folded better than any undertaker could have folded them. Everything happened for the best.'

'I suppose she mentioned my name, did she? Near the end I mean.'

'No, the last time she spoke about you was so long ago I couldn't rightly say now when it was. It may have been one night that I went up to tidy her room. I was doing out her cupboards and looking through the chest of drawers. She wasn't paying attention, but was staring into space, until I plumped up her pillows and settled her down in bed. Suddenly she turned towards me as if I had interrupted her dream, and asked me how old you were now. It gave me such a start to hear her

mention your name after all those years that I couldn't
remember what age you were, so I just said the first thing that
came into my head.'

'What did she say?'

'She said nothing for a while, and then she began to ramble
about something under her breath. I couldn't catch the words.
She used to wander a bit in her mind, now and again, especially
if she had lost her sleep the previous night.'

'Why do you think it was me she was talking about under her
breath?' beseeched Lally. Her eyes seemed to beg for an answer
in the affirmative.

'Oh, I don't know what she was rambling about,' said Kate.
'I had my mind fixed on getting the bed straightened out so
she could lie back at ease. I wasn't listening to what she was
saying. All I can remember is her mentioning blue feathers.
Blue feathers, I ask you. Her mind must have gone astray for
the moment, I suppose.'

At this, tears gushed in Lally's eyes again.

'I had two little blue feathers in my hat the morning I went
into her room to tell her I was getting married. I had nothing
new to wear but my old green silk costume, and my old green
hat, but I bought two little pale blue feathers and pinned them
on the front of the hat. I think the feathers upset her more than
going against her wishes. She kept staring at them all the time
I was in the room, and even when she ordered me to get out of
her sight it was at the feathers in my hat she was staring and not
at me.'

'Don't cry, Lally.' Kate felt uncomfortable. 'Don't cry. That
was long ago. Don't be going back to the past. What is to be, is
to be. I always believe that.'

Matthew and Nonny believed that too. They too told her not
to cry. They said no good could be done by upsetting herself.

'Not that I ever regretted it,' said Lally. 'We had a hard time
at the beginning, but I never regretted it.'

Kate moved over and began to straighten the red plush
curtains as if they had been the sole object of the change in her
position, but the movement had brought her close to her
brother, Matthew, where he stood fingering his chin

uncertainly. She gave him a sharp nudge. 'Say what I told you,' she urged him, speaking rapidly in a low voice.

Matthew cleared his throat. 'You have no need for regret as far as we are concerned, Lally,' he said, and he looked at Kate who nodded her head for him to continue. 'We didn't share our poor mother's feelings. Of course we couldn't help thinking that you could have done better for yourself but it's all past mending now, and we want you to know that we will do all in our power for you.' He looked again at his sister Kate who nodded her head more vigorously to indicate that he had left the most important thing unsaid. 'We won't see you in want,' said Matthew.

When this much had been said, Kate felt that her brother's authority had been deferred to sufficiently, and she took over the conversation again. 'We won't let it be said by anyone that we'd see you in want, Lally. We talked it all over. We are going to make an arrangement.' Once more she looked at Matthew with a glance that seemed to toss the conversation to him as one might toss a ball.

'We were thinking,' said Matthew, 'that if each one of us was to part with a small sum, put together the total would come to a considerable amount.'

But Lally put up her hands again.

'Oh no, no, no,' she said. 'I wouldn't want anything that didn't come to me by rights.'

'It would only be a small sum from each person's share but put together it could be a tidy amount,' said Nonny placatingly. 'None of us would feel any pinch.'

'No, no, no,' Lally repeated. 'I couldn't let you do that. It would be going against her wishes.'

'It's late in the day you let the thought of going against her wishes trouble you,' said Kate with an involuntary flash of impatience for which she hurried to atone by the next remark. 'Why wouldn't you take it? You are as much entitled to your cut as any of us.'

'You might put it like that, anyhow,' said Matthew, 'as long as we're not speaking legally.'

'No, no, no,' said Lally for the third time. 'Don't you see? I'd hate taking it and knowing all the time that she didn't intend me to have it. And anyway, you have to think of yourselves.' She looked at Kate. 'You have your children to educate. And Matthew, you have the house to keep up. As for you Nonny, you have no one to look after you at all. I won't take a penny from any of you.'

'What about your own children?' Kate asked. 'Are you forgetting them?'

'Oh, they're all right,' said Lally. 'Things are different in the city. In the city there are plenty of free schools. And I'm doing very well. Every room in the house is full.'

There was silence after that for a few minutes, but glances passed between Kate and Nonny. Kate went over to the fire and picked up the poker. She knelt down and drove it in among the blazing coals, rattling them with such unusual violence that Matthew looked at her. 'Do you have to be prompted?' Kate snapped when she'd got his attention.

Matthew cleared his throat, and again Lally looked at him expectantly. 'There is another factor to be considered. We were talking about it before you arrived,' he said, speaking quickly and nervously. 'It would be in the best interests of the family if you were to give up keeping lodgers.' He gave her a covert glance to see how she took what he said.

While Matthew was speaking Kate had remained kneeling by the fireplace with the poker in her hand. When he stopped she made a move to rise but her stiff new mourning skirt got in her way. And so instead of rising very quickly she listed forward with the jerky movement of a camel. It couldn't be certain whether Lally was laughing at Matthew's words, or at the camelish appearance of Kate, who immediately took offence.

'I don't see what there is to laugh at, Lally,' she said. 'It's not a very nice thing for us to feel that our sister is a common landlady. Mother never forgave that. She may in time have forgiven your bad marriage, but she could never have forgiven you for lowering yourself by keeping a lodging house.'

'We had to live somehow,' said Lally, but she spoke lightly, and as she spoke she was picking off the green-flies from a plant on the table.

'I can't say I blame Mother,' said Nonny, breaking into the discussion with a sudden venom. 'I don't see why you were so anxious to marry the man when it meant keeping lodgers.'

'It was the other way round, Nonny,' said Lally quickly. 'I was willing to keep lodgers because it meant I could marry him.'

'Easy now!' said Matthew. 'There's no need for us to quarrel. We must talk this thing over calmly. We'll come to some arrangement. There's no gain in doing everything the one day. Tomorrow is as good as today, and better. Lally must be tired after travelling all the way down here, and having to attend the funeral without five minutes' rest. We'll talk it all over in the daytime tomorrow.'

Lally looked back and forth from one face to another as if she was picking the face that looked most lenient before she spoke again. At last she turned back to Matthew.

'I won't be here in the morning,' she said hurriedly, as if it was a matter of no consequence. 'I have to go back tonight. I only came down for the burial. I can't stay any longer.'

'Why not?' demanded Kate, and then as if she knew the answer to the question and did not want to hear it, she stamped her foot. 'You've got to stay,' she said. 'That's all there is to say about the matter.'

'There is nothing to be gained by my staying, anyway,' said Lally. 'I wouldn't take the money, no matter what you said, tonight or tomorrow.'

Matthew looked at his other sisters. They nodded encouragingly.

'There's nothing to be gained by being obstinate, Lally,' he said lamely.

'You may think you are behaving unselfishly,' said Kate, 'but let me tell you it's not a nice thing for my children to feel that their first cousins are going to free schools in the city, mixing with the lowest of the low, and running messages for your seedy lodgers. And as if that isn't bad enough, I suppose you'll be putting them behind the counter in some greengrocer's, one of these days.'

Lally said nothing.

'If you kept a small hotel, it wouldn't seem so bad,' said Matthew looking up suddenly with an animation that betrayed the fact that he was speaking for the first time upon his own initiative. 'If you kept an hotel we could make it a limited company. We could all take shares. We could recommend it to the right kind of people. We could stay there ourselves whenever we were in the city.' His excitement grew with every word he uttered. He turned from Lally to Kate. 'That's not a bad idea. Is it?' He turned back to Lally again. 'You'll have to stay the night, now,' he said, enthusiastically, showing that he at least had not believed before that she would comply with their wishes.

'I can't stay,' said Lally faintly.

'Of course you can.' Matthew dismissed her difficulties without hearing them. 'You'll have to stay,' he said. 'Your room is ready. Isn't it?'

'It's all ready,' said Nonny. 'I told them to light a fire in it and to put a hot jar in the bed.' As an afterthought she explained further. 'We were going to fix up a room for you here, but with all the fuss we didn't have time to attend to it. We're putting you in the Station Hotel. We sent word that they were to fix up their nicest room. They have it all ready. I ran down to see it. It's a big airy room with a nice big bed. It has two windows, and it looks out on the ball-alley. You'll be more comfortable there than here. Of course, I could put a stretcher into my room if you liked, but I think for your own sake you ought to leave things as I arranged them. You'll get a better night's rest. If you sleep here it may only remind you of things you'd rather forget.'

'I'm very grateful to you, Nonny, for all the trouble you took. I'm grateful to all of you. But I can't stay.'

'Why?' Kate voiced the look on every face.

'I have things to attend to!'

'What things?'

'Different things. You wouldn't understand.'

'They can wait.'

'No,' said Lally. 'I must go. There is a woman coming tonight to the room on the second landing, and I'll have to be there to help her settle in her furniture.'

'Have you got her address?' said Matthew.

'Why?' said Lally.

'You could send her a telegram cancelling the arrangement.'

'Oh, but that would leave her in a hobble,' said Lally.

'What do you care? You'll never see her again. When we start the hotel you'll be getting a different class of person altogether.'

'I'll never start an hotel,' said Lally. 'I won't make any change now. I'd hate to be making a lot of money and Robert gone where he couldn't profit by it. It's too late now. I'm too old now.'

She looked down at her thin hands, with broken fingernails, and a fine web of lines deepened by dirt. And as she did so the others all looked at her. They looked at this sister that was younger than all the others, and a chill descended on them as they read their own decay in hers. They had been better preserved, that was all. Hardship had hastened the disintegration of Lally's looks. Although the bending of the bone, and the tightening of the skin, and the fading of the eye could not be guarded against, there was an unaccountable youthfulness about her. A chill fell on them. A grudge against her gnawed at them.

'I begin to see,' said Matthew, 'that Mother was right. I begin to see what she meant when she said that you were obstinate as a tree.'

'Did she say that?' said Lally, and her face lit up for a moment, as her mind was filled by a wilful vision of tall trees, leafy, and glossy with sunlight, against a sky as blue as the feathers in a young girl's hat.

Nonny stood up impatiently. 'What is the use of talking?' she said. 'No one can do anything for an obstinate person. She must be left to go her own way. But no one can say we didn't do our best.'

'I'm very grateful,' said Lally again.

'Oh, keep your thanks to yourself!' said Nonny. 'As Matthew explained, we weren't doing it for your sake. We wanted to put a stop to people coming from the city and telling us that they met you, and we knowing the ragged old clothes you were likely to be wearing, your hair all tats and taws, and your face dirty maybe, if all was told.'

'Tell me Lally, do you ever look at yourself in a mirror?' said Matthew. 'I don't mind admitting I was ashamed to be seen next to you at the graveside.'

'What came over you, that you let your teeth go *so* far?' Nonny asked.

Then through the curtains the signal lights on the railway line could be seen changing from red to green. Through the silent evening air there came a faraway sound of a train shunting. Even when the elderly maidservant came in with the heavy brass lamp the green railway light shone through the pane, insistent as a thought.

'What time is it?' said Lally.

'You have plenty of time,' said Matthew. 'That was only a goods train. Your train isn't due for two hours. His words marked the general acceptance of the fact that she was going, but tea was hurried in on a tray. A messenger was sent running upstairs to see if Lally's gloves were on the bed in Kate's room.

'Where did you leave them?' someone kept asking every few minutes and going away in the confusion without a satisfactory answer.

'Do you want to have a wash?' Nonny asked. 'It will freshen you for the journey. There's a jug of water in my room.'

And once or twice, lowering his voice to a whisper, Matthew leaned across the table and asked her if she was absolutely certain that she was all right for the journey back. Had she a return ticket? Had she change for the porters?

Lally didn't need anything though, and when it came nearer to the time of her train, it appeared that she did not even want the car to take her to the station.

'But it's raining,' said Matthew.

'It's as dark as a pit outside,' said Kate.

And all of them, even the maidservant who was clearing away the tray, were agreed that it was bad enough for people to know she was going back the very night that her mother was lowered into the clay, without adding to the scandal by giving people a chance to say that her brother, Matthew, wouldn't drive her to the train in his car, and it pouring rain.

'They'll say we had a difference of opinion over the will,' said Nonny, who retained one characteristic at least of youth, its excessive sensitivity.

'What does it matter what they say?' said Lally, 'as long as we know it isn't true?'

'If everyone took that attitude it would be a queer world,' said Matthew.

'There's such a thing as keeping up appearances,' said Kate. 'By the way, is that coat of yours black or is it blue?' she asked suddenly, catching Lally by the arm and pulling her nearer to the lamp to examine the sleeve.

'It's almost black,' said Lally. 'It's a very dark blue. I didn't have time to get proper mourning, and the woman next door lent me this. She said you could hardly tell it from black.'

Nonny shrugged her shoulders and addressed herself to Matthew. 'She's too proud to accept things from her own, but she's not too proud to accept things from strangers.'

'I must go,' Lally said at last.

She shook hands with them all. She looked up the stairway, down which the coffin had been carried that morning. She put her hand on the door knob. While they were still trying to persuade her to let them take her in the car, she opened the door and ran down the street.

They heard her footsteps on the pavement in the dark, as they had heard them often when she was a young girl running up the town on a message from their mother. And just as in those days, when she threw a coat over her head, the sleeves dangling, she left the door wide open after her. Matthew hesitated for a minute, and then he closed the door.

'Why weren't you more insistent?' said Kate curtly.

'With people like Lally there is no use wasting your breath. They have their own ways of looking at things and nothing will change them. You might as well try to catch a falling leaf as try to find out what's at the back of Lally's mind.'

The three of them stood in the cold hallway. Suddenly Kate began to cry.

'What's the matter with you?' Nonny asked. 'You were great at the cemetery. You kept us all from breaking down. Why are you crying now.'

'I'm crying because of Lally,' said Kate. 'None of you remember her as well as I do. I made her a dress for her first dance. It was white muslin with blue bows all down the front. Her hair was like light.' Kate sobbed with thick hurtful sobs that shook her whole frame and shook Matthew's thin dried-up body when he put his arm around her.

When she got outside the front door, Lally ran along the dark street of the country town as she had run along years ago as a young girl. She had plenty of time before her train was due, but the excitement of running now was caused by a terrible throbbing of her heart. She hardly remembered to slow up and slacken to a walking pace when she came into the patches of yellow lamplight that flooded out from shop windows and from the open doors of houses near the Square. As a child it had been an excitement of the mind that had caused her to run, for then it had seemed to her that the small town was ringed around by a bright world that was lit by day and by night. And in that bright world around, one could not fail to find joy and hope, one only had to run on, through the old town gate, over the dark railway bridge, keep going along the twisty road and you would reach the heart of that excitement. Some day she would go beyond it.

And one day she went. But now there was no joy anywhere. Beyond the pools cast by the yellow glare of street lights, there was to be no lasting joy anywhere. Life was just the same, whichever way you looked at it, in the city, in the town and in the twisty countryside. It was probably the same in the fields and villages although she knew little of them. Life was the same in the darkness and in the light. It was the same for the spinster and for the bedraggled mother of a family. You were yourself always, no matter where you went or what you did. You didn't change. Her brothers and sisters were the same as they always were. She herself was the same as she always was, although her teeth were rotted, and a blue feather in her hat now would make her look like an old hag in a pantomime. You might think beforehand that something you'd do or somewhere you'd go would make a great change, but it wouldn't make any real change at all. There was only one thing that could change you, and that was death. And no one knew what that change would be like.

No one knew what death was like, but people made terrible torturing guesses. Fragments of the old penny catechism she had learned by rote in school came back to her, distorted by a faulty memory and confused emotions. Pictures of flames and screaming souls writhing on gridirons rose before her mind as she ran. She was nearly at the station when she stopped running, and turning rapidly around she ran back a few yards in the direction she had come. She groped along a dark wall that rose up to the side of the path at this point until the wet black railings of a gate came in contact with her fingers. This was the gate leading to the parochial house, the residence of the parish priest. She banged the gate back against the piers with the fierce determination with which she opened it. She ran up the wet gravelly drive to the priest's house.

In the dark she could not find the brass knocker and she beat against the panels of the door with her hands. The door was thrown open after a minute with a roughness that matched her knocking.

'What in the Name of God do you want?' asked an elderly woman, who was the priest's housekeeper, with an apron that blazed white in the darkness.

'I want to see the parish priest!' said Lally.

'He's at his dinner,' said the woman, pointing aggressively, and went to close the door.

'I must see him,' said Lally, and she stepped into the hallway.

'I can't disturb him at his meals,' said the woman, 'unless someone is dying,' she added. Her anger at the disturbance was being driven out by curiosity when she saw the other woman was a stranger. 'What name?' she asked.

'Lally Conroy,' said Lally, the old associations being so strong that her maiden name came more naturally to her lips than the name she had borne for twenty-four years.

The housekeeper went across the hall and opened a door on the left. She closed it after her, but the lock did not catch and the door slid open again. Lally heard the conversation distinctly, but with indifference, as she sat down on the polished mahogany chair in the hall. Because nothing was going to thwart her from her purpose.

'There's a woman outside who insists on seeing you, Father.'

'Who is she?' said the priest, his voice muffled, as if he was wiping a serviette across his mouth.

'She gave her name as Conroy,' said the woman, 'and she has a look of Matthew Conroy, but I never saw her before and she looks as poor as a pauper.'

'I did see a strange woman at the graveside with the family but I wasn't speaking to her.' The priest's voice was slow and meditative. 'I heard that there was another sister, but there was a sad story about her; I forget what it was exactly. I'll see her,' he said. The sound of a chair scraped the floor and soon his feet rang on the polished wood as he crossed the room towards the hall.

Lally was sitting on the stiff chair at the fire, shielding her face from the heat of the flames that dragged themselves like serpents along the logs in the fireplace, but she sprang up as the priest approached. He was going to see her. In her mind she heard the train whistle once more, it was still far off, but it was instilling its presence on the country evening.

Lally was insistent. 'I'm in a hurry, Father. I'm going away on this train. I'm sorry to have to disturb you. I only wanted to ask a favour.' Her voice was uncontrollable as the flames leaping in the grave. 'My name is Lally Conroy.'

'Sit down, sit down.' The priest took out a watch from under the cape of his soutane. 'You have six minutes yet,' he said.

'No, no, no,' said Lally, 'I mustn't miss the train. I wanted to know if you will say a Mass for my mother first thing in the morning. I'll send you the money for the offering the minute I get back to the city. I'll post it tonight, from the GPO, there's a collection at midnight. Will you do that, Father? Will you?' As if the interview was over she stood up and began to go backwards, moving to the door. Without waiting for an answer she repeated her urgent question. 'Will you? Will you do that, Father? First thing in the morning!'

The priest looked down at the shabby boots and the thick stockings. 'There's no need to worry about Masses being said. Your mother was a good woman,' he said. 'And I understand that she herself left a large sum in her will for Masses to be said for her after her death.'

'Oh, Father, it's not the same thing for people to leave money for Masses to be said for their own souls, it's the Masses that other people have said for them that count.' Lally's thoughts leapt ahead in her excitement. 'I want a Mass said for her with my money. I want three Masses said. But I want the first one to be said at once, the seven-thirty Mass. And it has to be said with my money. My money!' Lally emphasised.

The priest leaned forward with an ungovernable curiosity.

'Why must it be your money?'

'I'm afraid,' said Lally, 'I'm afraid she might suffer. I'm afraid for her soul.' The eyes that stared into the flaming heart of the fire were indeed filled with fear, and as a coal fell, revealing a gaping abyss of flaming fire, her eyes filled with absolute horror at the heaving reflection of her idea in the red flames of the fire. 'She was very bitter.' Lally Conroy broke down for the first time since she had news of her mother's death. 'She was very bitter against me for twenty or thirty years, and she died without forgiving me. I'm afraid for her soul.' She looked up at the priest. 'You'll say them as soon as ever you can, Father?'

'I'll say them,' said the priest. 'But don't worry about the money. I'll offer them from myself.'

'That's not what I want,' Lally cried hastily. 'I want them to be paid for with my money. That is what will count most, that they are paid for out of my money.'

Humbly the priest accepted the dictates of the bedraggled woman in front of him.

'I will do as you wish,' he said. 'Is there anything else troubling you?'

'The train! The train!' Lally cried, and she fumbled with the catch of the door.

The priest took out his watch again.

'You'll just have time to catch it,' he said, 'if you hurry.' And he opened the door. Lally ran out into the dark street again.

For a moment she felt peace at the thought of what she had done, and running down the wet gravelly drive with the cold rain beating on her flushed face, she was able to occupy her mind with practical thoughts about the journey home. But when she got into the hot and stuffy carriage of the train, the tears began to stream down her face again, and she began to wonder if she had made herself clear to the priest. She put her head out of the carriage window as the train began to leave the platform and she called out to a porter who stood with a green flag in his hand.

'What time does this train arrive in the city?' she asked, but the porter could not hear her. He put his hand to his ear but just then the train rushed into the darkness under the railway bridge. Lally let the window up and sat back in the seat.

If the train got in after midnight, she would ring the night bell at the Franciscan Friary and ask for a Mass to be said there and then for her mother's soul. She had heard that Masses were said night and day in the friary. She tried to remember where she had heard that, and who had told her, but her mind was in great disorder. She leaned her head back against the cushions as the train roared into the night, and she feverishly began to add up the prices that were due to her from the tenants in the top rooms. She then subtracted from the total the amount that would be needed to buy food for the children for the week. She would have exactly two pounds ten. She could have six Masses said at least for that much. There might even be money over to light some lamps at the Convent of Perpetual Reparation. She tried to comfort herself by these calculations, but as the train rushed through the night she sat more upright on the red-carpeted seats that smelled of dust, and clenched her hands tightly as she thought of the torments of Purgatory. When flakes of soot from the engine flew past the carriage window, she began to pray silently, with rapid unformed words that jostled themselves in her mind with the sheafs of burning sparks.

The Little Prince

I

About four o'clock in the afternoon, while she was upstairs giving her father his medicine, Bedelia thought she heard her brother's voice in the shop below her. She hurried down. There was no one in the shop but Daniel.

'I thought I heard Tom's voice,' she said. 'Did I?'

Daniel was reluctant to betray Tom, but he would not tell a lie. He nodded his head.

'So he broke his promise!' she cried. 'What did he say? Who was with him?'

Apparently, however, it was the same old story. Her brother Tom had been doing the good-fellow again, as usual, walking into the shop, and up to the counter, with a crowd of good-for-nothing companions, and standing drinks all round as if he were a customer! If business came into his hands, he'd make short work of the profits, at this rate.

'Oh, how can he be such a fool!' she cried, and the impetuosity of her cry seemed to imply that there was a time when better might have been expected of him. But it was not a time for sentiment. She had to concern herself with the practicalities of the situation. 'I'll have to speak to him,' she said decisively. 'It's plain to be seen that he has become a regular toper.'

But as she uttered it, she knew that the word toper was neither just nor suitable to her brother Tom. His faults were not such as could be described by any word that connoted age or decay; they were still the faults of youth, and were it not that she and

Daniel would be involved in his downfall, she might have found something appealing in his reckless prodigality. As things stood, he could not be allowed to go on.

'Something must be done and done at once, Daniel,' she said. 'I didn't get a chance to tell you earlier in the day, but the doctor's report on Father was not so good this morning. He said that we could not expect him to last much longer.' She paused. 'And you know what that means,' she said significantly. 'You know what has to be done.'

Daniel knew. 'All I wish is that I could do it for you, Bedelia,' he said, 'but I explained my position to you and –'

'Oh, that's all right!' she said impatiently. She fully understood his position. If her brother failed to see things in a proper light, it would not do for him to get a wrong impression about Daniel, particularly when, like everyone else in the family, he was unaware, as yet, that there was anything between herself and Daniel. It might be different if Daniel were already his brother-in-law. Although, even then, it would probably be more delicate for her to handle the situation in her own way. Not that she felt it to be an unduly difficult task! There was no real harm in Tom. He would be the last in the world, she felt sure, to wish to hurt anyone, much less his own sister and her future husband. He might not, perhaps he could not, be made to mend his ways, but he could be made to see how his ways and theirs ran counter to each other, and how advisable it was that, if he was bent on pursuing his fully, he pursue it in some other clime. 'He will listen to me, I know he will,' she said. 'I know him inside and out. I can read him like a book. Didn't I tell you he would never be able to keep his promise? Didn't I tell you it would be a waste of time giving him another chance.'

For it had been in deference to Daniel's scruples that Tom had been given a last chance. It had been a mistake though as Daniel must now see. It had only postponed an unpleasantness that would otherwise be over and done with by this time.

'I won't let this night pass without making my mind plain to him,' Bedelia said. 'I'll bring him out here, when the shop is shut, where we won't be interrupted. While the rest of you are at supper would be a good time, wouldn't it?' 'There he is now!' she cried, as at that moment, beyond the green baize door that led from the shop into the dwelling quarters of the premises, they heard his voice raised in horse-play with his younger sisters. Bedelia glanced at the clock. 'Don't you think you could start to put up the shutters?' she said, and as Daniel set about doing as she suggested, she watched him irritably. She was eager to be rid of him, and to advance upon her designs.

Yet, when a few minutes later Daniel was gone, and she stood alone in the darkness, she did not immediately move, but, involuntarily in the gloom, her eyes turned towards where upon the wall behind the cash-desk, there hung an illustrated calendar from one of the numerous shipping companies for which her father had been an agent. On the yellowed and flyblown print her eyes had rested daily since she was a child, and as clear as day she could, in the darkness, make out the great liner afloat on its cerulean ocean. Tom would not be the first black sheep to be sent across that ocean. Far away though the New World was and though it could be reached only by crossing the vast Atlantic, what other remedy was there for a spendthrift like Tom who had no sense of what was due to his family? Many a young man like him went out in disgrace to come home a different man altogether; a man to be respected, a well-to-do man with a fur lining in his top-coat, his teeth stopped with gold, and the means to hire motor cars and drive his relatives about the countryside. Might not Tom make good there too? It did not seem likely, but it was at least possible.

Abruptly cutting short her meditations, Bedelia went through the baize door into the small parlour behind the shop. Supper had already started. Liddy was pouring out the tea, and Alice was cutting the bread. Tom himself had started to eat, and his mouth was full when he looked up in answer to his name.

'I want to talk to you, Tom,' said Bedelia. 'Now!' she said relentlessly, when he protested that he was hungry, but she felt bad when he put his saucer over his cup of tea that Liddy had just poured out for him, as if he thought he'd be back in a minute.

'What's up?' he said, following her out of the room. 'Hey, what's the idea of coming out here?' he cried, as she opened the door and stepped into the shuttered darkness of the shop.

'I don't want to be interrupted in what I have to say,' his sister said shortly, and she held the door open for him, as she would for a child.

'But it's pitch dark in here,' he protested, making his way awkwardly between the numerous display cases disposed about the centre of the floor.

Bedelia, on the other hand, made her way unerringly, and as she heard him stumbling against one thing after another, it was with difficulty that she restrained herself from commenting on his unfamiliarity with his surroundings.

'Come this way,' she said, when they reached the other side of the shop, where, behind the bar, there was a small room set aside for the use of customers desiring privacy, and commonly called the snug. Here too the small window giving on to the backyard was shuttered for the night, but unlike the plain wooden shutters on the shop front, in the centre panel of the shutter on the snuggery window, someone in a flight of fancy had cut a vent in the shape of a heart. Through this little heart-shaped vent there came sufficient light for Bedelia's purpose. When she turned around she could see her brother's face.

His was a surprisingly handsome and, she had to admit, undissipated look. But that will not last long, she told herself, and at once she broached her subject. 'Well, Tom! I suppose you know why I want to talk to you?'

To her annoyance, however, he did not seem to be listening to her. Instead, he had lifted up an old cracked jardinière of yellow glaze that stood upon a rickety bamboo table, and into which had been rammed a large badly fitting flower-pot, containing a single wretched stalk of geranium. 'Are you listening to me?' she demanded, because he seemed to be absorbed in looking at the wretched pot plant.

Still he didn't answer, but lifted the flower-pot out of its holder and held it up to his nose, passing the dried-up stalk under his nostrils as if it were a sweetly-smelling flower. She began to think that he might be trying to make a fool of her.

'Perhaps you think I am not aware of your having broken your promise?' she snapped. 'I heard that you and your friends were here all afternoon.'

She had the satisfaction of seeing him look up startled.

'You don't miss much, do you?' he said. 'I suppose the faithful Daniel gave you a full report of my conduct?'

'It's none of your business where I got my information,' she snapped, trying hard not to lose her temper at this stage.

'On the contrary, it is very much my business, dear sister, because you see, it happens that you were misinformed.'

She was taken aback, but only for an instant. 'Are you accusing Daniel of telling lies?'

'I am accusing no one,' said Tom, with the quiet of one who has something in reserve. She began to feel uneasy. 'I have my faults, Bedelia, but I do not break my promises.'

That was true. As a small boy he had always been truthful, but was it not said that drink broke down a person's character? She looked fixedly at him. 'Which of you am I to believe?' she said.

'Why not believe me, Bedelia?' And then, abruptly, he took up the flower-pot out of the jardinière and pushed it under her nose. 'Do you smell anything?' he demanded.

Instinctively she recoiled, but not before she had got the acrid odour that arose from the cracked clay. 'It smells like whiskey?' she said, surprised. Tom laughed. 'There's nothing wrong with your nose, Bedelia,' he said gaily. He was restored to his usual easy manner. 'Now do you believe me when I say I kept my promise? It's true I was here with my friends this afternoon, and I filled up my glass every time I filled up theirs, but I didn't drink a drop. Not a drop! When no one was looking I poured the stuff into this,' he brandished the flower-pot again. 'It looked as if it needed watering too,' he said. 'Not that it looks anything better now.' Light-heartedly he laughed. Light-headedly, Bedelia thought.

She was aware of a bitter feeling of disappointment. Her plans were set at naught. There was no immediate justification now for the suggestion she had been about to make to him. Or was there? Suddenly she saw a loophole in his justification of himself. 'I suppose you think you were very smart?' she said.

'I suppose you think I ought to be tickled to death to hear how clever you were. Well, I'm not.' She didn't look at him, but she sensed she had disconcerted him, and it gave her confidence. 'I might think more of you if you drank the stuff,' she snapped. 'You must be an out-and-out fool to pour away good whiskey like that. Don't you realise it was money you were pouring away. Money!' She almost screamed the last word. 'Well, isn't it true?' she said defensively, because she was frightened for a minute at the look upon his face.

He lowered the jardinière. 'I'm sorry, I thought you'd be so pleased, Bedelia,' he said.

She bit her lip.

As a little fellow he used to say that to her when she caught him out in some small misdemeanour and it always won her heart. But now she forced herself to believe that he was only trying to make things difficult for her.

'I'm afraid, Tom, that you are one of those people who have to be protected – from themselves, I mean,' she added quickly, as she saw him raise his eyebrows. 'It was fatal for a person of your character to be put in the position in which you were put by Father's illness. I was never one to beat about the bush, and I may as well tell you that when I called you out here I thought you had broken your promise, and I was determined there was only one thing for you, and that was to get you away from this town altogether, away from the bad company you've been keeping, idlers and spongers, who knew they had only to rub you down with a few soft words, and they were sure to have their bellies filled with drink. No, don't interrupt me! I know there are some of your friends who may not have been as ready to soak you as others, and have even lent you money, but believe me, they know that they didn't stand to lose on the deal. A young man with your prospects! Your friends were always your worst enemies. Well, that's what I was going to say to you, but after what you've just told me I am beginning to think that your very worst enemy is yourself. Pouring good whiskey into a flower-pot! I can't believe it.'

Tom was looking down at the floor while she was speaking.

'I suppose you are right, Bedelia,' he said quietly. 'But what's the remedy? I take it that since you had a remedy in the first case, you will be able to provide one in this case also. Indeed, the same remedy may be used in both cases.'

Was he being impertinent? Only for the delicacy of the situation, and the need for handling it carefully, she would have lost her temper. 'This town is not the place for you, Tom,' she said, coldly. 'If you were to go away, for a time anyway, make a fresh start as it were, maybe –'

But he interrupted her. 'So the remedy in either case is the same?' He laughed. 'That's a good one, you know. It reminds me of a joke I heard the other day. Would you like to hear it?'

Bedelia wasn't in the mood for jokes, but when he had a good yarn to tell there was no stopping Tom.

'Don't look so sour. Wait till you hear it. There was a little fellow one time, and he was married to a big bully of a woman, who hardly tolerated him about the place at all, except on pay nights. She had to give the poor devil his meals, of course, but I believe she never sat at the table with him, but just slapped them down in front of him, without a word, and all the time he was eating she'd go about the kitchen, banging away with the sweeping brush, or whatever she happened to have in her hands, and taking no more notice of him than if he were a dog.

'Well, one day, anyway, when he came home to his tea, she slapped down his cup and plate in front of him as usual, and threw a few cuts of bread on the plate, and poured out a cup of tea from an old brown pot that was stewing at the back of the range, maybe for hours. It was a big brute of a teapot, with a big awkward spout on it, and the tea used to belch out of it as if it was choked with something, as was probably the case.

'Anyway, this day when she had splashed out a cup of tea for him and given the milk-jug a shove in his direction, she went back to her work as usual, but although she wasn't taking any notice of him, after a bit she got a feeling there was something wrong. Maybe she didn't hear him stirring the spoon around in the cup. Or else she didn't hear him sucking the tea off his moustache, but anyway, she threw a look at him, and sure enough, he hadn't touched the tea. And after a few minutes when she looked again the cup was still before him full to the brim.

'"Well! What's the matter?" she said, stopping her work, and putting her hands on her hips. "Why don't you drink your tea?"

'The poor fellow got as red as a lobster, and he looked up at her apologetically. "There's a mouse in it, Maggie," she said.

'I suppose she got a bit of a start at that, because you must admit it wasn't a thing a woman would expect to happen. And so, after giving him a glare like as if it was his fault in some way, she stepped across and looked into the cup. And sure enough, floating on the top of the cup of tea was a dead mouse; it must have got into the old teapot while it was standing at the back of the range – and come down the spout – maybe it was that was clogging it all the time. Well, there it was, anyway, a mouse.

'"Hmm!" she said, and she took up the cup and carried it over to the sink, and taking up a spoon she fished out the mouse and threw it into the pig's bucket. "There!"

'But, like the last time, it wasn't long until she began to feel that he was still sitting in front of the cup without touching it, and she looked back at him. Right enough, he hadn't touched the tea. He was just sitting in front of it. The very sight of him drove her into a rage. "Well, what's the matter with you now?" she demanded. And she raised her eyes to heaven. "I declare to God I don't know what kind of a man you are! You won't drink your tea with the mouse, and you won't drink it without the mouse." '

It was a good story. Or so Tom had thought when he first heard it, and even now as he came to the end of it, he was inclined to laugh again, but at the sight of Bedelia's face, his own face sobered. He made no attempt to bring home to her the application of his parable. Instead, as if he took a bitter pride in doing what was expected of him, he drew himself up. 'When and where do you want me to go?'

Bedelia's face twitched at the question.

'America,' she said, flatly. But she almost broke down when she saw the look of disbelief, and then, worse still, belief, dawn in his eyes. 'It's the obvious place,' she murmured. 'A new country, a fresh start –'

But he put up his hand and waved away her words.

'Oh, yes! Yes! My dear sister. I know you think me singularly uninterested in the business, but I have occasionally flicked

over the pages of the shipping catalogues, and I know all about
the brave new world. We can take it as said. Let us get down to
more practical matters.' He looked down at his waistcoat, on
which there was a speck or two of clay from the flower-pot, and
he brushed it off. 'What a good job I have this suit in condition.
Saves buying a new one.'

Was this to be his attitude? Then he was going to make it
seem like she was driving him out. 'Anyone would think you
were going in the morning,' Bedelia said.

'And am I not?'

'You know very well that there will be a lot of arrangements
to be made. We'll have to come to some sort of agreement.'

'Arrangements? Agreement?'

'You'll be entitled to your share of the business, of course,'
she said, coldly.

'Oh, yes. Well, run up and tell the old man I'll take it now,'
he said. 'How is he this evening, by the way?' he asked suddenly,
in a different tone of voice. 'I haven't been up to see him all
day.'

'Oh, he's all right,' said Bedelia impatiently, 'but you know
right well he doesn't know anything about all this. I'm not
speaking of the present; I'm speaking of the time when –'

'Oh, I see. I'm glad the old man isn't a party to it. You're
talking about when our poor father is out of the way,' he said,
looking up at the ceiling over their heads.

'Quite naturally, there will have to be changes made when
that time arrives,' she said stiffly.

'Naturally!' Tom said dryly, but it seemed to Bedelia that he
was beginning to see things reasonably. 'As Daniel said   ' she
began.

'Oh, so Daniel is in this too?'

Bedelia bit her lip. She had made a slip there, but it was not
time for prevarication. 'You may as well know that Daniel and
I are going to be married,' she said curtly.

'Good God!'

Bedelia saw that she certainly had given him a jolt. But he
controlled himself.

'I suppose you mean afterwards,' Tom answered, jerking his thumb upwards towards the ceiling. The next moment he shot out his hand. 'Oh, well! The best of luck to both of you. Sorry I won't be here for the wedding.'

'Oh, but that's what I'm trying to explain,' she said. 'There's no need for you to go away until afterwards. All we want, Daniel and I, is to know where we stand financially. And even then we will certainly not be married for some time to come.'

But Tom was not listening. He had raised his head and although it might be an absurd fancy, she felt that, in imagination, he was already far away from her, standing perhaps upon the deck of an outgoing Atlantic liner, such as was pictured in the shipping calendars, breathing in the deep sea breezes that she supposed must for ever blow on the wild Atlantic. Then suddenly he came back to earth, back to the little dark snuggery.

'You and Daniel have everything nicely fixed for yourselves, I must say,' he said, and he smiled, this time – she was sure of it – absolutely without malice. 'But I don't think that I'll be able to fit in with your arrangements. If I have to go at all, I'll go at once.'

'But what about your father? How can we explain to him?'

Tom smiled again. 'I have no doubt you'll be able to find some satisfactory way of fixing that too.'

'What about your share of the business?' Bedelia cried, 'we'll have to fix up that. How can you get your cut without letting Father in on things. You can see our hands are tied. You can't go before he goes.'

Tom did not seem to see any great difficulty in the situation. He looked around him. 'Have you got a pen?' he asked. 'I'll make over my share to you and Daniel. How would that be? Won't that straighten out everything? It will be a little wedding present from me, or if you like to put it another way, it will be a little farewell present.'

But Bedelia had her pride to safeguard, or perhaps it would be more correct to say she had Daniel's sense of honour.

'Daniel would never agree to that,' she said stiffly. 'I'll have to speak to him about the matter. I dare say we will be able to come to some temporary agreement. And afterwards we'll get a solicitor to draw up a proper document. Meanwhile we'll send your money to you every year.' Just then, however, another aspect of the situation struck her. 'That's another thing,' she cried. 'We'll have to settle on what part of America you'll go to at first. In the ordinary way, people usually go to some part where there are other people from home, but in your case I thought it might be wise –'

'Oh, that's right, a fresh start for me! I see your point, my dear, but I think you can leave me to settle that matter for myself. And now?' He glanced at the door.

Bedelia was not satisfied to end the interview so abruptly. 'As soon as you get settled, you'll be writing to us, of course?'

In the dusky light of the snug, Tom moved, so that for the first time his face was out of the patch of light from the shutter.

'Let's leave it at that,' he said. 'As soon as you know my address – my permanent address that is to say, you can write to me.'

She thought for a moment there was a curious expression on his face, but the next moment he spoke so normally, and she decided she must have been mistaken.

'And now, if you don't mind, Bedelia, I'll go back to my supper.'

After he had gone, Bedelia felt so tired that she leant back against the wall of the snuggery, out of the shaft of light that had, all during their colloquy, fallen intermittently, in broken lines, upon her brother's face, but which now fell upon the opposite wall, unbroken in outline, a perfect little patch of golden light in the shape of a heart.

II

Although her father had lived for seven months after Tom had left for America, and although they had not heard from him once in all that time, it was impossible not to think that on this occasion at least they would not have some word. 'You'd think we'd hear from him at this time, wouldn't you?' Bedelia said to

Daniel, who was now her husband, as they came out of the church. It was the anniversary Mass for her father's death.

Up to this, Tom's silence could have been put down to carelessness, but now it seemed as if it must have another cause. Nor could they console themselves that he had not heard the news of his father's death, because in addition to requesting the American papers to please copy the announcement of the death, they had sent him a cablegram in the care of Mary Conaty, a former servant who had emigrated to Boston some years earlier, and who, in a recent letter to her sister at home, reported having met Tom Grimes in the street, not once, but on two or three occasions. He had promised to visit her, and although he had not done so up to the time of her last letter, it might reasonably be assumed that she had been able to communicate to him the sad tidings.

So certain were they that they would hear from him, that Daniel had anticipated the event by including his name in the newspapers among those from whom messages of sympathy had been received, although afterwards he had been a bit scrupulous about the matter. Bedelia, however, scoffed at such scruples. 'I would have included his name in any case, even if I knew we were not going to hear from him. We could not let people think that he had dropped out of our existence.'

Daniel sighed. He was afraid that was what Tom Grimes had done. Bedelia, however, was not at all reconciled to such an idea. 'He'll write yet. We'll get a letter out of the blue one of these days,' she maintained.

Meanwhile, pending their getting hold of his address, every month Daniel conscientiously set aside a percentage of the profits, and this money was lodged in an account he himself had opened in Tom's name the day after his father-in-law died.

'He can't want money very badly, that's one thing certain,' said Bedelia caustically, at the end of the second year, when they were making up the books, and she saw the amount that had accrued to her brother's credit.

'I wouldn't be sure about that,' said Daniel. 'He was deep, Tom was.'

Just what he meant by this, however, Bedelia did not wait to find out. 'Oh, depend upon it, we'll hear from him when he needs it,' she said.

But in this estimate of human nature, she was basing her judgement upon the generality of men, not upon the particular individual in question. And although he did not altogether agree with her, Daniel conscientiously lodged the money every month.

And so he was not taken completely by surprise one afternoon when, regardless of who was in the shop, Bedelia, an excited flush on her face, came to the green baize door and beckoned to him. When he saw that she held a letter in her hand, he jumped at once to the conclusion that it was from the outlier.

But it was not from Tom Grimes. It was from Mary Conaty. She wrote to say that she had met Tom again, and had a long chat with him. She knew they were worried about him at home, and had written to tell them there was no need for concern.

'He is perfectly well, and seems to be prospering,' said Bedelia, quoting from the letter, an excited flush on her face. 'Wasn't it good of her to write?' she cried. 'And to take so much trouble to describe the whole thing. She was walking down Tremont Street – that must be a street in Boston – and who did she see looking into a shop window but our Tom. Can you imagine it, Daniel, such a coincidence!'

Although Daniel was disappointed, having thought the letter was from Tom himself, he did not want to dampen Bedelia's pleasure, and so he tried to appear hopeful. 'So we've traced him at last,' he said. 'Well, tell me everything. How is he? What is he doing?' He put out his hand for the letter.

But some reticence seemed to come over Bedelia, and, appearing not to see his outstretched hand, she moved away. 'Oh, I'll give it to you later,' she said. 'I didn't read it properly yet, I only glanced through it.'

Her evasiveness was not lost on Daniel, and momentarily he was saddened. Before they were married, before her father died, there seemed to be a greater bond between them than there had been ever since. He used to think it was a bond of trust, of wanting the best for Tom, but now he thought it had been only a bond of connivance against him.

It was not until he went in for his dinner that he heard any more about Mary Conaty's letter.

'About that letter I got this morning, Daniel,' she said. 'I think it would be just as well if we didn't mention it to anyone, for the present, anyway. After all, it's very backhand information, not much better than gossip really, and for all we know, Mary Conaty might be misinformed about some of the things she said about him.' She paused here, and Daniel knew that she had reluctantly made up her mind to impart to him something she had found unpalatable in the letter. 'It's quite possible that she may have been mistaken about his employment, for instance,' she said, going slowly and carefully, as if, between each word and the next, she was trying to take a sounding of his reaction.

What a born conniver she was, he thought, with mixed emotions. She could not really think that she had told him what her brother was doing. But if it made things any easier for her, he was prepared to play her game, and he made no protest.

'It hardly seems possible that he would have taken a job as a waiter, does it?' she said.

'A waiter!'

In spite of his determination to play her game, Daniel couldn't keep back the exclamation of incredulity, but he regretted his indiscretion when he saw her wince.

'Ah well, we must not forget that it must take some time to get a footing in a strange country,' he said quickly.

Bedelia eagerly took up this support of her brother. 'People look at jobs differently in America. Over there people take all kinds of employment, and no one thinks any the worse of them. It's not like here! It seems to be a very classy hotel too.' Here she dived her hand into her pocket and took out the envelope of Mary Conaty's letter on which she had transcribed the name of the hotel. 'The Parker House it's called,' she said, as if this ought to impress him. 'Mary Conaty spoke as if it was a great achievement to get into the Parker House.'

It was a difficult moment for Daniel, who wanted at one and the same time to be kind, and to be truthful.

'I suppose to a person of Mary Conaty's origins a waiter's job would seem a superior position, but I'm afraid there's no denying it's a comedown for your brother, Bedelia.'

Instantly Bedelia flared up.

'Oh, but it isn't only Mary Conaty who thinks it. The Westropps who are the people she's working for over there – she mentions them in all her letters – they told Mary Conaty that it was very hard for a young man to get a job in the Parker House. It seems Mary told them about him, because she knew they used to be in and out of there, and they asked her to describe him, and when she did they remembered him at once. They had already picked him out, I suppose, as different from the others. Anyway, they told her she could be proud of him. They said he was like a little prince.'

As she repeated those words of the unknown Westropps, Bedelia's voice suddenly faltered.

'What's the matter, Bedelia?' Daniel cried.

'Oh, nothing, nothing,' she said. 'It's only that I just remembered something that people used to say about him long ago, when he was a little fellow, I often told you about it. When Mother began to ail, I used to have to mind him, and I used to dress him up in a little velvet suit with a white lace collar, and people were always stopping me in the street to look at him, and admire him, and that's what they used to say – that he was like a little prince. I had forgotten it until this minute.'

To his astonishment, she took out a handkerchief, and pressed it to her eyes.

'Oh, come now!' he said, and he put his arm around her shoulder. 'This is not the time to cry. On the contrary. Now we have his address for the first time, we don't have to depend any more upon roundabout methods of getting in touch with him. Who can be sure if he ever got any of those other messages? Now we can write to him direct. A letter addressed to the Parker House will certainly reach him.'

He was so confident that Bedelia put away the handkerchief. But the letter which was despatched to the Parker House Hotel that very day came back unopened, with a note on the back from the management to say that Tom Grimes had left their employment without giving them any address to forward his mail. The hotel was unaware of his present whereabouts.

'Now what will we do?' cried Bedelia, as she stared at the returned letter.

It was a bit of a blow all right, Daniel had to admit, but he was determined not to take it too seriously. 'Never mind,' he said. 'We'll hear tell of him again before long.'

It was, however, twenty-seven years from the day that Daniel made that singularly unprophetic remark, before they again got news of the little prince. Not that he was ever out of their minds for long, in all those years. For one thing, they had a constant reminder of him every month when they lodged money against his name in the bank, although their reactions were not identical, and Daniel's indeed had changed out of all recognition with the passage of the years. At first he had been concerned only with his own honesty and integrity in lodging the money so scrupulously, and also it had pleased him to see it accumulate in the beginning. Every month as he completed the transaction at the bank, he made the same remark to the cashier. 'Well,' he'd say complacently, 'it's there for him if ever he comes looking for it.' And as he went his way home, he used to reflect, with a certain amount of pride, on the way a comparatively small amount of money increases when it is left untouched, and computed at compound interest. It had grown into quite a considerable amount already.

But somehow, as the money accumulated, Daniel's attitude began to change. Scruples that might have been supposed to decrease with the years, were magnified. And where it had not seemed a great matter for a man to abandon a small share of a small business, the true nature of a man's loss now reached gigantic proportions, to all concerned, but Tom himself. 'I don't suppose he has any idea how much it has amounted to by now,' Daniel remarked to Bedelia. And he began to vary his talk at the bank. 'He'll get a surprise when he turns up and finds what's waiting for him.'

Then as the years since Tom had left began to be measured in decades, Daniel began to dwell on the diminishing ratio between the sum and the years at Tom's disposal for the enjoyment of it. Even if he turned up that very day, what use would it be to him at all. A feeling of great pity for Tom took hold, interrupted with pity for himself. For Tom would be a richer man than he himself would ever now become. For things had not prospered, as augured in the old days when Matthias Grimes was alive, and he himself was a raw shop-boy, greatly in awe of the premises in which he humbly served. Sadly now he used to look around the little shop and wonder how he had ever thought it was a big and flourishing business, for particularly in the twilight hour, before the lamps were lit, it sometimes seemed to be only a small box of a place, and it was hard to credit that one-third of the profits from it had been able to accrue to a sum as large as that which stood in Tom Grimes's name in the bank. He and Bedelia had nothing like it to show for their profits. Why, it was unlikely that the whole business, premises, stock, and goodwill, would be worth half as much as that sum in the bank. And although he had always been considered good at figures, his mind was confused by what seemed a mathematical fallacy. How had it come about that the part was greater than the whole? He and Bedelia had done their best. What had happened to make their achievement fall so short of their ambition? Or was it that their ambitions had been distorted, and out of proportion to what it was possible to attain?

Was it perhaps always a little box of a shop, and his feelings about it, long ago, no more than the illusions of a penniless shop-boy?

But what immense illusions they must have been to make him covet it, so much, and to make it seem so important that Tom Grimes be prevented from squandering it!

And as he lingered in the shop at night until later and later, it sometimes crossed his mind to wonder what might have become of him if Tom Grimes had proved obdurate, and failed to part with his birthright? But he did not ponder it deeply, because it was unlikely that his life would have been very altered. He might have left the employment of Grimes & Son, but only to go behind the counter of some similar concern, probably in the same town, for although it now appeared to him that there was nothing very noble or exalting in life as he had led it, he knew that this philosophic knowledge had only come to him as the fruit of age and experience, and that there had been nothing within himself in his youth to engender it. He had taken the only way that was open to him at the time.

There was just one thing that consoled him, and that was the thought of little kindnesses he had been able now and then to do for people, by which he meant the credit that he occasionally extended to the poor wretched creatures who came to him, shamefaced, without money to pay for the food they needed. If he had continued all his life to be a paid shop assistant, he would never have had the power to do these little kindnesses. So, down in the shop at night, long after closing-time, thinking of some of those poor people whom he had befriended, he roused his spirits sufficiently to end his gloomy meditations, blow out his candle and fumble up to bed.

Bedelia's attitude was altogether different. Even at the beginning it had seemed to her that it was not necessary to have given Tom so large a share in the profits. After all, he was putting nothing into the business, a factor which she felt ought to have been taken into consideration when calculating the percentage due to him. And so, right from the start, it galled her slightly every month to see Daniel put on his hat and go up the street to the bank. During the first years after her father's death, she did her best to stifle her misgivings. She could see that the business was doing fairly well, but it did not continue to flourish. One day when Daniel showed her the ledger, she said, 'Shouldn't Tom contribute something towards stock?'

But she accepted Daniel's argument that it would only complicate the book-keeping, because she was getting heartily sick of the way his head was eternally stuck in the ledgers. She shrugged her shoulders. After all, he must know what he is doing, she thought, recalling his competence in her father's time.

When time went on, however, the promise he had shown then seemed only to have been the ability of a servant. Why else had they not prospered more? It was not that he lacked industry, but sometimes when she watched him sprinkling sawdust on the floor, putting up or taking down the shutters, it occurred to her that it was not the business he cared for, but the shop itself, the tangible thing upon which he could lavish his care and attention.

There was also the matter of his not hesitating more to take the initiative of a proprietor with regard to giving credit. This worried her so much that the doctor warned her against annoying herself in any way. And in the years following the birth of an only son, she kept her thoughts engaged on routine domestic matters.

Later on, having been shown the ledgers, her misgivings grew into resentment. The shop had recently been repainted, both inside and out, and this made large inroads into their profit. She turned to the column of figures recorded in her brother's name. 'So he's to get off scot-free this time too,' she said angrily. She swung around to Daniel. 'I wouldn't mind if he needed it,' she cried. For it was her rooted conviction that her brother had done well for himself in America, and that that was the reason that he never bothered to write or come back to claim his share. 'He would probably laugh at the thought of it now,' she said. 'It would be a mere nothing to him. Americans have an altogether different scale of value from us, whereas –'

She looked disconsolately around the shop. Paradoxically, since it was painted it somehow looked less prosperous than before, and on the brightly painted shelves the newly arranged stock looked smaller than it used to look, she thought. Or was it only her fancy? On an impulse, she went out to the storeroom at the back of the premises and looked around her. Surely there used to be a bigger reserve of stock. She came back, determined to demand an explanation from Daniel, but when she came back into the shop and saw him deep in the ledgers as usual, the explanation occurred to her. It was not possible to have money laid out in two directions at the same time, and there was, as she knew, a considerable amount outstanding in credit.

The matter of credit had caused heated arguments when her father was alive. 'I'm sorry,' she used to hear Daniel murmur, 'but I'm not in a position to give credit upon my own responsibility.'

Sitting behind the counter at the other side of the shop, taking care not to be seen, she had applauded his tactful handling of a difficult situation. Perhaps that's what she took it to be, for it never occurred to her that he was speaking no more than the simple truth, and that no sooner would he be in full command than he would begin to extend credit on all sides.

At first it had only been to an odd person, now and then. She would find an entry in the ledger, and when she questioned him as to the advisability of trusting a certain person, he would only shake his head.

'But they were in a very bad way, Bedelia. If no one gave them credit they would starve.'

'But why did these people have to come to us? Why couldn't they go somewhere else?'

Daniel always had the same reply. 'I believe they will pay us back if they are ever in a position to do so.'

'If?' She was hardly able to contain herself with irritation.

Soon the ledgers were bursting with debts. With so much money tied up, how could she expect the stock to be fully replenished as it used to be in former days. Perhaps, as Daniel said, it would all be repaid in time, but meanwhile, where was money to be found for advancement?

At such times it was very trying to think of Tom's money, lying idle and useless in the bank. If it had even been lodged in their names, it wouldn't have been so bad, but nothing would have satisfied Daniel but to lodge it in her brother's own name.

'We could have made temporary use of it,' she complained bitterly one day. That they were unable to do so seemed but another proof of the way Daniel's conscientiousness had set limits to their ability to further their own interests.

But Daniel was adamant.

'It's safer never to meddle with things belonging to other people.'

'Belonging to other people!' she said starkly. She could only echo his words indignantly. Because indeed she was coming

more and more each month to regard the landlocked money
as theirs, which they were only prevented from making use of
by reason of a technicality.

'It is my belief he intended us to keep his share as a wedding
present,' she said one day. 'When we said we would send it to
him as soon as he sent his address, all he said was to leave things
as they were. I didn't pay much heed to it at the time, but I
remember distinctly now that he had looked at me with a
peculiar expression, and although I didn't understand it at the
time, it seems now that he never intended to send the address.
In other words, that was his way of telling me to keep the
money.'

To Daniel, it seemed quite possible that Bedelia might be
right. Such behaviour would have been compatible with Tom's
generous nature. But they could not count on it now, it would
have no bearing upon their present circumstances, whatever
this interpretation of his character might mean to them. 'What
you say may be true, Bedelia,' he said, a trifle dryly, 'but I'm
afraid your words wouldn't cut any ice with the bank manager.
You made a mistake not to get him to make a written statement.'

As if this might still be possible, Bedelia sighed. 'Oh, if only
we could get in touch with him,' she cried.

Their discussions always boiled down to that wish in the end,
with just one difference, that whereas Daniel wished to in the
hope of benefiting the absent one, Bedelia did so in hope of
gain for themselves.

'Ah, well, who knows! One of these days we may hear from
him out of the blue.' He had said it so often it had ceased to
have any meaning other than that it had come to be regarded
by both of them as a terminal phrase for a painful conversation.

On this occasion, however, Bedelia sneered openly at him.
'How often have I heard that? Do you know what I think? Well,
I'll tell you. It's my belief he's dead.'

Shocked at her bluntness, Daniel looked up.

'He may have been dead for years,' she cried. 'After all, it's
a queer thing Mary Conaty never ran into him again, or that
no one else from Ireland met him. Oh, to think of that money
lying there idle when it could be of so much use to us.'

Daniel was stunned. Had she no feeling at all, that she could speak of her brother's life so callously. It was altogether different for him to make up his costs. It was a matter of business to him. There was no blood between them. 'If he was dead the money would be ours,' he said, 'unless he married or had children.' That was yet another factor.

On this point, however, Bedelia reassured him, confident that her brother was not married. 'You'd find that he'd have made a claim quick enough if that were the case,' she said. 'Whatever foolish notions he might have had himself, you'd find his wife wouldn't be long in ridding him of those. No matter how much he made on the other side of the ocean, you'd find she'd grudge leaving us the few pounds on this side of it. And if he died, she'd certainly instigate proceedings to lay hands on our money. Oh, I think you can take it that he never married.'

Since his knowledge of the female mind was confined entirely to his contact with her mind, Daniel was inclined to believe Bedelia might be correct in her reasoning. 'There might be some way these things can be ascertained, and of putting in a counter claim for expenses due to us. We could get control over the money if there were a court order made to presume death.' Daniel had stored up this odd bit of knowledge in case it would one day be useful to them both.

'Where did you hear that?' she exclaimed, incredulously, but there was a gleam of interest in her eyes. Not that she intended to seek the assistance of the law as yet. It was indeed as if there were two compartments in her mind. In one compartment she was not only able to tolerate, but even to welcome, the idea that Tom was long gone to his reward, but in the other she steadfastly refused to believe such a thing. The habit of years could not altogether be broken. How many times in the years that were past had she not started at the sound of a voice in the shop, and thought it was the voice of her brother? And in the days that followed Daniel's suggestion that they get an order to presume him dead, a kind of guilty nervousness made her start violently at the sound of every strange voice. 'We'll wait another while before we take any step,' she said.

In the meantime, Daniel suggested they might write to Mary Conaty again.

Bedelia wrote that night.

It was four months, however, before a reply came to their letter, and it was not from Mary Conaty.

'Poor Mary Conaty is dead, Daniel,' she said, after scanning the words of the first page.

'Well, that puts the lid on it,' said Daniel, somewhat coarsely for him.

'No, wait a minute,' cried Bedelia, her eyes running on over the letter, and then leaping to the name at the end. 'This is from her daughter Biddy, and Biddy says –' She looked back to the beginning again. 'Isn't that good of her? She's going to look him up for us. And what do you suppose? She was with her mother that day long ago when Mary met him outside the Parker House Hotel. Isn't that extraordinary! Of course, she was only a child at the time, but she says she remembers him well. He was really striking-looking, Daniel, wasn't he? He had a kind of presence about him, I always thought. Anyway, he must have been remarkable in some way for a child to remember him like that. I dare say he made a deep impression on her when she's so willing to be a help to us in the matter, although I dare say she's doing it for her mother's sake too; she knew how devoted Mary Conaty was to our family. I must write at once and thank her for her offer.'

There began a frantic correspondence between Bedelia and Biddy Conaty, letters from both of them going off regularly, at set intervals, like cannonballs, without even waiting for a reply-volley.

Daniel was inclined to be sceptical of this young girl succeeding where her mother had failed, but he had to admit her efficiency. For in her third letter, Biddy told them how, having taken into consideration that Tom Grimes might well be dead, she had looked up the register of deaths right back to the last time he was positively known to have been alive. That was a remarkably thorough piece of work for a young girl to execute, thought Daniel. And furthermore, not having found any record of the demise of such a person, she quite properly concluded that there was a good chance of his being still alive. But, she added, and this Daniel thought very astute, he must be an old man now, and very likely incapacitated, and so her next proposal was to make enquiries at all the large State hospitals, homes for incurables, and even institutions that took in elderly people if they were destitute.

'My poor brother,' said Bedelia, as they came to this part of the letter, and she tried hard to feel compassion, but all she really felt was a renewed exhilaration in the chase. 'Isn't she wonderful, Daniel?' she cried, as letter after letter fell into the letter-box, now giving rise to little hopes, and now to little fears. 'What a nice girl she must be. When this is all over, we ought to invite her to come for a summer. She has people outside the town belonging to her mother, of course, but she doesn't seem the kind of girl who would enjoy being in the heart of the country, with no conveniences. We will ask her to stay with us.'

'She's a great girl all right,' Daniel agreed. 'She'll find him yet.'

'She will, she will,' said Bedelia.

All the same, it came as something of a shock when a cablegram arrived in which Biddy Conaty purported to have indeed done that very thing that they had predicted so light-heartedly. She believed she had found Tom Grimes.

Daniel was unaccountably perturbed by the news.

'She's found Tom Grimes,' Bedelia reported. 'He's ill,' she went on excitedly. 'Biddy found him in a hospice for the dying.'

She spoke as if she felt nothing, and Daniel noticed that she used her brother's surname. But Daniel was not surprised because he himself felt nothing. 'Was she talking to him? What did he say?' he asked at last.

'Oh, she hasn't been to see him yet,' said Bedelia. 'She just dashed off a letter to let us know she was on his track. The home is in a place called Norwood. She's only been in touch with the officials through the post, and by telephone.' Suddenly struck by some new aspect of the affair, she stopped short. 'We'll have to compensate her for all postage and cables,' she said. 'We can't let her be at a loss. Let's hope she will not have involved us in too much expense.'

Daniel brushed this aside. 'Oh, don't worry. We'll see that as a small matter, if he's been located.' There was always Tom's own money upon which to draw, but there might be a lot of red tape before they could lay hands on it. In the meantime ready money might have to be found in advance. They would have to borrow on the strength of a return being made for Tom Grimes's estate.

'It's a pity she didn't wait to write until after she'd seen him,' he said.

'Well, Daniel, I must say I think that's the most ungrateful thing I ever heard. The poor girl thought she'd never get the news away quick enough to me. Not that I can expect you to understand. After all, he's not your brother.' She pulled out her handkerchief. 'My only brother!' she sobbed. 'And to think he's dangerously ill in a home for incurables. Dying!'

Daniel, however, remained cool.

'A man named Tom Grimes is dying,' he said soberly. 'It's not at all impossible that it may be your brother, but neither is it impossible that it is an altogether different person who happens to have the same name.'

So astonished was Bedelia, that she could only gape at him dumbly, and a look that bordered on imbecility came over her face.

'Oh, I dare say it's him all right,' he said hastily, 'and I was wrong to criticise the girl. I must say she handled the whole thing well.'

Yes. Biddy Conaty had certainly spared no pains. She had done all that could be done. It was the facts which she disclosed which turned out to be unsatisfactory, as her next letter revealed.

My dear friends,

I went out to Norwood last Saturday, as I wrote you I intended. I found that, as the authorities had informed me, there was a patient there who went by the name of Thomas Grimes. They were not able to give me much information about him, as he was a casualty case that had been brought in by ambulance from a lodging-house in a poor quarter of the town. It appears he had collapsed from exhaustion, the poor man.

Bedelia bit her lip at these words, but read on:

> When he was brought in I was not able to see him. He was in a
> bad state of debility, but was able to give his name, which was the
> same as that he had given to the lodging-house keeper, who called to
> enquire for him some days later. When the authorities interviewed
> this woman, however, she was unable to give them any useful
> information about him, as he had only just moved in the night before
> his collapse. This person, whom I will endeavour to go to see myself,
> evidently knew nothing at all about him. She only called at the
> hospital in case she would be implicated in any charges of neglect, as
> he was very thin and undernourished looking. She went to hand over
> his luggage.
>
> I thought there might be something to identify him among the
> luggage, but the authorities had evidently thought the same, and gone
> through everything, with no success. There were only a few personal
> effects, nothing but a woollen sweater, showing signs of wear, a small
> roll of red flannel with two safety-pins fastened in it, a razor, a
> shaving-brush, a spare pair of boots, and a railway time-table. The
> contents of his pockets were of no importance from the point of view
> of identification.

At this point, there had evidently been a break in the writing
of the letter, which when it was taken up again, was in ink of a
different colour, and ran as follows:

> Since I began this letter I had several interruptions, and I am sure
> you are asking yourself why I do not hurry and tell you if I had gone
> out to Norwood again, which I did.
>
> Well, I'm afraid my visit wasn't as satisfactory as I hoped. The
> poor old man tried to be as co-operative as possible, but it was true
> for the authorities that he was in a very low state and failing rapidly.
> The nurse said he was perfectly normal mentally when it was a
> question of obeying instructions about medicine and the like, but he
> seemed totally unable to comprehend why I had come to see him.
> Naturally I couldn't ask him too many questions, but I gradually
> managed to introduce a few names into my conversation to see if they
> were familiar to him. I mentioned my mother first, and then I
> mentioned your name, taking the liberty of referring to you by your
> Christian name. Then gradually I began to talk about Ireland. I

think it was when I mentioned 'the old country', as my mother always called it, that his face seemed to alter in expression, but then, of course, it's very hard to judge the mood of old people, and the nurse said it might be only a twitch.

I do think myself, though, that his face did alter, and so I ventured to say something else about the old days that I remembered my mother telling me, and this time he definitely gave a sign of recognition. At least, he put up his hands to his face like a child. I think he must have felt bad or something. I was sorry for him anyway, and what is more, I was absolutely certain at that moment that he was your brother.

O dear, I'm afraid this letter is not very satisfactory for you, but I can only hope you will believe me when I assure you that I did my best. I will call to see him again, of course, and I left my address with the hospital authorities, who will notify me if there is any change in his condition. Perhaps if he gets stronger, I will be able to question him a bit about his early life.

Hoping you are all well. I wish I had more details.

Yours truly,
Biddy Conaty

PS. It has just occurred to me that you will wonder that I have said nothing about whether or not I recognised him, having already said that I had met him when I was a child. But I am sure you will understand that the years would have made a great change to him, to say nothing of sickness and poverty. Then, too, I always think people never look themselves when they are in bed, particularly in hospital. After all, I was very young at the time I was supposed to have met him, and I dare say in the interval I could have mixed him up in my mind with someone else.

B.C.

'Did you ever know such nonsense,' Bedelia cried in the same breath that she read the last line. 'I think she must be a bit stupid after all. Either that, or else she never met him. I don't care what she says about age or anything else: if she ever laid eyes on Tom Grimes she ought to be able to recognise him again unless she's a fool.' She flicked back through the letter with an exasperated look on her face. 'Couldn't she tell us whether he was the same build as our Tom, had he the same features? Was he Irish at all?' But it was too exasperating to contemplate.

'Now where are we?' she cried. 'What do we do next?'

It was an extraordinarily trying situation. Even Daniel saw they were in a pickle. 'We'd better send her some money, anyway,' he said at last. 'Tell her to see that he has whatever he wants.' For one thing was clear, if this man was her brother, he had not become the millionaire Bedelia had so often fancied him to be.

'But supposing it's not our Tom?' cried Bedelia.

Daniel shook his head.

'I don't think we'll be under much expense one way or another,' he said. 'Or not for long, anyway,' and he put out his hand and took the letter.

'I don't know so much about that,' said Bedelia. 'The girl said something about going to see him again when he got stronger.'

'If, not when, he got stronger,' Daniel amended. 'And somehow I don't think he will,' he added.

'You don't mean to say you think he'll die, and leave us in the ridiculous situation of not knowing for certain whether it is my brother Tom or not?' It was as if all the years, with their varying degrees of suspense, had been pressed into one unbearable moment. 'Oh, how can that girl be so stupid.' She wrung her hands. 'To think that it all could be settled in an instant if I could as much as get one glance at him, just one glance!' It was only an exclamation, only an expression of irritation and annoyance, but in it was the seed of an idea that had only to be released to germinate.

'You wouldn't think of going over there, Bedelia?'

'Are you out of your mind? Is it me?' To Bedelia, at that moment, it seemed incredible for her to travel to America.

Yet it was only five days later, Daniel, as agent, having been able to expedite matters with the steamship company, that he and Bedelia set out for Cork to board S.S. *Samaria* bound for Boston Harbour.

It was a bad crossing. The fog in which they set out from Cork did not lift the whole way across, and the foghorn sounded continuously. It nearly drove Bedelia crazy. For the first four days of the voyage she stayed down in her cabin, deadly sick.

Daniel fared a bit better. He got his sea legs after a day or so, and he was able to engage in such mild dissipation as shuffleboard, and guessing how many knots they had travelled each day. He also kept a sharp watch out for porpoises, and he took a great interest in passing ships, particularly at night when they were lit up like floating hotels. Once he believed he saw a disturbance in the water, which might have been a whale. He also made a few friends, but he did not speak about them to Bedelia, it would only annoy her.

On the fifth day, Bedelia came up on deck, weak and watery-looking in the face.

It was characteristic of Bedelia that her first and only encounter with the other passengers was with an angular figure dressed entirely in deep mourning. Her husband had died in the course of their first trip home to England in forty years, and she was now bringing his body back to America for burial. He was in the hold.

Up to meeting Bedelia, this woman had spoken to no one in the course of the voyage, but she made fast friends with Bedelia. They were constantly to be seen promenading round the deck in dismal discourse. After a day or two, Daniel began to feel that a slight revulsion that the other passengers felt for the bereaved woman, had extended to Bedelia also, for she was also wearing black for the voyage. Indeed, as he stood in the bar one afternoon, where although he was a teetotaller, he spent a lot of his time, the bulletin-board being there, on which the results of the various competitions were posted, an Englishman whom he had not met till then, jerked his glass in the direction of the two women, who could be seen through the portholes, slowly pacing up and down the deck outside.

'Rum thing to think of that chap down in the hold, isn't it?' the man said. 'I should think it would have been better to have put him down on the spot, not tote the poor devil about like this.'

For a moment, both men had a gloomy vision of the coffin down in the hold, stoutly propped no doubt, and corded down, but within which they visualised the dead man, like a shuttle, rattling backwards and forwards with the uneasy movement of the water. They laughed awkwardly.

'Bet my woman wouldn't go to all that trouble,' said the man, but the warmth of his voice implied such a good-humoured relationship, that Daniel's mind immediately conjured up a picture of a large woman, red in the face, her big bosom always lolloping up and down with laughter.

As if the Englishman read his thoughts, he pointed out again to where the two women in black, having made a round of the deck, were starting off upon a second round. 'She looks a cold fish to me. I bet she has some shrewd motive for taking the poor stiff back to the States. Look at the face of her. I can't stand a conniving woman.'

It was with a start Daniel realised that the Englishman had mistaken Bedelia for the owner of the corpse. Too awkward, too embarrassed, to put things right, he mumbled an excuse, and went out of the saloon. But he couldn't rid his mind of the derisive description of Bedelia.

Poor Bedelia, she was at her worst during the trip. Later on while he was trying to compose his mind long enough to make out his forecast of the ship's speed for the day, he caught sight of her again. The other woman had evidently gone below. Bedelia was alone. He was struck by how poorly she looked, the harsh salt winds were blowing her lank hair back from her thin face. How she had aged in recent months. She was not herself of late. Perhaps he had neglected her. He hurried out to join her up on deck.

'Oh, there you are, Bedelia,' he cried. 'There's going to be a ship's concert tonight,' he said. 'I was thinking we might stay up for it?'

Bedelia looked at him with scandalised eyes. 'I'm afraid I cannot forget the object of our trip as easily as you, Daniel,' she said. And turning aside, she began again to pace the deck with mournful steps.

Looking after her, Daniel reflected that in a certain sense her words were true. He had enjoyed the voyage, very much indeed, but he could not see that to do so was in any way culpable. Of course, Tom Grimes was only a brother-in-law to him. All the same, it was forty years since Bedelia herself had seen him. Who would imagine that her feelings could still be so quick.

If, however, Daniel had enjoyed himself mildly on the voyage, when they arrived on the other side he was no whit less lost and unsure of his ground than her.

To begin with, they had never heard such a din in their lives. As they drove away from the dockside, sirens were screaming, and just as they supposed they were getting away from the babel of dockland, their taxi-cab shot into a street above which ran an overhead electric trolley car, with a noise so deafening that they sat dumbly side by side, and waited with desperation for the real character of the city to manifest itself to them. But as Biddy Conaty had chosen their hotel for them solely on the merits of its nearness to the hospital, which was situated in a poor quarter, in a few minutes they found themselves drawing up in a street little better than any of those through which they had driven, and they began to think the whole city must be clamorous and deafening.

And then, just before their cab stopped on the other side of the street, where a short alley led off the main thoroughfare, they saw that a crowd had gathered.

'Oh, was there an accident?' cried Bedelia, hesitating to get out of the car.

But Daniel hurried her out, and up the steps of the hotel. On the top step, however, she stopped and looked across the street, and having now a full view over the heads of the crowd, she could see clearly what was going on, could see, yes, but understand? No. Bewildered, she pressed against Daniel, for through a hole in what seemed to be an ordinary white sheet, that had been sketchily erected on a wooden frame, a black head of hair protruded, and just as she was looking, a man in the crowd took up something, she couldn't see what it was, it looked like a stone or a turnip, it was big and round anyway, and aiming straight, it seemed, at that sweating black face, he missed it by only an inch.

'Oh, my God, what are they doing?' she cried, feeling sick and faint.

Confused remnants of things she had heard about lynchings and mob-law flashed through her mind, and she put up her hands to her face, and then, quickly, one after another, half a dozen men were raising their arms and flinging missiles at the pilloried head. 'Oh, what is it, Daniel?' she cried again.

'Come away,' was all Daniel was able to say, but neither of them could move a limb.

Then, peeping out between her fingers, Bedelia saw the round object flying through the air again, and this time she saw it smack with a nauseating sound, as it landed right on the negro's face, and burst open, splashing everything, the sweating face, the sheet, with a soft pulpy mess.

Her heart turned to stone. For a moment she thought it was the living fleshy face of the victim that had burst into pulp, then she realised it was some kind of grotesque unnatural-looking gourd, with which she was unfamiliar. And the negro, unable to wipe away the mess about his eyes and mouth, was shaking his head to rid himself of the splatters of the nauseating mess. But before he could utterly free himself of the pulp, as he stood there, she could see his great mouth open in a laugh. While in front of the booth a showman in a white coat proceeded to make ostentatious payment to the successful shier, the crowd roared applause.

It was a side-show. When in disgust and contempt Bedelia turned into the hotel, Daniel followed. It was unfortunate that she should have witnessed such a thing at such a time. Yet, it was only a public exhibition, but it gave them an indication of some difference in attitude, for which they would shortly be made accountable, in the private domain, for events that were to come. Were they expecting it to be a side-show, they had come to the right place for this to happen.

It had been arranged that Biddy Conaty would meet them at the hotel, so as they went into the vestibule, they were prepared when the young woman who had been seated there got to her feet and came towards them. They were not so prepared for her agitation.

'Oh, I'm so glad you got here at last,' she cried, and a painful flush spread over her pretty face.

He's dead, thought Bedelia, and said so.

'Yes, the night before last,' said the young woman, almost indifferently, and then she rushed ahead with the rest of her story, as if the death were a mere detail, a thing of small importance, beside the rest of what she had to tell them. She didn't even give Bedelia time to recover from what, after all, she ought to have known would be a shock. She seemed to be thinking only of herself for some reason or another. She was actually trembling, and hardly able to speak coherently.

'You must forgive me,' she cried, 'but the most awful thing has happened. I didn't tell you in my letters, it didn't seem important then, but I realise now that perhaps I ought to have mentioned it. You see, as well as me, there was a man who used to go to see your brother, I keep calling him that, no matter what. This other visitor was a very well-off man, a farmer from the middle-west who came to live on the east coast, and one day, I don't know how exactly, he happened to find out about your brother being in hospital, and he came to see him, because it seems Tom – as he called him – used to work for him years ago, and he had a great regard for him. I must say I thought he was a very generous man. He brought the dying man fruit and magazines and all kinds of things, and told the nurses not to stint him in anything, but just send the bill to him. I didn't say anything, because of course your brother could easily have been in the middle-west all those years that no one knew where he was, and if he had been prepared to work as a waiter, he could just as well have taken a job as a farm labourer.'

Biddy didn't seem to be aware of the effect her words were having upon Bedelia, whose agitation was increasing. What had passed in their eyes as being a fit occupation for someone trying to get on in the world, did not seem to be the thing to do in Biddy Conaty's eyes. After all this time, Daniel recollected his own remark that Mary Conaty might think it a good thing to be a waiter. Well, her daughter certainly had a different view.

Bedelia kept her head high and responded in kind. 'Whatever job he held, he is still my brother, and deserves to be held in esteem by us.'

Daniel felt a flush to his cheeks. In his wife's self-importance, even here, even in the States, where things counted differently, she was so proud.

Biddy went on. 'To be truthful, I didn't see much harm in this other man being kind to your brother. If you were in my place maybe you would have arranged things differently, but it took a different aspect when I realised that he was making a claim on the body. He took over the funeral arrangements, and I had to intercept him. I went down to the hospital and told the authorities that you were on your way over here, and intended to get here in time for the burial.'

'Well, what did they say to that?' Daniel asked.

'Oh, there's no use in giving you every word,' said Biddy delicately, but when Daniel frowned she overcame her scruples about their feelings.

'Well, what he said was, "Who the hell are they?" I'm afraid I misjudged him at the beginning, you see. He is really a bit coarse, and not the kind to be crossed lightly. I explained, at once, of course, and then he said something that took the ground from under my feet. He said that as far as he knew, Tom Grimes was never in Ireland in his life, that Tom himself had given him to understand that he was born in America – out there in the middle-west as a matter of fact. "Oh, that couldn't be!" I said, and began to tell him all I knew about your brother.' She faltered. 'About our Tom Grimes, I mean, but he only laughed. I don't think that was very nice of him, do you? And he said he knew Tom Grimes for thirty years, and he never once heard him mention the Old Country.'

Bedelia could listen to no more.

'Do you mean to say you've brought us all the way across the Atlantic on a wild-goose chase!' she cried. In spite of Biddy's fine appearance, Bedelia remembered that her mother had once been their servant. 'I must say –' she began.

But the events through which Biddy had passed within the last few hours had transported her to a state of excitement that made her impervious to Bedelia's anger. Indeed, she brushed it aside like a mere nothing. 'Oh, you don't understand,' she said impatiently. 'It's much worse than you think. I wasn't able to communicate with you all the week while you were on sea,

but in the last few days before he died, I mean, although there
was nothing positive to go upon, I got a feeling, only a feeling
of course, but you know how absolutely reliable feelings can
be? Well, as I say, I got a feeling that the man from the
middle-west might not know it all. He said he never heard the
poor old fellow mention the Old Country. Well, if it was your
brother he could have had his reasons for that, couldn't he? It
might have been a matter of pride with him not to let people
know he'd sunk to being a common workman. He might even
have had some idea in his mind about not wanting to shame
you and your family. You'd never know! And here's another
thing that I didn't think of until just now! I was judging the old
man by things my mother, and other people I'd met from
Ireland, had said. They were always going on about the old sod,
but of course they lived in the country, so why wouldn't they be
always talking about it, and thinking about the hawthorn
bushes and the cuckoo and the corncrake, the bogs and the
little boreens? But your brother only lived in a town, isn't that
all? There wouldn't be anything much to remember, would
there?'

Involuntarily it flashed into Daniel's mind that Bedelia had
made a miscalculation about the second generation of Conatys,
when she spoke of how much the girl would appreciate staying
with them instead of with her mother's people.

'Well, as I was saying, I began to have those feelings that
perhaps I wasn't so wrong about the poor old man after all, and
then, the very last time that I saw him before he died, although
he was a lot weaker, of course, and couldn't talk at all, I was
almost absolutely certain that he was your brother.' She
shrugged her shoulders. 'It was only a feeling, of course, but as
I say –'

But Bedelia was a woman too. She knew those feelings. 'I
know!' she cried.

Daniel saw that in Bedelia's eyes Biddy was completely
exonerated, she was reinstated to her former position of
confidant and ally. Bedelia gripped her by the arm. 'Do you
mean this man is an impostor?' she cried. 'Do you mean he's
trying to make a claim on our Tom?' Feverishly two spots blazed
in her cheeks, and she turned around to Daniel. 'Oh, what a

mercy we came over?' she cried. 'All I suffered on that awful ship, in that stuffy cabin, with the foghorn going all the time, was not for nothing. It was Providence, an Act of God. This man found out about the money, I suppose,' she cried feverishly, 'and he thinks he'll get hold of it. That's it! He thinks that if he can make out a good case he –'

Daniel's voice, however, had remained steady.

'Calm yourself, Bedelia, I beg you,' he said. 'Don't you see that if this man found out about the money, which is very unlikely, I must say, and if he had designs upon it, which is also unlikely, since Biddy here says he is a very wealthy man, but if such a thing were possible, can't you see that he's going the wrong way about advancing his interest? He is doing quite the contrary. It is our Tom who owns the money. His Tom Grimes couldn't possibly have any claim to it. No, my dear, I'm afraid we're up against something harder for us to understand.'

'But why –' began Bedelia.

Daniel shrugged his shoulders. And even Biddy seemed unable to supply a reason for the convincing attitude of the man from the mid-west.

'He says he only wants to do right by a faithful servant,' she said, but in looking at Bedelia's plain but respectable attire, she blushed at having used the word servant. Some of her excitement was ebbing. A little nervously, she went on. 'He's bought a plot in the cemetery, and he's ordered a lovely coffin, and he says –'

But before she had told them anything about a memorial monument, a sample picture of which she had seen, she recollected something else, and diving into her purse somewhat shamefacedly, she drew out a little roll of notes. 'This is the money you cabled to me for the funeral expenses,' she said. Clearly she had not been a match for the man from the middle-west. 'Oh, I hope you don't think I was in any way to blame,' she said, and not only did she look very inexperienced, but it was plain to be seen that at that moment she was sorry she had got involved in the affair in the first place. Then she rallied somewhat, almost to the point of defiance. 'I don't see that it really matters, one way or another,' she added, 'so long as he's dead, and the monument this man is putting up is really beautiful. He showed me a picture of it in the mortician's catalogue. You really couldn't have chosen anything better. He certainly didn't spare expense.' She implied that it, alone, cost more than all the money they had sent. 'He has arranged to have Masses said for him too,' she added, after a minute. 'It was I suggested that to him. You see, there was a medal around the old man's neck. I didn't know about it when I wrote to you the first time. I was only told about it after he was dead. The nurse asked me what she should do with it. I said to leave it on him, of course, but I didn't think any more about it till I was back in my apartment. Then all of a sudden it seemed to me that the medal was a proof he was our man. But when I got in touch with Mr Coulter – that's the rancher's name – he said it didn't signify anything. He said he never knew a Paddy who didn't have a medal pinned on to him somewhere. He said if a Paddy ever got drunk, or knocked down, the first thing you'd find when you opened his shirt was a medal. I did my best, but he put me down every time.'

Then, realising perhaps that the responsibility that had rested so heavily upon her, was hers no longer, she brightened. 'You may get the better of him, now that you're here,' she cried. 'He may listen to you. I told him you were arriving today.' She looked guiltily at the clock. 'I said we'd go straight to the hospital the minute you got here.'

Solicitously Daniel put an arm around Bedelia. 'Do you feel able for it, Bedelia?' he asked.

Of course there could only be one answer to that question for Bedelia. Everything hung upon her evidence. She stood up. 'Let's go at once.'

Daniel wanted to soothe both women at once. How he disliked melodrama. 'I think this stranger from the mid-west will hardly gainsay the word of the man's own sister.' He had only one worry, and that concerned the hospital authorities letting them see him.

'They assured me they won't close the lid until you get a chance to identify the body. They don't coffin them until the hearse arrives at the morgue,' added Biddy.

The porter hailed a cab.

Daniel placed the two ladies in it. He sat beside Bedelia, but naturally, it was not to be expected that she would feel like talking. She turned her face to the window. Daniel, who felt under an obligation to be civil to Biddy, inclined his ear in her direction.

'The hospital authorities were very decent about the whole matter, being so irregular,' Biddy prattled. 'As a matter of fact, they thought I was awfully silly to take exception to the other man's offer. So long as he was getting a Catholic burial, they didn't see why I should make a fuss.' In spite of the solemnity of the occasion, she giggled. 'They thought I ought to be glad he was getting such a fine funeral at someone else's expense.'

Seeing the look on Daniel's face, however, she became more subdued.

They were nearing the hospital. Bedelia, who had listened, as in a dream, to the prattle of the girl, was looking out of the window of the taxi-cab, where on the crowded sidewalks an immense number of people seemed to be coursing up and down. Among them, here and there, on more than one occasion, it seemed to her that she saw young men that bore a strange resemblance to Tom, though not one was as fine a man as him. He had been so handsome, she wondered if that was part of his undoing. She wondered if his good looks had worn well in the years that had passed since they had last stood face to face? She must be prepared for a great change in him, she told herself, but that idea did not really penetrate her mind. She kept seeing him as she had last seen him, young, gay, and mocking, and the words that had been used to describe him on so many occasions came into her mind. He had been a little prince. Slowly, tears welled into her eyes, and spilled down her cheeks. For the first time since she was a girl, there was no connivance in Bedelia's heart. All considerations of money had faded away. It was as if an angel of light had come and sat down beside her in the dark cab, illuminating everything with a blinding radiance.

Daniel, who looked at her covertly, saw a great change in her, and didn't know how to account for it. He only hoped she was not going to break down. They were nearly at the hospital now.

He reached out to reassure her with a pat on the knee. 'You're not sorry we came?' he asked, and he was surprised at the vehemence of her answer.

'Oh, no, I'm glad, so glad, Daniel,' she answered. And it was true. Her heart was filled with love for her brother, her little brother that she had cared for when he was a child, her gay, reckless brother, whose charm had been so great a danger to him that she had to take a hand in his destiny for his own good, her own brother, who at one word from her, had severed all ties of home and family, and come away to this alien land.

For years she had thought never to look upon his face again, and now it had come about that she was, after all, to gaze upon it. In death, no less than in life, compared with the agony of never seeing that face again, to see it would be a sorrow so exquisite as to be almost a joy. For it was her Tom. In her heart she was certain about that.

The taxi stopped.

'We're there!' said Biddy.

'This way, Bedelia!' said Daniel, as they went up the steps.

'This way, please!' said a nurse, as she led them down a long white corridor.

'Now!' exclaimed Daniel involuntarily, as the nurse opened the door of the morgue where the corpse was waiting for them.

Now! It was forty years since Bedelia had last seen the wasted form that, heavy as stone, lay uncovered before her. It was forty years since she had last seen that face. Or had she ever seen it? Before its implications of poverty and illness, she took refuge in a sudden doubt.

Could it be possible that those other people were right, and that it wasn't her brother at all? Surely no one could change so much, even in so long a time, even in death?

That nose! Tom never had that tightened drawn look about the nose. The hair, although it was white, was stiff and strong like Tom's hair used to be. But wasn't Tom taller? Desperately her eyes fastened on detail after detail. And then a voice, no, several voices, began pressing upon her. 'Well?' they said, Daniel, and Biddy, and someone else at whom she did not bother to look. 'Is it him? Well, is it?'

She looked again into the dead man's face. But if it was her brother, something had sundered them, something had severed the bonds of blood, and she no longer knew him. And if it was me who was lying there, she thought, he would not know me. It signified nothing that they might once have sprung from the same womb. Now they were strangers. Bewildered, she turned to Daniel. 'I can't say for sure, Daniel,' she whimpered, 'I don't know.'

She felt them all staring at her, and a nasal voice, now loud, now faint, like a voice heard under the first influence of an anaesthetic, kept saying the same thing over and over again.

'It ain't natural, it just ain't natural!'

And then, as she was being led out of the ward, she heard a woman begin to scream hysterically, and only confusedly did she comprehend that she herself was the woman who was behaving so unseemingly.

Bedelia stumbled eagerly forward, and let the others help her into the cab. For was it not in there that the angel had come and sat by her side, shedding about him the radiance of love. And might she not feel again as she had then, going for Tom? For now, too, all connivance dead, she had laid her heart open to her grief in losing Tom. But her heart was too old and cracked a vessel to hold any emotion, however precious, however small a drop.

There was no angel in the cab. It was stuffy and close, and smelled strongly of feet.

Trastevere

The lights were changing at the corner of Madison and Sixty-ninth. To get across in time, Mrs Traske walked fast. Then, just as she reached the other side, she heard her name called. How nice to be hailed in the street like that on her first day back in New York! She turned expectantly. But the young man who called out had missed the light, and a river of cars now flowed between them. From the far bank he was waving frantically, and although she could not quite place him, Mrs Traske stood and waited, smiling reassurance.

Who was he? His face was certainly familiar, so she kept smiling. He was pleasant, eager and intelligent-looking. When the lights changed again, he bounded across.

'Mrs Traske! You remember me? Paul Martin. We met in Rome.'

Given an instant more she'd have placed him. He was one of the young poets she'd met this summer. Rome was full of them, but this one was much the nicest.

'Of course!' she said. 'You took me to Trastevere – myself and my daughter.'

She'd been particularly grateful that he'd included Gloria; pretty young daughters were sometimes harder to entertain than people were aware. On the other hand, it must have been easier for him to be nice to Gloria than to a middle-aged novelist! Most of the poets in Rome were a bit contemptuous of Mrs Traske, especially when they heard she was staying on the Via Veneto. Fortunately, she had reached an age at which she was able to absolve herself for putting comfort before atmosphere. Their stay in Rome had been nearing an end when

they met Paul. Hearing that they had never been across the
river to Trastevere, he promptly offered to escort them. He
planned an interesting afternoon, and – what they appreciated
most – suggested they end the day with a visit to friends of his
who had an apartment in a magnificent old medieval palazzo
in the quarter.

'I thought you were still in Rome, Mr Martin,' she said, and,
assuming that they were both going the same way, she started
to walk on. But he did not move and did not let go of her hand.
In fact, he gripped it tighter, and she realised that he was upset.
The odd thing was that he seemed to connect her in some way
with his distress.

'Oh, Mrs Traske, you don't know how good it was to look up
and see you. I was in a telephone booth across the street. You
of all people, I thought. I didn't know you were in New York. I
just *had* to call out to you. You remember those friends of mine
in Trastevere, the ones we had dinner with that evening –
Simon Carr and Della?'

He was really very disturbed. He kept wiping his forehead.

'To look up like that and see you!' he cried. 'Someone who
knew them! I'd only just heard, you see – just a minute before.
I don't know any details yet, but oh God, Mrs Traske, she killed
herself – Della did – last night!'

'Oh, no!' Now she gripped *his* hand. 'How terrible. I can't
tell you how sorry I am.' Sorry for him, she meant; he was so
upset – the young woman she'd only met on that one occasion.
Naturally, she was sorry for her, too, and for her poor husband.
Yet her immediate sympathy went out to the young man in front
of her. He was so *very* young in his grief. 'What happened?' she
asked. 'Was there another woman?'

Paul was shocked. He threw up his hands in protest. 'He was
hers, body and soul!' he cried.

'What was it, then?'

'That's what's so awful!' the young man cried. 'I don't know.
I only heard she was dead. I was just going to put in a call to
Rome – over there,' he said, nodding back, 'when I saw you.
Oh, God, isn't it hard to believe? They were insanely in love.
You must have seen that for yourself the evening in Trastevere.'

With both hands now, he held on to her. 'What frightens me is that Simon may kill himself. He won't be able to live without her.' A wild look came into his eyes. 'And Della won't rest in the grave without him She'll –'

But at this point Mrs Traske disengaged her hands. 'Now, don't talk rubbish,' she said. She was suddenly impatient with him. 'Let's walk on,' she said. 'Better still, come along to my hotel and have some lunch. It's quite near. You'll feel different when you've eaten something. We can talk.'

But Paul sprang away. 'I can't,' he cried. 'I've got to put in that call to Rome. I may have to go back there at once.' For another instant, he stood in front of her. 'Thank you again just for being here!' he cried. Then he was gone.

Shaken, Mrs Traske walked on alone. The poor girl, she thought – young woman, rather, for surely Della was a little older than her husband. Or was she? It may only have been his dependence on her that gave that impression. No matter, it was all very sad. As to Mr Martin's fears of a double suicide, however, she would not, quite frankly, give a fig for them. Widowed young herself, and having enough good sense not to make public by marriage a second, late but deeply satisfying relationship, she had her own concept of love.

What *had* happened, though? All she could recall of Della was that she was beautiful, with fine eyes and shining black hair. The evening Gloria and she had spent with the three young people ought to have been entirely enjoyable, but somehow it was not. Once or twice, it had seemed Della was too dominating, but since the young men didn't seem to mind – quite the contrary – Mrs Traske had seen no reason to let it worry *her*.

Walking along Madison Avenue, she began to wonder. No more than Paul did she feel like lunch. She had an impulse to rink Mack, but she resisted it. He'd barely be back in his office, having met her at the boat and stayed to settle her in at the hotel. Anyway, she'd be seeing him for dinner. She stopped. She must be near Central Park. Ah, yes, she could see the tops of the trees. Perhaps she'd walk for a while in the sun there. According to her New York friends, Central Park was dangerous, but surely not in broad daylight? If one was to believe Mr Martin, not as dangerous as love! For although she'd snubbed him, Paul had made her think, with his fanciful notions of love. Crossing the avenue, Mrs Traske went in the direction of the Park. She'd miss out lunch altogether. After forty, it did no harm to skip a meal. She'd never been able to do that in Rome. There, she was hungry all the time. It made her ravenous just to walk down some of those narrow streets dedicated entirely to food – whole shops given over to one commodity: cheese, pasta, salami; stalls of fruit and vegetables arranged with as much regard to colour, shape, and size as the mosaics in the Vatican workshop. Passing them, her fingers used to itch to press a fleshy fig or a fat peach to see if it was as prime as it looked. But she was scared she'd set off an avalanche that would bury her up to the neck in apples and pears, figs, tomatoes, pomegranates, melons, aubergines –

The day in Trastevere, they had eaten an excellent luncheon at her hotel, and yet they had no sooner crossed the Ponte Palatino than she was famished again, tantalised by the smells that came streaming out of apartment windows – the smell of hot cooking oil, garlic, oregano. All the walking they did made her twice as hungry. Paul had shown them everything – basilicas, crypts, palaces, fountains, piazzas. He was tireless. What they loved best were the narrow streets, like the Via dell' Atleta, that plunged them into the atmosphere of Trastevere, with orange peel underfoot and gaily coloured washing strung across overhead like bunting.

   Thinking of what happened to her in one of those little streets, Mrs Traske had to smile. It was intensely hot and they were all perspiring, and so, although she was wearing only a light silk dress, she was relieved, really, when out of the sky a few drops of rain fell on her bare arm. She turned her face upwards to receive them, 'as if,' Gloria said afterwards, laughing, 'as if you were a flower, Mother!' Only it wasn't rain! Overhead, high above, when she looked up she saw the bare bottom of a man-child, held out by his mother in her strong brown arms.

How they laughed. Then Paul tactfully suggested that perhaps they ought to be getting on, as Della would be expecting them. She liked to eat early, because she had a job, he explained; she was always ready to eat the minute she got home from the office.

'Oh, we mustn't keep her waiting,' Mrs Traske said, for from the first she had assumed they were going to eat in the apartment. That seemed the whole point of the visit. They had seen the outside of enough old palazzos.

'Wait till you see their apartment!' Paul cried. 'I told you, didn't I, it's in one of the oldest palazzos in Rome, with balconied windows and studded doors – and they have a terrace garden on the roof. There it is!' he announced as they entered a *piazzale* off which ran a street as narrow as a gully.

Impressed, they stood and stared at the massive ornamented façade that projected over the thoroughfare.

'There are disadvantages, of course, as you can see,' Paul said when they got nearer and an acrid odour assailed them from the brimming garbage bins that had not yet been emptied. Like cornucopias, the bins spilled out a largesse of lobster claws, fish heads, egg-shells, decayed flowers, and the pulp of rotted fruit. And from the lavish heap, as they went past, a swarm of flies rose into the air with an iridescent glitter, hissing like geese.

'Sorry for that,' Paul said easily. 'It's the price for living in the quarter. But look at the carving!' He pointed up at the magnificent portico.

They were having trouble, however, getting past the garbage bins, and in the hallway itself they had to push their way through a horde of small children playing on the marble floor and the lower steps of the great marble staircase. The hallway was infested with children. They were very sweet, very appealing, but she had to hold her skirts clear of their grubby little fingers. When they reached the stairs she had to laugh out loud at one small fat infant who was trying to get up the great marble step. His diaper, heavy with urine, hung down under him like an udder, and left a wet track after him wherever it touched the steps.

'Like a snail!' said Gloria, and she lifted him to one side so they could pass, although in fact the wide staircase was so broad they could easily have got past him. All three of them could have gone up it abreast. A magnificent staircase. And on the walls, set in plaster, there were wonderful ceramic medallions, although elsewhere on the plaster, up as high as they could reach, the children had been busy with chalk and crayon.

'I don't advise looking too closely,' Paul cautioned uneasily. And, indeed Mrs Traske had just seen a very crude drawing. It wasn't all the work of children, not by any means. Not wishing to embarrass the young man, she launched into a generality. 'Graffiti fascinate me,' she said. 'I read a most interesting article on the subject recently.'

The words were hardly out of her mouth when a door opened overhead and a voice called down. 'What kept you? We're starving.'

Such familiarity was warming, and the Traskes hurried up, but when Mrs Traske got to the landing she couldn't help stopping again and exclaiming at the rich Venetian red of the walls that was so well set off by the pure white of the door and the pedimented architrave. 'What glorious colour!' she cried to the young man standing on the landing – Simon?

He smiled. 'It was extravagant of us to decorate the landing, because it doesn't belong to us legally. It's supposed to be communal, but as we're at the top we took a chance and did the landing, too, when we were doing up the rest.'

Gloria and Paul had joined them.

'I always say,' said Paul, 'that this landing sounds a trumpet for what is to come!' Stepping past Simon, he threw the door of the apartment fully open.

At the sight of the room within, Mrs Traske gasped and gave another rapturous exclamation.

'You sound surprised, Mother,' Gloria said sharply. 'Mr Martin did try to prepare us.'

Mrs Traske smiled at her daughter, grateful to her for helping her transform her surprise into more tactful terms of appreciation.

'But how could anyone be prepared for such dramatic colours?' Mrs Traske said quickly. 'That glowing ruby, and now this green. It's as green as the campanile,' she added when, stepping into the room, she saw the dome of Santa Maria in Cappella through one of the great windows at the far end. She turned back to her host. 'Is your wife an artist?' she asked.

For no reason that she could see, Simon and Paul both laughed – quite loudly, too.

'Well, then, it is the room of a poet,' she murmured. The room demanded a fitting tribute.

At this point, the door of a kitchenette opened and a young woman came out. Della? Like her husband, she dispensed with greetings and joined at once in the conversation. Again, the familiarity had the effect of putting the Traskes at ease. 'The room of a poet?' the young woman repeated, questioningly, and she looked around it like a stranger. 'You should have seen the room where he lived before we were married,' she said, but she took her husband's arm and squeezed it affectionately. She nodded at the prints on the wall. 'The prints were Simon's, of course,' she said. 'I only reframed them. And the old desk was his – I just had it stripped and waxed. And the books are his.' But she frowned slightly, because some of the books looked a bit ragged. She hugged his arm tighter. 'I think the colour was your idea, too, wasn't it? Or was it Paul's?' She reached out and drew Paul to her. 'I only paid for things!' She turned to Mrs Traske. 'Perhaps you're right,' she said. 'Perhaps it is the room of a poet, but with the tone raised an octave or two – by money.'

The mention of money in this way would have made Mrs Traske uncomfortable if it were not that the young men – both of them – were so obviously delighted with Della.

'I must tell you,' Paul said. 'Della has one of the best jobs in Rome.' He laughed. 'That's why they came here – and me, too.'

Did he live with them? Mrs Traske wondered. This room was so spacious there could not be very much sleeping accommodation beyond it.

Paul seemed to read her mind. 'I don't live *with* them,' he said. 'I only live *off* them.'

At this, again all three laughed, and Mrs Traske laughed with them. She could see, though, that Gloria found Della rather overpowering. What a strong personality. Standing there in the middle of her beautiful room, with the two young men linked to her, she suddenly presented an extravagant image to the mind of Mrs Traske – an image of a Maypole, festooned with ribbons, which, as they gyrated, bound the young men closer and closer to her.

'Simon, aren't you going to offer them a drink?' Unlinking herself, Della picked up an empty glass that had evidently been her own, then put it down again. 'I won't have any more,' she said, and it was hard not to feel this was a reprimand to them for being late. All the same, Mrs Traske and Gloria took the drinks that without choice, were offered to them, and Mrs Traske began at once to sip hers as an example to Gloria, who loathed Campari and found it as hard to swallow as cough syrup.

'It was good of you to come,' Della said then, unexpectedly. 'We've heard a lot about you from Paul.'

Mrs Traske had started to give the self-deprecated smile with which she usually acknowledged over-facile praise of her work when Della continued. 'About your generosity to young people, I mean,' she said.

How glad Mrs Traske was then for those frank admissions concerning Della's salary, because if money had been in short supply she would have thought the young woman was leading up to a request for a loan. As things were, it did cross her mind that they might be expecting something other than money from her. She turned to Simon. 'I regret to say I haven't read any of your poetry,' she murmured.

Della took her empty glass. 'How could you?' she said. 'It's never been published,' and before Mrs Traske could say anything more she put up her hand as if in warning. 'Don't suggest reading it in manuscript,' she cried, 'unless you are an Egyptologist or a hieroglyphist,' and, reaching out, she joined the two young men to her again. 'They call themselves writers, and no one can read their writing.' She laughed. 'And they can't spell.' She laughed again. 'They don't even know the meaning of words. Do you know what this fellow here thought?' She hugged Paul tighter to her. 'He thought temerity meant timidity! And this fellow here' – she hugged her husband's arm – 'this fellow thought a hysterectomy was a lobotomy! Not that one can blame him too much for that; the medieval philosophers all thought the womb was the centre of the emotions.' She let them go. 'Oh, they are hopeless cases. I don't know what they'd do if they didn't have me to look after them.'

And, indeed, to Mrs Traske it was beginning to seem as if she did give them strength. In the large room where she and Gloria stood apart as separate people, the three young people seemed to stand as closely grouped together as when they were linked.

'Take the girl's glass,' Della said to Simon. 'And if we're ready, let's go and eat.'

But it was over to the door through which they had come in she walked, and, opening it, she led them out on to the landing.

'Are we not going to eat here?' said Mrs Traske. Too late she knew she'd let slip that she was disappointed. She hadn't seen the room properly, hadn't looked at the prints or the books, and, above all, she hadn't had time to look out of the window at the wonderful view of Trastevere. She glanced regretfully around.

'Do you mind?' Della said, almost offensively, and she held the door open. Mrs Traske couldn't help feeling she'd been put under a compliment.

'We'd be happy to take pot luck, you know,' she said nervously. 'Gloria wouldn't mind giving a hand. She's quite a good cook. She makes a delicious omelette.' The truth was that after months of living in hotels and eating out, she herself would have enjoyed helping with a meal. She thought again of the vegetable stalls, and she could almost feel the snap of young beans under her fingers, and the swish of spinach.

Della however had turned away. 'We never eat in the apartment,' she said. 'There's a trattoria in the cellar of the palazzo – you must have seen the sign in the hallway when you were coming up here. We eat there every night – in fact we only eat up here on very rare occasions.'

'Sad occasions, not joyful,' Paul explained quickly. 'If one of them is sick, or something like that.'

'The smell of cooking hanging around the apartment all evening would disgust me,' Della said.

Still Mrs Traske was not happy. 'We shouldn't have come for a meal at all,' she murmured.

'But why should you think that?' Simon said. 'It's not that Della is tired or anything; it's just that we can afford to eat out – because of her job.'

'That's right,' Della said more graciously. 'If it weren't for my job, we probably wouldn't be able to eat at all!' She saw Gloria look surprised, and she gave a little laugh. 'Don't worry,' she said, and she nodded at her husband. 'He pays in other ways.' She paused. 'He washes the nappies.' When both Mrs Traske and Gloria failed to conceal their surprise at this, she shrieked with laughter. 'Figuratively speaking!' she cried. 'We haven't any little nappies.'

Mrs Traske looked nervously at Simon. As both he and Paul laughed, however, she tried to laugh, too. Gloria only stared.

'Don't worry,' Paul whispered reassuringly as they went down the stairs. 'Della knows what she's doing. Other people's extravagances are her economies.'

But it was no longer her social obligations that concerned Mrs Traske. 'Are they long married?' she asked.

'About three months,' Paul said. He leaned closer. 'They were living together for some time in London, but when Della got this great job in Rome they decided to get married.' He lowered his voice still more. 'I don't think Simon liked the idea of marriage at first – that's what Della meant about the little nappies – but he knew he couldn't live without her.' He grinned. 'I can hardly live without her myself. I'm over here on a grant, and I'm staying in a good enough pensione, but – well, I spend all my time here in their apartment. I'm afraid I lean on her, too. She's that kind of person. I'd heard of people like her before, but I never met one – people whose strength is a kind of magnet for people like Simon and me, who are pretty helpless when it comes to living. It's true!' he said when Mrs Traske looked quizzically at him.

They were at the bottom of the great stairs, and now she could see that there was a greasy sign on the wall and a steeper, darker stair leading down to the trattoria in the cellar.

The trattoria was small but packed with people. When Della appeared, however, the little fat patron, his face glistening with sweat, ran forward at once to meet them, as if he'd been rolled at them like a ball, and began to bow them toward the only empty table in the room, way at the back near the service doors.

'*Signore! Signora!*' He beamed until suddenly he saw Mrs Traske and Gloria. Thinking them a separate party, he was thrown into confusion, and more sweat broke from his face – it might have been rubbed all over with oil. For a moment, it was as if he were some lower form of life that would divide in two, both halves able to go forward and bestow welcomes alike on the two parties at the same time. But this being impossible, he clapped his hands and, summoning a waiter in a long lank apron down to his boots, ordered him to attend on the strangers. '*La carta per gli Inglesi!*' he cried. Then, as he realised that they were together, one single party, a beatific smile of relief broke over his face. '*Momento!*' he cried to the waiter. '*Carta per tutti.*' Without waiting to be obeyed, he dashed over to a service table and rushed back with a fistful of menus so greasy and wine-stained they were positively succulent, and dealt them out.

'*Prego.*' He gave one to Della. '*Prego.*' One to Mrs Traske. '*Prego, prego, prego,*' he cried, dealing one to each person. But the next instant he gathered them up again and discarded them. Like a conductor disdaining the score, he began to extol from memory the delights of his kitchen. '*Pollo al diavolo? Saltimbocca? Abbacchio alla cacciatora?* Tonight it is tender' – he bowed to Gloria – 'like the eyes of the *Signorina.*' Then, conspiratorially, he lowered his voice. '*Osso buco,*' he whispered. 'Tonight it is –' He stopped, and, placing a kiss on his fat fingers, he blew it heaven-ward. As there was still no response, he was silent for a moment. Then he raised his voice again. 'Steak!' he cried. Just the one word. But now he was no longer a restaurateur; he was a generalissimo. He held up his hand for their attention. '*Momento!*' he cried, and he stumped off through the service doors. When he emerged again, it was triumphantly, with a piece of raw steak on the palm of his hand; blood from it oozed through his fingers. 'Never a steak like this,' he said solemnly. 'Never!'

All except Mrs Traske and Gloria gave the steak a close scrutiny, Della even lifting it up and turning it over. But Simon winked at Gloria, and put on a face of mock dismay. 'What good is that when there are five of us,' he said.

'*Scusi?*' Angelo did not immediately catch that a joke was meant. Then, offended, he frowned. 'I speak of the little Florentine heifer from which we take the steak!' he said with dignity. '*Molto* steak, *molto!*' he corrected. And, assuming that an order had been given, he handed the meat to the waiter. His hands free, he clapped them commandingly. 'Steak *per tutti!*' he cried.

Mrs Traske would have preferred an omelette, and Gloria loathed steak. To make matters worse, Della had called 'Underdone!' after the little patron.

'*Capisco!*' Angelo cried, and was about to scuttle off.

'But I –' said Gloria.

Angelo stopped.

It was Simon, though, who had arrested him. 'Wait a minute, Angelo,' Simon said. 'Tonight I think I'll try the *osso buco.*'

'Simon!' Della was astonished. 'You know you hate sloppy dishes.'

'*Osso buco,*' Simon repeated.

'Simon!' Della caught him by the arm. 'It will take ages – twenty minutes, at least – you know that? You don't want to wait that long.'

But Angelo was all eagerness to comply. 'For the *Signore* – no!' he cried. Prudently measuring the distance between him and the other tables, he lowered his voice. 'For the one who comes in off the street, yes, maybe, but *per il cliente – il Signore –* no, no. I fix it myself, at once.' He held up five fat fingers. '*Cinque minuti.*'

Della sat back. 'Well, bring ours when it's ready, Angelo – without waiting,' she said. She still looked puzzled. She turned to Mrs Traske. 'I don't believe I've ever known him to eat *osso buco,*' she said. Then, as Angelo was hurrying away, she called again, 'Underdone!'

Mrs Traske looked at her. No matter what the two men said, it seemed to Mrs Traske that Della did look tired. It could, of course, have been that she was hungry, because she had picked up a roll and begun to pluck out the soft inner dough.

'It's all very well for Simon and Paul,' she said. 'They lunch here, too – that is to say, if they get up for lunch at all.' Suddenly she looked strangely at Mrs Traske. 'What time do you begin your day?'

Surprised, Mrs Traske hesitated. 'Do you mean when I'm at home, or do you mean here in Rome? This morning, we didn't get up very early, because Paul warned us that we'd have a tiring day trudging around and seeing the sights.'

As Paul nodded, Della gave him an affectionate smile. 'Did you really show them everything?' she asked him. 'For you the day must have been exceptionally exacting.'

Paul laughed. 'Della doesn't think writing poetry is work at all,' he said.

'But she married a poet!' Mrs Traske said, feeling she had to defend the young woman.

It was a shock to find that instead she had annoyed her. 'I married a man – a man like any other man, I hope,' Della said sharply. 'I don't see why allowances should be made for him on account of his work. I'd be insulted if anyone made allowances for *me* on account of *mine*.'

'Oh, but –' Mrs Traske began, when Gloria spoke up.

'Mother never expects allowances to be made for her, either,' she said hotly. 'But it's not the same as if she was just a lawyer or a paediatrician! When she's working she can't sleep and she can't eat and she gets upset over nothing. Writers are sometimes working when we think they're only standing looking out of the window! Didn't you know that?' she demanded crossly, and so like a small child her mother had to smile.

Fortunately, Della was not offended. On the contrary, she was amused. 'Do you mean that Simon here may be working when he's fast asleep at three o'clock in the afternoon?'

Gloria was not to be put off so easily. 'That's not fair,' she said. 'It *is* true his mind could be working – unconsciously – and that takes a lot out of a person. The artist has always been regarded as a sacrificial figure and – '

'Gloria!' Mrs Traske just couldn't let her go on. 'She has been reading *The Wound and the Bow*,' she said to Della by way of apology.

Della brushed the apology away, however, and actually encouraged the girl. 'Go on,' she said. 'I'm interested. I take it that you feel my husband here is some special kind of being.'

Uncertain suddenly, Gloria looked for help from her mother, but the ice was thin; it would never bear the weight of two.

'Well,' said Gloria slowly, to gain time as she searched around in her mind. 'Writers and artists, and people like that – they do have special insights, don't you think?'

Della looked at her with a grave expression. Then, equally gravely, she looked at Simon. 'You think' – she paused – 'you think he may be some kind of a nut?'

Here Paul exploded with laughter, and Mrs Traske would have laughed if she weren't a bit anxious about Gloria, who could easily have burst into tears.

The girl felt too strongly for that, though. 'Put it that way if you like!' she cried. 'I suppose some people *do* think poets are nuts. Just because they don't measure success by money!' Her cheeks were flaming.

And Della was apparently touched. She laid a hand on the girl's arm. 'How nice it must be to have you for a daughter,' she said with real sweetness, but then she turned sharply to Mrs Traske. 'Of course, it's true you writers *are* above money, isn't that so?' she said, and to Mrs Traske's amazement her eyes travelled – really quite insolently – over her dress, and came to rest on her opal-and-diamond brooch.

Compelled now to speak up herself, Mrs Traske looked Della in the eye. 'My husband was a stockbroker,' she said.

At that moment, luckily, the steaks arrived.

'Let's begin, shall we?' Della said when, except for Simon, they were all served. 'Poor Simon,' she said. 'I told you it would take twenty minutes. Now aren't you sorry you're not one of the common herd?'

'*Momento. Momento,*' Angelo clucked.

'Go easy, Gloria. You'll get indigestion,' Mrs Traske said trying to slow her down, although she sympathised with her motives for gulping it off – the steaks were positively blue.

Slow as they all went – and even Della ate slowly – they were finished before Angelo came back proudly bearing, breast-high, the platter of *osso buco*.

'It looks good,' Gloria said as she handed her empty plate to a waiter.

'It smells delicious, Simon,' Della said, and as Angelo took her plate she reached out and snatched her fork. Leaning across the table, she stuck the fork into the *osso buco*. To the astonishment of all of them, Simon, who had just picked up his own fork, threw it down on the plate with a clatter.

'Why, Simon, what's the matter?' Della cried. 'I only wanted –'

Simon didn't look at her. He pushed his plate across the table. 'If you wanted it, why didn't you order it? There. You can have it.'

'But Simon!' Della was so taken aback she held her fork in the air, half-way to her mouth. Unnoticed, the meat fell from the prongs. Then, quietly and carefully, she picked it up and put it on her side plate and laid the fork back on the table, straightening it as if she were laying a place setting. 'I only wanted to see if it tasted good,' she said, in a voice that for her was low and indistinct.

'I don't want it,' Simon said.

Stupefied, they all stared.

'Will you have a steak, then?' Della asked.

'No. I'm not hungry,' Simon said. 'You eat it if you want it.'

Della looked down at the full plate in front of her. 'But I don't want it,' she said. 'I had what I ordered – I only –' Then she didn't attempt any more apology. 'Don't be absurd, Simon. We'll wait for our dessert until you've eaten. Eat it up,' she said, pushing back the plate. She turned in exasperation to Paul. 'What's the matter with him?' she cried. 'Tell him not to be childish.' She turned to her husband. 'Eat it up, Simon.'

Simon, however, had leaned back and was calling Angelo. 'Take this away,' he said, pointing to the plate.

Angelo stared at him.

'Don't worry, Angelo,' Della said quickly. 'It's just that he's not hungry.' As the patron took up the plate but stood uncertainly with it held low, like a collection plate, she jumped up from her chair and whispered something into his ear. 'Go along, Angelo,' she said then, out loud, 'and bring our dessert.' She turned back to those at the table. 'What will you have? Fruit? Cheese?' To Gloria she spoke kindly, as if she were a child. 'How about a *cassata* for you?'

Embarrassed, they all nodded acceptance of what apparently was decreed for them.

It hardly seemed possible that the awkwardness would pass. Thinking of it now, Mrs Traske, walking in the sunlight, felt that there, in that incident – if anywhere – was a hint of why the young woman had killed herself. But no. As she recalled it, after that things had gone well. Nothing more was said about the *osso buco*. Simon was suddenly in better form. Indeed, the next quarter of an hour was the most pleasant of the whole evening. They were all soon at ease, and for the first time Simon showed a real interest in the Traskes and their travels. 'How long are you going to be in Rome?' he'd asked.

'I'm not sure yet,' she'd replied without much thought, eager only to keep the conversation on a safe topic. 'We intended going to Milan the day after tomorrow, but somehow or other, on the way here from Florence, we missed out on Viterbo, and I'm told –'

'Oh yes, yes. You can't leave without seeing Viterbo.' He laughed. 'Though, mind you, I was only there once, years ago, and I didn't see much of it. I was drunk. Very drunk.' He turned to Paul. 'You remember that day?' He turned back to Mrs Traske. 'We'd hired an old car and we were supposed to turn it in in Rome, but we didn't really expect it would last out the trip. We were driving along when we saw the sign for Viterbo, and felt we ought to see it, so we turned off the main road. We thought we might eat there. But after we'd driven down some of the old streets – Viterbo is *all* old streets, and they're *all* crooked, *all* dark, *all* damp, even on the hottest day – well, we didn't think much of it, and we certainly didn't feel like eating there, and so we were trying to find the way out again when the old car gave a jolt. Blump it went. And then blump again. Blump, blump, blump. Paul, you remember?'

Paul was convulsed with laughter. 'Go on!' he cried.

Simon went on. 'Can you imagine a flat tyre in a place like that? We looked at each other in despair, threw up our hands, and decided to drive on. Blump we went, blump, blump, blump, blump, blump. We began to think we'd punctured all four tyres. And then to make things more hectic, although when we first drove into the place it was like a city of the dead, not a living soul in sight, *now* from all sides people appeared. Men, women, children – especially children. The children started running after us, shouting and yelling. I stepped on the gas. In a backward place like that, a pack of children is as bad as a pack of wolves. We tried to put a bit of distance between us and them, and I thought we were getting up speed when all of a sudden the kids dropped back. They stopped dead, in fact, and huddled together. The last I saw of them they were staring with their mouths wide open. Then I was jerked back as all of a sudden the ground went from under the car. Next thing there was a loud smack and a great almighty splash. We hadn't a puncture at all. We'd driven down a flight of steps into the river. That was all!'

'Oh, Simon, you never told me that story,' Della said. 'I want to go there. I want to see those steps.'

She was laughing so happily Mrs Traske thought that perhaps after all no harm had been done by the incident of the *osso buco*.

'How did you get the car out of the river, Mr Carr?' Gloria asked.

Dear girl. How they laughed at her.

'You must never look beyond the end of a good story, Gloria,' Paul said. 'Your mother could have told you that.'

They were all happy again.

'We certainly won't miss Viterbo after this,' Mrs Traske said, and she began to draw on her gloves. 'Which means we will be staying another day in Rome, so why don't you all have lunch with me tomorrow at my hotel?'

'But Della doesn't eat lunch,' Simon said in dismay.

'I have a snack at the canteen,' Della explained.

'Oh, what a pity,' Gloria said, and Mrs Traske turned to Paul, whom Angelo had released from his chair by pulling the table out from the wall. 'Perhaps you and Simon –' she began.

Uncertainly, both men looked at Della.

'Why not?' Della said. 'It would be a change for Simon.' She paused. 'A change from lying in bed, I mean.'

Once again for a moment, Mrs Traske's heart sank at what sounded to her like an unnecessary gibe, but again the young men seemed to see it in some other light, because they both laughed. It seemed settled that the young men would come to lunch.

Meanwhile, they were moving towards the stairs, and Paul had run up the steps to call a taxi.

'What time?' Simon said.

'How about noon?' she said, and she was just about to compliment Angelo on the meal as he bowed them out, his face now in the heated room glistening as if he was sweating glycerine.

Della, who had been looking at the little patron, suddenly turned to her husband. 'Simon! I forgot. You can't go. You've got to lunch *here* tomorrow. Isn't that right, Angelo?' she asked, smiling at him.

'*Si, si, Signora.*' Angelo bobbed his head up and down.

Della reached out and patted him. 'You are a dear, Angelo,' she said, before she took Simon's arm and began to move towards the door. 'Angelo is keeping your *osso buco* for your lunch tomorrow,' she said. 'Those sloppy dishes improve by keeping – the flavour comes out with standing overnight.' Then she turned to Mrs Traske and put out her hand. 'You'll be in Rome again,' she said indifferently.

Simon said nothing, and somehow Mrs Traske didn't look at him as she shook hands. He had pulled away from Della, Mrs Traske saw out of the corner of her eye. She started to go up the dark stairs, and when she reached the street Paul was there with the taxi. She thought it best to let the others explain about the lunch to him. She and Gloria got into the car.

As it drove away, she looked back at the three of them standing on the kerb. Simon seemed taller than she'd realised, and Della was really quite small. That Maypole image had been absurd, she thought, and even Paul's description of her as a tower of strength didn't seem right any more. Mrs Traske stopped. Was it possible that Della wasn't strong at all – that she had all the time been taking strength, not giving it as the young men thought?

Mrs Traske was surprised to find that her eyes had filled with tears. She wiped them away and looked around for a seat. She'd exhausted herself with her efforts to probe human motive, and now she felt curiously lonely. She sighed, and looked at her watch. She never liked to ring Mack during office hours, but perhaps just this once she might do so. He might slip out for a cup of coffee with her. It would be nice to meet him at this banal time of day and not wait for the more circumspect hours of evening.

She sighed again. Life was so short. And she remembered something Mack had once said, to which she had not attached importance at the time. She had said that she did not see much point in getting married at their age, when they had not much left to give each other, and he had shaken his head in disagreement.

'At least we do not diminish each other,' he said.

Were they making a mistake, she wondered, she and Mack? In spite of how often they thrashed things out and discarded the idea of marrying – laughed at the mere notion – perhaps after all —

She had come to a gate leading back into the street, and there would be a phone booth close by. She'd call Mack anyway. Even on the phone he was able to cheer her up – make her happy, make her laugh. She walked faster. For a woman of her years, her step at that moment was light.